GHOST GIRL, BANANA

A NOVEL

WIZ WHARTON

HarperVia

An Imprint of HarperCollinsPublishers

GHOST GIRL, BANANA. Copyright © 2023 by Wiz Wharton. All rights reserved. Printed in the United States of America. No part of this book may be used or reproduced in any manner whatsoever without written permission except in the case of brief quotations embodied in critical articles and reviews. For information, address HarperCollins Publishers, 195 Broadway, New York, NY 10007.

HarperCollins books may be purchased for educational, business, or sales promotional use. For information, please email the Special Markets Department at SPsales@harpercollins.com.

FIRST EDITION

Designed by Yvonne Chan

Library of Congress Cataloging-in-Publication Data has been applied for.

ISBN 978-0-06-323974-6

23 24 25 26 27 LBC 5 4 3 2 1

For Mumma, of course

"No such fat goose lies in the road."

QUESTIONABLE CHINESE PROVERB

One Hundred Miles Short of Heathrow's Second Runway

1977

From here, they descend at speed, her eardrums swelling like corn in a saucepan, *pop, pop, pop.* The world reappears through the oval of the window: toy cows glued onto Astroturf, a *Blue Peter* landscape of tinfoil lakes and cereal-carton houses. Her red sandals crush the crayons at their feet, rolling the lashes of wax into a puddle of long-cold gravy.

Not far now, the woman says. She has traveled with them and her face is kind, but she is not their mother. And what about their father? He is on the ground with the lakes and the cows. He is waiting on an oily tarmac. They have done wrong and he is their punishment. Remember this.

Her sister's hand grapples for hers beneath the blanket, the tiny nails scabby and fringed around their cuticles, and although the feeling disgusts her it is the only thing that seems familiar—that will continue to be familiar—for all the years to come. Remember this. Hold it close.

From here, they will descend at speed.

Part One

BEGINNINGS

ONE

Lily

London 1997
12th Day of Mourning

By the time I was twenty-five, there were only two things I remembered about Mumma. The first was that she smelled of watermelons; the second was that we were happy.

We'd taken our father's name, of course, but a name is only half a story. The other half existed in that strange hinterland: hushed questions, Chinese whispers, that had faded over the years to silence. And that was the problem. Like a dripping tap or an unpaid bill, Mumma was the squatter at the back of my brain forever waiting for the moment to surprise me.

THE BEGINNING OF my ending is easy to mark. I was standing at the living room window, watching my neighbor's funeral procession make its third lap around the estate. Brixton rain. The sort that gets nothing clean, only picks up the grime and the stink and drops it somewhere else.

A small crowd had gathered in the car park, pretending not to get wet beneath their Tesco shopping bag rain hats and broken-winged umbrellas, but it seemed dishonest of me to join them. I didn't even know the dead man's name although we'd looked at each other often. Our flats faced onto each other, separated by the scrubby excuse for a square, and sometimes—when I'd wake up in the night—I'd see him propped against the mirror of his glass. *Ferret*, I used to think: the way his hands were always in motion, his bony fingers plowing troughs through his hair, or stroking gray skin through the fabric of his vest. One day I'll go over there, I told myself. He might have a story, too. We could become friends. But I never did.

The too-long rattle of the letter-box drew me away from the window, accompanied by the postman's tuneless whistle. I waited for him to retreat, listening for the tight wet loop of his footsteps fading across the landing before I wandered into the hallway.

On the mat was a single envelope. I'd never been a person who got excited by the mail; someone who expected flowers or cards from boyfriends, or *round robins* from girls I'd been at school with. Mostly it was menus or my appointments, perhaps one of those anonymous invitations for self-defense or the local jamboree at which no one awaited my attendance. I kept them all, nonetheless. Positioned right at the entrance to the flat, it demonstrated to the people who came by—my landlord, the pizza delivery boy sopping wet from his piddling little moped—that mine was a busy life, populated with busy people.

I threw the letter on top of the pile and went back to spying on the car park. The funeral procession had moved on but the crowd hung around in their clusters, chatty and reluctant to disperse. Maybe they were waiting for an encore, a second chance to reflect on their mortality. *But he looked so well when I saw him. One minute he was here and then . . .*

Gone.

Fuck it. Today was the day. Six years without the curb of routine had made me a woman of jagged risings, allowed the indulgence of watching the world change through the prism of my bedsit window. I knew the thrum of my neighbors' engines, the precise flourishes on the tags of graffiti, the fractals of the cracks in the walls. In another life these skills might have been useful. In this one I was merely a clock-watcher.

I gathered the mail from the hallway and began to sort it on the living room table, matching it up as I went: Dave's Disco, takeaway, therapy, like that game we used to play called Remember. That only left the newest envelope, which didn't fit with anything. I picked it up and examined it. It was yellow and thin in my hand, the paper the wrong side of luxurious, as was the careless slant of its address. I shook it free of the rain and then tore at an unlicked gap in its corner and pulled out the letter within. *Commissioner for Oaths*, it said, along with the details of a London solicitor located at Gray's Inn Road.

> RE: In the matter of Miss Lily Miller, formerly known as Li-Li Chen, daughter of Sook-Yin Chen, of Castle Peak Road, Kowloon.

Phrases jumped in and out of my vision, the black ink morphing into shapes across the paper. *We are writing to inform you . . . An inheritance . . . Please call us at the number below.*

It had to be some kind of scam. You heard about these things all the time: soft approaches by so-called Good Samaritans; innocent people giving up their life savings. As if.

Despite this, something small and barely perceptible tried to creep past my notice and take root in the darkest of spaces. I perched on the sofa and shut my eyes.

Five things I can see, four things I can . . .

Did that technique really work for anyone?

Dr. Fenton said I worried too much and maybe I should stop overthinking things—one of those typical therapist mantras, along with *no caffeine after 4 p.m.* or being grateful for the person I was. Easy for him to say.

The day that letter arrived, I hadn't been allowed to think of my old name, or any of the memories that went with it, for more than twenty years.

TWO

Sook-Yin

Kowloon, June 1966

On the morning of Sook-Yin's exile, the harbor was fuller than the gutters on market day. The islanders had always taken their status seriously. If you could get into the sea you could fish, they said, and if you could fish you would never go hungry. A family's survival depended on money—people casting their hopes to the tide aboard dinghies and leaky sampans—and now she was paying the price because she had never been able to make enough of it, or at least not the right kind for her brother. She could have scrubbed floors till her fingers bled, boiled laundry from Kowloon to Guangzhou, but she would never become an intellectual, a person that he could respect. *Numbskull, shame of the family, a woman of twenty-two with no more than a fourth-form education.* Isn't that what ah-Chor had said?

Some money was more equal than others.

PASSENGERS HAD STARTED to board the liner. As Sook-Yin peered up from the shadow of the dock, one hand shielding her eyes from the sun, they looked like minnows in the palm of a giant. *The*

Carthage—Pacific and Orient. The same words she'd read on her ticket when she'd gone with ah-Ma to the embassy that morning. Later, she'd looked them up in her dictionary:

> **Carthage**
> proper noun
> 1. An ancient city on the coast of north Africa.
>   Founded by the Phoenicians. Finally destroyed by
>   the Romans at the end of the Third Punic War.

She considered the gleaming paintwork, the shiny reflections piercing its windows, the muscular heft of its ropes. Nothing about the ship looked destroyed. A lucky omen, perhaps—the same way Kowloon had risen from its ashes.

Panic wrenched her from her distraction as passengers appeared from all directions. Where was her family? She fought her way back along the pier, searching for her brother's hat, her mother's hand on her pink umbrella, until through the swell of the crowd she saw a face she recognized, even though she doubted her instinct. *Ba-Ba?*

"Sook-Yin, good," he said. There was the familiar tightness to her father's jaw, and the heat of her anger resurfaced from the last time that she'd seen him. Was it four or five years ago? She'd gone with ah-Chor for ah-Ma's housekeeping and woken their father's mistress even though it was almost noon. Sook-Yin had dared to protest and her father had slapped her with an outstretched hand. Once. Twice. Now he'd grown fat and she resented his happiness.

"So, you're really going?" he said.

"Why? Did you come to make sure?"

"Sook-Yin, no hard feelings, okay?"

He reached for his wallet and pulled out a foreign note. It was pink, with a portrait of the Queen on it and a single word that she recognized: *Ten.* "This is all I can give you," he said. "Ah-Bao's funeral took most of our savings."

Her father's secret son. Ah-Ma had mourned him for all of a minute, and not in sorrow, but only as a woman.

When she shook her head, he pushed the money toward her. "You are still my daughter," he told her. "No matter what ah-Ma tells you."

For a moment, she dared to hope. "Ah-Ba . . ."

He turned his face toward the ship. "Prove you can do better, ah-Yin. Make your family proud of you, and perhaps we will see you again."

Ah-Chor appeared through the throng, grabbing at the neck of her coat as he shouted above the noise. "Deck D! Deck D, silly dreamer! Are you trying to waste our money?" The effort strangled the words in his throat before he turned and saw their father. Bent his head. "We didn't expect you today, sir. Did you want to speak to Sook-Yin?"

"I have said what I came to say."

"Very good then, sir."

Sook-Yin looked from one to the other, at her older brother like their father's shadow and herself without a voice. "Goodbye, then, Father," she said, but when she turned, he had already gone.

STANDING ON THE approach to the deck, people pushing her this way and that, she didn't know what to say to ah-Ma. "Write to me often," she told her, and then to ah-Chor, "Please look after our mother."

"Yes, stop fussing! We'll be fine."

Thrown forward by the weight of the crowd she had no option but to follow it upward to the gaping mouth of the ship.

It was a long way down to the harbor. Her brother was still on the dock but ah-Ma had moved farther away. She could see the retreating shape of her raincoat with its red chrysanthemum pattern. Was her mother cold? Were her shoulders shaking?

Sook-Yin waved her arms and shouted, her words lost among

the others louder and more excited than her own. *Goodbye! Goodbye! Goodbye!* Some of the passengers had brought colored streamers— bright reams of red and yellow that exploded from their hands like fireworks. She picked one up at her feet, hoping it would reach her own family and let them reel her back to safety. *We didn't mean it. We love you. Come home.* She held the end and cast it out, but it was too short and her voice too faint for anyone to come to her rescue.

THREE

Lily

—————————
—————————

12th Day of Mourning

I was still holding the letter when the phone rang, tinny and muffled beneath the sofa cushions. That's where it lived in those days, amid the dust and the rot and stray candy because it was disgusting and the bringer of bad news and I had no desire to talk to anyone. "No one's asking you to marry it," Maya said. "You only need to answer when I call you." I pulled out the handset and there she was. Had to give her that, I suppose. Despite my sister's faults she'd maintained an uncanny ability to know when something had happened.

"Hey," I said when I answered. I wanted to blurt out the words *guess what, the strangest thing . . .* but she was in a hurry and interrupted me.

"I need you to come by the office."

"What, right now?" I said.

"There's something we need to talk about."

I'd become inured to these occasional summonses: fools' errands to check her back door or make sure she'd turned the oven off. In lieu of me having a proper job my time was considered fluid, each task a pointed reminder of my own alarmless existence.

In spite of this, her urgency threw me. And why the need to go to her office?

"As soon as you can," she said.

I glanced down at the letter again, my hand sliding against the receiver. The reason was obvious, wasn't it? She must have got one too.

BY THE TIME I emerged from the tube at Camden, I'd talked my panic into a kind of relief. Maya would sort it all out. She'd probably called the number already, solicitor to solicitor and all that. It's what she'd trained for, wasn't it—First at Oxford, imminent partnership—at least until that last year when she'd decided to give it all up to play happy families in her husband's business.

Maya's worse half, Ed, was some shit-hot world-class architect. He was also about a hundred and three. I always knew she would land on her feet with someone super-rich and super-successful but she'd made a Faustian bargain on that one.

Their office was in one of those mews houses, meddled to fuck in the eighties with glass bricks and windows for doors. I never understood it myself, all that interfering with social history for a genteel tantrum in the guise of progressiveness.

They'd got some new mousy-haired Sloane in reception. "Mrs. Redgrave's with a client?" she said, practically cross-eyed from looking down her nose at me. She'd already assessed me as someone unimportant, and without the steer of prior knowledge no one ever guessed we were sisters. Petty in my annoyance, I slid against the fiberglass sofa and flicked through *Architectural Digest*, making little cracks of thunder with the pages.

EVEN IN HER office, Maya kept me waiting, marooned behind the hull of her desk as she wrote in her man-sized diary, her center parting as neat as an airstrip. "Dyed your hair?" I said.

She frowned but kept her eyes on the page. "Can you not be weird for five minutes?"

I squinted. It was definitely blonder. "Not trying to hurry you," I said, "but I've got somewhere to be at two."

"Where?" It was a miracle she didn't give herself whiplash.

"Hot date with Robert De Niro."

"So you *are* still seeing Dr. Fenton?"

She placed a tick in the page's margin with a furious flourish of responsibility. "You do realize it's meant to be tricky, Lils? If therapy was easy, it wouldn't be worth it."

I rested my arms on the desk, the letter crackling its disapproval in my pocket. "Go on, then. Spill," I said.

She pressed her temples. "Something weirdly awkward has come up."

In the matter of Miss Mei-Hua Chen . . .

"Ed's planning me a secret party."

"What?"

"I know. It's horrendous. I hate it."

"Sorry, no, I meant what are you on about?"

"He's been threatening to do it for months, cozying me up with all his associates. Says it makes sense to keep me in the 'network.'"

"Hostage network?"

"Funny."

But it wasn't, was it? This couldn't be the reason she'd called me here. She was warming up to it, easing me in. "And I'm to do what, exactly?"

"I need you to talk to him, Lily. Pretend that his assistant let it slip and you want to plan it yourself because you know me, blah blah blah . . . At least then I can control the invites."

"Right."

"Don't panic, I've done it. It's done. Food and guests and everything, so it's not exactly lying." She flicked me with a petulant gaze. "That won't be a problem, will it?"

"Couldn't you have told me this on the phone? You made it sound really urgent."

"Well, no . . . it has to look *plausible*." She paused as though realizing something. "I don't expect you to *come*. I know you despise these things."

"Why not get one of your lackeys to do it?"

She straightened the pens on her desk, lining their lids up like little soldiers. "I can't trust them. Not like you. They'll only blab to Ed."

Something unreadable crossed her expression. Had something happened between them? I made a useless mime toward her belly. Still as flat as the Fens. "Everything all right . . . down there?"

"Thank you, everything's great."

"Has Ed been going to the scans with you?"

"God, no! He just wants to know if it's all fine."

"And is it?"

"Yes, it's fine . . ." She blinked at me. "I mean it. Everything's fine."

"Sounds like it's fine," I said.

We played these games, Maya and me. When we were younger, I struggled to read her but the years had worn down her armor and revealed her emotional leakage: the subtle grind of her jaw; the indisputable flicker at the corner of her eye that she liked to attribute to aging but which I suspected was a different kind of badge. One that, until now at least, had always had my name on it.

I couldn't leave without one last try. "So, there's nothing else you wanted to tell me?"

"No. Like what?" she said.

"Nothing . . . through the post this morning?"

The vein in her neck jutted out. "You're not in trouble again, are you, Lily?"

I feigned a bark of outraged laughter. "No! Why would I be?" I said, and in that moment it was important I convince her, a strange reversal that had started that last year. She'd seemed relieved at first when Dad died—having one less person to care for—but sometimes she'd get this look in her eyes and I couldn't be sure anymore which of us was protecting the other. "I sent you a card, that's all," I said. "*Mumma Maya*, the Abba singing nun. It'll come tomorrow, most likely."

WALKING BACK TO the station, I tried to analyze things more rationally. Maya's reaction meant one of two things: either she'd yet to receive a letter or someone had singled me out, which made no sense. What we'd been through, we'd been through together.

THE VICIOUS OVERNIGHT storm had wreaked havoc with the roads around Clapham and all across the Common lay the fractured corpses of oaks and sycamores, all their years of hard work felled in a single night of furious devastation. I wasn't in the mood for Dr. Fenton. By that stage, I'd been seeing professionals on and off for six years, ever since the debacle at university. If you were to plot my progress on a graph it would resemble an errant sound wave, lilting as a Chopin nocturne with a schizoid Liszt phrase somewhere in the middle.

The waiting room toilet was engaged when I got there. I checked my watch as I hovered outside, listening for the sound of the flush and the asthmatic wheeze of the dryer before at last a man stepped out. He couldn't have been more than thirty but there was something unraveled about him: the finger of grime on his collar, the mismatched socks, like a detour from the vanity of youth. Is that how I looked to others? Even at twenty-five, was I pushing the boundaries of appearing ironic?

"Sorry," he said. "Hello." We tried to maneuver ourselves unsuccessfully.

"I'm late—if I could just—"

"Seeing Dr. Fenton?" he said. "It's okay. We've only just finished."

Fenton appeared at his office door. "Ah, Scott, I've caught you," he said. "The number for that group I was telling you about."

He didn't look like a Scott. During their furtive exchange of paper I sensed the man glance at me again, but not being in the mood to satisfy his curiosity, I kept my eyes on the floor and waited to be let into the room.

"I WOULDN'T WORRY," Dr. Fenton said when I mentioned the trees on the Common. "Nature tends to take care of itself, irrespective of others' intentions."

He seemed distracted that day. His pen, which I could never keep up with, remained at a lazy angle, his eyes drifting toward the window. Not that I blamed him. How many shopping lists and plans for home improvements had been gestated during similar tedium?

In an effort to pass the time I decided to show him the letter. I followed his eyes as he read it twice and then put it back on the table. "You made the call?" he said.

"I just assumed it was one of those cons. Like that bumf they send you in the post. *Reader's Digest*. The pools. *You're* a winner!" He didn't laugh when I gave it the jazz hands.

"The man's name didn't ring any bells?"

Hei-Fong Lee. Deceased.

I shook my head.

"Have you spoken to your sister about it?"

"I was hoping she'd get one too, so we could decide what to do. Together."

"And what if you couldn't agree?"

"That's not going to happen," I said. "I mean, obviously we have differences of opinion . . . telly and books, that sort of thing. But never about the important stuff."

He smiled. "Like coming here, for example . . ."

My armpits prickled under my jumper. I shouldn't have sat so close to the radiator. "Look, maybe I *wasn't* that keen to begin with, but that's my point about Maya. She's always known what's best for me."

His pen sprang to life across the page. The most it had moved in ten minutes. "So those initial feelings you expressed here, that your sister was attempting to control you—"

I started laughing. "I didn't say that!"

Fenton raised an eyebrow in contradiction. "If I remember correctly, you were quite angry about a list she'd made in order to help your recovery."

Try to go out for a run; stop examining yourself in mirrors; practice having conversations with others.

I shuffled against my seat. "If I said it, it was out of frustration. I'm a very frustrated person. Isn't part of that blaming each other?"

"Sometimes, yes," he said. 'But it makes me wonder why you didn't make the call. As something you could do for yourself." He gestured to the letter. "As far as I can tell, this could have any number of outcomes available."

"As in, the cat is both dead and alive?"

"If you like."

I knew what he was getting at. If the inheritance *was* connected to Mumma, it would be a chance to find out about her, learn something about myself: where I came from, where I fit in, especially as Maya and Dad had never talked about it. But as usual with Dr. Fenton, such a proposal relied on the binary.

"You're forgetting something," I said. "Knowing after the fact is one thing. But you can't unopen the box."

"Fear didn't stop you before."

"I don't know what you mean. Aren't I here *because* I'm frightened?"

"And when you hurt yourself at Cambridge? That must have taken guts."

I pinned my elbows against my sides, trying to hide the dark circles of sweat that had started to leak from my armpits. "That wasn't bravery," I said. The same petulant tone of voice as if he'd bested me at marbles. "And I was a different person then."

He crossed his legs and his notebook fell, its landing deafening and infinite in the silence. "Were you—really?" he said.

FOUR

Sook-Yin

June 1966

The boat was a foreign country, and though Sook-Yin was not fluent in its language she knew that some things were the same the world over. There were fishermen and captains here too, and First Class was for the people at the top. Theirs was the gold-ceilinged dining room, the dance floor that shone like a conker, the bluest swimming pool with its deck chairs and parasols where pale-skinned women shrugged off their clothes and tried to marinate their flesh in the scorching sun.

She was happier down below. The room on Deck D where she stayed was only one floor above the workers and she enjoyed the vacancy of its days, the way come nightfall she could lie in her bunk and feel the ship's belly vibrating like a heartbeat.

All the women in her cabin were Chinese. Two of them—like herself—were going to London to train as nurses, although in a different place to Sook-Yin. The third, it surprised her to discover, was a woman with whom she'd once been at school.

Florence Ho was two years her senior and was to marry a man from Lamma who'd settled in London some years ago. Aside from this basic fact, the details seemed to change with her mood. First he was eighty and then a hundred years old; he had four children, or perhaps it was two; his wife had died in the midst of childbirth and then later, a terrible accident. Whichever version Florence chose to relate was always met with the other women's sympathy, Sook-Yin alone in her relief that that there was someone more stupid than herself.

None of them had traveled long-distance by ship before, a disadvantage that slowly became clear in the sickness that befell their cabin. Only Sook-Yin remained unscathed, but each morning she woke to the engine fumes mixed with the smell of vomit, the air cloying and thick with its sourness. When the women cried for their mothers, it was her they came to rely on, fetching flannels and bowls of soup or ice chips scooped into paper cups at whatever time they cared to demand them. Used to her life belowdecks, she always felt exposed in these errands, her ticket tucked firmly in her bra in case she was called for questioning.

AT SUEZ, the heat was dazzling but any hopes of finding respite on dry land were disappointed by orders to stay on deck. The view was meager consolation, taunting Sook-Yin as it did with its promise of the markets in the distance, with their scent of incense and ripe fruit and the enticing calls of the vendors. She was delighted when an hour later a group of women came waddling toward the gangplank. "Lady! Lady!" they called. "Come and see the pretty necklace we have."

Sook-Yin ventured down from the deck, mesmerized by the large wooden tray that each of them wore around the neck, holding strands of polished beads that glinted and winked in the sunlight. She took one of the necklaces and held it against herself, marveling at the ripples of green and ocher that followed her fingers like water. "How much?" she asked the woman.

"Ma'am, for you, ten shillings. I give you very good price."

The only money that Sook-Yin had was the note her father

had given her. Ah-Ma had put the rest in a bank in London. She returned the necklace to the tray. "No. Is impossible," she said in English.

"Okay. How much you give me?"

Sook-Yin had already turned back to the ship, but stole a glance over her shoulder and held up the fingers of one hand.

The woman pulled a face. "Starve my children?" she said.

"Five." Sook-Yin was adamant. Hadn't ah-Ma taught her as much? Who at home had shown *them* pity when they'd trawled the streets looking for work, her feet burning through the soles of her sandals and her throat scratchy as the rind of a kumquat? From the slums of Diamond Hill to the penthouses high in the Peak, people would always take advantage if you let them.

She made sure she counted the change. She didn't know what five shillings was worth, only that it was half of what it could have been, and she congratulated herself on her bargaining.

Later, as her cabinmates passed it between them, its value only grew in their envy. "You should take it to a jeweler," one said. "Those stones must be worth a fortune."

"I would rather have the money," Florence barked. She had refused to touch the necklace, dismissing it with a cursory glance as the others cooed around her.

"But I would never sell it," said Sook-Yin as she tucked it deep into the neck of her undershirt. She'd already decided that it was her talisman, a totem to the person she would be, and she vowed to keep it safe, always.

THE ENGLISH SKY was the color of a fresh bruise as they landed at Tilbury Docks. Sook-Yin squinted and blinked in the murky light, the taste of dirt on her tongue as she boarded the waiting minibus. Florence, with her purse full of money, had barely stopped to share her details—her new address and telephone number hastily scribbled on a torn receipt—before she'd hailed a taxi and left.

The scenery changed as they drove away. Roads as thin as noodles flashed past in a blur of grime: ashy concrete, blinded windows, the abandoned skins of washing on balconies. A wave of panic ambushed her. Before she'd stepped foot on the ship, the farthest she'd traveled was Cheung Chau Island, ninety minutes away on the ferry, and even then she'd managed to get lost. But ah-Chor had been adamant. She could return only in an emergency. Losing your way was not an emergency.

THE NURSE'S QUARTERS were not at the hospital but in a place the driver called Hammersmith. Sook-Yin had looked forward to her own room but when she arrived that evening another woman was already waiting there: small, with yellow hair and eyes as pale as a ghost. She jumped up and held out her hand.

"Hello, who are you?" she said.

"My name is Chen Sook-Yin."

The woman let out a laugh, revealing an enviable arc of perfect teeth. "I'll never remember all that! How about I call you Chen?"

"Chen is family name. Unless we in army now?"

She said her name was Peggy, drawing out the syllables with effort as though she imagined Sook-Yin was deaf. "Well, come in and take the weight off your feet, love. I hope you don't mind I took the bed by the window so I could have a crafty fag now and then."

Sook-Yin had no idea what she'd said. The woman's voice was like Gung-Gung's rifle—*tatatata*—so fast! She looked around the room, mouthing the words that Sister Catherine had taught her: *a desk, a chair, a window. Dirty stain on carpet.* She didn't understand the bed with its sheet tight-tight on the mattress, stiff and rough as a coffin.

She'd arrived too late for the canteen dinner, so Peggy took her to a stand-up restaurant and bought her fish wrapped up in newspaper that left a ticklish smell in their room. Sook-Yin gasped as she opened the parcel. A whole cod! Back home, she was always the last to the rice bowl after ah-Chor and ah-Ma had finished, and she couldn't believe her luck. She ate at speed with her fingers, her heart beating as fast as a runner's.

"What do you think?" Peggy asked.

"Yes, I really like. And funny potatoes too."

"Ooh, yeah. Chips are great."

Peggy stood and addressed their reflections as she tidied her hair in the mirror. "D'ya reckon they put us together on purpose? Two foreigners, if you know what I mean."

"But you not foreigner," Sook-Yin said. "You are English lady."

"I'm from the *north* of England. That's like Timbuktu to a Londoner, although it must be worse for you. Are you feeling very homesick?"

Sook-Yin considered the word, imagining ah-Chor and Ba-Ba's faces. Sick *for* home, or because of it? Shook her head. "No. I come for adventure."

Peggy turned to her open suitcase and began pulling out dresses and thin coats, which she hung in the small shared wardrobe. "Don't you have anything?" she said.

"Is too late fetch luggage now. Man put it inside basement."

Her enormous bull leather trunk. The name of its first owner had been crossed out and replaced in a dull blue paint: *Chen, Sook-Yin, bound for England.* Ah-Chor had written it in his scrawling handwriting, the letters big enough that it wouldn't get stolen or, most likely, so she couldn't forget. Now, as she stared at Peggy's clothes—bright as the apartments in Wan Chai with their blues and pinks and yellows—she was relieved her own clothes were hidden. There was something shameful about them: the long johns, the fisherman's sweater, the four pairs of thick wool socks bought at the Army and Navy store. How many pieces of strangers' underwear had passed through her and ah-Ma's hands in order to afford them? *England is cold,* they'd said. For the first time since her departure, a small, sharp stab of resentment settled above her chest at the realization of her family's ignorance.

Peggy took a handful of pictures from her case and pinned them to the large cork noticeboard. Sook-Yin got up to look closer. "That is Marilyn Monroe," she said.

"Aye. Do you like her, too?"

"Oh, yes. She very famous in Hong Kong. Like James Dean and Cary Grant."

"*Love* James Dean," Peggy said. "And that Clark Gable's a bit of a dish."

Sook-Yin put her hands to her face. For all the weeks leading up to her trip, she had only imagined the bad things: the vast oceans between the continents, the barriers of language and culture. And yet here they were joined in this room, by the cold air that lay thick as a blanket and some strange desirous instinct programmed by films and music and shared dreams. "In my language is funny," she ventured. "Clark Gable is same as this." She gestured to her armpit and said the words in Cantonese, and Peggy howled until she cried.

AT EIGHT O'CLOCK the next morning, she was summoned to meet Matron Connolly. Earlier, she'd collected her uniform, dismayed to find that aside from the paper caps there was nothing small enough to fit her. She fidgeted outside the office, the starched innards of her new dress swinging around her like a rice sack.

"Come!" a voice called when she knocked. She opened the door and waited, curtsying when the woman looked up. "Ah, you must be Miss Chen," she said. "For goodness's sake dear, I'm not the Queen. Come in and shut the door." Sook-Yin sat with her hands in her lap, avoiding the inquiry in the woman's gaze and uncomfortable in the silence.

"So, what makes you think you would be a good nurse?"

Sook-Yin had not prepared for this question. She knew that A and B equaled C, but not why it should be this way. Her brother had got rid of her and she had come.

Her mind snagged on the memory of Florence bent double over the toilet. "On ship, I look after sick people."

"You were a nurse on board a ship?"

"Not nurse, exactly. Passenger. But I care for women in cabin. Bring soup and washing their . . ." She paused as she searched for the word. "Knickers."

Matron cleared her throat. "I see. And what about the rest of your family? Was your mother a nurse, for example?"

"My mother is cleaner," she said. "Washing people's—"

"Yes, yes, I understand. But washing is only part of your job here. In ten weeks, you will sit exams. Will you be able to manage the lessons?"

"I promise I very hard worker."

She pursed her lips at Sook-Yin's dress. "Is that the smallest uniform they had?"

"Yes. I sorry for look bad."

Matron checked her watch and stood. "Come with me, Miss Chen."

Sook-Yin followed behind at a distance toward a small annex at the back of the building that, judging by the odor from its chimney, was fueled by cabbage and strawberry jam.

"This is Nurse Chen, a new student at the hospital," Matron said to the woman on duty. "I want you to give her three portions of everything until she fills that uniform."

SURPRISED BY THE matron's kindness, Sook-Yin returned to her empty room and began a letter to ah-Ma. *London is fine*, she wrote. *People are being very kind to me so perhaps I belong here after all.*

She stopped and reread the words, the characters blurring and swimming in front of her as her tears cockled the airmail paper. She crossed through them and started again. *Ma-Ma*, she scribbled, *you were right. England is cold and wet. I am homesick. Please write back to me.*

FIVE

Lily

15th Day of Mourning

I was on my shift at the charity shop. The volunteering had been Maya's idea—a way of spitting me back at the world when the worst of my illness was over but I couldn't face getting a "real" job. Three years later and I was still there.

It suited me, I suppose, being surrounded by dead people's things. Most of the donors weren't really dead but it was amazing the stories you heard, the gaps you filled in their absence: the unworn mother-of-the-bride's dress, the single stiletto missing its twin in some gutter in Shaftesbury Avenue.

The people suited me, too. All of us were drifters in some way, trying to navigate our way back to life or stopping ourselves from falling out of it. Babs was one of the former. Her husband, Reggie, had died four years earlier but she was only now managing to bring his stuff in. It was the little things at first—a mug or a handful of paperbacks—but that last month she'd let go of the jigsaw he'd been doing the week that he passed. She'd even taped a note to the box— *may be missing pieces*—because, as she explained to me later, no one wanted to spend all that time trying to put something together only to find out it was never a possibility.

28

When the shop got quiet, I showed Babs the letter. It wouldn't hurt to get another opinion, and she enjoyed giving the benefit of her experience, like when someone tried on a secondhand suit and needed a woman's eye, or if she thought it was likely to rain; the hope that she remained useful to the world.

"It might be a tax thing," she said. "From when your parents were living there. Now that things are changing, I mean."

In less than two months' time, Hong Kong's ownership would revert back to China. Somewhere in my mind I knew this. I knew the name Deng Xiaoping and that in the eighties he appeared on the news with Thatcher to discuss the colony's Handover. Chinese faces on the telly were rare back then, unless it was an attempt to make fun of them, and it had surprised me. Being seen. I'd looked up at the news like a dog who only halfway knew his name and was trying to make the connection, but then Dad had turned it off and gone to cry alone in his room.

"It won't be that," I said.

"How old were you again—when your mum died?"

"Barely five. We were *all* in Kowloon when it happened." The telling had become routine, although never as painless as I hoped.

"Not much time to make memories, then?"

Do you ever get déjà vu, Maya? Sometimes I'm sure there are things I remember.

You're imagining it, Lils, conflating. Everything you remember is what I've told you.

"No. Not really," I said.

Babs sighed with the impressive despair that she reserved for moments of shared distress. "At least Reggie had a few good innings."

"Yeah, that's always—oh, *shit* . . ." My gaze froze on the front of the shop as a woman pushed through the door, weighed down by bags. She didn't see me at first, but then—

"Lileeeee? Oh my God!" she cried. "It must be absolute *years*." She stepped back so she could take in the sight of me. "Wow! You're looking . . ."

29

"Alive?"

"*Great.* I was going to say *great!*" She attempted an air hug, her arms akimbo. "What are you doing here, anyway?"

I shrugged. "Volunteering. Sometimes." I turned and pulled Babs towards me. "This is Elise," I said. "We were at uni together."

Babs offered a tight-lipped smile as she leaned over and reached for her bags: Waitrose, Armani, Paul Smith. "Should I take those from you?" she said.

"That would be fabulous, thank you. About time I had a clear-out."

Babs hefted them away to the back room, leaving us lingering like driftwood on the carpet. Elise fingered a brooch on the counter. "God, you're good," she whispered. "Giving your time up, I mean."

"Some of us have it, I suppose."

"What else are you up to these days?"

I fought my urge to view this as rhetorical. It couldn't be. By that point I hadn't seen her in five years, as evidenced by the change in her appearance. She'd lost a fair bit of weight, along with the white-girl dreadlocks and the *58% Don't Want Pershing* T-shirts, replaced by court shoes and pin-striped power suits.

"I'm trying to open a music school."

"Lily! That's crazy!" she said. Terrible choice of words. As was obvious by the way she cringed.

"I don't mean anything ambitious. A small studio or something would do me. For the local kids who can't afford lessons. Slow, though—red tape and all that."

She gave an approving little nod. "In that case I should give you my details. I'm sure I could pull a few strings."

Out came the card from her handbag, which I read only out of politeness. "Dizzy heights, already."

She threw her head back and laughed. *Ma ha ha.* "Remember how I swore off corporate law? Used to say it was a sign of selling out, but God, the injustices we uncover!"

"Yeah, I bet," I said.

Still fighting the good fight, of course.

ELISE WAS IN her third year when I met her at Cambridge. Freshers' Fair, 1988. I'd already spotted her on the margins of the hallway, between the Rowing Club and Millais poster sellers, desperate to drum up interest for her causes: Socialist Rights at Oxbridge; the Ethnic Womens' Reading Group. By contrast, I was fresh out of my London comprehensive, sneaking past the table for the Oriental Society pretending I was a goth.

Nevertheless, she persisted. Apparently, we were in this together, a sorority based on God knows what. *We have to be visible*, she'd always say. *Fight the good fight.* I never summoned the courage to tell her that I'd already surrendered a long time ago; that my immigrant mother had died and left me with half an identity about as useful as a broken mug; that my dad, with his grief and refusal, had killed all the fight left in me. Instead, I did what I always did and made it all about me in the most spectacular way I could think of, just so Elise and everyone else would stop telling me what they wanted me to be and leave me to be nothing at all. Like I'd told Fenton. The coward's way out.

ELISE TURNED HER gaze to the shelves with the faux decorum of approaching something delicate. "And how's everything else been going?"

"My health, you mean?" She stared. "Yeah. All better," I said.

"Because you had us all very worried back then." She grazed my arm with the tips of her fingers. "And I was devastated to hear about your dad." I thought I'd misheard her at first but then she went on. "He was such a lovely man. I mean, I know it happened last year, but—"

"How did you know about that?"

"Oh!" She shifted her weight to her hip. "I suppose it must have been Maya. We had a few phone calls and dinners. Nothing major."

"Right." I could just imagine the two of them together, sipping their warm white wine at Langham's, retailing my humiliation. *Oh, isn't it awful? Poor Lily. All that wasted promise.* "Well," I said. "Mustn't keep you."

"Oh, yes. Right." She made a show of checking her watch and then reached over and touched my arm again. "You look well, Lily," she said. "It really was lovely to see you."

"Yeah. You too, Elise."

I watched her walk out of the shop, quickening as she crossed Brixton Road. She still had a fat arse, actually.

Babs scuttled out from the back room. "Everything okay?" she said.

"Yeah. No worries. All good." I fetched my coat from behind the counter and shrugged it on.

"I knew I recognized her," she said.

"What's that?"

"Your friend. She's been here a few times, by my reckoning. Spends ages looking around. Bought a Gloria Steinem once, as I recall."

"Right." It all made sense, now. I wasn't surprised that she and Maya had become friends. My sister may not have been made from the same stuff—our silver spoon decidedly plastic—but she worked hard to convince you otherwise and maybe that was the point. That the illusion of life took work. That being part of the world *took work*.

Still, having an accomplice was cheating.

Babs rearranged Reggie's jigsaw for the tenth time. "Go home and sort out that letter."

"You reckon?"

"Yes. I do. It's like that old movie," she said. "In all that shit, there must be a pony."

SIX

Sook-Yin

August 1966

Sook-Yin had been at the hospital for eight weeks. Some of them—the ones spent in pediatrics and maternity—had passed with ease, the inbuilt vulnerability of women and children making their gratitude toward her instinctive.

The general wards were something else. They were invariably the preserve of old men traveling headlong toward their own ending and determined they were going to shout about it. To them, Sook-Yin's care was an insult. They had neither the time nor the patience for her English and no problem in telling her so. At their service she was not even "nurse," but "Here!" or "Woman!" or "Wei-Wei Wong." Why did they call her Wei-Wei Wong? Wei-Wei Wong was a prostitute's name.

This wasn't her only problem. Their first exam was in less than a fortnight and Sook-Yin could remember none of it. She could set tea trays and wash a hundred bedpans, fold a sheet until its edges were like knives, but each time that she sat down to read, the words would float from her mind like balloons, mocking and eluding her grasp. It would have been easier to run to the moon and bring back a star in her pocket.

SHE'D JUST RETURNED from breakfast that morning when Peggy appeared with a parcel. "For me?" Sook-Yin dared to ask. In the two months since she'd been in London, she'd not heard a thing from ah-Ma.

Peggy shook her head. "Sorry, love, not today. Do you want me to open it elsewhere?"

"No. I like to see." In spite of her disappointment, Sook-Yin could never begrudge her friend's joy.

Together, they sat on the bed and Peggy let her untie the string. Beneath the crackled folds of brown paper it was like Christmas and New Year together: a bright red lipstick and four pairs of stockings along with Sook-Yin's favorite magazine, *Cosmopolitan*. She'd never seen such things in Hong Kong: perfect instructions on how to eat and dress, how to wash your face in four different ways. Sometimes there were naughty things too, which she read behind the shield of her hand: pictures of naked body parts and how important a woman's pleasure was. Mostly, these things confused her.

"Still no news from your mam?"

"No. I think she forget me."

Peggy picked up a pair of the stockings, and then went across to the noticeboard and took down the photo of Marilyn Monroe before handing them both to Sook-Yin. "For you. They're a present," she said. "You'll always be Marilyn to me now."

Sook-Yin rolled the shape of the name in her mouth like a taste she was unfamiliar with. "Marilyn Chen," she said, deciding she liked its flavor. Her face fell. "But I have nothing to give back you." What did *she* have that anyone could want?

"Don't worry about that," said Peggy. "Although there is *something* that you could do for me." She paused. "How about you try and join in more? Have a laugh and a dance with the rest of us?"

That past month, a record player had appeared in the common room and on weekends there would be parties: crowds and smoke and noise and the sound of glass on glass like the sunset call of cattle bells, the licorice circle of records where men and women sang nonsense songs. *Da doo ron ron. Mashed potatoes.* Sook-Yin had watched through a crack in the door once but despite the number of people had never felt so lonely.

"I can't. I have so much study."

Peggy looked down at her shoes. "I'm not only asking for me . . . some of the girls have been talking, like. Saying you don't want to fit in."

"Why they say that about me?"

"Because you're always in here, for one thing. And for another, girls can be bitches."

Sook-Yin lay back on the bed. It was the math problem all over again; that elusive missing ingredient that others had to make sense of the world. And in the same way that her homework defeated her, she feared she would never find the right answer.

ON THE DAY of their written exam, all the nurses gathered in the canteen. Matron Connolly stood at the front, a long wooden baton in her hand to mark the time at thirty-minute intervals: thirty minutes for basic anatomy, thirty minutes for common diseases, thirty for protocol and practice.

Sook-Yin took her seat at the back. It was lucky that earlier in the week she had surprised herself in the practical. Her lunch tray was a thing of neat beauty, her skill with a bedsheet exemplary. Now all she needed was a nominal pass and her place on the course was secure.

She said a prayer and turned over the paper.

Complete the diagram below, showing both the location and relative size of the gallbladder, kidneys, and spleen.

She looked up and gazed at the room. Everyone else's head was bent, their concentration drifting in waves and carrying the smell of Lux and Juicy Fruit, of minds cleaner and fresher than her own. She read the question again and then drew a small round shape with an arrow. *This is Spleen*, she wrote. She squinted and rubbed it out, changing the word to *gallbladder* before adding *God help me* in the margin in the smallest Chinese characters.

Afterward, pleading a headache, she went alone to her room and hid herself under the covers. She must have fallen asleep, because by the time she finally emerged the sky through the window was dark and someone was knocking on the door. When she didn't answer, it opened anyway.

"Hello? Is anyone in here?"

Sook-Yin scrambled to get to her feet as Matron Connolly came into the room. "Are you ill, Nurse Chen?" she said. "You do realize that supper is over?"

She perched on the edge of the bed and patted the space beside her. "You came top on the practical this week. The written paper, I take it, was hard for you."

Confronted by the proof of her stupidity, Sook-Yin pressed her nails into the flesh of her palms.

"Do you want to stay at the hospital?"

"Yes! I want very much for staying!" It felt like a rock had been thrown at her stomach. How could Matron doubt it? And, more important, how could she prove it to her?

Numbskull. Shame of the family.

She stood and put her fists beneath her rib cage. "*Here* is kidneys," she said. She pressed the upper left of her abdomen. "And this is where you find spleen." She slid her hand to the right. "Here, I know, is gallbladder."

Matron watched her performance in silence. "I see," she said at last. "There is clearly nothing wrong with your brain. Your problem, Miss Chen, as I see it, is merely your fear of being tested." She pinched the bridge of her nose. "From Monday, I will tutor you myself and then you will resit the exam and get the full marks that I know you can. Do I make myself understood?" Sook-Yin nodded. "And in the meantime, I want you to buck up."

"I do not know this 'buck up.'"

"It means whenever there's a storm we smile. *Even* as we get wet." Matron stood and reached into her pocket. "I almost forgot," she said. "A letter came for you this morning." She laid it on top of the desk. "I believe it's from your mother."

As soon as she was alone again, Sook-Yin collapsed on the bed. She had earned a second chance. And a letter from ah-Ma, too! She fingered the airmail envelope, caught between excitement and wanting to savor the moment, and then tore it open along its edges.

Ah-Yin, how are you, dear daughter? I enjoy reading your letters very much, and the photograph of yourself in your uniform. You look fat.

It is only now that I've been able to write to you. I don't know if you heard it on the wireless, but there is a revolution happening on the mainland. Mao Zedong has been destroying all the statues and gathering an army of Red Guards to spread his message of communism. In Harbin City they rounded up the intellectuals and made them stand with signs around their necks like naughty children in school. I do not like these "Struggle Sessions." President Zhou says it cannot happen in Hong Kong, but there has been talk of riots in the villages. There is so much anti-British feeling and now the moderates are getting nervous because of the way they rub hands with the banks. Ah-Chor says it is not safe to be a teacher. I do not know what to make of it.

Better news, I went to yum-cha with Mrs. Chee. I told her it was too expensive but she wants us to be lonely together, so what can I do about it? Sui Je from the Army and Navy store wants a picture of you in your new socks so she can get customers into her shop. You should get one at Buckingham Palace.

I am praying for you at the temple, although last week I paid the villain beaters to put a curse on your father. Today I heard a rumor that his whore lost a fortune on mahjong. I am very glad about it.

There is no need to worry about me. It is better that you have a good job and earn money for the rest of the family so your brother has nothing to complain about. One day, he might even be happy.

With love as always, from Ma-Ma.

SOOK-YIN READ AND reread the words, her heart clenching. What if war came back to the island? Would the Red Guards confiscate their chickens? And what would happen to her family then? She pictured ah-Chor disgraced on a stool. So much for his boasts about being an intellectual!

The only thing that could help them was money, but she already sent home most of her salary and there was no prospect of a raise till she qualified. She glanced at the books on the table. Now, more than ever, she needed to prove herself.

THE FOLLOWING MONDAY she was called to the office. Her timetable was clear that morning and she took along her nursing manual, eager to start her tuition.

"Yes?"

Sook-Yin balked as she looked into the room. Matron Connolly was nowhere to be seen and in her place was an older woman, as thin and veined as a string bean.

"Ah, Miss Chen, come in." She pointed to the seat in front of her. "Matron Connolly has had to take leave and will be absent for the foreseeable future. My name is Matron Baxter. Do you know why I asked to see you?"

Sook-Yin clasped her book as she sat, her damp fingertips sliding on its cover. "Matron . . . *old* matron," she began, "arrange to give me lesson."

"Lessons? What sort of lessons?"

"To help me pass exam."

"But you sat the exams, did you not?" Whenever the woman spoke, her left eye veered around in its socket while the right remained frozen and glaring. She opened the notebook in front of her and ran a ruler along its columns. "Ninety-two percent on the practical, yet only fifteen on the written exam. I must confess, Miss Chen, I can't recall a more blatant discrepancy. Did you receive any help on the practical?"

Sook-Yin's eyes widened. "No! I did it by my own . . . Matron Connolly said—"

The woman held up a hand. "As Matron Connolly is not here to defend herself, I can only go on what's in front of me. I take it you remember the conditions of your training here? The contract you signed when you entered?"

"Yes. I must pass exam."

"On the *first* attempt, Miss Chen." She closed her book with a dull slap. "Sadly, as a result, I have no option but to end your place here."

Sook-Yin's mouth fell open, all semblance of decorum forgotten. "Wait now, please!" she said. "There must be other way around this."

"I'm sorry, but that is impossible. Exceptions would only set a dangerous precedent." The woman got up and walked to the window and then turned and faced her with a taut smile. "You will have twenty-four hours to pack. Please return all items of hospital property, including any keys you hold to the building." She resumed her place behind the desk but remained standing until Sook-Yin rose. "I wish you good luck, Miss Chen. I'm sure one day you will find where you belong."

SEVEN

Lily

20th Day of Mourning

When the week ended with no news from Maya, I made an appointment with the solicitor on the letter.

Greene and Nesbit was a swanky anomaly on a tatty corner of Gray's Inn Road. Like the neighborhood it fought to contain, the street had grown jaded with age, its grand rows of terraced houses now blighted by the neon of grocers' shops and the murky tide line of the passing traffic.

Mr. Nesbit greeted me himself. He was a balding, middle-aged American with the manner of a game-show host and a suit as vivid as a hangover. "Miss Li-Li Chen?" he said, as he leaned forward to shake my hand.

"Actually, it's always been Miller."

He smiled. "Shall we step into my office?"

This was only the first of many entrances I was required to pass through that morning as he proceeded to excavate my existence with the scrutiny of an anthropologist. *What was your father's name? Who are your siblings (if any)? What was your last address?* He'd also asked me to bring in my passport, which his secretary took away and copied.

"Congratulations," he said at last, with an effusive spread of his arms. "I'm pleased to confirm, Miss Miller, that you've been named as a beneficiary in a will."

"This Hei-Fong Lee?" I said.

He shot me with an invisible pistol. "Chinese banking magnate."

"Sorry, but I still don't get it. Why leave anything to me?"

He pulled a folder from the drawer in his desk. "The bequest appears as a codicil. That on completion of a certain task you'll become fully entitled to the inheritance."

I had visions of the Labors of Heracles, Atlas with the world on his back. "What sort of task?" I said.

"Principally, that you go to Kowloon and sign your acceptance in person."

I blinked at him. "I'm expected to go to Hong Kong?"

"Mr. Lee was very insistent." He opened the folder and read. "'With the express purpose of reconnecting with your roots.' Specifically, in relation to your mother."

I wiped the slickness from my palms. *Obviously* this would be about Mumma. What other connection could there be? "I suppose I'm free to refuse?"

Mr. Nesbit stared at me. The same look I'd seen all my life from Dad and Maya and Elise. The one that said, *Are you mad?* "Miss Miller, perhaps I should have been more specific. The bequest is for half a million pounds."

I know what most people would have done on hearing this. How most people would have reacted. Except my family were not most people. For twenty years we'd barely talked about Mumma. It was "too upsetting" for Maya and Dad, which had turned into an unspoken agreement that we never look back at the past. It was only me who'd wanted to remember—*maudlin, morbid Lily. Always trying to be different.* Was it any wonder I grew afraid of asking?

"Want some advice?" Nesbit said. "Take the money, have a nice holiday, pop in on a few of your relatives, if only for appearance's sake. Nobody's grading you on this. It really is a win-win situation."

He hurried a small card towards me. "The details of his executor. The eldest son, I believe. He'll be your person of contact."

I glanced at the boldness of its typeface. *Daniel Lee. Futures*, it read, along with his various numbers.

"There's one other thing I need to mention. Mr. Lee's family is in a period of mourning—a cultural thing, I'm guessing—which adds a note of urgency to the proceedings. They need you to complete the task within the first forty-nine days of the death." He flipped through the diary on his desk. "What with the admin and your delay in coming here, tomorrow is day twenty-one, so while you're at liberty to think things over, please do so with that consideration."

ON THE TUBE, the rocking of the carriage took on a strange, seductive lullaby: five hundred thousand pounds. Five hundred *thousand* pounds. They called it life-changing money for a reason, and it wasn't as though I didn't need it. The money Dad had left me was almost gone. It would barely support me for a year, especially if I didn't find a job. With that amount, I could start up the music school. Prove I wasn't useless after all.

I allowed myself to indulge in the fantasy. It had been embellished over the years, playing out like a scene from a movie, from the *shush shush* of its velvet curtains to the fat bellies of cellos and French horns and the sigh of ivory on wood; the fascination of children's fingers, eager and mute in their discovery. A world where everyone was welcome.

I almost forgot I was going to Maya's. I stood up into someone's armpit as the doors were closing at London Bridge—*sorry, sorry, sorry,*—and wrestled my way to the door, landing breathless and panicked on the platform. How the hell would I tell her about Hong Kong and why was I even doing this when I could just go home and think? I trudged toward the overground. Because I'd already sworn that I'd be there. Another in a long line of family (dis)agreements.

In the month before Dad died, he made us promise to meet

up occasionally, an idea born out of the belief that, denied his ar-bitration, our relationship inevitably would disintegrate. The other reason I couldn't put it off was because Ed was working late and it was the only night I would get her alone.

I actually enjoyed it sometimes—watching a telly that was big-ger than my head and drinking soup that wasn't from a cup, but I suppose it was the other stuff too—the comfort of having a sister, the effortless safety of someone knowing you and knowing them back in return. Before Ed came onto the scene it was the most faith-ful relationship I'd ever had.

I wasn't surprised that marriage had changed her. I was more bemused that they'd settled in Forest Hill, which was barely a blip on the map of the nouveau riche. Naturally, Ed had razed the place, built umpteen glass extensions and a subterranean *viewing room* to differentiate himself from the proles. When questioned about the expense, Maya referred to it as their *forever home*, a sickeningly lib-eral phrase encompassing a life barring all possibility of the shit ever hitting the fan.

Apart from the way we looked—my changeling, genetic freak of a sister with her green eyes and dark blond hair—this was merely the most obvious of our differences, the ones that people on the outside might see, but there'd always been others of temperament: dominant versus subordinate, serious versus irreverent, living their best life and barely existing.

While Maya never deigned to give me my own key, she did—on these prebooked occasions—leave one behind for me at the front door, concealed beneath an ancient Fray Bentos tin. The tin was a humorous nod to our past, the key her quiet acknowledgment that in my inadequacy I was still living it, and arriving early and indulg-ing myself was the closest thing I ever got to a holiday.

I LET MYSELF in and pottered about. Much as I hated to admit it, I *was* still in thrall to its novelty—the pure, indulgent space of it—and an hour passed with ease, creeping around the various rooms like a burglar at the Louvre. I had my feet up in the living room, watching the end of some awful quiz, when the events of the morning rushed back to me. It must have been all those winners on screen. The relief of money.

One look. I wonder if.

I made my way to the basement. Ed's home cinema took up most of the space here, but there was a room at the end of the corridor that Maya had earmarked for a nursery. I opened the door and looked inside, relieved to find it the same.

It was a storage room of two halves. The front was neatly swept and full of tidy stacks of baby things—a cot, a mobile, a designer pram—new inside their packaging and bearing price tags that made my eyes water. Behind these was a jumble of odds and sods, an abandoned repository of regrettable purchases and vacuum-packed victims of the seasons: jacquard curtains, dour-looking bedsheets.

I inched my way to the back, the tramlines of dust at my feet announcing its seldom-used status. Most of the stuff from Dad's house was here, a buckling tower of cardboard boxes that Maya and I had somehow filled together in our haze of indeterminate grief. It was behind these, tucked away in a corner, that I saw it—the raised hands of its green vinyl straps announcing its impatience to be collected.

Mumma's suitcase.

I'd opened it only a handful of times, and always like this. In secret. I carried it to the front of the room and coaxed the rusty locks, disappointed when they at last came free with a waft of age and mustiness. I didn't know what I'd expected: sunshine and watermelons, perhaps.

My heart snagged as I opened the lid. Our old clothes were folded on top, laundered and replaced by Dad in the days after we'd come back from Kowloon: a tiny short set and thin cotton dress, two pairs of red sandals in different sizes. The only things he'd kept. My scant memories of what else had existed had all but vanished on Mumma's death. New Year had reverted to the first of January without the prospect of *lucky money* or the chance to utter a catch-phrase in a sticky, forgotten language. If we'd ever known a tongue different from our dad's it would be as rusty as the case's locks now and probably sound as ugly.

I TURNED MY attention to the things beneath—the random treasures thrown in by our grandmother when she knew we were being sent away: an ID card in Mumma's name, the printing crazed and blurry, her canceled passport, her death certificate. Alongside, there was a small silk pincushion with a circle of bobble-headed children surrounding a pale red pumpkin, plus a larger framed photo of Mumma. She must have been a schoolgirl when it was taken. Her hair, in its two fat braids, had the sheen of molasses poured fresh from a tin, and there was the suggestion of mischief in her eyes, which were black and brackish and impenetrable. It was painful to see it again: her youth, how alive she looked.

I ferreted through the rest of the case, afraid I'd imagined what I was looking for, but no, there it was at the bottom—Mumma's floral address book, sheathed in its yellowing plastic. I leafed through and scanned the entries, careful to avoid the pages where the tiny stitching had started to come loose, but aside from the numbers and English addresses everything had been written in Chinese. Fat chance of finding Hei-Fong Lee.

I flicked back to the inside cover. Under *In case of emergency* were two entries written in capitals: our dad's name—Julian Miller—along with our Brixton house plus another located in Kowloon under the name of Wing Chan Chen and then, in brackets, *my mother*: Flat 10, 430 Castle Peak Road. The same address as on Nesbit's letter.

It's not stealing, I told myself. These things belonged to both of us. I tucked the address book into my bag and returned the suitcase to its dusty rectangle before I went back upstairs for coffee.

I opened the fridge and searched the shelves. No milk. I couldn't be bothered walking down to the shop, especially now that it had started to rain. Wine would have to do. I poured a glass from the Riesling at the back and sipped it as I stood at the window, watching the drips running races down the pane.

Guilt arrived and squatted in the corner. *Poor old Maya*, it said, not coming home to a decent brew, for buying you a slap-up meal, for not knowing that you've been snooping. Fuck's sake.

I checked my watch. She wasn't due back for half an hour but it was probably better to leave her a note. She'd only panic if she got home early and both me and the key were missing.

I went to her office for paper, but aside from the obligatory banker's lamp and an extravagant vase of lilies, the desk was bare. I rifled around in the top drawer, my fingers washing against pens and batteries, a single condom still in its wrapper. Ugh. That horse had bolted.

In the second drawer down was a notebook. It was one of those hardback things, its plastic spiral jammed into the space, and I had to wrestle it free. It released at last with a crack, bringing with it a spill of papers. Shit. Why were tidy people always such frauds?

As I bent to gather them up, an envelope broke free from the pile and slid out onto the carpet. The same anemic yellow. The same careless slanted address. My stomach jolted at the clean slice at the top, and I opened it and pulled out the letter.

RE: In the matter of Mrs. Maya Redgrave, formerly known as Mei-Hua Chen, daughter of Sook-Yin Chen, of Castle Peak Road, Kowloon.

The same words, just a different name. I checked the postmark on the front of the envelope: June 6, '97. Exactly the same date as mine.

EIGHT

Sook-Yin

September 1966

Sook-Yin stared out from the taxi, one eye on the meter as the concrete landscape of Hammersmith gave way to the tree-lined roads of central London. Florence hadn't seemed that pleased to hear from her, but after a brief conversation from a phone box had told her to come to a place called Swiss Cottage.

Marriage had done her no favors. Though she'd never been blessed with real beauty, there'd been a handsome solidness about her. Now, when she stood in a certain light, you could hardly tell her neck from her face.

"You can blame Harvey for that," she said as she poured them tea in the kitchen. She slid a gold-colored box across the table—pineapple cakes and custard tarts. "I think he's trying to fatten me up."

Sook-Yin took one of the buns. Its warm crust smelled of home touched by the hands of someone familiar, and she let the crumbs linger on her lips, afraid to lose the sensation.

It felt good to be speaking Cantonese again, although she was alarmed at how once or twice her mouth grasped at the air for the right word; the way an English verb or noun would lurk like an imposter. "The children must keep you fit, though."

Florence snorted. "Harvey has spoiled them too much. The two of them are practically savages." She peered out from under her lashes. "Plus, I found out that he lied to me. His wife's not even dead. German woman," she said. "Rose and Michael are half-breeds." She showed her a photograph that was sitting on the dresser. The children's hair was the color of dried clay, a contrast made all the more striking against their Asian features.

"But Je Je, they are so beautiful!"

Florence frowned as she looked at the picture as though struggling to see her point. "What a simpleton Harvey is. To be fooled once by the woman is bad enough. How are the children supposed to know what they are? Like stepping in the gap between paving stones." She returned the photo and shrugged. "What do I care, anyway? Harvey has plenty of money and he lets me do what I want."

"His restaurant is doing well, then? That must make you happy, at least."

"What is happy?" Florence said. "All I know is there was nothing at home for me." She let out a mournful sigh. "I should have married Hei-Fong."

"Hei-Fong Lee?" Sook-Yin's cup almost slipped from her hands. What a strange ghost from the past.

"Hah. I should have asked your brother to fix us up. Face like a film star," she said, "and I always knew he was sweet on me."

Part of Sook-Yin wanted to laugh. In all the years she had known Hei-Fong he'd never once talked about Florence. Nor did she mention the face *she* remembered: his cheeky swagger around the Walled City, hustling dollars from anyone who visited in return for watching their cars, childhood picnics in Kowloon Park, their laughter bright as the moon as they caught crickets and threw them at ah-Chor. The very last time she had heard from him had been the letter she'd read, her hands shaking: *My parents are sending me away. Don't forget me, Sook-Yin, I'll come back for you.* August 1959—practically a lifetime ago, so why was her own face burning now? "Didn't his parents send him off to the States? I heard he was in some kind of trouble."

"What do you expect?" Florence said. "You can't move in the Walled City for criminals, and his family as poor as chickens. They were so eager for him to disappear that they had to sell their shoes for his ticket. Still, all that's changed, apparently. My mother says he's back in Kowloon now and hanging out with your brother again. He'll be a millionaire before we know it."

As much as Sook-Yin doubted this, it wasn't beyond the bounds of reason. Why else had ah-Chor bothered to stay friends with him beyond the obligation of childhood? You had to be special to escape such a past—ambitious or deluded, perhaps. Nothing if not resourceful. It was the other side of the bargain that perplexed her. What had her brother ever done for Hei-Fong?

"I heard he's engaged as well."

Sook-Yin blinked. "Good for him," she said.

Florence examined her over her cup, her eyes narrowing. Had she seen her blush-hot skin, the quickening of her adrenaline? "And what are *you* going to do with your life now?"

Sook-Yin's relief was short-lived. She'd been too preoccupied with leaving the nurses' home to even consider her next move, but now the urgency of it pressed in on her. Her family would react badly to the news, and what would she do about money?

She glanced again at the photograph. "What about children?" she ventured. "The caretaker at my mother's apartment—Mrs. Chee—often babysits for the neighbors. I could look after Rose and Michael."

"Because you did so well as a nurse . . ."

Sook-Yin resisted the urge to retaliate. All Florence needed was a little push, a little flattery. "A wealthy area like this? I bet all the women have help here and you wouldn't want them to think they can laugh at you." She traced a finger across the tablecloth. "They probably think *you're* the nanny."

"Juk sai! As if marrying an old man isn't punishment enough!"

Sook-Yin gave a sober little nod. "Well, exactly!" she said.

Florence gnawed at the skin around her thumb. "This house *is* big enough for ten . . ." She drained the rest of her tea, suddenly pleased with herself. "Yes, what a clever idea I've had. I will talk to Harvey about it tonight."

HARVEY WAS NOT only happy to let Sook-Yin stay, he was also nothing like she had imagined. For a start, he wasn't even forty yet and although he was no Jimmy Yu, neither did he have reason to be intimidated by Florence's misplaced vanity. The children, too, seemed to take to her, and so began their mutual agreement: board and a wage for Sook-Yin in return for looking after them.

She had been there a little over a month when Harvey invited her for dinner at his restaurant. At first heartened by the prospect of an evening out, Sook-Yin spent an hour perfecting the beehive that Peggy had taught her on one of her visits.

After her unceremonious departure from Hammersmith, it had been a relief to reestablish their friendship, and now, as well as the visits, they spoke once a week on the telephone. Peggy's training was progressing at speed, and as much as Sook-Yin was delighted for her she couldn't help feeling her own failure in its aftermath. The memory dulled her excitement for the evening. What did it matter *where* she was living when she remained dependent on the goodwill of others, waiting for the rug to be pulled from under her?

Nor was Florence disposed to help matters. Ever since Sook-Yin's arrival she'd been disappearing from the house each morning and not returning till late afternoon. Where she went remained a mystery, but Sook-Yin soon understood that Florence's contentment with these outings seemed to go one of two ways: either she would smile and be generous on her return, or her expression would be sullen and silent as she retired upstairs to her room.

That day had been one of the latter, but never one to suffer in silence, the trip to the restaurant only fueled her complaints. The children were quarrelsome and annoying; each dish that was brought to the table too salty or bland for her taste. When a plate of oranges was served between courses, Florence greeted the plate with disdain. "Are they sweet?" she demanded in English.

"Yes, madam," the waiter replied, "although I am sure you will find them very sour."

If she had bothered to work on her language skills, Florence would have demanded that Harvey fire him. As usual, however, the indictment of others eluded her and she gazed around the room with a bored sneer.

"That man has been staring all night," she said.

"Which?"

"The English one by the window, over there."

Sook-Yin followed her gaze to where a young man sat alone at a table, his strong jaw partially hidden by an unruly mop of yellow hair. He seemed immersed in the book beside him, which he consulted between mouthfuls with a thoughtful, serious expression occasionally broken by laughter. She tilted her head left and right, trying to catch the shape of its title, but when he looked up and caught her eye she flushed and turned away.

Not long after, the waiter reappeared carrying glasses of cola for the children and a bottle of wine for the table. "Mr. Miller sends his compliments," he said. He waved in the direction of the window.

"Do you know that man?" Florence said.

"Your husband says he is a regular here. A very successful financier."

Florence reached for the menu and ran her finger along the prices of the bottles. "Tell Mr. Miller to join us," she said. "The conversation at this table is boring."

The waiter relayed the message, and after he'd finished whatever he was reading, the young man turned down the corner of the page and walked over to where they were sitting. He was taller than Sook-Yin had imagined. Handsomer in the glare of the light.

"Julian Miller," he said, offering his hand. Florence, misjudging his distance, awkwardly pumped his knuckles.

"I very pleased meet you," she said.

"And these must be your children?"

Recognizing his tone of admiration, she nodded with faux humility. "Yes. Very lucky. Very beautiful." Her smile dimmed as he turned to Sook-Yin. "This children's nanny," she said.

"Well, I shouldn't intrude on your family meal."

Even as he said this, however, his arm was already on the back of the empty chair, and before Florence had quite relented, he sat down. In truth, his eyes had never left Sook-Yin but now he addressed her directly. "I didn't quite catch your name," he said.

She hesitated. She was still unused to the Western convention of putting her own name in front of her family's—of *I, myself* not *we, the people*—but given her experiences at the nurses' home, she was forcing herself to get used to it. He picked up the bottle of wine and attempted to fill her glass, but she covered it with her hand.

"My name is Sook-Yin Chen," she said. "And I do not drink on duty." It was something she'd heard on TV—some hospital drama or crime show—and although she felt a little foolish saying it, part of her hoped that it sounded impressive.

MR. MILLER STAYED for another two glasses, hanging on Florence's words while delighting Rose and Michael by making paper animals out of their napkins. Sook-Yin observed him from a distance. What was it about the English that they preferred smoking and drinking to eating?

"I hear you are businessman," she said, during a lull in the conversation.

He nodded. "Particularly Oriental investments. I find the Chinese such beautiful people."

She ignored his deliberate stare. "Oh. Then you speak Cantonese?"

"I'm ashamed to say that I don't, although I've always found it fascinating. Why is it, for example," he said, "that apart from the character for zero, there are no circles in your language?"

Accustomed to the drudge of her days, Sook-Yin had forgotten the excitement of thinking and she clutched at the edge of the tablecloth, determined not to disappoint him. "I cannot tell you exact answer," she said, "but according to Confucian philosophy, the square is more important as shape. In the same way as old fortified city, it give idea of stability, strength—each mark like building houses. They add and communicate each other, but same time have no sense till finish. If one stroke appearing in wrong place"—she drew with her finger on her napkin—"the character and meaning collapse."

Mr. Miller said nothing at first, but then delivered a smile so broad, she assumed he must have wind. "I don't care if that's true or not," he said. "That's the most perfect answer I've ever heard. You must have the soul of a poet."

Sook-Yin pinked with pleasure. With no one but the children for company, she couldn't imagine she'd grown more intelligent, so what had changed? Was it simply that she'd managed to express herself; the fact that with no preconceptions he'd allowed what she'd said to have value?

"What on earth are you doing as a nanny?"

She lowered her voice. "Harvey and Florence have been very good to me. They took me out of a bad place."

"Do you mean Hong Kong? Or a bad situation?"

She wasn't sure if there was a difference but she erred on the side of caution. "When I first arrive in London, I did not know any people help me."

"Well, now you've met me," he said, "and I believe that you could do anything. In fact, if it's not too bold, you should allow me to make some introductions."

Newly aware of Florence's scrutiny, Sook-Yin withered. "Is very kind," she said, "but I think I happy with children."

"That's a shame, but I understand. Will you take my number, at least?" He produced a card from his pocket and slid it to her across the table. "Call me anytime. Office hours."

"WHAT DID HE WANT?" Florence asked as they rode back in the taxi that evening. Away from the gaze of the restaurant her mood had reverted to its state of sullenness.

"Nothing. He was just being friendly."

"Foreign men are only interested in one thing."

Sook-Yin turned and smiled at the window. The small-mindedness of Florence's words reminded her of ah-Ma's warnings as they stood at the harbor in Kowloon. *No drinking from English taps. No standing on corners alone at night. Never trust a man with a shaky leg.* But how could they know any better when they had no interest in integration? The English weren't the enemy, they were merely a different culture with their own identity firmly at their heart.

Despite this, it was ironic how Mr. Miller's flattery had made her realize how lucky she'd been in securing the job at Florence's. Rose and Michael were rarely a bother and she was earning much more than she had been, so why had she continued to lie to her family? She clasped her hands in her lap. "I'm going to tell ah-Ma I've left the hospital."

Florence's mouth flopped open. "*Aiya!* Are you really that stupid? Why would you tell her anything?"

"But what if she thinks I've forgotten her? She must have sent hundreds of letters to Hammersmith."

Florence scoffed. "I wouldn't bet on it," she said. "Isn't your brother some big success?"

"So what? I'm working too."

"You wash my children and cook my dinner! Is that what they want to hear? Trust me, they may be kind to your face but behind your back they're talking—*ba ba ba ba*, all their voices." She pinched Sook-Yin on the arm. "Why bother adding feet to the snake? Especially if you want to go back. Do you ever hear me talking about my life? When my mother asks me how marriage is treating me, I don't go *boo hoo hoo*, I say everything is wonderful. So."

Sook-Yin examined her lap. Florence might well have a point, at least where ah-Chor was concerned. He'd only twist the facts against her. Use his influence as "man of the family."

Your life belongs to me now.

She pressed her fingers into her pocket and grazed the edge of Mr. Miller's business card, reassured by its presence if nothing else. In that moment, like the rest of her life, all she wanted was some proof of her existence.

She'd rallied by the time they'd got home, however, and after she'd put the children to bed she went to her room and wrote to ah-Ma. She'd made duck soup from a broken egg! Why shouldn't she be proud of her resourcefulness?

It was only after she'd finished the letter that she realized how careful she'd been. She hadn't mentioned Florence by name, only referring to the rich Chinese family who'd offered her a better-paid job in London. To underline the point, she enclosed a five-pound note before licking down the edges of the envelope and setting it on her dresser. As she got into bed that night, she was convinced that they would praise her.

NINE

Lily

20th Day of Mourning

Half an hour after finding the letter, I was sitting with Maya at the Golden Bacchus, listening as she grilled the waiter about the likelihood of seafood in the ginger sauce. I'd promptly jumped to the wine menu, having already—much to her disgust—had a whisky chaser while we waited for a table. They'd turned up the air-conditioning, and now she sat with her coat across her shoulders like some insouciant Aquascutum-wearing Shiva.

At least we were out of the house. The volume, if not the content, of what I'd planned to say to her would be tempered by the pressure of an audience, and if that failed, I could get up and leave.

"Can't be too careful," she said, setting the menu back on the table. "I had the most terrible shits after Daphne's."

I was making headway toward the haze of a second glass before I finally summoned the nerve. "Why didn't you tell me you kept in touch with Elise?"

"Who?"

"Elise Treyger. She came into the shop."

Her fingers dangled over the olives. "What on earth did she want?" she said.

"She popped by to shed her old skin. And to say she was sorry about Dad."

I could've said she'd come to do Maya's dirty work, but I still wasn't sure that was true. Something about it was all Elise. A persistent itch that she'd needed to scratch, fueled by the flea of gossip.

"Why are you making it sound so devious? To be honest, it went out of my head. I've seen her"—she counted on her fingers—"three times in the last five years? It was a solicitor-solicitor thing. A stupid occupational hazard." She dabbed her mouth on her napkin. "Don't tell me—she's started to chunk up again. See that arse coming from Mars." And that was the other thing about Maya. In matters of personal safety, she would throw anyone under the bus.

She was clever, too. Instead of obviously changing the subject she proceeded to springboard away from the topic, wittering on about the fake virtues of corporate law while managing to boast in the process. My inner censor broke. "I know you got a letter," I said.

Her hand paused on the way to the butter knife. She even attempted a laugh. "What?"

"The solicitor told me. Nesbit."

This was a gambit, given Maya's ex-profession. I had no idea about client confidentiality, whether Nesbit would've told me if I'd asked, but I wasn't about to out myself and lose the moral high ground.

"Done anything else behind my back?" I'd expected some diatribe about Nesbit's ethics and was quite impressed when she launched into mine. I held her gaze over my glass. She wouldn't get away that easily. "Fine. I got a letter. But we're not going to do anything about it."

I pressed the tines of my fork into the tablecloth. "Maya. Some stranger has left us a fortune! Five hundred thousand quid."

"Actually, it's a million. Half each." She swiped at my wineglass and drained it. "And I want nothing to do with it, okay?"

"How are you not even curious?"

She laid her palms on the table. "*No such fat goose lies in the road.* Do you remember who used to say that?"

I rolled my eyes. "Plato?"

"Mum. It was Mum who said it. And as much as I dislike such folksy bollocks, it actually happens to be true. What she meant was there's always a catch. Perhaps not now, but somewhere. That's how desperate people get caught out." She looked at me. Lowered her voice. "*We* are not desperate people."

"All right, married a millionaire . . ."

"Oh, for God's sake, Lil, be reasonable! When have I ever not looked after you?"

"But that's exactly my point. It's always been that way around."

"What does it matter? I'm *family*!"

"Yes," I said. "A part of it." I gazed at the space beyond her shoulder. "Tell me more about Mumma," I said.

"Why? So you can torture yourself?"

"Because I *miss* her. I've always missed her. And this letter . . . it's brought it all back."

She poured a glass of water. "You can't miss someone you don't remember."

"Why do you *always* say that, when I know there are things in my head! I remember the smell of the gutters, riding the ferry across the harbor, the way the rain feels hot in a monsoon."

"You know them because I told you."

And there it was—that wall. Her experience versus mine, as if she owned that part of history and I could only receive it second-hand. Sometimes. Rarely. Never.

"Fine. Then 'tell' me again. Was Mumma tall? Was she kind? Am I like her?"

"She could be bloody annoying, yeah . . ."

"Mays, I'm being serious." I'd become obsessed through the years with this last one. Nor was it simply the *idea* of her legacy. It was a concrete memory of lying in bed, drifting to sleep while Mumma sang to us. I'd never mentioned it to Maya before because I was afraid that she would pollute it. Claim ownership. But I'd always wondered if it had driven me to music.

Maya searched my face. "Yes, she was kind. And funny. And you already know how much you look like her."

"So why stop talking about her? Why did Dad get rid of her things?"

"You know why. Because it was really hard for him."

"But what about me?" I said. "I wanted to know where I came from. The other half of our heritage. What if this Hei-Fong Lee is our chance?"

"Lily—" Her fist tightened against the tablecloth. "We don't know this person from Adam! I mean, where has he come from all of a sudden?"

"He's obviously Chinese."

"So?"

"So, what if we're related?"

"Well, where has he been all these years? And where were the rest of Mum's family? We were *children* and our mother had died and they sent us away like rubbish. They couldn't even wait for Dad to come back for us. All these years, and not even a letter!"

"How can you be so sure?"

"Because Dad told me they didn't. And I should know—I'm the one who looked after him . . ." She paused. "I know it wasn't your fault, but I *was*."

A familiar sensation rose from my stomach—not the wine or the whisky or hunger but undigested guilt; all that anger and regret and jealousy rolled together into an acidic splinter. It didn't make it untrue, though. I couldn't claim the moral victory on that one.

Maya bit her lip. "Look, of *course* I've considered the money, but this can't be good for us, Lil." She bent her head toward me. "What if he was the person who was driving the car?"

I pulled away. "Jesus, Maya!"

"Well, someone was," she said, "and it's amazing what guilt does to people."

"Why do you always assume the worst?"

"Because maybe then I can't be disappointed." She raised her hand to her mouth, as though trying to push the words back. "Sorry, you know what I mean, though."

"That's my thing," I said. "Get your own neuroses."

She checked, and then mirrored my half smile. It was a gesture we'd practiced that last year, the one that said *we're okay*. And we were. I knew we were. I knew Maya wouldn't let me fall again; that I'd never go hungry or homeless or have to beg anyone for anything. We would survive as well as we always had.

"I'm going to give you the money for your project."

"What?"

"The music school. I'll set you up with a business manager and give you the money to start it. It won't be half a million, I'm afraid, but enough to get you off the ground."

"Why would you even do that?"

"You're my sister, aren't you? And because it's what Dad would have wanted."

I shook my head. "Well, I wouldn't feel right about taking it, not with the baby on the way. Plus, you don't have that kind of money."

"I do. I've been saving for years."

"For what?"

She shrugged. "It seemed a good idea at the time. And now it is, okay? I know you'll make it back. We'll probably get loads of sponsorship, the press love a sob story, don't they? And I believe in you, all right? I mean, you saw what happened when *I* learned the piano, whereas you became bloody Mozart."

My sister had never been big on compliments. It was one of the rare things we had in common, and it was a currency I didn't know how to spend. "Your doula's going to hate me."

"Oh, fuck off!" she said, but she laughed.

The waiter arrived with the food and to my surprise I was looking forward to it. Maya leaned over and nodded at my plate. "Looks good," she said. "Let's eat."

TEN

Sook-Yin

—————————————

November 1966

The children had been sick for a whole week. At first, Sook-Yin's worry had overridden her exhaustion, but once she learned it was no more than a tummy bug, she grew frustrated with cleaning up their messes: the constant bed changing, the bleaching of floors, the need to open all the windows in winter. It didn't matter how much money you had; everyone's shit smelled the same.

Part of her blamed Mr. Miller. She'd grown used to her life in London, reconciled to its routine boredom, but now she felt the itch of restlessness, the sense of her own potential encouraged by what he'd said to her. Nor was it only this. Almost every day since their meeting at the restaurant he'd telephoned the house from his office, asking if she'd like to meet again, and although her answer was always the same, she was starting to enjoy the attention.

That morning, she was making eggs and toast for Michael when the telephone rang in the hallway. Both children were now out of bed and she rushed to pick up the receiver, anxious in case Rose should answer it.

"You sound out of breath," he said. "Have I caught you at a bad time?"

When was it he'd stopped announcing himself and merely started to speak, knowing that she'd expect it? "I making snack for children."

"I can call back later, if you like?"

"No, is fine, is over."

"In English we say 'all done.'" She liked the sound of his smile.

"Yes. I all done," she said. "And how are you, Mr. Miller?"

"I'd feel better if you called me Julian."

"Okay."

"You will, or you know that I wish it?"

Sook-Yin examined herself in the mirror. It wasn't wise to encourage men too early, to let them think you were simply waiting for them. *Cosmopolitan* had taught her that. "Yes, I thinking about it."

"Hmm. So, look," he said, sounding a little deflated. "Since you seem so against the pub, why don't I take you to the pictures instead? We'll sit in the dark and not talk to each other."

"Pictures is cinema, yes? We go to see *Mary Poppins*?"

"I was actually thinking of something more grown-up. There's that Lawrence of Arabia thing replaying near you at the Odeon in Swiss Cottage."

Sook-Yin frowned at the receiver. "How you know where I live?"

"You live with Harvey, don't you? How else would I have got your number? . . . So, is that a yes to the film?"

"Maybe."

He sighed. "Well, it won't be on forever, and to be honest I'm getting the message."

"Message?"

"That you're not interested in being my friend."

"No, Mr. Miller . . . Julian . . ."

"Anyway, I've got a meeting to go to. Call me if you change your mind, but if I don't hear, I won't ring again."

He hung up without saying goodbye, the dial tone droning like an accusation. Sook-Yin replaced the receiver just as Michael yelled to say he was finished and needed her to clean up after him. *Spoiled sprat*, she said under her breath.

She was rinsing a dishcloth at the sink when the telephone rang again and she almost fell in her rush to answer it. "Julian? Mr. Miller?" she said. Static fizzed over the line.

"Wai? Sook-Yin?" a voice said.

Ah-Chor? Her brother had never called before, and she felt a prickle of panic in her chest. "Yes, it's me. Is ah-Ma all right? Is Chairman Mao causing trouble in Kowloon?"

"Never mind all that," he said. "All this talking is very expensive. And what is this nonsense I hear? Is it true you've given up nursing?"

Sook-Yin twisted the wire around her fingers, watching the skin as it bulged and purpled. "It wasn't that," she said. "Unfortunately, I failed the exam."

"You didn't study?"

"I did!"

"In that case you must be an imbecile! No wonder you've become a servant." He spat out the word like a bad prawn.

"Not a servant, a nanny," she said. "I'm working for a good Chinese family."

"So *you* say. What is their name?"

Sook-Yin's mind went blank. Almost anything sounded fancier than Chen. What about Cho, or Lum? "It's Florence," she conceded at last. "I don't suppose you remember—"

"That idiot Florence Ho? Juk Sai, Sook-Yin!" he said. "All that money we wasted? You will put our mother in her grave."

"But I can't see what difference it makes. I've been sending my wages regularly and you must be earning good money . . ."

She regretted it as soon as she'd said it, the way she always did whenever she tried to stand up to her brother. It was a trick that God had played on her: to let her be born with fire in her belly but not the intellect to let it burn.

"Eh?" He made a noise like he was going to explode. "What the hell do you know about anything—all this time you've been wasting in London. Do you expect us to keep you forever? You are nothing but a cockroach, Sook-Yin!"

The room wobbled behind her lashes. Even after all his years of bullying she hated the fact that she still craved his approval. "I can get more money, I promise. I've met someone who will give me a better job."

"A likely story—"

"It's true! His name is Julian Miller and he's been trying to help me for weeks but I felt bad about letting Florence down."

"Florence Ho is not your family."

"Yes. I realize that."

"Then realize by proving it," he said.

SOOK-YIN'S FINGERS TREMBLED as she dialed the number. She'd only intended to leave Julian a message and was caught out when he answered immediately. "I thought you in meeting," she said.

"No. They postponed it till later. What's wrong? You sound upset."

"I was just talking with family." She touched the wood of the console, begging the gods not to punish her. "My mother is not very well."

"I'm so sorry to hear that," he said at once. "Is there anything I can do?"

She hesitated. "Remember when we talk in restaurant and you say you can find me a better job?"

"Yes, of course. I told you."

"Thank you. Then I would like."

"All right. I'll make some calls. Can you meet me tomorrow evening?"

"Yes, okay, I come."

"We'll see that film," he said. "You sound like you need cheering up. Don't worry, we'll sort it all out."

ELEVEN

Lily

22nd Day of Mourning

Maya had blown me away with the offer of the money. Though her concern for my health through the years had signaled an emotion close to affection, it also carried the weight of something else: filial duty perhaps, a fear of somebody watching.

Despite what had happened with Mumma, she'd never been someone who lived in the moment. Even as a child her caution was evident. Spoiled Christmases littered our past with her joyless habit of opening things one by one—sometimes with weeks in between.

One year, I'd gotten a book on Medieval history. I'd been reading about the Flagellants, faintly obsessed with whippings and hair shirts. "Is Maya doing penance?" I asked Dad. Given how annoying she'd been about the gifts I thought she might be punishing herself but Dad had only laughed. "Your sister has marvelous restraint," he said. "She believes in a future that's worth holding out for." I'd tried to absorb this lesson, learn from it, but all I heard was *not like you.* The fact she now saw me in this future was revelatory; the thought of us taking the world on together, intoxicating.

I decided to pop in and surprise her. Two days after the events at the restaurant, I went to a florist at London Bridge and bought her a

ridiculously frou-frou bouquet—tropical, with leaves like vaginas—
along with some overpriced snake oil at Neal's Yard, before getting
the train to Forest Hill.

THE HOUSE WAS lit up from fifty yards away; the shadowy strobes
and wispy afterglow of bodies caught in motion as they moved to
and from the roof terrace. Fuck it. Maya's party. I let myself into the
gate, crouching like a fugitive from Colditz as I propped the flowers
on the step and turned back.

"Not coming in?" a voice said.

Ed stepped out from the ornamental juniper, one hand cradling
a half-spent cigarette and the other nursing a drink. By the state of
him, it wasn't his first.

I pulled my coat tighter around me. "Not my thing, I'm afraid.
I'm just leaving something for Maya."

"Risky around here," he said. "Never know who's lurking. Come
on! At least bring them inside. She's literally standing right there."
He pointed to one of the windows and I saw Maya with her back
against the bookcase, looking thoroughly miserable.

"Five minutes. Okay?" I said.

THE HALLWAY SEEMED to have shrunk with the sheer weight of
people within it, the air thick with the boom of fake laughter and the
dizzying scent of Kouros. I was right about the people they'd invited:
corporate suits in fancy dress who had swapped their hedonistic days
for conversations about pensions and cashmere combs. And always
there was money. And canapés.

Growing up in the midst of the seventies, Maya had been grateful for the Janets and Jasons. I'd watched her roam in the grime of
council estates in patched-up, cut-off denims discussing the latest
people she fancied—*Lee Majors or William Shatner?*—white-toothed,

all-American golden boys. I was invariably ousted from these discussions, forced to sit on my own until someone was called for tea and I'd be offered a marginal part in some fake wedding ceremony or other. I had no firm notion—or should I say, consolation—of being popular or unpopular in those days. It was more a proof that I was testing out: that to invite either envy or derision it was necessary to first be seen as something other than what was skin-deep. Twenty years later, I had my answer. Maya's world was now a place of esteem and I was still stuck playing Mr. Sulu.

o o o o o o

Ed threw the flowers onto the console and then beckoned to a passing man. "Tristan! Come and meet Maya's sister!"

The man's handshake was like a well-done steak: firm, but juicy with fat. Ed patted him on the back. "I'm just off to freshen my drink. Help her find Maya, will you, old boy?"

As soon as I arrived in the living room, I saw that the fragment from the window had been illusory. Maya was separate, yes, but un-alone, holding court amid a gaggle of admirers. Before I knew what was happening, the man—Tristan—had pulled me to the front. "Maya, you dark horse!" he bellowed. "Apparently, this one's your sister!"

The change in her expression was immediate, the way light travels faster than sound. Panic. I dragged my finger across my throat. *I'm not staying*, I mouthed for good measure.

Champagne arrived in my hand. "So what field are *you* in?" the man asked.

"I work in a charity shop."

"Charity sector, you say?"

"No. The Age Concern. In Brixton."

His lips grappled for a suitable expression. "But—who do you work for otherwise?"

I shrugged. "That's it," I said.

He took a swig of his drink, his face reddening. "God! How sporting of you."

"I don't know. I bet it's a hoot!"

I turned toward the voice and saw a woman on the edge of the circle, resplendent in Biba and Gypsy Rose headgear. She came forward and offered her hand. "It must be wonderful not to have all that pressure."

"You'd be surprised," I said. "Dead people's things are a huge responsibility."

Out of the corner of my eye I spotted Maya creeping toward us. "Lovely!" she cried to the woman, depositing dry kisses to the sides of her face. "I didn't realize that you were coming."

"Well, you know I find these things tiresome." She pointed her glass in my direction. "But this one here's a tonic. Where have you been hiding her, Maya, and can I please have her as soon as you're finished?" She leaned over and whispered conspiratorially. "How strange that your sister's never mentioned you. Is this a recent revelation in your family? One of those delicious *This Is Your Life* moments?"

I glanced at Maya. "I'm sorry?"

Mistaking my question for deafness, her voice grew shriller. "Different father or different mother?"

"Neither."

This was even better than she'd expected. "You were *adopted*?" she said.

"Uh, no . . . We're *biological* sisters."

"No!" She looked genuinely confused. "But you look totally different," she said. "Maya has that delightful English burn, but you're so . . . *exotic*-looking." She got grabby with a tray of vol-au-vents. "Aren't genetics *fascinating*."

The rest of the room had fallen silent, as though they'd tuned in to some yokel radio station on a desolate road to Nowheresville.

Maya colored as she cleared her throat. "All our differences are fascinating, actually."

"You might have to elaborate on that one!" someone said, and they all laughed.

"Well, Lily's a genius at the piano, for a start. I mean, we both had lessons as kids, but—"

"Face it, Maya, you were crap!"

She turned and faced the man, a weasel-faced toff in blazer and loafers who had clearly forgotten the purpose of socks. "There's a certain grace in knowing when you're beaten. Which *you* should have known when you asked me to marry you."

The man withered and then saluted the joke as the room erupted into hoots and howls. Maya smiled as she sought out Ed. Until then I'd forgotten his presence, hadn't noticed him propped against the sofa slowly getting plastered. He looked even older than usual, like a dad collecting his kids from a party, awkwardly swinging his car keys.

A cry broke out among the guests. "Duet! Duet! Duet!"

Maya's smile wavered as she raised her hands. "I reserve the right at my party not to make a total arse of myself."

"Boo!" they shouted back. Then—"Sister! Sister! Sister!"

I was back in the Common Room at Cambridge: the baying, the nastiness, the privilege. Knowing she was the architect of my coming misfortune, Maya looked nervous. She jerked her head in the direction of the piano and all of a sudden we were kids again.

Back and back and back.

Please get it over with, Lily. Do it so we can fit in.

I pushed my way through to the instrument. Obviously, it was a Steinway and, like everything precious that Ed had bought, I couldn't touch it without his permission. I lifted the polished lid, and as the smell of spruce enveloped me there was a moment of almost calm.

"Play something *exotic!*" someone called, and everyone laughed again. They wanted Salieri, not Mozart, did they? A measure of who I was? I raised my hands to the keys and played "Chopsticks," precisely and perfectly.

o o o o o o

I cadged a cigarette and snuck off to the garden. One of the stones on the path had come loose and I rocked my feet against it, enjoying the distraction of its slow synchronicity from the trembling that had started in my legs. *Five things I can see, four things I can feel, three things* . . . Had Maya really told no one about me? And because of my health, or something else?

The back door slid open behind me. "This one's taken," I called out.

Ed's voice emerged from the shadows. "Don't mind me if I stand in my garden."

I scoffed and turned my back to him and a moment later I heard him laughing.

"Maya's not wrong, you know. You really *are* a genius. Even at your own sister's party you managed to make it about yourself."

"Thanks for setting me up," I said.

"Maybe she's setting us both up."

I paused as I dragged on the cigarette. Was this about the party or the baby, or what? Not that I cared either way, especially if it implied some kind of alliance. "It's fine. I'm used to it," I said. "It's called being part of a family."

"Meaning?"

"Oh, I don't know . . ." I said. "Have you even *been* with her to the hospital?"

"Did she tell you she wanted me there?" I hadn't expected to hear hope in his voice and I made the mistake of looking at him. I almost felt bad when he winced. "No, didn't think so," he said.

"I'm presuming you had *something* to do with it."

"Yeah, for about five minutes, which is about as long as she can take of me these days." He tipped his glass at the skyline. "Sometimes

I come out here," he said, "and see all the buildings I've made. You think I'd be proud of that, right? But in the end it's just concrete and steel. Everything happens after I leave." He smiled and shook his head at me. "Don't worry, I'm not looking for your sympathy. In fact, it's the thing I like most about you, Lil—how you manage to be so *empty.* How's that working out for your love life?"

He was so close I could smell his breath. The cloying sour-sweet tang of it, slightly rancid with hunger. "Somewhere between why and none of your business."

"Shame. We could have made a great team, you and me. Even now I could stretch to the both of you. I mean, you share these things, right? Like your sister's boyfriend at Oxford? Naughty naughty Lily."

He sprang forward and tried to kiss me. It was vicious rather than lustful, born of aggression as much as opportunity, but he was too pissed and I caught him with my elbow.

He reeled away, doubled over with laughter. "Your face!" he said and pointed. "You don't think she tells me these things?"

I ground the cigarette under my shoe. "I'm going to leave now," I said.

"Fine." He scratched his eyebrow. "Just one thing before you go. You do know that she lied to you, right? That little inheritance from Daddy? Fantasy! He didn't even leave a pot to piss in."

My biceps twitched as I folded my arms. "Are you that jealous?" I said.

"That money came from *us,* you doofus! The only reason Maya's been carrying you is because you're too flaky to handle the truth. She doesn't want your blood on her hands again."

It took me a second to absorb this, to recover enough to get close to him. "I hope she leaves you," I said.

"Not before she leaves you. And that will make it almost bearable."

I WAS HALFWAY down the road when Maya finally caught up with me. "Hey!" she called. "Lily, wait, hey!" I stopped, but didn't look at her. "Why didn't you tell me that you were going? Also, you forgot your coat." She fussed it around my shoulders, trying to button the neck. "Remember how I used to do this when you were little? You secretly loved it when I used to mother you."

She flinched when I pulled away from her. Dared to look hurt. "Look. I'm sorry, okay?"

I pulled my arms through the sleeves, tugged the sides down. "Sorry you never told them about me? Or sorry about something else?"

"Look, it's not what you think . . . But it *is* complicated, isn't it?"

"Being my sister?"

"Explaining the past to people. It's like some stranger looking through your photo album. It doesn't mean shit to them, and I value you more than that." She glanced back over her shoulder. Shivered. "Look, can we talk about this later? Ed's as pissed as a fart and they'll only trash the house if I leave them."

"Fine."

It would take the whole night to talk about it: why she'd pretended I hadn't existed, why she'd kept Dad's poverty a secret, why she'd really offered the money for the music school. Maybe her strength wasn't blagging, after all.

She reached in and gave me a hug, pressed her lips to my forehead. *Judas kiss*, I thought.

TWELVE

Sook-Yin

November 1966

Sook-Yin studied the posters in the foyer. She liked the look of Lawrence of Arabia, with his blue eyes and windblown face, but when Julian came back from the booth he told her they'd missed the start of the showing. "I got us tickets for *The L-Shaped Room*," he said. "It's a political drama. You'll like it."

As they sat in the almost empty cinema, Suk-Yin did not want the film to end. She wanted to stay in the blackness forever, so people wouldn't see her red face and bruised dignity. Though her English wasn't perfect by any means, she knew what *political* meant, and this wasn't it.

She watched the story unfold with a mixture of horror and outrage, occasionally glancing at Julian. Lit up by the flickering light, his profile revealed no emotion, and she was angry about this, too. She wanted to rescue the character called Jane—unmarried and pregnant and lonely; slap the bigotry from the man called Toby. Why had he treated Jane this way when all she'd wanted was love? And why had Julian assumed she'd enjoy it?

THE NIGHT'S CHILL relieved the burn of her skin as they stepped into the darkness of the street. Julian strolled beside her, oblivious as he checked his reflection in the blackened shop windows they passed. "So, what did you think?" he said.

"Really? I think is depressing."

"Yes, but that was the point. An honest piece of social commentary."

"But Toby only love Jane when is easy. All he want is own success. When he find out she pregnant, he turn nasty."

"I don't think that's very fair . . ."

She wasn't sure if he was joking or not. He'd always liked it when she'd spoken her mind before, but now he looked like Michael when he didn't get the toy that he wanted. "I sorry I disappoint you," she said.

"Don't be silly. You haven't. Besides, it would be a bore if we agreed on everything."

Sook-Yin dared to glance at him. Despite her discomfort at the cinema, she had not forgotten the point of the evening. "So is okay we talk about job?"

"Ah, yes. I almost forgot. I meant to make some inquiries this afternoon but I'm afraid it got rather busy. I'm sure it's better this way. They'll probably want to talk to you."

"Oh! But my English is not good."

"Stop worrying. You'll be fine. In fact, if I hadn't left my address book at home, I could've taken you now to the office." He pulled back his sleeve and checked his watch. "I suppose we could always prepare. So you're ready when we make the calls."

"Prepare at office?"

"My flat. It's only gone eight," he said, "and it'll be another week before we're both free again."

Sook-Yin hesitated. She hated to waste the evening but was it wise going back to his house? She considered ah-Ma's warnings, but this time they were countered by other threats: another week of holding off ah-Chor, of Julian thinking she was being ungrateful. And she really *did* need this job. "I suppose is okay," she said.

"That's the spirit, Sook-Yin." He whistled at a passing taxi. "I'm not that far away."

JULIAN'S FLAT WAS in a terrace on Gower Street. Even given the faded glamour of its architecture, it didn't resemble the home of a financier—the expected warmth of a bright chandelier, the soft sounds that spoke of thick carpets. Yet even these minor disappointments were nothing compared to the shock of its interior. Sook-Yin held her breath as just beyond the doorway the skinny, littered hallway gave out to a stairwell that smelled of piss where grubby people in unwashed overcoats sat drinking and rolling cigarettes.

The room itself was no better. With its dripping walls and stink of fried grease it was even worse than the shanties in Yuen Long. Her mother would have had a fit. And where was all the furniture? Her gaze moved from the stool beside the bed, which held a lamp and a dull silver kettle, to the handle of the open window where a bottle of milk hung sadly from a sock.

Julian leaned out to retrieve it. "My fridge broke down," he said, with no apparent sense of self-consciousness, "and the shops take forever to deliver at Christmas." He pointed into the distance. "But look here, you can see the lights."

She followed his finger to the street, where in between the roofs of the terraces hung garlands of artificial baubles: holly and candles and berries gently glowing as they heralded the season. Julian's eyes seemed to brim at the sight.

"It's the one thing I've always hated about London—the fact you can't see the stars for the streetlights—but Christmas makes everything seem hopeful. Big dreams, big plans, big life . . ." He turned away and clapped his hands. "Right. First things first," he said. "If we're going to impress these friends of mine, we have to brush up on your vocabulary."

"What does this mean, to 'brush up'?"

"It means to get better. To improve oneself. The first rule of life is pretending."

Sook-Yin's instincts, vague at first, took on a more familiar shape. Julian's expressions may have been different but there was something she recognized about the sentiment: Matron Connolly telling her to *buck up*, ah-Chor's coronation as man of the family, Florence's vanity in her Swiss Cottage kingdom. *The first rule of life is pretending.* It was all a charade, a big bluff. The most surprising thing, however, was that as much as these people had deceived her, they seemed to have deceived themselves, too. Was *this* the secret to belonging? Her cynicism turned to curiosity. Maybe Julian could teach her something, after all.

He fetched a notebook and pen from his briefcase and then wrote out a list of words before inviting her to sit on the bed. Without so much as a chair in the room she had no choice but to perch beside him. "I want you to read these," he said, "and see if you know what they mean."

She attempted to say them out loud. "Debt collection. Loan. Interest payment. Mortgage. Profit. Loss. Lia . . ."

"Liabilities."

She gave an irritated sigh. "I do not know what this mean."

"That's all right. Take your time. Say them over again."

"Debt collection . . . Loan . . . Interest payment . . ." She froze as he touched her hair. "Mortgage payment . . . profit . . ."

"Loss, and liabilities." He leaned over and kissed her cheek. "The more you say it, the more natural it sounds." She turned her face away. "It's just a little kiss, Sook-Yin."

"But all I looking is friendship and job."

"Are you saying that you've never kissed a friend?" She closed her eyes and reddened. "I bet you've dreamed about it."

"I am only a good girl," she said.

"It doesn't make you bad. It's when you worry that you don't enjoy it." He leaned over and kissed her again and she pressed her fists into the blanket. *I am here for my family*, she told herself. *I am doing it so they have a better life. Hadn't ah-Ma done worse in the war?*

Realizing the inevitability of what was coming, she buried her mind in a memory: ah-Chor playing houses with Hei-Fong one summer on the balcony of ah-Ma's apartment. Sun rippling against the rooftops. The sounds of their joy in the warm air. Herself alone behind glass. *Go away, Sook-Yin, go away.* The shape of ah-Chor's mouth through the window, teeth bared. *You're a pest, a nuisance, a cockroach. Ah-Fong chose me in the end.*

When they'd grown bored and left the apartment, she'd tried to continue their game, touching everything Hei-Fong had touched and setting light to a bundle of hay beneath the belly of ah-Ma's cooking pot. The laugh of the wind as it caught the flames and threw its anger toward the washing line; gold-rimmed embers of black floating heavenward and becoming one with the wavy sky. If their mother hadn't returned from the market the entire apartment would have been an inferno. Sook-Yin remembered the burn on her skin and the way ah-Ma had shaken her bones. *Had she asked for trouble? Had she wanted it?*

AFTERWARD, SHE LAY in the bed as Julian dozed beside her. She reached for her knickers and wiped herself down, feeling heavy with the ache inside her and wishing she could make herself small enough to slip through the bedsit window. How many steps had she walked up? How far would she have to fall?

She got dressed and crept to the door.

"I'm sorry we didn't finish our studying."

When she turned, his eyes were open. "Is okay. Is fine. I go home now."

"Promise you'll call me tomorrow?"

"Tomorrow."

"I really *do* like you, Sook-Yin." He pointed to his jacket. "There's money in the pocket," he said. "Take a taxi back to Harvey's. I would hate anything bad to happen to you." She nodded and took some coins, not through any desire to please him but because it was the only way that she knew how to end things.

THIRTEEN

Lily

23rd Day of Mourning

Knowledge changes your perception of things. In the space of less than an hour, Maya had become my bailiff, my flat no more than a lending library. Past conversations took on new meaning: the shaggy rug that she so detested, the expensive coffeemaker I'd bought as a rare treat; things I'd assumed had been a question of taste now transformed before my gaze into objects of frivolous economics indulged at her and her husband's expense.

My initial instinct—that Ed had been bullshitting—was also dismantling at an alarming rate. Wasn't it obvious Dad had died with nothing? Two kids, a single parent, a shitty job at the local referral unit teaching English lit. to truants? He'd done his training later in life but despite being offered numerous jobs had instinctively gravitated toward the dropouts, as if in granting them a second chance, seeing the awful hardships they'd gone through, he somehow saw a reflection of himself. "The council doesn't even care," Maya told him, furious on his behalf whenever his applications for more funding were overlooked. "They're practically telling you to get out and save yourself."

"Then who will make the difference?" he always said.

With anyone else it would've seemed like posturing, but it's not like we were rich to begin with, not in the way that other people were, with their ponies and holidays in Malaga, something I'd not even questioned in the ruthless solipsism of youth. Yet now I thought about it, Maya and I still had everything we wanted, and that was even before his cancer and the extra gifts and handouts he'd given in his efforts to resurrect me. Where else had I thought it had come from if not overdrafts, credit cards, the never-never?

What hurt most was that Maya had carried on the lie. Was it something she'd recently found out, or something she and Dad had decided together—their blond heads joined in conspiracy? And was I angry or simply jealous? Moot point. Being a liability to Dad was one thing; continuing the legacy with my sister was different. I held her back. I filled her swamp. I made her see the monsters. And despite her patina of good cheer, her lovely smile, and her *nothing fazes me* attitude, I realized now that they terrified her.

The next morning I woke in a sweat, my cuss thick and sour with saliva as I remembered my appointment with Fenton. It would be good to see him, I supposed, if only to tell him I'd got it wrong.

SOMETHING FELT OFF about the clinic that morning. Even though the place was half empty there was a disconcerting feel of activity, the staff milling in groups behind glass screens, engaged in urgent conversations.

I hadn't even made it as far as the front desk when a therapist I'd sometimes seen around—a young woman in a too-tight sweater and self-consciously artisan earrings—came up to me. "It's Lily, isn't it?" she said. "I've been asked to see you today. If you hang on, I'll check if the room's free."

She walked off through one of the doors, leaving me stranded in the middle of reception. When I turned to look for a seat, I recognized the man called Scott in the corner, went over, and tapped him on the shoulder. "Hey. All right?" I said. His expression morphed into a semblance of acknowledgment. *What's going on?* I mouthed.

"Dr. Fenton's gone," he said.

"What do you mean he's gone?" I imagined him pinioned by some random car or flattened by a tree on the Common. Maya always said I had a grotesque imagination.

"He's gone, man. He's left the clinic."

The roil that had begun in my stomach threatened to reach my bowels and I crossed and uncrossed my legs. Didn't they have to give us notice about these things? "He can't have gone. I need him."

The young woman reappeared through the door and glanced uneasily between the two of us. "You can come with me now," she said. "We'll be in room number three today."

But I didn't want room number three, nor this woman barely five years older than me with her sorted life and her look-at-me earrings. I wanted to be back in Dr. Fenton's room, with its smell of book dust and pencil shavings. What use was clean? Or temporary?

"Fuck that," I said, and walked out.

I WAS MARCHING toward the high street when I heard the sound of footsteps behind me and Scott appeared over my shoulder. "Everything okay?" he said.

"Yes. I'm fine. Go away." I kept walking, faster this time, until after a moment his voice called out again.

"Someone reported Dr. Fenton . . ."

When I stopped and turned around, he was so close he almost headbutted me. "He threw a book at the bloke."

I gave him a cynical look. "Fenton. Threw a book. At someone?"

"Honest to God," he said. "That receptionist—with the really loud voice? Said he'd been sleeping in his car for a week. His missus left him, apparently."

I paused, trying to get my head around it. It was hard to think of Fenton in that way: that he existed outside of his room and had a messy, ordinary life. I didn't like it.

"The rest of them are having a right mare trying to find someone new for all of us. You have to go back, put your name on the list."

"Not me," I said. "I'm done with it." I started walking again and this time he kept pace with me.

"How come?"

"While the lunatics are running the asylum?" I laughed. "I refuse to join any club that would want to have me as a member."

"You quoting Marx at me now?"

"Groucho, not Karl. So you're sure." To be honest, I was quite impressed.

"Aren't we all in the club already?"

"And paying someone to examine your misery when they're just as miserable themselves is the definition of a frivolous expense. Is it any wonder the world is up shit creek?"

"I dunno, I find it helps. Knowing I'm not alone."

"We're all alone," I said. I slung my bag across my shoulder. "Better get on with it, anyway. Good luck with your life and all that." I tried to skirt around him, wrong-footed when he stepped in front of me.

"I don't s'pose you fancy a coffee?"

"Excuse me . . . No . . . What for?"

He shrugged. "I just thought we could chat for a bit."

"Not a big talker. Sorry."

"Yeah, I did get that impression . . ."

I stopped then, despite myself, and sneaked a crafty look at him. He wasn't bad-looking, as it happened, now that his nose had stopped whistling. Decent shoes. With socks. I stared down the abyss of the afternoon and a familiar specter crept over me: that craving to take control. Primal and automatic. "I don't like cafés," I said. "But I might have coffee at mine."

WE NEVER GOT around to the talking. Was I a reckless person by nature? Perhaps. Sex itself had never meant much to me and I'd grown fearless about its safety. Maybe it was a delayed reaction to Dad's death, or maybe it preceded this: a learned capacity to feel things only in an immediate and visceral way—through heat and breath and sweat and the sense of your own body in danger.

Mumma's gone. Mumma's gone. Mumma's gone.

I once read that survivors of plane crashes sometimes experienced this feeling too—the endless ways that normal life disappointed them—and how they spent the rest of their days chasing that joy in aliveness again. All I knew for sure was that sex was the only act when I ever—even for a moment—felt like I existed.

WHEN MORNING CAME, however, whatever smidgeon of comfort I'd derived from it had well and truly evaporated. I stared at Scott's face against the pillow, pale in the unkind slivers of daylight. What the hell had I done?

The night's memories returned with a creeping dread: the wonder of his fingers on the map of my scars, the kind words, my unintentional surrender. I needed to get rid of him. Quick. I pulled on whatever I could find and rushed to the kitchen to make coffee.

Half an hour later, I banged on the bathroom door. Did he think this was going somewhere? I sensed it in his lover's shower, the way his hand lingered too long on his coffee cup as he gazed at me across the table. The moony eyes. "I've got work today," I told him.

"My GP signed me off." There was an almost smugness about it—a child holding a tinny medal for coming first in the egg-and-spoon race—that transmuted to a wet-lipped pout.

"Some of us prefer not to dwell." It sounds cruel, but I didn't care. I needed to create some distance between us. Yes, we might have had something in common, we were both messed up in our own ways, but his playing field was not my field.

I got up and started washing my cup. Around and around with the scourer. "I really do have to get going," I said.

"Sorry, yeah." He made a show of pulling on his shoes, making sure his laces were lined up before uttering those awful words: "Let's exchange numbers, at least."

He picked up a pen from the counter and scribbled something on an abandoned envelope. Waited for me to reciprocate. Why did he have to draw things out? When I didn't move, he rubbed the back of his neck. I wouldn't miss that horrible mole. It had a hair growing out of it, for fuck's sake.

"Well, don't I feel a dick now?" he said. He turned and sloped out of the kitchen and a few seconds later I heard the front door. He didn't even have the guts to slam it.

FOURTEEN

Sook-Yin

January 1967

Sook-Yin spent the next weeks reflecting on her mistake. Her days were kept busy with the children—cooking, cleaning, walking—but at night the memories would return with a darkness that kept her awake or crept into her dreams like weeds: wet and dirty and tangled. How could she have been so stupid?

She hoped time would help put things behind her and found that each day she didn't hear from Julian was like a boulder being lifted from her back. She stopped watching the phone with fear, stopped asking Rose if she could answer it because her hands were full of dishes or messy from chopping vegetables. Christmas came and went and suddenly it was the middle of January.

But just as her anxiety about the telephone lessened, she discovered another problem. Her period was late. Not only this but she'd been sick to her stomach. She tried to deny the knowledge from her nursing days. She had caught a cold, a virus. It was impossible to have a baby from your first time. Wasn't it? Wasn't it? Wasn't it?

She was bent double across the toilet voiding yet another wasted breakfast when Florence came past the door. "What is that stink?"

she said. She took a can of Glade from the cupboard and emptied it into the air, which made Sook-Yin vomit again. "Anyone would think you are pregnant!"

Sook-Yin started to cry and Florence pulled her up from the floor and made her sit on the closed lid of the toilet. "What have you done, ah-Yin?"

She put her head in her hands. "Mr. Miller," she said.

"You slept with him without a commitment?"

"I didn't intend it to happen."

"You think soup can go back in a broken pot?" Florence rubbed her face. "And who is supposed to look after the children?"

Sook-Yin's stomach cramped in panic. "Please do not sack me, Je Je. There must be doctors who know about these things . . . who help women to lose their babies."

"Are you mad? What you're saying is illegal!"

"Then what am I going to do?"

Florence slumped against the edge of the bath, tracing loops around her mouth with her thumbnail. "There *is* one thing I can think of. My friend Mrs. Lim is a very good herbalist. She could probably suggest a recipe." Sook-Yin raised her head. "It's just a shame I can't ask her right now."

"Why not?"

Florence rubbed her slipper back and forth against the carpet. "All right. Since we're trading secrets, I lost some of Harvey's money. A bad run at the mahjong table."

All those days she'd disappeared from the house, *that* was where she'd been going? The game had haunted Sook-Yin's childhood; the brittle deafening of the tiles through the ceiling; the trading of wives and houses; her father's blood on the stairwell in the morning. She wished that she could shake her! "Why would you do that?" she said. "I could have told you it would lead to trouble."

Florence pouted. "At least *I* can undo my mistake." She rubbed the pale band on her wrist where something had obviously once lain.

"Where is your bracelet?" said Sook-Yin. "Your wedding present from Harvey?"

"The last game. I told him it was getting mended at the jewelers." She rubbed her chin. "If only I had some more money. Then I could kill two birds with a single rock."

It was obvious what she was hinting at, and what choice did Sook-Yin have? Florence wouldn't think twice about letting her go, giving her job to some other poor refugee, and at least this woman might be able to help her. "I have my savings," she said. "You could use some of it to replace Harvey's money, buy your bracelet back from them."

"Would you really do that for me?" Florence turned to her with a sweet smile. "Just give me enough to get back in their good books. I'll ask Mrs. Lim and then call it a day."

SHE DIDN'T RETURN until seven that evening. "Where have you been?" Sook-Yin asked. "The children have been waiting to eat."

"Don't worry about that," Florence said. "We'll take them to Wimpy for dinner."

Sook-Yin caught the glint of gold on her wrist. "Is that your bracelet?" she whispered. She frowned at Florence's smug expression, an uneasy feeling inside her. "Did you buy it, or win it back?"

"I won it. And more besides. You should have seen their faces. It won't be long before I'm ahead again."

Sook-Yin's cheeks grew hot. "And the other thing?" she said.

"Oh, yes. I brought it up, but the names were too difficult to remember. *Pen-ny-roy-al*, that was one of them." The English words thrashed like a whale in her mouth.

"You didn't ask her to write them down?"

"Right in the middle of a game? It was very awkward, I tell you. She probably thought I was asking for me." She stroked the ditch in Sook-Yin's elbow. "I'm sorry, sister," she said. "If you can give me a little more money, I promise to ask her tomorrow."

Sook-Yin pressed her hands to her face. Ah-Chor had been wrong about Florence. It was herself that had been the idiot. Always and only herself. "Leave it. It doesn't matter."

"But what about the baby?" Florence said. "The rest of Harvey's money?"

"Just put back what you won today and tell Harvey you spent the rest. Say the jeweler charged you too much."

"But he checks every little thing like a miser!"

"Then tell him you lost the receipt!"

"Are you saying you're not going to help me?" Florence sat up, affronted. "After you've lived here for close to six months with food and wages and board?" She got up and stormed to the door. "Your brother was right," she said. "You really *are* a cockroach!"

WHEN SOOK-YIN RETURNED from the school run the next morning, she found Harvey alone in the kitchen. "Gho, Gho are you ill? Why are you not at the restaurant?"

"Sit down, ah-Yin," he said. His voice made her mouth turn dry. Had he discovered the missing money? And where was Florence, come to think of it? Perhaps she had run away, or Harvey had sent her away and now would dismiss her, too, for joining in the conspiracy.

"Why don't I make you some tea?" She went to pick up the kettle.

"How far along in the pregnancy are you?"

Sook-Yin stopped and put her hand on her belly. Too flat for him to have noticed. "Florence told you," she said, and there was no need to make it a question. It was her punishment for not giving her the money.

"Did you think I wouldn't find out? Why didn't you come to me first?"

"I didn't want people to know. I didn't want *Florence* to know."

"In that case you should have moved to Mongolia!" They exchanged the faintest of smiles, a shared understanding. "You've not told Mr. Miller, I take it?" Sook-Yin shook her head. "I thought as much. He has been at the restaurant every night, drinking and smoking and eating like pleasure is going out of fashion."

"Please don't tell him, Gho-Gho."

"Why? Is the baby not his?"

She didn't answer at first. Whatever was inside her, she didn't think of it as anyone's possession. Not even hers. "I could go away," she said. "At the hospital they taught us about clinics where women have their babies in secret. Afterward, I could get it adopted."

"White people don't want half-breeds."

Sook-Yin balked at the tremble in his lips. Gentle, sorrowful Harvey. What weight had he had to carry? What dreams had he been forced to give up?

"There's a chance Mr. Miller may be different. We must give him the opportunity to answer." He stood and went to the fridge. "I brought *sui mai* and I want you to eat," he said. "And no more looking back at the past. You will end up killing yourself."

FIFTEEN

Lily

24th Day of Mourning

Mr. Nesbit had left three messages on my answering machine. I stared at the blinking light, listening to his drone, his urgency. I'd been so close to turning him down. I'd even practiced my speech: an expression of gratitude for his client's generosity but my ultimate refusal to be beholden to anyone, all the while preparing to take Maya's offer.

I'm going to give you the money for the music school.

If we'd never received those letters, would the thought have even occurred to her?

All the joy of that day washed away. If Maya could lie about Dad, what else had she been hiding in order to make my life easier? I had to show her I could manage on my own. That I could find answers to the void of my past. That I was no longer her sick little sister.

THE TRAVEL AGENT on Electric Avenue was as crowded as a beach in Magaluf, everyone looking for last-minute bargains to where the sun would be less disappointing. The staff were sweaty and harassed, the man who dealt with me sullen and uncommitted. Maybe I wasn't asking the right questions, or else the answers I gave made no sense to him. Was I aware this was the year of the Handover? What did I intend to do on my budget? Was there anyone there I could stay with? *Yes. I don't know. Maybe.*

Once I'd handed over my credit card, however, his surly concern evaporated. I was young, after all, he said, and young people did reckless things; if they didn't, they were doing something wrong. I don't suppose it was part of his intention but as I left with my ticket that morning, I tried to take comfort from that.

I popped into the Age Concern. Given her encouragement about the letter, I wanted to give Babs some credit but she greeted the news with silence. "It's not really about the money," I told her. "More that I'd like to find out about Mum. You never know, I might discover I fit there."

Babs fussed at the floss of her hair. "I forgot to tell you," she said. "Those bags your friend brought in. I put them straight in the corner for collection—nothing decent or useful among it. Bit cheeky, if I'm being honest."

"Babs—"

"I'm sorry I pushed you now. I'm going to miss you, Lily."

I put an arm around her and squeezed. "Don't be silly. I'll be back before you know it."

"That's what I mean," she said. "When you get back, I'm going to miss you."

MY PARANOIA ABOUT Maya lingered when I called her that afternoon.

"Has something happened? Are you dead or on fire?"

"Er, not yet," I said.

"In that case, you'll have to give me two minutes. You're currently number three in the queue."

I heard the click as she put me on hold again, her tone of habitual busyness newly transformed in my mind to her expectation that I wanted something and therefore deserved to wait for it. I was reminded of the old sign on Dad's office door, erected to keep us at bay while he privately attended to his sanity with the *Guardian* crossword and a bottle of Blue Nun: *I can please only one person per day. Today is not your day. Tomorrow's not looking good, either.*

Maybe I was being unfair. I knew that my sister *was* genuinely busy, and had been for as long as I'd known her.

I listened to *The Four Seasons* on loop and thought of her alphabetizing Dad's collection of LPs. It had been one of her obsessions as a kid, graduating in complexity as she aged—from artist to title to genre—like some anal, protracted party trick. It had gained her entry to the sanctum of his office, a privilege kept out of my reach but which she shared when the fancy struck her and Dad happened to be out at work.

"Is Lindisfarne prog rock or folk?" she'd said. This happened sometime in the eighties, during a half-term sweatfest of boredom. We'd been hiding out from the mini-heatwave and all I'd wanted was ice baths and Fab lollies; to have blond hair that didn't absorb the sun.

"Lily? Are you there?' she said. *The Four Seasons* had ended abruptly.

"Whatever happened to Lindisfarne?"

"What?"

"Did you ever find out where they fit?"

She emitted a breathy sniff. "Is this important? I have to go to a meeting."

"Sorry, yeah, you go," I said. "And don't bother about ringing me back. I just called to remind you I'm going away for a bit."

Her leather chair did a squawk of protest. "No. Hang on. Away where?"

"Don't you remember?" I lied. "That therapeutic retreat in the country . . . Like the one I did at the hospital. It was Dr. Fenton's idea. Nothing but nuns and chores and three weeks of silent contemplation. Anyway, now it's happening."

"Three weeks? But that's a shit ton. I'm sure I would've remembered."

"You're getting dementia," I said. "Look, I probably *didn't* make a big deal of it because they don't choose everyone to go and I assumed I wouldn't get picked, but apparently I've made excellent progress."

Silence. She wasn't convinced.

I injected a note of offense. "I thought you'd sound a bit happier. You're always saying I should be more proactive. I might even get out for a run."

"Right . . . Well, obviously that's brilliant. Remind me again where it is?"

I racked my brain for somewhere restful and green that was likely to have an excess of nuns. "Somewhere in the Cotswolds, I think." I winced. *The fucking Cotswolds?* "They don't like to give the address out—"

"So you can't be distracted, I suppose."

"Yes, exactly!" I said. "It's like the Masonic arm of the Priory. They've got your number for emergencies."

I heard her tapping her pen on the blotter. "So—do you need me to pay for it or anything?" She could've *tried* to sound snide about it.

"No. It's all been covered, thanks. Sponsored by some pharmacy company."

"Ugh. Make sure they don't spike your beans."

"'Soylent Green is people.'"

"'*There was a world once, you punk!*'" Her laugh dimmed and then disappeared. "Hang on a min, Lils," she said. Her hand rustled against the receiver as she muttered an acknowledgment to someone. "Bloody meetings, sorry. But listen, that all sounds great . . .'"

Her mind was already on other things. I was almost home and dry. "And we'll sort out the money when you're back, yeah? I've got the check ready and everything."

I closed my eyes. "Sure . . . that's great."

"But you have to promise me, Lils . . ."

"Promise you what?" I said.

"I mean the Cotswolds *are* lovely, but promise you'll ring me if it all gets too much."

SIXTEEN

Sook-Yin

January 1967

The days blurred without reason or purpose; mornings transformed into night like soy sauce spilled onto a watercolor. When Sook-Yin cooked or played with the children, when she walked them to and from school, it was with the dull mechanics of habit. Harvey's mission was a foolish errand, but most of all, it felt humiliating. If Julian had regretted his actions, if he'd had any feelings at all for her, wouldn't he have made some effort at contact? Instead, as she had suspected, now that the chase was over the dog had no interest in eating the rabbit.

Though it hadn't changed the horror of her predicament, the acknowledgment of her own stupidity had allowed her some closure with Julian. Harvey was a different matter. She was both alarmed and afraid by his persistence. To be ashamed of herself was one thing, but the idea that he was trying to get rid of her was like speaking the words out loud, the same way ah-Chor had spoken that day when he'd told her she was going to London. *You are nothing but an embarrassment to the family. Nobody wants you anymore.*

Exiled. Abandoned. Rubbish.

A fortnight after the confirmation of her pregnancy, Harvey

telephoned the house and asked Florence to bring the family to the restaurant. Was her banishment to be so public? "Did he say why?" Sook-Yin asked. She could barely speak for the fear in her throat, hot and viscous as blood.

"Am I his keeper?" Florence said. "That's the only thing he told me."

Standing alone in the bathroom, Sook-Yin startled at her reflection in the mirror. How long had it been since she'd washed her hair? Since she'd brushed her teeth with the light on? She went out to the landing and called over the banisters. "Tell him we're going to be late."

"WHERE HAVE YOU BEEN?" Harvey said. His urgency bordered on fluster, and Sook-Yin bit at the stain of her lipstick, glad she had made him wait. If he was determined to make this a battle then she would go into it dressed as a warrior.

She barely disguised her shock when he led them to the center of the restaurant, where Julian sat alone at a table.

"Sook-Yin, it's been too long," he said. He stood and kissed both her cheeks, newly flushing in the knowledge of her stiffness.

"I'm hungry!" Michael whined.

"All in good time," Harvey said as he pushed his son into a seat. "Mr. Miller has something to say."

Everyone took their places, the heat reigniting Julian's face as he stood and addressed the table. "You must forgive my absence, Sook-Yin. I fear we've been the victims of a terrible misunderstanding. After our trip to the cinema that evening, I thought we'd agreed to speak again, but when there was only silence . . ."

He groped blindly for his glass before he saw it was already empty and was forced to put it back down again. "The truth is, I'm not very good at expressing my feelings, especially if it seems like I'm being rejected. Call it British reserve if you like, a certain cautiousness at appearing a fool, but when Harvey told me what had actually happened, I knew I'd have to take my chances." He ran out of breath and gulped. "What I'm trying to say is . . . I love you, and I have from the moment we met. You are extraordinary and clever and beautiful and I would be an idiot if I never told you so."

"I can't hear what he's saying!" Michael said.

Sook-Yin pulled the boy onto her lap, as much a shield between her and Julian as any attempt to calm him. She had no idea what was happening. "Now, we all hear," she said, although her mouth was so dry she only whispered it.

Florence let out a small gasp as Julian took something out of his pocket and knelt on the carpet beside them. "Please would you honor me by being my wife?"

Sook-Yin looked at his outstretched hand and the open box that lay at its center. Inside was a thin band of gold, set with a tiny diamond. Twinkling under the dim light, it looked like a raindrop held up by a star, and as much as it was only an illusion, so too did it bring possibilities: a father for her unborn child, a husband to bring home to her family, the prospect of a life for herself. Perhaps she'd been mistaken about him and this was simply the way of things.

"What do you think?" he said. "Will you give me this chance to prove myself?" Sook-Yin looked at Harvey and Florence, too afraid to answer at first. There were "right" things and then there were "only" things, and she was running out of chances for one of them. And he'd said he loved her, hadn't he? She couldn't remember the last time she had heard the words.

Finally, she swallowed and nodded. "Okay. I marry you," she said.

AN HOUR AFTER Florence and the children had gone home, she found herself alone at the table. The restaurant had all but emptied and the shock of the sudden quiet—the silencing of glasses and cutlery, the burst bubble of chatter around her—made her mind feel chaotic by comparison. Thoughts tumbled in and confronted her, and like in one of the children's puzzle books she tried to find the connections between them: *man* and *woman* and *marriage*; *money* and *future* and *safety*; *brother* and *mother* and—what? She didn't know the ending of *that* line and was half-afraid to tug at it; afraid she would find a blank image for *home*. Wasn't that the reason she was here in the first place?

She pulled the compact out of her handbag and passed it over her reflection: red eyes, red face, red neck. The same color she'd seen on ah-Ba when he used to come home late from the factory. She was her father's daughter all right.

She shook the thought from her mind. The champagne must have gone to her head, dulled her senses. What was Julian's proposal but a new start—a chance to prove her family wrong?

Strengthened by this resolution she glanced at the bar and saw him standing alongside Harvey, seemingly engaged in a heated conversation. Only when Julian got up for the bathroom did Harvey come back to sit with her. "Are you happy, ah-Yin?" he said. "Now everything will be all right."

A sudden jolt in her throat. Why had he said it like that? "What were you discussing?" she said.

"When?"

"The two of you there, at the bar."

Harvey gave a laugh of surprise. "Just two men talking business," he said. "So, when will you tell your family?"

She knew it would have to be soon. Apart from the fact of her pregnancy, there would be so much for her to arrange: invitations and dresses and flowers; a proper winter coat for ah-Ma and shoes that hid her toes.

"Has Harvey been leaking my plans to you?" Sook-Yin shook her head as Julian reappeared beside her.

"Actually, we talk about wedding. My mother never been to this country before."

Julian tugged at his ear. "It's a long way to travel," he said. "Not to mention expensive. Wouldn't you rather we save for our new life?"

She pictured his room in Gower Street, how unsuitable it would be for a family. "Yes. I suppose that is true."

He kissed the top of her head. "Don't you worry. We'll send them photographs. Great big ones, to put on the wall."

Sook-Yin turned the ring on her finger. Inasmuch as she'd imagined these things, they had seemed less plain, less *gray*. Photographs were only for shrines. She pictured her mother's disappointment. "I suppose is very different in Hong Kong. To us, wedding is always big celebration."

"I understand," he said, "but your family will be there in spirit. Besides—" He leaned over and drained the rest of his glass. "We're hardly in Kansas anymore."

SEVENTEEN

Lily

29th Day of Mourning

Heathrow Airport was an assault on my senses, a human fruit machine of alarms and flickering lights surrounded by hot plastic seating. I'd arrived too early, of course, a hangover from my five-day panic about the enormity of what I was doing. Earlier, I'd called Maya from a pay phone and told her I would see her in three weeks, but now I glanced at the exit signs, trying to resist the mucky loop of the escalator that would take me back down to normality.

As soon as I boarded, I took a Valium and let the first hours of the flight drift by until the stewardess woke me for food and I picked at a pancake roll and a piece of apple from the plastic tray. I studied my fellow passengers. Most of them were Chinese, and the rapid gunfire of their conversations nudged at the edge of my sleep, the sharpness of their intonations like anomalous peaks in a sound wave. I turned on the screen in front of me and watched a film without the headphones, trying to read the actors' lips.

Once we were over Mongolia, I took out the list of guesthouses that I'd printed out at the Brixton library and circled the one at the top with my pen: Chungking Mansions. The photos of the rooms seemed fine, and best of all, I could get there on the shuttle bus.

It was eight in the morning local time when we began our final descent toward the perilous strip of Kai Tak's runway. I gripped the arms of my seat as the plane tipped like a marble in a funnel toward the right turn at Checkerboard Hill, skirting the roofs of the nearby apartments and sending the doll's house miniatures of their furniture trembling within the open windows.

o o o o o o

A heavy fug, slate as a pigeon's wing, enveloped the morning sky as I followed the crowds through Arrivals. The lucky ones were met by family, while others—sheened with their travelers' tans—hurried in search of transport, their backpacked walks a timpani of metal cups and the rough slough of mats and waterproofs. Why the hell had I done this? *Breathe, for God's sake. Get a grip.*

I was calmer once I'd boarded the shuttle, peering out through the dust-streaked windows as the squat exterior of hangars succumbed to the arteries and bustle of city streets.

I needn't have worried about losing my way. Getting off at Tsim Sha Tsui, the hotel was nothing if not conspicuous. If Heathrow Airport was like a casino, Chungking Mansions was where you went to lose big. It was more Blackpool seafront than urban metropolis; a hive of noise and activity selling foreign currency, knock-off Gucci, and almost everything else in between.

I gazed up from across the street to the shabby, gap-toothed residences that rose like the maze of a prison. Errant laundry and people alike hung from the peeling windows punched into the building at random; the guesthouses coexisting with sweatshops, the scars of their changing identities carved into the fascia of the brickwork: Chak Mei Ivory Factory. Yum-Yum Filters. Still, there was something seductive about it, a medusa exerting her pull on those who dared to turn in its direction. Grimy and exhausted by the journey, I wasn't about to argue.

As soon as I approached the entrance, I was ambushed by a

middle-aged Sikh in a *Relax, Don't Do It* T-shirt. "Need place to stay? Good price. Best guesthouse in Chungking Mansions."

I assumed he must be an anomaly, a traveler who'd decided to stay, but I was wrong. Inside was a veritable microcosm of the immigrant experience: kimono shops, African food stalls, a Bangladeshi tailor bent over the bones of a suit accompanied by a chorus of steamy presses. "Elevator this way," said Good Price.

We queued for twenty minutes as the two sluggish elevators arrived, filled up, and deposited people in an endless, congested circuit. I glanced toward the stairwells, where a knot of wiring and bamboo water piping coexisted in frightening proximity, while mere meters away from my feet thick layers of leaky rubbish oozed stench and maggots onto the concrete. Notwithstanding its buzzing strip lights, it seemed mathematically impossible to create a more depressing interior. *Just like home*, I thought.

I was finally escorted to a place in Block C, a runnel of identical doors embedded in the walls of its corridor. "Welcome to Happy Guest House. Lovely room for you, lady."

He opened the door and I peered inside. The adjective was obviously relative. A single bed took up most of the space, flanked by drawers and a small TV and overlooked by a doorless toilet and makeshift shower. Six feet beyond, at the airless window, more wires and bamboo pipes crisscrossed at an eye-stabbing angle. I suspected a deliberate ploy to sell me a more expensive room, but slow from the effects of the Valium compounded by my jet lag, I said thank you and paid him anyway.

I DOZED OFF, and when I woke up it was two in the afternoon and the streets were humming with traffic. At the window, I peered down at the pavement with its homogenous rush of dark heads taunting my lack of a plan. Time to get my bearings.

I took everything I had of value—my passport and travelers' checks, along with a handful of cash—and went down onto the street.

The earlier smog had burned away and the June heat descended like a wall. Monsoon season had yet to arrive, and the dry air sucked the spit from my throat even as I sweated, the air a soup of clove oil and talcum.

I followed the herd along Nathan Road, through the miasma of shops and eateries, my throat itchy from hunger and thirst. At a café in Ashley Road, the smell of pork buns and ramen drew me in and I ordered one of each with a Coke. The place was clearly an oasis for Westerners, and it was only as I paid my bill that the waiter examined me closer. "Filipina?"he said. "Taiwanese?"

I grinned. Though not definitive proof of my looks, I was pleased that he thought I fitted. "My mother is from Kowloon."

Over the years I'd evolved into the present tense and used it now by default. I found it more accessible for strangers, people more amenable to what they expected rather than the things that might have been true.

My pride was unearned and short-lived as he let forth a torrent of Cantonese. "You don't speak?" he said to my silence. His harsh expression was an insult, not a question, and as I limped away with my change its wound remained like a deep regret.

Twenty minutes later I was in Kowloon Park, my muscles driven by some primitive memory, although I knew how unlikely that was. Whatever had brought me, I was glad of it and I wandered for close on two hours, through the mazes and man-made islands, through the aviary with its hornbills and parrots and the tai chi corner alongside the pavilion, where men and women dressed in yoga pants practiced their delicate human grace.

The sun was setting when I arrived at the pier and the city's complexion had changed again, its occasional drabness newly transformed in the emerging firework of lights across the harbor. Again there was the pull of something familiar: the shape of the skyline like a pattern in my mind, the outlines of junks and sampans, a sweetness to the smell of the water, just as it had been in my memory. The activity even at this hour made London seem like a parochial aunt who had stayed up past her bedtime, and it was then I started to realize how Hei-Fong Lee had made his fortune. Sleep, I realized now, was a dirty word for Hong Kongers.

Chungking Mansions never slept either, and by the time I got back to the foyer it was as rowdy and packed as ever, the queues for the elevators even longer albeit with a different crowd. Nighttime had exiled the casual shoppers and brought out the hustlers and dealers, girls leaning against the shutters in colored vinyl miniskirts, dancing to fuzzy boom boxes. I was surprised when I returned to my room and found it the same as I'd left it.

I sat down and worked out a plan. I would wake early and wander the streets, acquaint myself with their layout and the routes on the MTR. I'd ride the ferry to Central and back again, and at night I'd return to the guesthouse, finding dinner in the buffet of samosas or baskets of cheap dim sum in the mall at the base of the building.

The only crack in the gloss of this plan was that it didn't include Daniel Lee even though he was the reason I'd gone there, and as I sat in my room that night, I admitted that I was afraid. Distance hadn't lessened my shock about Dad, but worse was the implicit suggestion that there might be more revelations to come.

I'd turned off the light in my room when I heard a commotion outside in the corridor. It began as a drizzle of sobs that slowly crescendoed into a wail. I got up and pressed my ear to the wall and then cracked open the door and peered out.

No more than five feet from my room, a young woman was facedown on the carpet, naked except for her underwear. My stomach turned. I've never been a person with an appetite for trouble. I've closed doors on rowdy parties, walked away from fights on the bus, but this was different. I came out and crouched beside her. "Hello? Are you okay?"

She was barely older than a teenager. Old bruises scattered her chin, the crusting scar of a once-split lip. I gestured to my room. "Come inside and let me help you."

She shook her head. "Too dangerous, you," she said. "Better for man downstair."

She was right, and I was relieved. There would be men, other *people*, in the lobby. Always better to have safety in numbers.

For once, I was lucky with the elevator. Downstairs, the floor thrummed with the heat of bodies, and I fixed on a group of Europeans hanging around the shutters of the tailor. "A woman needs help," I told them. "Upstairs in the hall of Block C." They crossed their arms and turned away from me. "Can't you understand what I'm saying? A woman is hurt. Please, help me."

I spotted Good Price at the entrance of the building, smoking as he scouted for taxis, and ran to him. "Do you remember me?" I said.

"Yes! Hello, Block C. Is everything all right with room?"

"I think a woman's been attacked in the hallway. Please can you come and help me?"

"English woman?" he said.

"Chinese . . . or Korean, I think. Does it matter what color she is?"

Good Price ground out his cigarette. "Yes. It matters," he said. "Did you remember to lock your room?"

Fuck.

"Come on. Perhaps you are lucky."

By the time we ascended the stairwell—Good Price quick and automatic in the darkness—it was clear that luck hadn't favored me. The woman had vanished from the corridor and the door to my room stood open. He walked ahead of me to check and then called me back inside. "Anything missing?" he said.

I pulled my rucksack from behind the shower curtain, where I thought I'd been clever in stashing it, and turned it upside down. "Passport, cash, and travelers' checks." The backs of my knees were shaking, my fear of being sick a poor relation to my stupidity. It was the oldest scam in the book.

"You must go to the embassy," he said. "Get up and go early as possible." There was something practiced about the instruction, even as he stopped short of admitting liability. "It is a terrible thing, Block C. But the police will not listen, you understand?"

I searched for something to calm my panic, saw a fly capsized on the sill. Six legs, six wings, black body. Shattered eyes of a monster. *We have flies in London, too.*

"You want I find you another room? No charge. No charge," he said.

I turned to him, caught by his kindness. "Please," I said. "If you can."

Good Price was as good as his word and found me a room on a different floor. Once he'd left, I turned out my pockets. Ninety dollars and not even a passport. I threw myself onto the bed, fetused against the pillow, my stomach a web of panicked knots. How was I going to stay now? And how the hell would I get home?

EIGHTEEN

Sook-Yin

January 1967

Sook-Yin woke with a throbbing head, relieved when she called down the stairs to find that the house was empty. She suddenly remembered that it was Saturday, meaning Florence and Harvey must be out with the children. Had she really slept till noon? She took two aspirin with a glass of water and then pulled the phone to the living room and dialed her mother's number. "I have some news," she said, when she answered.

"You have found another job, ah-Yin?"

"No . . . I'm getting married." She closed her eyes at the cavern of silence coiling itself through the wire. "He's from a very successful family. Business people," she said. Whispered exchanges rippled in the background and Sook-Yin strained to make out the other voice. "Is Mrs. Chee visiting so late?"

"No, your brother just brought me home. We've been on a trip to Lychee Garden . . . He says he wants to talk to you."

"All right." Sook-Yin picked at her lip and then arranged her mouth in a smile, surprised when she heard his laughter.

"Ah-Ma must be joking around. She said you were getting married."

"His name is Julian Miller."

The levity curdled in her brother's throat. "The man who was giving you a job?"

"Yes. The same," she said.

"What do you mean by this? And what sort of name is Miller?"

"It means he is English, obviously."

"Listen, Sook-Yin," he said. "What is the point you are trying to make here?"

There were only two voices her brother knew: either he was as sharp and as brittle as a cane or, like now, he was condescending, as though trying to explain an easy problem to a particularly stupid child. "I must have misunderstood," she said. "Since you sent me away to London, I thought I was free to marry who I wanted."

"And to hell with your family, is that it? We paid so you could improve yourself."

His volume had risen to its default but she kept her own tone measured, aware that it would infuriate him. "Improve myself for whom? Ah-Ma and I were perfectly happy, but you turned her thoughts against me. Told her I was a no-good spinster-in-waiting." She pictured his look of betrayal. Yes, ah-ma had told her about that, so who was the stupid one now?

"And marrying a white dog is something better? Can you really not see?" he sneered. "Even in his own country he wants to colonize us! Keep an eye on the natives."

No. He was wrong about that. Though he sometimes spoke like a politician, Julian had never come across as a bigot. And when had her brother changed his song? Was he not an *English* teacher? Horrible, opinionated ah-Chor, as fickle as a blade of grass turning wherever the weather most favored him. So what if her engagement wasn't a fairy tale? All she needed was a chance to prove herself. "Then you won't be coming to the wedding?"

"And see what a traitor you are? Rub our noses, is it?" He said this last bit in English and this time she laughed out loud.

"Then I hope you will enjoy the photographs." She pointed her chin at the telephone. "Please tell ah-Ma to send me a cheongsam. My fiancé will send you the money."

SOOK-YIN WAS NOT long out of the bath when Julian turned up without notice, saying he had a surprise for her. They rode in a taxi to Islington and were dropped off at an abandoned building around the corner from the high street. Half of its windows were boarded up, the others bearing the weathered remnants of its former occupation: a sign for Meaty Bovril and a sun-bleached advert for Spangles.

"What do you think?" he said.

"I think why you bring me old grocer's shop?"

"It's not any old grocer's shop." Julian took a ring of keys from his pocket and opened the lock with the largest of them. "Welcome home, Mrs. Miller!"

They went in and he flicked on the lights, bathing the gloomy space in a wan yellow sheen of dust motes. If Sook-Yin stretched out her arms to the walls it was barely bigger than her room at Florence's. "We live in shop?" she said.

"No! We work in the shop. We live in the flat upstairs. Imagine the sign," he said, punctuating the air with his outstretched hand. "Millers. Grocers. Islington." When Sook-Yin failed to respond, his hand dropped with the suddenness of disappointment. "You could be a bit more excited."

"Sorry, yes, I more surprise. I thought you happy in office."

"But I can't be my own boss there."

"Are you not boss?" she said.

The tips of his ears grew red. "Well, not of the entire company, no . . . But this way we can be self-sufficient, no one telling us what we can and can't do. Wouldn't you like to run the show for a change—finally take charge of our lives?"

Sook-Yin cleared a circle of dust from the window. She had to admit it sounded good to her, especially after ah-Chor's lecture that morning. Imagine his face when she told him: the owner of a shop, no less! A proper businesswoman. And it was only sensible to start off small; protect themselves. She could even picture it now if she squinted: a vase of red flowers on the counter, some bunting along the shelves, a lucky cat to bring in the customers. Harvey had spoiled her, that was all, and she'd become used to living in luxury, forgotten where she'd come from.

She looked at Julian's face, full of hope and joy and excitement. She may not have dreamed of this bed she had made, but at least he'd stepped up and stood by her, and that was more than she could say for her family.

Lily

▬▬▬▬▬▬▬▬▬▬▬▬▬▬
▬▬▬▬▬▬▬▬▬▬▬▬▬▬

31st Day of Mourning

We don't issue short-notice passports."
        I stared at the man behind the desk, a fresh wave of
nausea rising in me. Given a different circumstance, the consulate
building would have seemed spectacular, with its sparkling façade
of white stone and its domed frontage of turquoise glass, but that
morning I'd woken at six, my night's sleep disrupted by panic, and
by the time I'd got to Admiralty—dragging my suitcase through the
crowds of the MTR—my head ached and I was sticky with sweat.

Things had only got worse from there. Despite my early arrival
I'd obviously missed the jump on the queue, and beyond the calm-
ing illusion of the building's exterior I'd entered a world of chaos.
The sizable reception was already half full, my presence another
brick in the wall of backpacks and high-carried toddlers, of crying
babies and pushchairs and sighs and the stink of sweat and frustration, cementing my long-held conviction that there was no comfort
in other people's misery.

After an interminable wait, I was processed and shown to an
office where I was forced to repeat my predicament to the sour-

faced Brit now in front of me. I pressed my nails into the flesh of my thighs. "So what do I do now?" I said.

"We can give you an emergency travel document that will be enough to get you back to London." He pulled a form from his desk and began to fill it out with a starched hand.

"Any idea when that might be?"

"A few days, once you pay the fee. The cost is eighty pounds."

I'd originally booked for three weeks. Even if I had the money to pay him, it would mean practically no time in Hong Kong. "I'll need to call my bank," I said. "Ask them to sort out the finances."

"You do realize today is Friday?" He followed my eyes to the calendar. I'd forgotten I'd lost a day to the time difference. "Is there anyone you can call in Hong Kong? Perhaps a friend or a relative in the UK who could wire you money in the meantime?"

The obvious choice was Maya, but two days into my trip I'd be buggered if I had to phone her. I considered calling Mumma's family but the address was two decades old, the chances slim that they'd be living in the same place, let alone be willing to help me.

That left only one person. I rooted around in my bag and fished out the card from Mr. Nesbit. "Would it be possible to ring one of these numbers?"

He took the card and read it, his lip curling with unguarded surprise. "May I ask how you know Mr. Lee?"

"We have some business between us."

"In that case, I'll take care of it personally." He stood and gestured to the telephone. "Zero gets you an outside line. Feel free to call your bank."

My eyes stung in the breeze of the closing door. Had I underestimated Daniel Lee's influence?

Much as the man had expected, my bank could do little until after the weekend, and I started to panic again. Would the embassy give me a loan? Would they know of a place I could stay?

I paced around the office. Unlike the grandeur of the building's façade, the room had been built for function, with its dull paint job and token rubber plant. On one wall hung a portrait of the Queen flanked by the regional and Union flags and alongside these an artless display of all the previous British governors, Chris Patten's photo the most recent among them. Strange to think that in less than a month the whole politics of the place would change, the colony becoming nothing more than an entry in the history books; crisp and new at first and then desiccated into the past. How would it be for future generations who had never known it this way? For all the people who were left behind with their stories tangled by memory?

The airless room was stifling and my lack of sleep was starting to catch up with me when a young woman came through the door. Everything about her was sharp and dry: the shadows of her face in the sunlight, the impeccable pleats of her black suit, the triangular feel of her hand when she reached across and shook mine. "My apologies for Mr. Lee's absence. I'm afraid he is busy this morning." She set a briefcase on the table and opened it. "So you are little trouble?" she said.

"I'm sorry?"

Her lips narrowed. "There are some very bad people in Hong Kong." She produced a large padded envelope. "Inside is prepay credit card. Also, some Hong Kong dollar for things that are little little."

I took the envelope and looked inside. It was an awful lot of money. "This isn't necessary," I said. "I've already been in touch with my bank. All I need is somewhere to stay."

"Mr. Lee has already book room. I will take you back and show you."

"I'm happy to stay where I was . . ."

Her smile wore the disdain of some secret knowledge. "Chungking Mansions impossible. Please now, you pick up suitcase."

A CHAUFFEUR-DRIVEN DAIMLER drove us back from the island, the woman frustrating my attempts to ask questions by spending all her time on the telephone. I was vaguely aware of the concept of drivers—used by soap stars and people in rock bands, even Ed, I supposed, once or twice when he was doing some palace in Mayfair—but the idea was somehow obscene to me. Maybe it was because of this, the notion that *staff* were viewed as unimportant, that I turned my attention to him. "What exactly does Mr. Lee do?"

His eyes flicked to me in the mirror, shocked that I had addressed him. "Mr. Lee in finance sector."

"You mean he works for a bank?"

He smiled. "Mr. Lee *is* bank," he said.

Directly on the harbor's north shore we pulled into the manicured forecourt of an imposing white hotel, its backdrop shadowed by a soaring tower in the same colonial style and its entrance guarded by an arc of Rolls-Royces. A porter stepped forward and opened the car door and the woman cupped her hand to the phone. "The desk expect you," she said. I stared at her, not understanding. "This is Peninsula hotel. You stay as Mr. Lee's guest." She pulled something from the pocket of the back seat. "Also, is mobile cell phone. Important numbers already in there." When I hesitated, she pushed it toward me in a semi-aggressive manner. "Mr. Lee is very busy," she said. "He cannot have any more trouble."

I continued to feel on the back foot as I was escorted inside to the front desk and greeted by a smiling receptionist. "Welcome, Miss Miller," she said. "Please allow the porter to take your suitcase. Mr. Lee has recently arrived."

"Mr. Lee?" I said.

"He got here five minutes ago." She pressed the bell on the counter and gestured beyond my shoulder. "He's waiting for you in the lobby."

TWENTY

Sook-Yin

February 1967

On the day she was to meet his parents, Sook-Yin took the tube to Fulham Broadway. She'd never traveled before on the District Line, and at Earl's Court she took the wrong branch and had to double back on herself. Julian was already at the entrance, the shine of his newly polished shoes dulled by a puddle of half-smoked cigarettes. "I wish you'd left earlier," he told her. "My mother is cooking us lunch."

He waited outside on the pavement as she went into a nearby newsagent and bought a cellophaned box of Black Magic and a wilting bunch of chrysanthemums. "This is Chinese way," she said. "It is bad luck to go empty-handed."

Julian fingered the inside of his collar. "Yes. About that . . ." he said. "It might be best not to mention such things. My parents are a bit old-fashioned. Fish and chips and holidays in Scarborough. Women must be seen and not heard . . . You won't be offended, will you?"

Having been inducted into Julian's liberalism, Sook-Yin was a little surprised, but given his buildup to the day and the trial of her journey that morning she agreed that no, she wouldn't be. The

Millers were an old English family and she was marrying their only son. It was natural that he should be nervous.

They broke away from the high street into a seedy row of terraces, their doorsteps blighted by cracks and the windows shrouded in laddered nets. Julian steered her into one of the entrances, where she was forced to pick her way through a graveyard of broken flowerpots and the splinters of a fallen trellis. "My parents have lived here for years," he said. "I offered to move them somewhere better, but they're stubborn and wouldn't hear of it." He leaned over and wiped her lips and she moved her head away.

"This is lipstick, not dirt," she said.

An older woman opened the door to them, dressed in an untidy apron and slippers. "Sorry we're late, Ma," he said, laying a kiss on her cheek. "This is my fiancée. Sook-Yin."

He presented Sook-Yin to the doorway as though she were a prize on a game show. And what was happening to his mother's face?

Mrs. Miller's lips opened and closed in silence, like a goldfish realizing its bowl was empty, before she turned again to Julian.

"I don't understand, love," she said.

THE BRUME OF vegetables boiled to surrender hung heavy over the table as Sook-Yin studied her plate of sloppy meat, trying to guess what animal it had once been. For almost an hour she'd sat in silence, her voice not asked for over the clatter or the fence of private conversation. She glanced around the table, resisting her instinct to laugh. With his red face and lumpy body, Julian's father looked like a sweet potato.

"So, what do you do?" she ventured, when he paused to belch in the silence.

"Me? I'm a builder," he said. He mimed placing bricks with his fists. "Build-ing hou-ses. You see?"

"Yes. I understand. We have many builders in Hong—" She stopped and checked herself. "Yes. I understand."

"And what about you, then, miss?"

"Right now, I am nanny in Swiss Cottage."

His father chewed with an open mouth. "You must have thought your boat had come in. Finding a nice young man like Julian."

"I did not expect it," she said.

"Isn't that why you came over?"

"No. I come here to work."

He nodded. "Escaping the Commies in China."

Sook-Yin pushed a carrot to the edge of her plate and watched it dissolve. "Actually, my family from Hong Kong."

He gave up on his lump of gristle, excavating its gungy remnant and flicking it onto the table. "Didn't know there was a difference," he said.

Beneath the graying puddle of the tablecloth she felt Julian's foot on her tights. *Let me handle this*, it said. "Dad, Hong Kong has been a British colony for over a hundred years. Remember the Opium Wars?"

"No one likes a smart-ass, Julian." Julian shrank in his seat as his father pointed his knife at Sook-Yin. "So really, we're your masters."

Julian's mother, who'd been eating in silence, rose like someone had poked her with a cattle prod and began to gather their plates. "Pudding, I think," she said.

"WELL, THAT WENT better than expected."

Julian's mood seemed buoyant as they headed back to the station. Sook-Yin walked five paces in front of him, her speed guided more by her simmering rage than the threat of rain above them. When he caught up, she stopped and glared at him. "Why you no tell them about me?"

"What on earth are you talking about?"

"I see your parents' face. They shock when they see I Chinese."

She had felt it all afternoon: their stares at the side of her face or her reflection in their fake crystal glasses like a mirror of their disapproval. The awful way his father had spoken to her. A foreign girlfriend was all very well as long as she returned to her terrible country.

Julian raised his eyebrows. "I *told* you, the pair of them are dinosaurs. They still think they're actually important—that the best thing I can do is be a brickie working all the hours God sends, and for what? To have a lace doily on my table?"

"Being builder is not the problem."

He laughed. "Oh, Sook-Yin, you don't have to forgive him. I know I haven't." He scratched the side of his neck. "When I was young, I used to think I was afraid of him until I understood I was actually ashamed. Ashamed of his ignorance mainly, but also that he should be in charge of me and there was nothing I could do about it. He lived for that power, too. Used to beat me senseless most days. Is it any wonder I wanted to escape?" His face darkened with the memory of it. "If it weren't for my mother, he'd be better off dead."

Sook-Yin flinched at the violence of his words. She'd never been a stranger to ah-Ma's slipper, but it was always in fear more than anger—when she'd put a finger too close to a socket or smashed the last of the eggs by not carrying them carefully enough. Still, it was true that fathers could be different. That ah-Ba had been different. "I understand," she said.

At the evidence of her sympathy he softened. "Yes. I knew you would. We're two halves of the same coin, aren't we? Both trying to improve our lives." He touched her belly through her dress. "But the best thing about being a grown-up is that now we have the power to change things. We don't have to turn into our parents." He reached inside his pocket and held out one of the heart-shaped chocolates from the unopened box she'd bought.

"You stole this from the house?" He'd sullied a gift without permission. Now the gods were sure to punish them, the same way they'd punished Florence.

Julian laughed at her outrage. "Don't worry, I left one for my mother—one each for the two women I love. And I only did it for you. Everything I do is for you," he said. "I want you to remember that."

TWENTY-ONE

Lily

31st Day of Mourning

The hotel lobby was as intimidating as the rest of it. Half conservatory and half museum piece, it had been designed both to see and be seen in, with its baroque chairs and gleaming tables and its panoramic views of the harbor. I paused in its cavernous entrance, cowed by the scale of its molded balustrades and its ceilings gilded with snaking vines, hardly able to follow its confection.

"You must be Lily Miller," a voice said. I turned in the direction of its source and shook the hand it belonged to.

"And you must be Daniel Lee." I lingered over his grasp, allowing me time to look him over: a ripening, boyish handsomeness augmented by a simple suit. Enough money to wear its privilege lightly.

"I'm sorry I couldn't make it to the embassy, but I trust my assistant looked after you?" His voice was as crisp as an autumn apple, accented by a curve of American. Not raised in Hong Kong, then. He gestured to a table by the window. "I took the liberty of ordering us tea."

FOR THE FIRST ten minutes he spoke only of himself. In addition to growing up in the States, I learned that he'd recently turned thirty, an apprentice and now the successor of his father's invest-ment company. "I started as an errand boy," he said. "I must've been twelve at the time and already eager to inherit the business, but my father insisted I serve others as he had. I'd come to his office during my summer vacations and had to remember how each man took his tea: oolong, lapsang, gunpowder, a dash of lemon or honey. Freshly brewed or steeped."

I wondered at the point of this story. Was it intended to put me at ease, to suggest we were equal in some way with my greasy battered sneakers, my T-shirt barely thick enough to conceal a body brought up on corned beef? Whatever it was, it wasn't working and his attention was making me nervous.

It was when he gestured to the teapot that I understood. Rather than assail me with a gesture of chivalry, I had taken his place as the errand boy and was now expected to serve *him*. I sulkily poured out two cups. "I'm sorry for your loss," I said, "and obviously grateful that you bailed me out today, but at the risk of sounding rude per-haps we should talk about the reason I'm here."

"Yes. My father's will."

"But this is what I don't understand. Why leave me and Maya anything?"

At the mention of my sister's name his gaze lingered over my shoulder, as if he expected her to appear at any moment. I almost turned myself, heart thudding.

He eyeballed the slices of lemon, bowing briefly when I picked up the tongs and then placed one in his cup. So much for wearing his privilege lightly. "Honest answer? I have no idea," he said, "al-though I know my father was a great philanthropist and met many people over his lifetime . . ." He pulled a photo out of his jacket. "This was among his effects."

I started when I saw the picture. It was a faded portrait of me and Maya, dressed in Chinese jackets sitting astride the statue of a lion. Judging by our ages, it had been taken when we lived in Hong Kong. The only photo I'd ever seen of us there. I turned it over and read the English inscription. *Mei-Hua and Li-Li Chen*. He shook his head when I handed it back. "Please. You must keep it," he said.

My mouth was suddenly dry. The tea was thin but curiously tarry; disgustingly harsh on the cardamom.

"How do you find the flavor?"

"*Delicious*." I returned the cup to the saucer and tucked the photo into my pocket. "So, are you saying your dad knew our mum?"

His lips narrowed as he topped up our cups. "You look different to how I imagined."

"Oh?"

"Yes." He touched his nose. "More . . . Western."

I gave an obliging smile. "You must be the first person ever to say that."

"Perhaps only someone Chinese can see it."

I knew then what I'd seen in his expression, the reason he'd been watching so attentively. *Fear*. "You wondered if we were related," I said. "That my mother and your father—" I almost laughed. Instead, I let the silence hang over us, a pause that at least for me turned into the murky discomfort of not fully grasping the measure of something. Could a problem as messy as that turn out to be simpler than the truth? "What does your family think? About the connection, I mean? It's hardly a small amount of money."

The angle of his legs grew wider, surer now of the territory. "As I said, my father was a generous man and made several similar bequests. The Chinese take death very seriously."

"It's a very serious matter."

"I meant the importance of discharging one's debts."

The word landed like a stone between us, garnished with the specter of Maya, hands on hips. *What if he was the person who was driving the car?*

"Debts as in money, or something else?"

He shrugged. "Money, quarrels, disputes. If a man argued over land or property, if he spoke in a bad way to someone. Everything must be resolved. That's why we open the will after death. So there can be no shame on the person who wrote it."

What about guilt, I wanted to ask, although I was certainly no stranger to that logic—the need to pour it out in the end without fear of recrimination: the people you slighted, the quarrels, who you loved, who you pretended to love. There was also the chance that he'd meant it metaphorically—the symbolic penance of a spiritual culture.

"All right," I said. "But why insist that I come to Kowloon?"

He turned and peered out the window. The Star Ferry was coming back to the harbor, a froth of white ribbons churning on a gray foam. "My father loved this island," he said. "He had an enduring affection for its identity. Perhaps, in wanting you to come here, he was hoping you'd feel the same. Respect the legacy of your mother."

A dank heat crept into my face. How dare he presume that he knew me? It was the Elise thing all over again: *Swear your allegiance. Prove yourself.* What made it even worse was that I'd signed up for this voluntarily, despite how evident an imposter I was; that beyond the accident of my features, the footprint embedded in the soil of my genes, I had no idea what it meant to be Asian.

"In any case, you're here now," he said, "and that's all my father wanted. We'll need your acceptance notarized and then my assistant will require your bank details." He drained the rest of his tea, noting with a wry smile that mine was unfinished. "Please stay here while we finish the paperwork. The hotel's a great base for Hong Kong and there are some beautiful things to discover."

He stood. I was being dismissed. This was even easier than Nesbit had imagined. Too easy. I put my hand in my pocket and touched the edge of the photograph. "Would you mind if I gave it a few days? This is all quite a lot to take in, and I don't only mean the money."

His jaw ground in little circles. "That is your privilege, Miss Miller, but it would help my family if this was over soon."

"Yes. I'm aware of the mourning period. And I'm really not trying to annoy you, especially given how much you've done for me."

He pressed his shoes together. "There's no annoyance on my part. If anything, I'm surprised. If there's one thing I've learned about the West it's that you prefer not to question your lives."

NOT LONG AFTER he left, one of the white-gloved sailor-hatted bellboys turned up to escort me to my room. And *obviously*, it was in "The Tower." I stood at the unlocked doorway, staring in at the suite of rooms that could have housed the whole of Brixton, or at least drowned it beneath all that marble. I went in and looked around, afraid at first to touch anything: the enormous pieces of furniture, the fireplace with its cleaved surround, the brass telescope *just so* in the window. At least at Chungking Mansions with Good Price and the rest of the woebegones I'd been invisible and sometimes righteous, but now my difference made me jittery. Part of me wished Maya *was* here: beautiful, sophisticated Maya, whose entitlement lay as easy as rain, who would take this all in her stride and speak for us both as she always had. Had anything been assumed by her absence, or was I merely seen as her ambassador—the incumbent of *Sino-British relations*, rather than the bewildered no one that I was?

No such fat goose lies in the road.

Maybe Mumma was right. Who left a million quid to strangers?

I curled up in the smallest of the armchairs and hugged myself. Yes, I wanted the money, but I also wanted to know what such a ridiculous gift came freighted with. I'd spent my whole life looking in from the outside, accepting what I'd been told as fact, and now I wanted the real history behind it. Who had Mumma really been and what was her connection to Hei-Fong Lee?

I pulled my diary out of my bag. The thirty-first day of mourning, meaning I still had time to think about it.

A few days here would be okay. A little memory to entertain

Babs with. I imagined what Dr. Fenton might say: Why are you making it so hard for yourself? After your share of terrible luck, it's only right you should have something good.

Poor old Dr. Fenton. In a way, he might have a point.

Almost as soon as I'd acknowledged this permission, my anxiety gave way to something else—a feeling akin to hysteria. I got up and ran the length of the floor, swan-diving onto the bed amid the silk of blankets and pillows. I turned on the shower in the bathroom and watched the water pollute the taintless glass, ate half a golden peach from the bowl. "Can you see me yet, Maya?" I said out loud. Like a dog leaving its piss on a lamppost.

TWENTY-TWO

Sook-Yin

February 1967

Sook-Yin stood beneath the Shaftesbury Memorial Fountain wait-ing for Peggy to arrive. They'd got a rare day off to go shopping together and Sook-Yin had even learned a new word: *trousseau.*

She looked up at the gilded statue. The first time she had come to Piccadilly she'd stood in wonder for a good forty minutes study-ing its details along with her guidebook. The nuns at her convent school—remarking on the dangers of love—had once shown them a picture of the sculpture in a yellowing newspaper clipping: Eros striking artfully at their hearts, loosening limbs and weakening their minds, and whether through fear of falling under its spell, or simply overwhelmed by the figure's nudity, the girls had succumbed to a fit of mass fainting.

Now, as she gazed at its pitted form and the bird shit gathered in its basin, she scorned her old naivete. The craftiness of the nuns. The figure was not even Eros but his younger brother Anteros—avenger of the unrequited—for whom the power of love's pointed arrow was nothing more than a sad misconception.

She turned her attention to the street as new bodies spilled out from the underground. A woman with Peggy's face, wearing a bright blue houndstooth coat, waved from across the island. It *was* Peggy but what had she done to herself? Her long yellow hair was gone, shorn to within inches of her neck. "I fancied a change," she said when Sook-Yin crossed the road to meet her." I'll show you the picture. You could get it done, too, if you like."

Sook-Yin shook her head. On her, it would look like a punishment.

In truth, her shock was envy. On the cold nights back in the nursing home the two of them would share a bed and sometimes she'd wake in the night and find Peggy's hair across her own shoulders, golden and bright in the moonlight. Imagined it as her own. How different life must be to have the privilege of being accepted with pink hair or green hair or no hair. To know your white skin would do all the talking.

For an hour they trawled Swan and Edgar, marveling at the toasters and pressure cookers and being sprayed by the assistants in Perfumery until, at Peggy's request, Sook-Yin gave in and bought a bottle of Madame Rochas. "Now, lady dresses," she said. "I want to look my best for reception party."

They wandered the rails of the first floor where Peggy selected a handful of possibles—demure shifts in ivory and duck egg, a tailored skirt suit and pale yellow twinset—before they went across to the changing room. Peggy settled herself on a stool. "So, dish the dirt, then," she called. "What's Julian really like? I mean, normally you tell me everything but I know next to nothing about him. Is he thin, is he fat, is he bald? I want to make sure I approve."

Sook-Yin frowned, one foot in and one out of her tights. "Why I need your approval?"

"This *is* the man who's marrying my best mate!"

What did Peggy expect her to say? That she'd been rattled by the visit to his parents; knew that as much as the engagement had saved her, she was making the best of a bad lot, choosing practicalities over emotions? Confiding these thoughts wouldn't change things. It wouldn't make the baby disappear, or her own fears any less urgent. Besides, there was her family to think about, even though history appeared to be repeating itself. She had never dared to ask ah-Ma outright, but judging by the family photos her brother's arrival had been similarly quick. Despite this, there *had* been good years, before her father turned his back on them. With time, and the appropriate mindset, perhaps love could grow after all.

She raised her chin to the mirror. "He look like film star," she said. "He very tall with blue eyes and yellow hair."

"Blimey, and money as well? He sounds too good to be true." Peggy whispered into the curtain: "There must be *one* thing about him you don't like. Is he a rotten kisser or something?"

Sook-Yin grimaced as she pulled at the skirt. The waistband was tighter than she'd expected. "This one no good," she said.

"Give us a look, at least."

"No! I say is not ready." She held the curtain closed, preventing Peggy from seeing the modest bump that made the fabric bunch up like a fist. "I try the blue one instead." The zip snagged as it went past her hips and she cursed in Cantonese.

Peggy gave a nervous laugh. "D'ya need a hand?" she said.

"I fine. Please give me minute." Sook-Yin exchanged the dress for another one but each thing she tried was the same. And why was she so itchy, so exhausted?

She folded herself on the stool as a single tear rolled out of her eye and dissolved amid the swirls of the carpet. Peggy's shoe appeared in the gap. "What's going on?" she said.

"Is too hot to try on dresses. I sorry I taking so long."

"It's not too late, you know."

Sook-Yin looked up between the rake of her fingers. "Not too late for what?"

"If everything's going too fast. I could sneak you away through the window, like that time you sneaked me into the nurse's home. Remember? We could run away and have fun instead."

Sook-Yin closed her eyes, ambushed by a different memory: meeting Hei-Fong amid the orchid trees at Kowloon Botanical Gardens. They should have been at school, but the day was too hot for their restless minds and beneath the shelter of the branches a kinder future beckoned them. Up and up they'd climbed, looking down like gods through the clouds and holding hands as they sang a childhood song:

> *What are you looking for, lonely one?*
> *I'm only looking for a friend.*
> *Let me salute you then and shake your hand*
> *I'll be your good friend till goodbye!*

They had been allies in their rebellion, living on their wits when their brains betrayed them. What was it that ah-Fong had said that day? *Let's run away to the circus. Let's never stop having fun.*

She pulled herself up from the seat. "Why you always try to go back?" she said. "We are not the way we were."

"Listen . . . I only meant—"

"I am happy. Please, stop talking."

Sook-Yin wrenched her clothes on again and then threw back the curtain with a flourish. "I take the black one," she said. She held out a tentlike smock that she'd grabbed when Peggy wasn't looking.

"Oh, God, did I really pick that?"

"Is nice and useful," she answered. "Black never go out of fashion."

"Nor do shrouds," Peggy said. She fingered the fabric, wincing. "Why don't we grab some tea and come back—find something a bit more *Marilyn*?"

Sook-Yin stared at their reflection in the mirror, knowing that the distance between them was bigger than it actually appeared. "But I not Marilyn," she said. "My name is Sook-Yin Chen."

TWENTY-THREE

Lily

―――――――――――――

32nd Day of Mourning

Outside the door of my room an army of vacuum cleaners whirred across carpets, their drone and whine and rumble fused with the crack of clean sheets and the bright clang of cups and spoons, sharp as a hangover.

I explored the suite again. Where else could I press ten buttons for coffee, for a bath at precisely the right temperature, for a choice of film in twenty different languages?

You're not to get distracted.

I pulled out the photo of me and Maya and propped it up on the desk. *Exhibit A.* What had it been doing with Hei-Fong Lee and, more pertinently, why had he kept it?

AFTER ASKING THE woman in reception, I took the bus to the library in Ho Man Tin and asked to search the newspaper archive.

The elderly clerk peered at me over her glasses. "English or Chinese language?"

"English, I'm afraid," I said, thinking of the man that day in the café. "Unless there's someone here who translates?"

The woman picked up the telephone and after a brief conversation with someone, a man emerged from the door behind her. Aside from the flare of a shaving cut he had the stoop and pasty complexion of having spent years on his knees in a basement.

"You ask for newspaper archive?"

I followed him to the back of the building where a large partitioned-off area held an arrangement of microfiche machines. "Which paper you looking for exactly?"

"To be honest, I'm not really sure. I'm doing a project—on Hei-Fong Lee?"

"Banking man?" I nodded. "Most recent will be obituary. *South China Post*, *Hong Kong Economic*. They may have some background history."

He left me and ten minutes later reappeared with a cardboard box before we sat at one of the machines. He took out the first sheet of acetate and held it up to the light. "This is *South China Morning Post*," he said. "English-language newspaper." He focused it under the glass and a perfect miniature of the masthead appeared, and beneath it a full-page article published the day after Mr. Lee's death.

"Wow," I said. "Big story."

I briefly scanned the page but it was nothing more than I'd expected: column inches of guff and bluster about one of the "giants" of investment banking. Only the last paragraph made me pause.

Mr Lee is survived by his mother, Mrs Jin Lee, his wife Mrs Jiao Lee and his son, Mr Daniel Lee (30), who will take over the running of the company.

I wrote the names in my notebook. If Daniel Lee was as in the dark as he claimed, I might need to search farther afield. "Are they all like this?" I said. "All following the official line, I mean?"

"Mr. Lee very popular man. Always give money to charity."

I chewed my lip. Was Mumma a charity? Were we?

Something else occurred to me, then. "How far back do the archives go?"

"Many, many decades."

"Could you search for something else? It's not related or anything. I just promised a friend a favor."

I wrote down the date from Mumma's death certificate and then tore out the page and gave it to him. "The incident happened on this day."

"What am I looking for?" he said.

"A road accident. Here in Kowloon."

"I can check, but it might take time. Exam season here. Very busy. Perhaps you leave telephone number and I call you when is ready?"

I'D PLANNED TO check out Castle Peak Road but had left Mumma's address book at the hotel. I'd just got back to collect it when the telephone rang in my room. "Miss Miller?" the voice inquired. "Mr. Lee is in reception. He wondered if you could join him."

I hung up and stared at the receiver. By falling on Daniel Lee's mercy had I also surrendered all ownership of my own time?

He greeted me down at the front desk, jacketless in shirt and trousers with a faint sheen of sweat on his brow from the emerging heat of the afternoon. "I hope you had a better evening, Miss Miller?"

"Yes, thank you, the room is unbelievable. The view, the bed, the facilities . . ."

Sensing I couldn't go on mining my amazement indefinitely, he pulled at his sleeve. "Yesterday, after we spoke," he said, "I wasn't sure I made myself clear about why my father's wishes are so important. If you've no other plans for today, I hope you'll accompany me somewhere."

Perhaps it was his candor that relieved my irritation, or the fact that without his suit he looked smaller, younger, so I could almost imagine the twelve-year-old boy he'd been with his tray of teacups, eager to please. At the very least I could quiz him further. "Yes," I said. "All right."

A different Daimler idled on the forecourt, an oversized basket of fruit propped up beside the driver. There were apples the size of two fists, dimpled oranges, a torture of lychees, all wrapped in a choke of ribbon like the grand prize in a hospital raffle. Was he intending to convince me with a picnic?

We spent most of the journey in silence, although occasionally he'd puncture the space by pointing out some place or other: the bustling markets or the towering estates that flashed past in a streak of balconies too much like home to interest me.

We were twenty minutes along the expressway when an incongruous maze of trees rose from the concrete in the distance. "What's there?" I asked and turned, pushing my finger against the window. He seemed surprised.

"The remains of the old Walled City. The Chinese built it as a military fort and it remained in their control even when they ceded the rest of Hong Kong. My father grew up not far from there."

"What a beautiful place," I said. His shoulder dismissed my approval. Perhaps I had spoken out of turn, pressed on the wound of colonialism with no respect for his political barometer.

I kept quiet for the rest of the drive, but as we approached the signs for Chuk Yuen, I experienced the strangest feeling. It seemed pretentious to call it déjà vu, but it got stronger as the car pulled over and the driver pulled the basket from the front seat. A name—a collection of words—bubbled up from the back of my brain. It was only once we'd turned the corner and were confronted by the square stone arch that it came to me.

"This is the temple of three religions." Straightaway it sounded right, like a piece finding its home in a puzzle.

"You know of this place?" he said.

I shook my head, half-afraid. Maya had never mentioned it. "I must have seen it in one of the guidebooks."

The temple rose in front of us, the vivid red and gold of its architecture anachronistic against the skyline and at the same time, perfectly in marriage. Suspended in line with its roof, pregnant lanterns swelled the sound of voices: the shouts of vendors selling fortunes from the sidelines, the chants of the faithful and hopeful blending together in apparent contradiction.

"*Wong Tai Sin* means 'Immortal Wong,'" he said, "the divine name of Wong Cho Ping, a Taoist hermit who became a deity. People come here to bring him their troubles and to ask favor for the souls of their ancestors. He's famous for granting wishes."

The smell of incense thickened the atmosphere as we approached the altar square where a patchwork of worshippers had laid out their offerings: cartons of plums and figs, the salty tang of roasted chickens, a whole suckling pig on a stick wet with its glisten of marinade. I'd never been a religious person. I'd been in a church maybe four or five times—baptisms, weddings, christenings, most of them under duress—and saw the scene now from a similar distance, my impulse driven by a touristic curiosity rather than any sense of spiritual longing.

I watched Daniel Lee pray at the shrine, the smoke curling as it carried his voice away. Alongside, men and women shook wooden canisters that vibrated with the sound of rain and cast numbered sticks onto the concrete, looking for answers. "We call this *kau chim*," Daniel whispered. "A form of Buddhist fortune-telling. It means 'what you request you receive.'" He gestured to one of the interpreters. "You don't need to ask in Chinese. Which answer do you wish for?" he said.

I shook my head as pleasantly as I could. "I'm okay. It's not really my thing." Expecting him to show me the same respect, I was shocked by his gnomic smile.

"Is it your mind that is closed, or your heart?" he said.

I KEPT MY distance from him as we walked on, making noises of dispassionate approval at the portrait of Confucius in the Three-

Saint Hall and the model of the Nine-Dragon Wall, privately fuming. Why couldn't I have rational objections that weren't rooted in fear or denial, as if what had stopped me belonging was my own lack of faith or broad-mindedness?

We emerged into the sunlit gardens, blinking like awkward teenagers after a disco and I hurried to the coolness of the stone bridge. He came to rest on the parapet beside me, looking down at the blackness of the lotus pond with its rainbow flashes of koi and terrapins.

"I didn't mean to offend you," he said. "Back there, when I invited you to pray."

"I wasn't quite ready to burst into flames."

He laughed. "But you're not a religious person . . ."

"I don't think you have to be, to experience Hell."

He drew two characters on the stone with his finger. "In our language we call this *diyu*. An earthly prison," he said. "I guess the closest is Dante's underworld—these eternal layers with their own kinds of punishments."

"What sort of punishments?"

"A gossip's tongue pierced forever with burning forks, a greedy man forced to eat iron filings." He shrugged. "The normal kind of stuff."

"Charming."

"It has to be serious to make us come here. By honoring the dead's wishes we are saving their souls. Setting them free to move on to a better world."

It sounded like propaganda to me. Catholic indulgences. "Do you *really* believe that?" I said.

"It has never been a question of belief, so much as conscience and tradition."

"And what about the people who rebel? Do *they* have a place in your Hell?"

He smiled. "The thing that people forget is that rebellion is not individualism. Whatever costume you want to dress it in, it's simply another form of belonging—to help us make sense of the world." He reached down for a stone at his feet and cast it into the pond, watching the ripples spread out on its surface. "Are you a rebellious person, Miss Miller?"

"No. I don't suppose so," I said.

"Yet you went to Chungking Mansions . . ."

"That was ignorance more than anything. I had no idea it would be so dire."

"Maybe we are always drawn to where we think we belong."

"What do you mean by that?"

"Chungking Mansions is a place for the lost," he said. "It's where people go when they want to disappear."

Part Two

MIDDLES

TWENTY-FOUR

Sook-Yin

London, September 1972

Julian's side of the bed was empty. Sook-Yin pressed her hand to his pillow, frowning when she discovered that it was cold again. She had been married for more than five years and for the past month it had been the same.

These morning disappearances seemed to have come out of nowhere, but now as she lay in bed, her mind drifted back to a past conversation. She had been tidying up in the living room while Julian sat at the table trying to "balance" the shop's books. She had never liked the term; the threat of its precariousness. "Any news from your family?" he'd said.

Sook-Yin turned the broom in her hand. "I spoke to my mother last week. She say that everything's fine." It wasn't strictly a lie, although she had no idea what her brother was doing. He hadn't spoken to her since the wedding.

"It's just I've been thinking," he said, "I don't suppose they could send us some money?"

Sook-Yin shook her head. "No. I think is impossible." She squinted over his shoulder. "Problem with book?" she said.

"Not at all, business is booming. In fact, I was planning on expanding our stock. Branching out."

"Why not ask Harvey's advice?"

Julian pushed out his bottom lip. "Ah, yes, your precious Harvey. With his *wonderful* Chinese restaurants. I suppose you wish you'd married him?"

"Why you say such things? Harvey been very good to us. He pay for wedding and everything!"

"And he who pays the piper . . ."

Sook-Yin studied his face, the familiar panic that had never quite left her rising again in her stomach like a bad dumpling. "You sad you marry me, Julian?"

He reached out and squeezed her waist. "Don't be silly! I'm simply being childish and jealous because I want you all to myself." He took her hand in his. "I just want you to be proud of me."

Was it really jealousy for her or something else? The sort of comment that came out automatically as you stood on the fringes of someone else's good fortune, hiding your own inadequacy beneath a thin veneer of distaste. She didn't dare say this out loud, however, too afraid that if she asked the question he might not give her the answer she wanted, which was that everything was going to be fine.

SHE GOT UP and emptied her bladder again. It had become her normal routine now that her second pregnancy was almost at full term. Next door, in the room that resembled a closet, Mei-Hua was already awake and giving orders to her collection of stuffed animals with the ferocity of a Communist general. Sook-Yin stood at the doorway and listened, marveling at the complexity of her sentences, at what a sponge she had turned out to be.

Her daughter had been slow to begin with, her walking months behind others at the clinic and her language even worse. Day after endless day, Mei-Hua would watch and laugh as Sook-Yin desperately mouthed the words at her: *Ma-Ma, Ba-Ba, Po Po.* Julian was unperturbed. "She'll do it when she's ready," he said.

It was around her second birthday when Mei-Hua had wandered into the kitchen on newly steady feet and spoken without pause. "I am hungry. Make me lunch now." Sook-Yin, standing over the sink, had dropped the plate she was holding and called Julian out from the shop. From then on, she'd become his world, Sook-Yin sidelined as they pored over stories of castles and dragons and princes. She knew that she should be pleased, but even so she couldn't help wondering what else her daughter had been hiding.

A LITTLE AFTER ten that morning, Harvey surprised her with a visit to the shop. It was rare to see him these days, now he had a second restaurant to take care of, and she quickly wobbled down from the ladder where she'd been busy refilling the shelves.

"How nice to see you, Gho Gho!"

He gazed in awe at her stomach. "Wah! Have you eaten a dragon?"

She laughed as she cracked her back. "I cannot wait for it to be over."

"It must be a boy to stay for so long." He looked around and caught sight of Mei-Hua, who was pottering alone in the corner, putting cans in her small toy cart. "And how are you doing, Mei-Hua?"

"My name is Maya, you silly!"

Harvey raised his eyebrows. "What is this *Maya*?" he said.

"It's my name, of course! English names for English people. The Queen commands it," she said.

Sook-Yin wiped the sweat from her brow. "The name was Julian's idea. He was afraid she'd get teased when she started school."

"What nonsense!" Harvey said. "Mei-Hua is a beautiful name. It's the name she was born with, after all."

Mei-Hua raised a finger in warning. "No talking Chinese!" she said.

"That one is precocious," Harvey whispered. He glanced at the apartment door. "And where *is* Daddy today?"

"Gone to earn money, of course."

"Oh! Well, that is good news." Harvey pulled Sook-Yin aside. "Business is bad?" he said.

"No, we've been pretty busy."

"Then why are you here on your own?" He tutted at her silence. "Julian always had the damned mind of a butterfly!"

She lowered her head. "But he has been a good worker," she said. "And a good father to Mei-Hua, besides."

Harvey batted the air. "You don't need to defend him, ah-Yin. The debt has been more than paid!"

"What do you mean? Whose debt?"

He bent down and readjusted a can. "How is your mother anyway?"

Sook-Yin stared at the back of his head. Had he not heard her or had he changed the subject? Despite this, his mention of ah-Ma intruded with a different concern. She chewed the end of her ponytail. "Ah-Ma and I have been talking regularly."

Harvey stood and smiled. "But that is good! Since when?"

"Since after Mei-Hua was born. She managed to find a job in a factory and has been sending me money now and then . . . Told me to keep it a secret. To be honest, I feel a bit bad about it."

"Well, your mother is her own woman, I'm sure. I wouldn't worry about telling your brother."

Sook-Yin moved a little closer. She had been wanting to unburden herself, especially after that conversation with Julian, but couldn't think of anyone to confide in. "I wasn't talking about ah-Chor," she said. "I've been keeping it secret from my husband."

If he was surprised, he kept it hidden. "That is nobody's business," he said. "Besides, you could do worse than to have a few savings. Why not use it to take a trip home? Let your mother see her grandchild at least?"

Sook-Yin rubbed her stomach. "I can't go anywhere like this. And there's always so much to do here."

Harvey sighed. "Don't be afraid of moving slowly, ah-Yin. Be afraid of standing still."

THE MORNING PASSED in an increasing blur of customers. Sook-Yin hadn't lied about that, for in spite of her initial worries the shop had been a surprising success. Nor had she lied about Julian's investment in it. Its condition had been worse than they'd imagined—the cellar held hostage by damp rot, woodworm in all the fixtures—but neither had been afraid of the work. In fact, she thought of those weeks with fondness, the camaraderie that had grown between them; the way she would be painting or cleaning a wall and Julian would come up behind her and caress her growing bump, whisper encouragement. *Things are going to be wonderful.*

And for the most part she admitted they had been, for Julian's optimism had been infectious. Something else that had surprised her too was how suited she was to this type of work. The advancement of the shop was her accomplishment. Like ah-Ma selling matches with her eggs, Sook-Yin had learned to anticipate wants and encouraged Julian to buy accordingly. It was her idea to sell sweets with tobacco, to put canned peaches alongside the dried custard, for if there was one thing the years had taught her it was that a person's bad habits seldom traveled alone.

It was their like-mindedness in the face of opposition that had made her agree to a second child as proof of their commitment to each other. As far as testaments went, and in the absence of comparable experience, it was the closest she imagined to love.

SHE WAS DEEPLY lost in this reverie when the bell above the door shook violently and three men sauntered into the shop. Sook-Yin was sure she didn't recognize them. She would have remembered their shaved heads and tight boots. The skull tattoos on their forearms. Her fingers worried the knot in her apron string. "Let me know if I can help," she called.

The men ignored her at first before the tallest one came up to the counter. "Where's *Mr.* Miller today?"

"Why? You have business with him?"

"Maybe."

Her heart skipped at the edge in his tone but she folded her arms against herself, widened her stance. "Then I am his wife. You can talk to me." Her gaze wavered as she sought out Mei-Hua, who had stopped playing to stare at the men, and she spoke to her in a sharp voice. "Maya! Go up to your room."

"Why?"

"Because I say so, okay?"

Mei-Hua took her time, puffing out her cheeks in mock outrage before she slipped through the door behind the counter. Only when it shut behind her was Sook-Yin able to breathe again.

She turned once more to the men. Without her notice, the three had separated and begun opening boxes of crackers and biscuits and the glass bottles of Tizer and R-Whites, shaking them up and opening them so they exploded in a fountain of pink foam. Sook-Yin pressed her hands to her stomach, her fear and rage colliding in a confusing storm of paralysis. Only the shake of her right leg betrayed her. "What this about, please?" she said at last.

The tallest man helped himself to a chocolate bar, unwrapping and biting into it before throwing what remained on the floor. Sook-Yin glanced out the window. Where were the other customers? Wouldn't anyone come in from the street? She considered screaming, making a run at them, but it would be impossible to tackle them all.

She walked around to the front of the counter so they could see the swell of her belly and was relieved when the smallest man spoke. *Leave it. Leave it. Enough now.*

The tall one leered into her face. "White blokes don't suit yeller," he said. He held her gaze, his breath metallic and hot on her cheek before he nodded to the others. One by one they left, slamming the door so hard the glass rattled within its frame.

Sook-Yin waited till they'd crossed the street and then ran over and locked the shop door and turned the sign to "Closed." Mei-Hua, hiding at the entrance to the apartment, peeped out and surveyed the devastation. "Who were they, Mumma?" she said. "Why have they made such a mess?"

"Nobody. Nothing. Don't worry." Sook-Yin reached over and pulled her close. Her own body was damp and empty, like a slaughtered animal drained of its blood. "They make mistake," she said. "Silly men just make mistake."

FOR TWO HOURS she paced the carpet of the living room until her shoes left tracks in its cheap pile, pale and flattened as her mood, but Julian didn't return. She ran a bath and made dinner for Maya, pushing the cooling shapes around her own plate until they congealed in a ball of dark wax. What if the men had found him? How would anyone know how to contact her?

As the evening continued, however, her worry turned into anger. How could Julian treat her this way? She took his shirts and threw them on the floor, imagining his body inside them as she stamped on them over and over. But when nine and then ten o'clock passed, her fear returned and she gathered them up again, pressing their folds to her cheek. *I'm sorry, I love you, I'm sorry.*

It was after midnight when he finally returned, his voice questioning the chain at the apartment door. She found him leaning on the wall of the stairwell, brandishing a bunch of flowers. "For you, my lovely wife."

Sook-Yin's eyes traveled over his face. No cuts, no bruises, no nothing. "Where have you been to?" she said. She recoiled at the fumes on his breath. "You spend all day in pub?"

"No!"

"Now I know is lie!" She beat his chest with her fists. "I wake up this morning you gone! Every morning you gone! You never tell me why."

"What's got into you?" he said. "And why was the door locked?"

She sank into one of the armchairs. "Because bad men come into shop today."

"What men?" Julian put the flowers on the table and then knelt on the carpet beside her. "Calm down and tell me properly. Are you and the baby all right? Did they do anything to Maya?"

"I send Maya to flat straightaway." Her nostrils flared. "Three big men. All together. They say they looking for you. What is it about now, Julian?"

He rubbed his temple. "I don't have the foggiest idea. They were probably pulling a prank."

"What is prank?"

"A joke."

"They not seem like they were joking."

"You've had a fright, that's all. If they come back, I'll handle it."

Sook-Yin shook her head. "But how will I know you be here? You never tell me where you going."

He cupped her chin. "From now on I'm staying put," he said. "And I couldn't tell you at first because I wanted it to be a surprise."

She turned her head away. "Maybe I have surprise. Maybe you come back and I dead! I be work work working all day."

"Well, I be work work working too." He pressed his forehead against hers. "Are you still my girl, Mrs. Miller? Only, I thought you might like this . . ." He produced a wad of money from his jacket. More than she'd seen in her life.

"Where you get this?" she said.

"An old business friend of mine. He's been giving me tips for investments and today I cashed them in. Aren't you a bit happy?" he said.

Sook-Yin brewed in silence, not quite ready to forgive him. Who did investments at six in the morning? She tried to ignore the image of Florence hunched over the mahjong tables, which had crept into her mind unbidden. Surely Julian wouldn't be that desperate. Hadn't he told her that business was booming? She sighed. Julian, Mei-Hua and the baby—they were all she had in this new world and she couldn't afford to lose any of them. "Come to bed, then," she said.

SHE COULDN'T SETTLE that night. Each time she arrived at the edge of sleep the three men would appear in front of her like they'd been lying in wait behind her eyelids. She got up and checked the locks on the door and then went to make tea in the kitchen.

She was fetching the milk from the fridge when she heard the shatter of glass in the shop below. She stood there, listening in the darkness, and then ran back and shook Julian awake. "I smelling smoke!" she said.

Julian sat up at once. "Put Maya in something warm and take her straight down to the basement. Don't open the door to the shop."

"What about you?"

"I need to gather our things. Our passports, photos . . . the money." He lifted her hand from his arm. "I need to, Sook-Yin," he said. "Go on, I'll be all right."

Sook-Yin wrested Mei-Hua from her bed and bundled her into a coat. She was still too asleep to walk quickly and Sook-Yin was forced to carry her, stumbling under her weight down the two flights of steps to the basement.

The back door was stiff from disuse and it took all her strength to pull at it before it came open with a shudder of wind. Mei-Hua, shocked awake by the cold, rubbed at her eyes. "What's happening, Mumma?" she said.

"There is fire. We need to leave."

BY THE TIME they were safe on the street, the front of the shop was already an inferno. Mrs. Deep, who ran the laundry opposite, came out covering her ears with a blanket as the fire engines screamed like a banshee. From as far as half a mile away, house lights popped on in their clusters as other neighbors got up to investigate. They came out in their dressing gowns and nightshirts, the radiant heat of the flames inviting and then repelling them like magnets against the violence of the smoke-streaked sky. A murmur became a wave as it quickly passed among the waiting faces. *Where is Julian? What is he doing?*

Minutes seemed to take hours to pass before at last he staggered out through the back door coughing and rinsed with sweat, clutching a small brown suitcase. His eyes streamed as they searched for his family. "Is everyone all right? Sook-Yin?"

Finally relieved of her fear for his safety, Sook-Yin merely nodded as she gazed sightlessly at the caved-in shop window; her mind fused as one with the scene. The charred bodies of cans were *her* body, the toxic stench of metal her own breath, for wasn't part of herself in this place? Her hopes, her dreams, her invention?

"Your wife is in shock, Mr. Miller." Mrs. Deep put her arm around Sook-Yin and then took her blanket and wrapped it around her. "Let me take your family to our house."

The three of them were walking away when Sook-Yin stopped and doubled over. *Not now. Not now. Not now.* She crouched down as another wave hit her, liquid pouring onto the pavement as sharp and forceful as a monsoon, and looked at Julian with helpless eyes. "The baby is coming," she said.

TWENTY-FIVE

Lily

33rd Day of Mourning

Dad liked to tell me I was born in a fire. He said it was the reason for my passion and sensitivity and once I was older why life disappointed me. Yet with each day that passed in Kowloon I got the sense he'd been wrong about one of them. I wasn't disappointed, I'd simply been missing out.

ARMED WITH THE things from Mumma's suitcase, I took the MTR to Cheung Sha Wan. I knew that it was a long shot, but if I was able to find my grandmother it would be the first step in reconnecting with my family. Maybe she could even tell me about the Lees.

The apartment building was in a down-at-heel street about ten minutes' walk from the station. I was amazed at how easily I found it; the familiarity of its cream plaster walls and its peeling concrete balconies, the colored shops around the marketplace. And everywhere the smell I remembered—from the gutters and kitchens and rooftops, heady and cloying in the sunshine: sour fruit and the dankness of raw meat. *See,* I wanted to say to Maya, *I wasn't imagining things. I know more than you ever gave me credit for.*

There was a narrow counter in the lobby of the building, half-covered by a sliding window. Beyond it I could hear a TV; the same cheerful, catchy refrains for mosquito cream and Vitasoy milk that I'd watched on repeat at the hotel; the words for "hurry" and "tasty" that I'd managed to teach myself. I pressed the bell on the ledge and a woman appeared from the inner door, a halo of white roots in her black hair.

"Castle Peak Road is here?" I drew the number in the air with my finger. "I'm looking for flat number ten. Grandmother," I told her. "*My grandmother.*"

"No understand," the woman said.

I wasn't surprised. With my gurning expressions and Western accent, I sounded like a reject from a seventies sitcom. I took out Mumma's address book and showed her the entry on the front page: *Wing-Chan Chen. Flat 10.*

The woman raised her hand to her mouth and then retreated at speed to her apartment. I was on the verge of ringing the bell again when the latch on the inner door opened and a younger woman looked out. "You are looking for Chen Wing-Chan?"

"Yes."

"You had better come in," she said.

She invited me to take a seat in the cluttered but homely living room. I stepped over ornaments of Buddha and plants big enough for a Kew Gardens hothouse before mooring myself on a wicker chair. The older woman sat opposite on a sofa, its fabric bleached into perfect rectangles from the shape of the windows in the sun, and regarded me with a wary curiosity.

"I'm afraid Mrs. Tam's English is poor." The younger woman gestured to her older companion as she poured tea in the adjoining kitchen. "We don't get travelers often."

"Do you live in the building, too?"

"Hah. At number sixteen." She brought a tray to the table and then reached over and switched off the TV. It set off a chain reaction in Mrs. Tam, who immediately came to life, tripping over her words in her eagerness. The young woman listened and translated. "Mrs. Tam's mother was good friends with Wing-Chan, all the time she live here."

"But now my grandmother's moved away?"

The young woman bent her head. "I am so sorry," she said. "She pass away six months ago, not long after Mrs. Tam's mother. Wing-Chan had bad stroke at end."

I sank into the back of my seat. First Mumma, then Dad, now our grandmother. Our family's proclivity for bad endings was something else. An unwanted image came to me: Maya sitting with Dad in our Brixton house, watching him wither away from his cancer like a faulty string of Christmas lights—on and then off and then on again. Like the attention I wasn't well enough to give him. "Was anyone with her. At the end?"

She nodded. "Wing-Chan has older son. A professor at Hong Kong University. He sold the apartment a month ago." Mrs. Tam interjected again. "Please forgive," the young woman said, "but she asking if you really granddaughter? She say this son does not have any children."

Realizing the misunderstanding, I took out Mumma's passport and ID card. Mrs. Tam held them up to the window, her eyes rounding before she spoke in hurried tones.

"She say you are daughter of Chen Sook-Yin? The Chen Sook-Yin who died?"

"Yes! We were living in the flat when it happened. Maybe Mrs. Tam remembers me—or my older sister, Mei-Hua?"

The two women consulted each other. "Mrs. Tam was not living here then but perhaps *you* remember her mother? Her name was Mrs. Chee?" She showed me a photo from the shrine above the console, its frame scarred by the stains of spent incense. I ran the woman's face through my mind, trying to catch the loop of its dropped stitch, but I couldn't be sure.

"I *was* very young at the time." I pressed my hands to my lap. "I hate to ask," I said, "but I don't suppose you have an address for my uncle? It's very important I get in touch with him."

Mrs. Tam handed back Mumma's things and instructed the young woman to write on a notepad. "Your uncle's name is Chen Chor-Kit. He lives in Wan Chai district, over on Hong Kong Island. When he sell your grandmother's apartment he give Mrs. Tam his address in case of important letters." She tore out the page and gave it to me.

"Thank you. I can't tell you how helpful you've been."

As I stood, Mrs. Tam spoke again and the young woman nodded and went out to the office. She returned a few moments later and held out a cardboard box "This is for you," she said.

"No, I couldn't . . . really. You've done so much already."

She smiled. "This is not gift. When your uncle sell the apartment he ask Mrs. Tam to clean for new occupant. People always leaving little traces but he never come back to collect them, so now we give them to you."

IN THE TAXI back to the hotel I tried to resist the invisible tide of foolish weeping and magical thinking. I was a detached and rational person; knew that my timing in receiving the box had been nothing more than coincidence, and that my excitement about what it contained hung only on the memory of me and Maya returning from school that day to find that Dad had gutted the Brixton house. Everything that Mumma had collected—the effort she'd made for our heritage to be visible—had vanished in a matter of hours. "We've been burgled," I'd said to Maya stupidly, conjuring a market for cheap plaster foo dogs and polyester tasseled lanterns rather than the TV and stereo, which lay untouched. "Mumma's gone, Mumma's gone, Mumma's gone."

They're just things, Maya said on repeat all the weeks I refused to be comforted. *Dad just found it too hard to look at them.* I tried to have that maturity, to see it from their point of view, but I could only focus on the things we had lost. I still did.

There was more than one way to rob a person.

I WAITED TILL I was back in my room before I opened it, sitting on the bed. The box had the same smell as Mumma's suitcase: of age and neglect and dust and someone else's memories. On top was another silk pincushion, identical to the one at Maya's house except the red pumpkin was worn and dusty, its surface pockmarked where once there'd been needles. Beneath this were two small photographs. The first was a picture of Mumma, her face cast in afternoon shadow from the wide brim of her floppy straw hat. *Lychee Garden*, the sign read above her. She must have been close to my age and I saw the resemblance in our features—the genetics in the bow of her lip, the quirkiness in the tilt of her eyebrow; understood why, when I was a teenager, my father would startle when I caught him unawares, his mouth opening and closing in silence.

The second photo was more of an anomaly. It was a studio portrait of Marilyn Monroe, the edges curled and yellowed with age.

"To Sook-Yin, with love from Peggy. London, August 10, '66."

Peggy, Peggy, Peggy . . . I tried to put a face to the name but came up blank. It seemed a strange thing for Mumma to have kept, although maybe I was overthinking things. Perhaps her reasons were as simple as mine had been with all those pictures that had graced my own walls in the days before I knew any better; before I realized all the things I couldn't be.

The next thing I pulled from the box was a piece of paper so thin I assumed it was tissue at first. I smoothed it out and held it up to the light. It looked like an invoice of some sort, the Chinese handwriting faded by time and marked by a dull copper stain. Halfway down, there was an amount in figures: 10,000 Hong Kong dollars. If the receipt was as old as it looked, ten thousand would have been a small fortune. I couldn't imagine what it might have bought.

I tipped out the other random objects—a hair clip, an ebony chop-stick, a folded box of matches from a place called the Lucky Seven Club, their tips worn and smooth from the damp where they must have fallen and been forgotten. To other people these things would be junk but to me they were as precious as a diary or bones thrown up by the earth. *We were here*, they said, *someone once had a use for us*, and I silently thanked Mrs. Tam for understanding.

I laid everything out on the desk alongside the picture of me and Maya and was just about to throw out the box when I caught sight of something else—a sealed envelope trapped in its base. I pulled it out and studied it: *To Mr. Julian Miller*, postmarked April '78. Five months after Mumma had died. Baffled, I turned it over and saw a message in dad's handwriting.

UNKNOWN. RETURN TO SENDER.

It didn't make any sense. The address was our Brixton address. I tore the perforations and opened it.

Dear Julian,

This is fifth letter I write you, but all of them been return. I try to explain you many time but still I get no answer and now my heart is very broken. One thing is lose my daughter. Second thing is lose my grandchildren. Please! Send letter with picture, so I see Mei-Hua and Li-Li again. With best wishes from Chen Wing Chan.

I read it over and over again, my fist bunching against the sheets. One letter might have been lost, but five? It was impossible. Dad had returned them to Hong Kong deliberately.

All these years, and not even a letter!

How can you be so sure?

Because Dad told me they didn't.

So Maya had believed it too, as much a victim to his narrative as I had been. What the fuck had he been thinking?

Calm down, I told myself. This wasn't the Dad I knew. His grief about Mum had been palpable, had lived in the walls and floors, been part of the air. The sort of mourning that could only be dealt with by erasing all memories of a person. That *had* to be the reason he'd returned them. Or maybe he'd seen them sending us home as a deliberate act of hostility and had shut them out as a punishment. Cutting his nose off to spite our faces.

For the first time since arriving in Hong Kong, I felt a real urge to call Maya, desperate for her to make sense of it, but resisted. I didn't yet have the guts to tell her I was here and I still couldn't explain the inheritance.

But at least now there was someone who could.

TWENTY-SIX

Sook-Yin

September 1972

H er second daughter took nine hours to be born that night, but as Sook-Yin lay in the freezing hospital any comfort from the ease of the birth was overshadowed by the horror of its circumstance. Everything they had worked for was gone.

She wrinkled her nose at the glass of stout that lay untouched on the table beside her. She remembered the same from Maya's birth— its bitterness that she'd drunk with vigor—but she had no appetite for its rank, stale odor now.

Harvey arrived at the first stroke of visiting. He leaned over the tank by the bed and peered at the sleeping girl with her wrinkled jaundiced face and her fists held tight to her cheeks. "Beautiful baby," he said. "And see how quiet she is! She must have the heart of a tiger."

Mrs. Deep, on Sook-Yin's instruction, had called Harvey when she'd gone into labor. She had told him about the fire, too, but Sook-Yin knew he wouldn't mention it, unwilling to jinx his blessing with unnecessary talk of tragedy. Instead, he showed her the things he'd brought: the woven swaddling cloth and the pieces of chicken and rice, traditional offerings on the birth of a baby, so they would never feel cold or hungry.

"Now something for ah-Ma," Harvey said. He pulled out a cardboard box and showed her the four plump buns, their golden crusts almost wet in the pale light. "Red bean paste. Your favorite."

Sook-Yin took one and bit into its center, and the smell, so redolent of her childhood, forced hot tears to her eyes. All at once, the sound of crying babies and the nightmare of the shop disappeared, replaced by the refuge of home.

Roused from her sleep by the smell, the baby's eyes popped open—*ping ping*—like two blackcurrants. "Eat, eat," Harvey said to Sook-Yin. "I will take your daughter for a minute."

He lifted the baby from the tray, her mouth pulled into the shape of an O by the sudden motion of flying. Harvey beamed. "She will not ask for anything, this one. Mei-Hua will take advantage if you let her. A strong name will see her right." He drew with his finger on the bedsheet. "One *Li* for beautiful," he said, "and one for reason and logic. See how it rises, like music! *Li-Li.*"

"Gho Gho, that is perfect," she said.

He inhaled the scent of the baby's head, which Sook-Yin already knew had the sharp, sweet bite of coriander, her hair as black as Maya's was golden. "Who else will visit today? Have you heard from Peggy lately?"

Sook-Yin shook her head. Their friendship had declined since the day of their shopping trip. For a time, they'd stayed in touch—a bunch of flowers when Maya was born, a card for her first birthday and Christmas—but over time the gaps had got longer, and now it was a year since they'd spoken to one another.

Harvey pulled a face at the ward. "It's so barbaric in here. Back home, you would sleep for a month and virgins would wash your body and clean up your daughter's do-do." He waved at the glass on the table. "They would feed you proper medicine, too. Not this thing that stinks like an ashtray."

Sook-Yin laughed, for she hated being here, too. "I will leave soon enough," she said before she remembered what she had to return to and her smile dissolved like sugar. Harvey cracked his knuckles.

"We will cross that black water when we come to it."

IT WAS NEARING the end of visiting hours and she was drifting through a restive sleep when Julian appeared beside her. Sook-Yin glanced at the still-swinging door. "Where is Maya?" she said.

"I left her at home with my mother." He mistook her frown of disappointment for anger. "She is tired, Sook-Yin," he snapped. "All of us are tired and busy."

She pinched the sheet between her fingers. Perhaps he would have liked her to get out of bed and sweep the ward to be useful. "Any news from police?" she said instead.

"They're still trying to find out what happened."

She leaned back and closed her eyes. "The shop will take so long to fix up again."

"Actually, Sook-Yin, I've been thinking. Maybe we should make a fresh start. Move out of the area altogether."

She opened her eyes and sat up. "You don't believe that business is good? Together we make it better."

Julian pinched the bridge of his nose. "Look, I was trying not to worry you but the police believe it was a racialist attack."

Sook-Yin's mouth fell open. "What you mean, racialist attack? We been there five years already! Mrs. Deep runs laundry on street and never experience such problem."

"It's different, though, isn't it?" he said. "She married someone of her own kind."

White blokes don't suit yeller.

Yellow. How had she not guessed?

"Don't worry, we'll show them what's what. The best revenge is success and we'll be better off somewhere else."

Sook-Yin turned away. "You mean somewhere to hide someone like me?"

He reached for her leg beneath the blanket. "Now, don't get all maudlin about it. We have Maya to consider, after all."

"Because she pass for 'your kind'?"

Julian had taken pride in his role as her savior; paraded Sook-Yin like a shield of moral virtue among the immigrant faces of Islington, but the moment that trouble came calling, it seemed his instinct was only to retreat.

He rubbed the back of his collar. "You can't begrudge her for wanting to fit in. I want Utopia as much as the next man, but if it's the only way that she'll have opportunities..."

Sook-Yin gazed down at her baby with her almond eyes and snub nose and black hair. "And what about this daughter?" she said.

TWENTY-SEVEN

Lily

━━━━━━━━━━━━━━━
━━━━━━━━━━━━━━━

34th Day of Mourning

I took the ferry across to the island and then followed my map to Wan Chai. Unlike the openness of Castle Peak Road there was a nervous security about my uncle's apartment block, cameras trained on its modern façade and a yellow guard box overlooking the car park. What would I say if somebody questioned me?

I'd been there about ten minutes when a little Datsun pulled into a parking space and a woman in overalls got out, carrying a bucket of cleaning supplies. I followed her up to the entrance, where she swiped the door with a key card and then held it open for me. "Ngoy, sin," *thank you*, I said.

I lingered in the pristine lobby. Two large elevators took up most of one wall, while on the other was a bank of mailboxes—one assigned to each apartment. I waited for the woman to disappear and then followed the rows of numbers until I found my uncle's. My stomach churned. Perhaps it would be more sensible to give him some notice.

I took out my notepad and pen. Dear Uncle Chor, I wrote. I'm sorry to trouble you like this . . .

Too apologetic. Maya would never have shown such attrition.

I was beginning the letter again when one of the elevator doors opened and a young girl glided out on roller skates. I supposed she was about thirteen, dressed in a demure little pinafore, her hair pushed back with a Hello Kitty headband. She took a ring of small keys from her pocket, each of them topped by a colored fob, and began emptying some of the boxes. When she got to Uncle Chor's, I stood. "Is that the mail for Chen Chor-Kit?" I said.

She spun around and stared at me. "Why? What is it to you?" Her accented English was immaculate.

"My name is Lily Miller. I'm sort of a friend of the family."

"Why didn't you ring the bell?"

I scratched my head. "I suppose I wanted to surprise him. Do you know if he's home today?"

She examined me between chews of her bubble gum. Smiled. "Follow me," she said.

We rode the elevator to the fourteenth floor and she skated ahead to a door that lay ajar at the end of the corridor. "Suk-Suk!" she called out at the entrance and then looked back and beckoned to me. "Well, come if you're coming," she said.

UNCLE CHOR MUST have been pushing sixty, his hair brindled with gray amid the black although his body was corded and muscular. I scavenged my memory for a hint of his face or a passing resemblance to Mumma. Saw nothing.

He listened while I spoke in the kitchen. I revealed only the basics at first: that Dad had died and I'd come to Kowloon to satisfy my curiosity about our cultural heritage. "I visited the flat on Castle Peak Road," I said.

His body half-turned in surprise. "That apartment was sold a month ago."

"Yes, Mrs. Tam told me. I'm sorry."

"So, you speak Cantonese these days?"

"There was a lady there who translated."

He nodded in that particular way that showed this was only what he'd expected. "You have certainly been busy, Miss Miller."

"Well, I have a lot to catch up on." I gestured to the door. "The young girl, is she a relation?" I already knew that he was childless but I was interested in what he would say, especially as the conversation was proving awkward.

"Feng Mian is my goddaughter," he said. "Her family moved back to Beijing but have allowed her to finish her education here."

"Any idea what she wants to do, yet?"

"She has mentioned an interest in law."

"Oh. Like Maya," I said, and then with only the slightest guile, "she did her degree at Oxford."

He raised an eyebrow, as though the puzzlement of this was large but not altogether unpleasant to him. "Very impressive."

"I did music. At Cambridge."

He paused to take this in. "I presume your sister is a good success?"

I laughed at the obviousness of it. Even here, dear Maya bested me. "Oh, yes. And filthy rich." He allowed himself a smile, and, emboldened by the advantage, I pushed. "Uncle, there *is* another reason I'm here. Are you familiar with the name Hei-Fong Lee?"

"The financier?" he said.

"Yes. I wondered if he had any connection with our family. Specifically Mum, I mean?"

"I think that is very unlikely. Even with my charitable connections, I've never met the man myself." He placed his palms on the counter. "Forgive me for being blunt, but my sister has been dead for two decades. What exactly is this about?"

I paused. "Okay, this is going to sound weird, but Mr. Lee named me and Maya in his will. He left us quite a fortune." I saw his shock behind a tight smile.

"Congratulations," he said.

"Yes, but this gift—it's a total mystery, and seeing as you're part of the family I hoped you'd know why he'd done it."

He shrugged his shoulders in surrender. "I'm sorry, I wish I could help you but I really have no idea."

"Okay. I see. That's a shame." I took out the phone that Daniel Lee had given me and wrote its number on the hotel notepad, along with the number of my room. "I'm here, if you do think of anything."

He glanced at the crest on the sheet. "Congratulations," he said again. He busied himself at the sink, staving off any further conversation. Not the best time to ask about the letters, then.

I braved a step toward him. "Uncle, I know my coming here must be a shock to you, but I really *would* like to stay in touch. It would seem a shame if we didn't after all these years. I bet you've got some wonderful stories about Mum."

He washed and dried his hands with even, careful movements. "It's true you have surprised me, Miss Miller. Perhaps I could think about it."

"Yes . . . Please do," I said.

There was nothing else I *could* say. I left him standing in the kitchen, pausing in the hallway to catch my breath. It was only when I turned at the front door that I noticed the young girl from the elevator, peering at me from around the corner.

TWENTY-EIGHT

Sook-Yin

October 1972

Four weeks after the fire at the shop, they were still living with Julian's parents. At first, Harvey had invited them to stay at Swiss Cottage but Julian had resisted the idea. He claimed that Maya disliked the food there, while Rose and Michael were now at an age where they'd grown precious about their belongings and had no desire to have a baby on the scene. There seemed no evidence for either of these things but, already exhausted by the demands of a newborn, Sook-Yin eventually capitulated.

The situation had made her ill. His parents' house was fit to bursting and her belly grew soft and flabby from their nightly diet of meat and potatoes. She'd been more than happy to cook for them but they had no appetite for her moo shu pork or her sweet and spicy sauces. "Bloody nightmare," his father said. "I'll be living on the bog for a week."

And then there came another blow. Julian had failed to get insurance for the shop—a misunderstanding in the terms of the lease, he said—meaning they would not be reimbursed for their losses. On the surface, Sook-Yin remained stoic but in private she pulled at her hair, cursed his carelessness and her own stupidity. If only she'd insisted on looking at the books they might have avoided the situation.

"It's not your fault," Harvey told her when she phoned and re-layed the news to him.

"But I should have looked over the documents myself."

"With your education?" he said.

Sook-Yin pressed her nails into the edge of the table. The knowl-edge that Harvey meant well, the soft way he always spoke to her, demoted her guilt to a level of shame far worse than when she spoke to her brother.

"I suppose he wants me to bail him out?"

She was pricked by the sharpness of the question. Julian was a dreamer but he wasn't a bad man, and his constancy should be ac-knowledged. Harvey's words had crossed a boundary. The sting of her husband's foolishness, her despair at the thinness of their fate, was hers alone to indulge in. "Not at all," she said. "Between us we have plenty of savings. I only called to tell you that we're making a new start."

Harvey didn't answer at first and she was glad in that moment to have silenced him. "I see," he said eventually. "Well, I hope it's not too soon. I was going to ask you a favor." She waited. "Florence plans to visit her mother but she gets so nervous whenever she flies and I would prefer it if she had some company. I would pay for all your tickets. Take the girls and have a holiday at the same time."

Sook-Yin felt the advantage swing away from her grasp. Given all the kindnesses Harvey had shown them, she couldn't in all con-science disappoint him. At the same time, the offer perplexed her. Florence had gone home three times already and had never needed a chaperone, so what was different now? "I don't know, Gho Gho," she said. "The children are so young to be flying."

"But your mother would be delighted to see them. You haven't been home since you left."

"Perhaps I can think about it."

He let the silence linger. "We are also making a new start," he said. "Planning on moving abroad."

"You are leaving London?" The floor shifted beneath Sook-Yin's feet, her anger forgotten. Harvey had been more of a brother than ah-Chor: had clothed and fed and nurtured her, shown her there was a meaning to family beyond blood. She would rather he berate her a thousand times than hear him say those words.

"I have the chance to work in Australia. I have already sold the businesses."

He must have known for months that they were leaving. "What about Florence and the children?"

"I'm sure the children will get used to it. And Florence will go where she's told."

Her breath snagged on Harvey's tone. Was this the result of Florence's gambling? How bad must things have got to move all the way to Australia? Bad enough to sell the businesses? "Will this really make you happy?" she said.

"To be happy is to learn from our mistakes." The pause hung heavy between them. "Are you still saving the money from your mother?"

"A little, when I can. Now and then." Why was he asking her that? She regretted telling him about Julian's investments—the one risk he might have taken. It wasn't fair to compare him with Florence, and besides, that was all in the past.

"Even a little is good," he said. "Who's to say when you might break a beggar's bowl?" His attempt to sound lighter failed. "So you'll let me pay for your trip home?"

"You make it sound like the last time I'll see you."

"Don't be silly. We'll keep in touch."

It was Peggy all over again. Hei-Fong. A letter here, a postcard there. The years stretching out between them.

Even so, her longing fought against Harvey's duplicity. What else had she dreamed of these past years but seeing her mother again? And how else would she justify the cost of it? "Thank you, Gho Gho," she said. "I will talk to Julian about it."

She hung up before she could cry, wondering if, despite her bravado and the chaos through the living room walls, he had sensed her hurt through the telephone.

TWENTY-NINE

Lily

―――――――
―――――――

34th Day of Mourning

I'd have to handle things better with Uncle Chor. Though I'd drawn a blank about Hei-Fong Lee with him, there was still lots he could tell me about Mumma. Eventually, he might even accept me. I imagined us going for dinner in Cheung Sha Wan, him showing me the places from their childhood. *These are the streets where we played; here's where we once went to school; these are the dreams we imagined.* Right now, though, it was all a bit raw—me opening the tomb of the past and raising the ghosts of what he thought he'd forgotten. To be honest, I knew where he was coming from.

I WAS HEADING out for lunch when the phone rang. "Miss Miller, it's reception," the woman said. "I have an outside call to put through to you."

She would have said if it was Daniel Lee, and aside from the rest of his family no one knew I was here except Uncle Chor. Perhaps he'd had time to process my visit and wanted a connection after all. The receiver clicked and burred in my ear.

"Is that Lily Miller?" a voice said. It was female—high and unfamiliar.

"Uh-huh. Who's this?" I said.

"It's Feng Mian calling, remember? From this morning at your uncle's house."

"Oh. Is everything okay?" I worried that I'd given him a heart attack.

"Yes, he's quite all right, but I couldn't help hearing your conversation." She paused. "Would you like me to tell you something?"

I gave a nervous laugh. "Tell me what?"

"It's difficult for me to talk now. Can you get to Causeway Bay?"

"What?"

"Exit C on the MTR. Chor-Kit is playing tennis this afternoon but it would be safer not to meet at the apartment." At my hesitation, her tone grew urgent. "Do you want my help or not?"

"Sure," I said. "All right." In the background, Uncle Chor called her name and she lowered her voice.

"I have to go," she said. "See you at half past three."

I was about to say goodbye when I heard the dial tone and realized she'd hung up.

I LEFT AND traveled to Central before changing onto the Island Line. I arrived early at Causeway Bay and made my way to Exit C, where Feng Mian had instructed me to meet her.

The walkways and stairwells were rammed; conveyor belts of ants in tailored suits squeezed tighter every three minutes as a new train disgorged its passengers with the astringent stench of electricity. I stood in a pocket by the doorway, my worry that I would miss her swiftly dispatched when she finally turned up. The demure little schoolgirl had vanished, hijacked by a lipsticked Lolita complete with knee socks and miniskirt. The only thing that remained were her roller skates. "You look different," I said.

She looped her arm through mine. "Thanks. Let's go get bubble tea."

Outside a nearby café, Feng Mian sat down on the curb and changed into a pair of Converse. "I can't wear them in there," she said, nodding at her skates. "They're assholes about the floor."

Inside, she ordered our drinks—coffee and some milky confection—in a brisk, harsh-sounding Cantonese before we slid into one of the vacant booths. She observed me over her straw. "I could tell you were related, you know. Even though you told me that phoney name."

I laughed in outrage. "That's my *actual* name," I said.

"Not the one you were born with." She shrugged. "I'm going to change mine too when I'm old enough. Patricia. I'll shorten it to Patty."

"Like Peppermint Patty, from *Peanuts*?"

She rolled her eyes. "Yeah. Exactly like that." She ran a finger along the rim of her plastic cup. "So, tell me, *Lily Chen*, was your uncle Chor ever cool?"

I smiled at the table. "I was too young at the time to know, although my sister probably remembers."

"Ah, yes, your wonderful, successful sister. I have one of those, too."

"Does she live with you at the apartment?"

"Uh uh. She's twenty now. Moved back to Beijing with our parents."

"They must have a lot of faith in my uncle. I mean, you being alone with him."

She smiled. "Why wouldn't they?" she said. "Chor-Kit always does what he's told. Plus my mom and dad couldn't wait to get rid of me."

Adolescents were well-versed in outrage. It came to them as naturally as hormones and was almost as indiscriminate in its battles: ten o'clock curfews, bad hair days, not wanting to eat their greens. What about Maya at that age—all that sneaking around with boys, reeking of Tweed and Wrigley's and hissing alcohol fumes through the letterbox. Now look at her. I wanted to tell Feng Mian this; that in the way of foregone conclusions this battle of hers seemed as pointless. "It'll turn out all right," I said instead. "Sisters and parents and stuff." It was bad enough that it sounded patronizing, worse that it sounded untrue, and I wasn't surprised when she looked insulted.

"Don't say you're not furious about some things. Isn't that the reason you're here?"

I studied the gap between my fingers. *Was* I furious? I filed it away for later. "Didn't you say you had something to tell me?"

She shrugged. "Tell you, ask you," she said. "What's the big scandal with your family?"

So that was it. Luring me here under false pretences on the off-chance of some titbit of gossip. "I wasn't aware there *was* any scandal."

"That's not how it seemed when you left. Chor-Kit was pretty mad. Opening drawers and throwing stuff around. Plus the things he said about your mother."

I stared at her. "What things?"

"I'm not sure how to translate it. Something like *hell-raiser*, maybe?"

"What?" I almost laughed.

"And now you've been left all this money? Sounds pretty dodgy to me."

She really *had* been listening. I swirled the dregs of my coffee. On the one hand it would explain his hesitation but it could just as easily be something else; the exaggeration of a childish mind desperate for the next thrill, the next *scandal*. Her flawless English was steeped in the same, honed through a generation's diligent exposure to Western telly and cinema.

"I like your jacket," she said then. Satisfied with the detonation of her bomb, her interest had predictably wandered. I glanced down at myself. It was something I'd swiped from the charity shop; a battered seventies leather that Maya said made me like Doyle from *The Professionals*. "My sis says it's hard to get cool stuff in China. Nothing my parents would allow her, anyway."

I got the reckless seed of an idea. "I'll trade with you," I said.

Her eyes betrayed her pleasure, even beneath their glaze of cautiousness. "For what?"

"My time in Hong Kong's ticking on and I need to know more about my mum and her connection to Hei-Fong Lee. Uncle Chor might have photographs or letters, but if he's really as upset as you say, he's unlikely to give them to me. You could help me look."

She frowned. "I don't know . . . He's pretty careful."

I made a point of staring at her outfit—the flagrant, practiced deception of it. "Something tells me you'll manage," I said.

WE WERE WALKING along Lockhart Road, heading back toward the station, when she stopped at an innocuous little doorway half-hidden between a clothes shop and a pharmacy. "I need to run an errand. Come with me?"

I followed up a flight of tiled stairs, its dark walls lined with papers and magazines displayed in plastic pockets. They were all in Chinese except for one: an English-language hardback of *Wild Swans*. "What is this place?" I said.

She paused on the step. "A bookshop."

We turned into a studio on the first floor. The place was a veritable library, crammed into half of the building's width with yellowing shelves and makeshift countertops. I wandered along its aisles, running my finger across hundreds of spines in a language I didn't understand and navigating the shallow corners where fusty academics and young people alike jostled for space like pinballs.

Feng Mian had disappeared. I emerged from the pillar of a bookcase and saw her standing in a shallow transept, seemingly engrossed in a large wooden noticeboard. I assumed she was reading the adverts but then she took a slip of paper from her pocket and hid it behind a postcard of Chairman Mao. What the hell was she doing?

She turned and walked back to the counter and, seeing her distracted with the clerk, I followed her path to the board. I pulled out the paper and opened it. It had been hastily written in Chinese, a red love heart drawn as its postscript. I smiled as I returned it, newly ashamed of my prurience. How many hours had I spent in the eighties making mixtapes on the floor of my bedroom for boys who didn't know I existed?

Once we were back on the street, Feng Mian put on her skates again. "Thanks for the coffee," I said. "And for agreeing to help me with Uncle Chor."

She raised a hand to me. "Jacket first," she said. I slipped it off and gave it to her. "You sure you want me to do this?"

"Why wouldn't I be?"

"Well—you know what they say." She stood and flexed her ankles, checking her straps were fastened. "Be careful what you wish for."

THIRTY

Sook-Yin

December 1972

Much to Sook-Yin's surprise, Julian seemed delighted about the prospect of her going home, and a few days later there was other good news: not only had he found a new job, but a new place for the family to live—a three-bedroom house in Brixton, complete with its own private garden. "I'll have time to decorate," he said. "Besides, you've needed a break for months."

A spike of panic at the extent of his enthusiasm. "But you will be all by your own at Christmas. Harvey tell me to stay for six weeks."

"I'll have to keep busy, then," he said. "You won't recognize the place when you get back."

Privately, she hoped this was true, for the new house was verging on derelict, its thin walls and Victorian windows no match for the inclement London weather, which sang cold through the cracks and holes. There were dandelions growing in the skirting boards. The mice were bold and plentiful. Also, at ten pounds and sevenpence a week its rent was even more than the shop had been. Even so, the relief of leaving Fulham had persuaded her, as had the knowledge of her secret savings and the cushion of Julian's investment money.

A FORTNIGHT LATER at the airport, however, when Sook-Yin saw the planes on the tarmac, her excitement curdled. How could such a thing get off the ground, let alone stay in the air? "You are still an amateur," Florence laughed when she saw the damp bloom beneath Sook-Yin's armpits. "Next time you should stay on the boat."

THE ATTRACTION OF flying was baffling. Its speed was all very well, but with barely a finger between one seat and the next and the stench of the nearby toilets it felt as comfortable as being in a strait-jacket. It was only when sunrise broke—pale lemon with its streaks of vermilion—and she saw the closeness of the wings to the clouds that her heart rose up to meet them, high on a wash of adrenaline and the promise of seeing ah-Ma again.

FLORENCE'S FATHER WAS already in Arrivals but there was no sign of ah-Chor. After half an hour, Mr. Ho took pity on them. "I can drive you to Cheung Sha Wan," he said. "It's not much out of our way."

Florence fanned her face in disagreement. "Cheung Sha Wan is the other side of town and I'm already so hot and fed up. Do we really have to?"

Sook-Yin read the expectation in her face. As usual, she wasn't really asking a question so much as allowing Sook-Yin to come to an obvious conclusion: that in allowing Harvey to pay for their tickets something was owed. "We'll be fine," she said. "'I'm sure my brother will be here any minute."

Abandoned to the chaos of the terminal, Sook-Yin attempted to pass the time by playing a game with Maya. They searched the faces of the people around them, trying to match them up into families: the Po Po with her trolley full of presents hurrying toward a woman with a cluster of children; the thin husband already palming his cigarettes as he strode toward his wife.

Sook-Yin's gaze lingered on the figure of a businessman. What if she saw Hei-Fong at the airport, flying in from one of his meetings? Would she ignore him, berate him, hug him? She shook his face from her head, blushing at the ambush of his memory. *What a silly idea*, she said out loud. *I probably wouldn't even recognize him.*

"Recognize who?" Maya said. Had Sook-Yin really spoken aloud in English? She had been away from home for too long!

"I make mistake," she answered. "Mistake a man for someone I know."

o o o o o o

It was another hour before ah-Chor appeared. *He has turned into our father*, Sook-Yin thought, as her annoyance gave way to relief. His wiry frame had filled out, his tanned scalp visible in the part of his thinning hair. Nor was her surprise one-sided, for it had been six years since they'd seen each other.

"You have finally become a woman," he said. He bent down and examined Maya like a new species on display at the zoo and then peered into Sook-Yin's sling. "And what is this little *gwei mui*?"

Exhausted by the journey and the wait, Sook-Yin struggled to contain her irritation. How dare he speak of her child like that? "Her name is Li-Li," she said. Maya tugged at the hem of her skirt.

"What's a gooey moy, Mumma?"

Ah-Chor laughed and tugged at her blond hair. "It means she is ghost girl," he said in English. "Not one living thing or the other."

HER HEART SANK when they got to the apartment and found that ah-Ma was not at home. "On Sundays she plays badminton," said ah-Chor. He dropped her suitcase by the kitchen and yawned. "And table tennis on Fridays at ten."

The evidence of these details—these simple, insignificant pleasures—wounded her more than her mother's absence; the idea that while she'd been homesick in London ah-Ma's life had gone on without her.

At least the rooms were the same. There was the same tired sofa she remembered, the same faded, peeling linoleum that led out to the edge of the terrace. Silenced by the foreignness of the space, Maya stood with one arm by her side, the other glued to Sook-Yin's sleeve, her eyes unsure. "This is where I grow up," Sook-Yin said. She recalled the long nights she had spent in her room, her stomach rumbling as she played alone, or later, dreading the next day's work scrubbing the floors of richer women and wishing she could return to childhood. She was glad that now she had children she could pass on this hindsight of gratitude. Glad that her children had the chance of a better life.

Tempted by the sight of a closed door, Maya at last broke free and began wandering through each of the rooms, peering into cupboards and fingering ornaments. She held her fingers to her nose. "This country smells funny," she said.

"That is the smell of my memories." Sook-Yin refastened the lock on the sideboard, disappointed at her daughter's reaction. "This house like history lesson."

She threw open the balcony doors and the heat and the sounds of the afternoon rushed in on a pungent wave. "The hens have gone?" she called to ah-Chor, stepping out and peering around. She'd been looking forward to seeing their stringy legs and kissing the quilt of their feathers.

"They were cooked and eaten years ago. There's no money in eggs anymore! Everyone goes to the supermarket."

"Is this to do with the Revolution?" Sook-Yin had been following events on the radio ever since the trouble in Beijing. She'd learned about the "Four Olds" that Mao had been trying to overturn: old ideas, old culture and customs. Old habits.

Ah-Chor snorted. "Your body may be different, little sister, but your brain is as empty as ever. Don't you realize we're protected in Hong Kong?"

Protected by whom, she wondered? The more she'd listened to the debates, the more she had started to realize that Britain was as guarded as China in its interests. Fortune was fickle and had a short memory, almost as short as her brother's with his new clothes and his car and his professorship. Hadn't he once pretended he wasn't a teacher? How quickly he'd changed his views again now he assumed that he was safe.

Ah-Chor twirled his car keys. "Ah-Ma won't be home till late and I have too many of my own things to do. You might as well sleep till she gets back."

SHE WOKE TO the sound of running water, and when she got up to investigate found ah-Ma at work in the kitchen, rinsing a bunch of radishes and chatting to Maya in Cantonese. "Ma-Ma! Why didn't you wake me?" Sook-Yin ran over and covered her in kisses.

"Aiya! You will squeeze the breath from me!" Her mother wriggled out of her grasp. "Can't you see I'm making your dinner?"

"But I am so pleased to see you!"

"All right. Let me look at you, then." Ah-Ma stood back and examined her at arm's length. "You have grown the body of a mother. We have the same soft belly these days, although you still have the neck of a giraffe."

Sook-Yin laughed. "Weren't we always the same?" she said. "I've known it more since I had to go away." She stopped and bit down on the words. No one wanted a child who complained. "Never mind, we are back together now."

Ah-Ma muttered something under her breath. *Back together, but different.* Was that it?

Maya tugged at her grandmother's leg and pointed to the waiting colander. "This one is bossy!" her mother said as she helped her shake out the vegetables. "And where are you hiding this baby?"

Sook-Yin roused Li-Li from the bedroom and brought her into the kitchen. Ah-Ma took the child in her arms. "As yellow as a stick of bamboo!" she said. "And hair as black as a crow. Are you sure this one is your husband's?"

Sook-Yin lowered her eyes and blushed. Though she knew it was only a joke, she had never heard her mother speak in this way before, as if in a secret club she didn't want to belong to. She wanted her ah-Ma of old, with her whispered warnings and cautionary tales that made Sook-Yin want to crawl back to her belly. *Tell me again about the Japanese soldiers. Did they really hang people at the boys' school? Did they really do that to the beautiful women?*

She had only been an infant when the war had come: small enough to conceal when the bombs fell, unworthy to be taken as a concubine. She had once been proud of her innocence. But now, as they stood in the kitchen—two mothers together at last—something told her those days were gone.

THIRTY-ONE

Lily

35th Day of Mourning

Wanting to thank Mrs. Tam for the box, I went early to Tsim Sha Tsui and visited one of the bakeries. At this hour the smell was intoxicating, the air heavy with its mist of flour and the warmth of vanilla and rose petals. As I pressed my face to the window, I had the weirdest sense of déjà vu, the same one as at Kowloon Park or that day I'd visited the temple. Untangling these memories was frustrating. Like composing a new piece of music only to realize that you'd heard it years ago. *Were* they mine or Maya's, after all?

I went inside and picked out a selection—steamed buns with salted egg yolk; tarts with larded crusts and sweet pastries with winter melon—before I hailed a taxi to Cheung Sha Wan.

Now that I'd spent nearly a week in the city, I'd started to ask for places in Cantonese rather than pointing to names on a map, and the drivers responded by charging me less, ignoring my New Territories accent to smile and nod in approval.

The market was already alive, the narrow sidewalks overflowing with vendors and the dangerous terrain of bamboo parasols because the day was turning out hot again.

Through the open door of the building, I spied Mrs. Tam behind the lobby window. I tried to picture *her* mother, Mrs. Chee, sitting beside my grandmother, their deep friendship over the years—the shared secrets, the gossip, the laughter—but the image still eluded me.

Mrs. Tam saw me and broke into a grin. "One minute! One minute!" she called. I heard the bolt slide from the door and then she appeared and ran past me to the stairwell, returning a few moments later with the young woman whom I'd met at her apartment. "Hey! Come in!" she said. She was trying to pull on a pair of flip-flops while keeping up with Mrs. Tam's chatter. "She say she been thinking about you, so the gods must have brought you back to us."

I laughed and showed them the box. "They did! And they sent me with cakes."

FOR THE NEXT hour I brought them up to speed with what had happened on my visit to Uncle Chor and what Feng Mian had told me afterward. Mrs. Tam listened, her features darkening until she spoke and the young woman translated. "She say your uncle is talking nonsense. From what her mother told her, Sook-Yin was a very good daughter. It was Chor Kit who was unhappy about it."

"Unhappy about what?" I said.

She reddened and dipped her head. It was clear they'd been talking about it. "The fact that your mother marry a Westerner. Her brother believed it was against our culture."

"*Gwei mui, gwei mui!*" said Mrs. Tam.

I looked from one to the other. "I don't understand," I said.

The young woman sighed. "It was something your uncle used to call you. It is a kind of insult. A silly word. In English you call it *ghost girl*. It means you don't belong here."

The start of tears hit the back of my eyes and I blinked them away. I'd guessed from my grandmother's letter that it wasn't her who had sent us back to London, so had it been Uncle Chor after all? Is that why he'd been so cautious on my visit, so apparently threatened in its aftermath?

Mrs. Tam put her hand on my arm. "Don't worry, don't worry," she said in English before she spoke again to the woman.

"Your *po-po* is in St. Raphael Cemetery. Here, in Cheung Sha Wan."

"My *po-po*?"

"This is how we say 'grandmother.' Perhaps you would like to visit her."

Something pulled at the anchor of my memory. Ma-Ma, Ba-Ba, Po-Po.

"I would really love that," I said. "Would I be able to walk from here?"

She frowned. "Is very difficult place, but Mrs. Tam say she will take you. Walking, perhaps thirty minutes?"

"I don't want to be a nuisance—" I began.

"No! She very insist. She is going to stay with her brother to-morrow and may not see you again. She say very important not forgetting your ancestor."

THE AFTERNOON WAS potent with heat as I set off with Mrs. Tam to the cemetery. Without the benefit of conversation, the journey seemed longer at first but after a while we fell into an easy step, Mrs. Tam stopping from time to time to comment or point to some landmark at which I nodded and smiled with gratitude. I went into one of the corner shops and bought flowers and two cartons of iced tea, which we drank in pleasant companionship.

Our strides became more of an effort as we got to the base of a steep slope. At the top it broadened out again, giving way to the view of a high wall—cobbled and ancient-looking—in the middle of which was a large door.

I wasn't prepared for what awaited me. The cemetery resembled an ancient amphitheater: a banked series of concentric semi-circles across which lay thousands of tombstones. The creep of its boundaries shocked me, spread out across a vast stretch of land far larger than the exterior had suggested. As much as the cemetery's arrangement, I was struck by its sound. There were hundreds of people in attendance: lighting incense, chanting their prayers, chatting and eating and singing in an anomalous vibe of celebration. There was a circus of wildlife, too: feral cats and exotic birds, the fuzzy nonchalance of a large macaque eating a discarded peach.

Rather than the dates that I was accustomed to, many of the gravestones had photographs on them, their faces preserved in all stages of life. I stopped at the figure of a rabbit carved out of blush-pink soapstone with a picture of a boy around four on it. His body was pale and thin, the plainness of his shorts and thin shirt atoned for by the beauty of his shrine like an overdue apology. An honored debt.

Mrs. Tam was already far ahead of me, striding along the ledges with even, doubtless steps as though with each movement of her feet she were striking some map in her memory. *Bam, bam, bam.* I hurried but struggled to keep up, my shoes slipping across the wet moss.

Finally, near the top of the highest ridge she stopped and pointed. The slab that rose in front of us was tall and pristine in its newness, its characters rendered in a dull gilded lettering. I was startled by the image in the photograph. Despite her wrinkles and the froth of her gray hair, she was almost the replica of Mumma. Yet it was more than this. I recognized her.

"Po-Po," Mrs. Tam said. She reached over and touched the stone and then took my hand and did the same. "Po-Po."

"Hai-ya." *Yes,* I said. I laid down the flowers I'd bought. "Hello, Po-Po." I sensed the shadow of her closeness, of someone I had known and yet never known, of time passing and how much I had wasted. I felt the injustice of Mumma's ashes, sent back to England by Uncle

Chor. They should have been here with *her* mother, not scattered beneath some oak tree, cast out and unloved by her family.

It was then, with my hand on that stone, that I was finally sure I'd always been part of this; of some lineage beyond what I'd imagined or ever been allowed to indulge; that I wasn't *half* of anything, but both.

My memories had been right all along.

THIRTY-TWO

Sook-Yin

December 1972

Sook-Yin had been back in Kowloon for a fortnight before she saw her brother again. Along with ah-Ma and the children they met at a restaurant in the center of town and this time he'd brought someone with him—a patron from the college where he now taught.

She was one of those pretentious women: the sort who dismissed her cashmere clothes—*This little thing? So old!*—and had her hair washed twice a week by a stranger. Within minutes of sitting down she'd already boasted about buying an apartment.

"The commute is so much better from Central." She slipped off her extravagant fur coat—clearly too hot for a Hong Kong winter—and made a point of moving it away from them. "Although to be honest, I prefer Happy Valley."

"I hear Central is very expensive now."

The woman tugged at her earring. "I earned it, I may as well spend it. I told Chor-Kit he must look for one too."

"If he can afford it, perhaps he should. Especially if it will stretch to a room for our mother."

Ah-Chor gave a squeak of outrage. "Ah-Ma is happy in Cheung Sha Wan," he said. "As people get older, they like what they know."

"If she is old, then what does that make you?"

Sook-Yin felt a pinch on her leg. "Your brother is right," said ah-Ma, turning her smile on the woman. "My son would do even better in Central."

"Like Ying and Ying," Sook-Yin muttered.

The woman appeared not to hear, too busy yawning as she looked around the table. "Whose are these children?" she said, as though she'd discovered some abandoned luggage.

"They are Chor-Kit's nieces. My oldest, Mei-Hua, and Li-Li."

Maya gave the woman an unsmiling stare. "I want butter and soy sauce and rice."

Sook-Yin looked across at her brother. "Yes, let's eat," she said. "If we're not waiting for anyone else."

The words had barely left her mouth when ah-Chor stood and pointed over her shoulder. "Everyone! You remember Hei-Fong."

Sook-Yin almost choked on her tea. All those years of imagining had finally made him real again. She turned around and stared. Same eyes, same smile, same face. *He has not aged a day*, she thought, before she said out loud, "You really *are* back from America."

Hei-Fong touched his heart and pointed at her. "This one has a long memory," he said. "Yes, I finally learned to behave myself."

"He's done better than that," said ah-Chor. "Got an excellent job at the bank now."

"If I do, it's thanks to Chor-Kit." Hei-Fong turned and grinned at Sook-Yin. "I had to come when he said you were back again."

Ah-Chor's colleague fanned her cheeks. She seemed offended that Hei-Fong hadn't noticed her, and as soon as he looked in her direction she pulled out the chair alongside her. When he took the seat beside Maya, Sook-Yin wasn't sure who was happier—herself or her lovesick brother.

Hei-Fong reached out a finger to Lily. "What beautiful girls," he said.

Ah-Chor gave a snide little laugh. "Finally, she found something she was good at."

"Is that any way to speak about your sister?" Hei-Fong swiped at ah-Chor's arm, albeit with the softness of a joke, and then bent his head and whispered to her. "Do you remember when I used to pull your hair?"

"Yes. You were quite the barbarian." This time, ah-Ma stamped on her foot beneath the table. Hei-Fong laughed.

"I even found a wife to drag back to my cave. We have a young son, now—Daniel. He must be around the same age as your eldest." Out of the corner of her eye, Sook-Yin saw the woman deflate.

"He is as feisty as his father," said ah-Chor, enjoying the renewed attention of his companion. "You'll need to send *him* to America, too."

"You sound like my wife, Chor-Kit." Hei-Fong lit up a cigarette. "I've always thought that it pays to be a fighter. Wouldn't you say, Sook-Yin?"

She glanced in her brother's direction. "I have to say I agree. Who else will help you if not yourself?" She took a sip of her tea. "I suppose you know that we live in London now?"

"Yes, no thanks to your brother. And how do you like it over there?"

"Oh, it's fine," she said. "And not as cold as people imagine."

THE MEAL WAS pleasant enough until Hei-Fong insisted on seeing them home. They rode in the taxi together, Sook-Yin keeping her face to the window to avoid the bullet of his gaze. "Ah-Ma," she said at last. "What is the story with ah-Chor and that woman?"

Her mother stroked her throat. "He is a little infatuated I think and she enjoys watching him dance like a monkey. I'm afraid she will break his heart."

"If he *had* a heart in the first place."

"Aiya! Hush now, ah-Yin. Your brother is not that bad. Think of all the things he has done for you."

Had ah-Chor twisted her mind that much? Sook-Yin pressed her back to the seat and endured the rest of the journey in silence. It was only once they'd returned to the apartment, tempered by her one glass of wine and Li-Li dozing beside her, that she softened a little. She supposed it natural that her brother had needs too, and who could say what was in the heart of a man? Perhaps even monsters got lonely.

SOOK-YIN PUT LI-LI to bed and then excused herself to ring Julian. He always called them at a particular hour, keen to speak to Maya, but it was late and they'd probably missed him. She knew he would call the next day but she was still smarting from ah-Ma's comments and wanted to know how the renovations were going.

She sat on the bed with the telephone and cracked open the spine of her address book, tracing her finger along the entries. She always dialed the number with care and was mortified when a woman answered. "Sorry, I think is wrong number."

"Oh! It's an awful line. Who was it you said you wanted?"

"No worry, is mistake,' she said. The wine must have gone to her head. "I looking for Julian Miller."

"Julian, you said? No, hang on, love." She called Julian's name in the background and then returned with a tone of apology. "He can't hear me—he's busy cooking. Do you mind if I tell him who's calling?"

Sook-Yin rubbed the side of her temple. "Yes, but excuse me, who are you?"

The woman didn't answer at first but then her voice became shorter and more annoyed. "It's Marie," she said. "His girlfriend."

Sook-Yin lowered the receiver as the pork she'd eaten for dinner rose hot and sour in her throat.

"Hello? Hello? Are you there?"

She put the phone back to her ear. "Yes, I am here," she said. "Is my mistake. I call wrong person."

She pushed the handset back in its cradle as Maya walked into the room. "Can *I* talk to Daddy?" she said.

"Sorry. Daddy not home."

"But I heard you talking to someone."

"Pajamas now, Mei-Hua," she said. "I will come and read to you soon."

Maya dragged her feet and left but straight after there was a knock at the door and Hei-Fong put his head around. Could she not get five minutes in peace? "I'm about to leave," he said. He frowned at her expression. "Is everything all right, ah-Yin?"

She flinched at the affectionate form of her name. Picked at her dress. "Yes, I'm fine. Why not?"

"Your face looks a little . . . upset."

Sook-Yin stood and tied back her hair in a single, aggressive motion. "You are mistaken," she said. She pushed past him into the living room and opened the doors to the balcony but it only brought a rush of the same air, the woman's voice like the buzz of an insect. *Marie, Marie, Marie.*

White name, white voice, white face.

But it's different . . . She married her own kind.

You won't recognize the place when you get back.

"It was nice to see you," Hei-Fong called.

She spoke without turning around. "Thank you. Yes. The same."

She heard the click of the front door as the stink of fish guts rose up from the gutters, the rotting sweet scent of bruised fruit. Like every child in Hong Kong she had learned to tell the time by smell, but she had no need for that now to know that the sun had gone down already.

THIRTY-THREE

Lily

35th Day of Mourning

The visit to the cemetery had changed me. Not only was I start-ing to understand where I'd come from but after hearing the news about Uncle Chor, the circularity of history, too.

Ghost girl.

Like the fault in the pattern of a fabric endlessly repeating itself. Mumma and I were more alike than I'd imagined. When was it we had both stopped belonging?

I KNEW I wasn't born unhappy. Even after Mumma had died I remember periods of invisible joy, whole stretches of feeling part of a family. Weeks in Scarborough, fish and chips on the beach, pad-dling in the sea with Granny and Grandad, with their varicose veins and knotted hankies. I never thought to question their complicity; assumed grief was a universal silence. *Mothers must be dead and not heard.*

And through it all there was Maya, and that helped things. She taught me how to tie my laces, amended my fashion mistakes with only half a roll of her eyes, was patient when I got the stomach flu, consigned for almost a fortnight to the short path between bathroom and bucket. Dad had always been terrible with body things—the messy details of shit or vomit—whereas Maya always managed to stay calm, keenly aware of human fallibility.

Nor was this limited to her knowledge of biology. She was in Juniors when I started school and already well-versed in the cruelty of others. Too fat, too thin, thick glasses. If they wanted to get you, there was always a reason. Maya, though, remained untouchable. She was the white girl whose mother had died—that uncrossable boundary of morality and pity—and at first she played it for both our benefit. She threw stones on my behalf, hit back at anyone who noticed our differences. *Yeah, she's my sister, so what? You should look at yourself in the mirror!*

Mumma Maya. My surrogate. My karaoke song.

It didn't last.

It's easy to conflate these things—the way the years can bleed into one, lose their edges—but like Uncle Chor and his views on Mumma's marriage, there was a start to Maya's betrayal.

It was the year she moved schools that things changed. There were new friendships and boys at stake, gossip she couldn't possibly miss out on, and all of a sudden I became a liability. "Ignore them," she used to say. "I'm too busy to come around and walk home with you." Her excuses became a habit, for she had learned something without me noticing, which was this: that life was safer within the majority.

Dad, of course, agreed with her. "Why don't you just try to fit in? They'll find somebody else to pick on as long as you don't show your weakness."

I started to wonder what my weakness was and I didn't have to go far to discover. It was in every joke about paddy fields and rickshaws, in the comedies on evening TV where hapless immigrants were forced back to school to learn how to speak "proper"

English, in the outrage of Deborah Kerr with Yul Brynner in the *The King and I*.

Chinese, Japanese,
What are these
Yellow knees?

Amid the fungible genes of my classmates my weakness became an infection, treatable only by denying its existence. I scoured the streets and the pages of magazines to find Western women like me who had been born with the accident of a monolid or a mouth too small for their face, whose jet-black hair would only change color with the liberal addition of peroxide and only then to a Tango orange. Meanwhile, Maya glided through school and then Oxford with her blond hair and green eyes and white boyfriends. I watched them come and go like the seasons, pinching her bum and wanting her, wanting whatever she had.

I taught one of them piano for a while. I remember the heat of his fingers on the keys, the fold of our bodies like a perfect C, the press of his kiss like the pedal. Sustaining, and then undoing me.

Sorry. I made a mistake. You're not really my type, after all.

It was then I realized the true source of my jealousy. It wasn't Maya's brain or her hair or her boyfriends, but her lifelong assurance that she would always belong.

I WAS BACK in my room at the hotel when someone knocked at the door and I found Daniel Lee standing in the corridor. We hadn't spoken since that day at the temple when our parting had been more than awkward. A choke of panic sat beneath my annoyance. What if he'd changed his mind, sorted the paperwork already and had come to escort me from the building?

"Hi. Am I intruding?" His hands were balled deep in his pockets, his shoe working against the carpet until its fibers stood up like brushed dog fur.

"Were we supposed to have a meeting?" I said.

"Not at all. I just get the feeling I've not been that welcoming."

I gestured over my shoulder to the suite. "You've been more than generous, Mr. Lee."

"I've come to take you to dinner," he said.

I exhaled, only partly in relief. I was going to get the talk again, wasn't I? The final countdown to D-Day. "Look, I do understand," I began, "and as soon as I get my card back—"

"You should bring a coat," he said, motioning toward the window. "The weather is going to change."

HE'D GIVEN HIS driver the night off, the unfamiliar concentration as he drove a convenient barrier to more conversation. Fine by me. We ended up at a restaurant at Hung Hom Bay that was surprisingly small and unshowy. I could tell he'd been there before, however, by the way the manager came out to greet him and immediately addressed me in Cantonese. Keenly aware of my embarrassment, Daniel Lee ordered for both of us, plus a bottle of red for the table. "Thank you. Again," I said, once we were alone on the terrace.

"I already know what is good here."

When the waiter returned with the wine, he kept his hand on top of his glass. "Worried about driving?" I asked.

"We're not supposed to drink during mourning."

"Please, have at it," I said. "I promise not to tell your mother." I immediately heard how crass it sounded, like telling an ex-smoker to have *just the one*. "Sorry. That was awful of me."

He reached over and filled his glass, as though he'd only been waiting for my permission. A vampire stepping over the threshold. "Actually, it's my grandmother you should worry about offending."

"Fourteen days. I'm counting."

"I wasn't talking about the inheritance. For some reason she likes the sound of you. Tonight was her idea."

"You mean you're here to do penance?" I clinked my glass

against his. "To your grandmother, then," I said. "Who is obviously something of a badass."

WHEN THE FOOD arrived, I tried everything: the stinky tofu, the fermented intestines, the bowl of hot noodle broth with its frilly, unidentified islands. In my search for a connection with Hong Kong, food had seemed an obvious outlet. It shored the gaps I couldn't broach with language and with every mouthful of something new I imagined filling myself with Mumma, building a bridge to her memory one dumpling or duck foot at a time.

Daniel Lee nodded in approval. "I'm impressed with your bravery," he said.

Unlike my attempts with the cardamom tea.

I shrugged. "I grew up in the age of Spam. We used to call it eyeholes, earholes, and . . . never mind." I stoppered my mouth with a wonton and he waited until I'd chewed it.

"Are you enjoying your stay in Hong Kong?"

"Yeah, it's amazing," I said.

AFTER MY VISIT to Wan Chai that morning I'd walked over to the Canal Road Flyover, remembering something I'd read in the guidebook. I'd missed the period of Jingzhe when the place was at its busiest but even then, with the commuters in their suits and the frenzy of the markets and shops, it was buzzing. The area was home to the Villain Beaters, a collection of Asian pensioners who for fifty dollars a throw would heap fiery curses on your enemies. You could hear their chants from fifty yards away. *Da siu yan! Da siu yan!* they called. *Beat the petty little people!*

The smog of incense hung drily in the air, parting with the choke of the traffic to reveal the lines of makeshift altars. Some of the queues were insane: housewives and men with briefcases clutching photographs or fragments of letters. Pieces of cloth. They took their places on plastic stools and the old women would take the item— the used tissue of a lover perhaps, the payslip of a spiteful employer, even a photo of Jiang Zemin—and beat it with the heel of a shoe, the thwacks resounding in a bitter percussion. Their prayers had a violence about them, the nightmarish rhythm of a song that shocked me back to my childhood. It was something that Maya used to sing:

> Beat your little hand,
> Your good luck will come to an end,
> Beat your little eye,
> Very soon you will die.

By the time the women were finished, all that remained were fragments, which they set on fire in a paper tiger. I'd watched as they burned in the bin, the golden glow of their embers flickering like pulses in the gloom.

"REALLY AMAZING," I said again. "Not least because this time I'll remember it."

Daniel Lee raised an eyebrow in question. "This isn't your first time here?"

"You didn't know?" I said. I lay down my chopsticks. Frowned. "We came out here when I was four. Me and my sister and my parents. We'd have probably stayed as well—if my mum hadn't died, I mean." I wiped my mouth on a napkin. "It was a hit-and-run. In Kowloon."

His face fell. "I'm so sorry, I had no idea . . . I can see now why you questioned the will."

I washed a spoon around the bowl of its dish. "That photo you gave me," I said. "Are you sure your dad never mentioned her? Or maybe your mum did, afterwards?"

"She's not said much since he died. Barely looked at the paperwork. Besides, as I told you before, my father was a generous man. He and your mother could have met in passing." He took a swig from his glass. "You've never spoken to *your* father about it?"

"He's gone too. And before that, only bits and pieces. I suppose he was a bit like your mum. He never stopped mourning, to be honest, and you try to get on with it, don't you—living, I mean?"

"But you were so young. That's rough."

I detected a prying disguised as interest and out came the Miller defensiveness: *Sit forward. Look ahead. Hide your weakness.* "Oh. We were fine," I said. "Our dad was pretty brilliant, considering. Maya ended up at Oxford and everything."

"Very nice. And you?"

"I sort of did music at Cambridge, although I left before it ended."

He smiled. "Your idea of teenage rebellion?"

"Yeah," I said. "Something like that."

WE CHATTED FOR another two hours, trading small, curated anecdotes greased by a second bottle of wine. I told him my plans to start a music school, I learned of his skill at pavement tricks that his uncle had taught him as a boy in order to sharpen his radar for business: Pig-in-a-Poke, Find the Lady. He was a surprising person, really.

Away from the restaurant's heat the navy sky was cloudless, revealing an ocher moon that infused the air with an odd chill. He was definitely too drunk to drive by then and we abandoned the car by the curb and went in search of a taxi. "You'll be hungover for work, Mr. Lee," I said.

He wagged his finger at me. "Mr. Lee was my father's name. To my friends I am always Daniel."

"Oh. Is that what we are now?"

"And I shall call you Li-Li." He conducted an invisible orchestra. "Your mother foretold your destiny. It's a very musical name." He hailed a passing cab and then once I was safely inside, closed the door behind me.

"Are we not sharing?" I said through the window.

"Sadly, we are going in different directions."

"Well, your grandmother should consider you forgiven. Tell her I had a good time." I waved as the taxi pulled away, pretty sure that it wasn't a lie.

THIRTY-FOUR

Sook-Yin

January 1973

Every day since the phone call to London, Sook-Yin imagined the conversation she would have with Julian. She'd not phoned him after that night, nor had he made any attempt to contact her. A mutual waiting game.

In contrast to this silence, her fantasies were vivid in their detail: arguments where she begged him to stay, her face pale and raw as a hungry ghost, her arms outstretched; others where she was manic or murderous. Far more frequently, however, it took the form of a simple dialogue in which she asked if he was going to leave her and he responded with a yes or no. It didn't matter which word he chose—where her mood took her on this day or that—for the deed had already been done, suggesting the answer was unimportant anyway.

At least Kowloon had given her distractions, the most surprising of which was that Hei-Fong continued to visit them, sometimes in the company of ah-Chor but increasingly on his own.

She was packing for their flight back to London when he returned. "One last trip," he said. "Your mother is happy to watch the children."

THEY DROVE ALONG the expressway, Hei-Fong's mood unusually somber as he tapped and then gripped the steering wheel. "I can't believe you're leaving," he said at last. "Just as we've found each other again."

Sook-Yin pursed her lips but could manage only the mildest of scolds. "Found each other again? You make yourself sound like a single man."

"Aren't I allowed to value you as an old friend?"

Her cheeks vied with the scarlet of the seats, mortified by the exposure of her vanity.

"Still, it's annoying," he said, "how you don't realize what you need until it shows up."

She laughed then. "Is it any wonder you're in finance, ah-Fong? You have all the chat chat chat. And where are you taking me anyway?"

"When I told my mother you were back in Kowloon she said she was desperate to see you. She's upset you didn't come earlier."

Sook-Yin sat up at the window. She'd not been paying much attention to their journey but now she recognized the shadow in the distance, crooked and gray as a sickness. "Your parents still live in the Wall?"

Hei-Fong smiled. "Damn, I was right about your memory!"

"I assumed—" she began to say.

"I know, but what can you do?"

AS SOON AS they pulled into the forecourt a group of children surrounded the car, a hundred soiled fingers on the heat of its hood as they fought for the right to guard it.

Hei-Fong got out and opened her door. "Not a dent, not even a scratch," he cautioned an older boy as he palmed him a handful of dollars. "You know what will happen if there is."

Sook-Yin watched the exchange with interest, seeing ah-Fong so clearly at the same age: his threadbare clothes and determined face jostling in the very same forecourt. He'd shown her his savings on a shelf in a glass jar—the thick glass rippled and dim, each milestone marked with a ribbon—until eventually, over the years, she understood he had no intention of spending them the way the other boys did but merely kept them as a kind of evidence.

She got out and peered at the estate. They'd always called it the City of Darkness, three hundred tiny apartments crammed into a space of less than three hectares. Ah-Ma had forbidden her to go there after ah-Chor had got lost in its stairwells more than once; nightmare legends about its black labyrinths where you could wander for more than an hour without seeing daylight or touching the ground. Stories, too, about the things that he'd seen there, nameless and baffling as a child but which she came to know in her own time as opium dens and prostitutes, as gangs and gambling houses.

A slice of rare daylight entered the space and then withered like the beam of a sundial as Hei-Fong led her through one of the entrances. Sook-Yin's memories unfurled in the darkness. The heat was the sweat of money and sex; someone's knock the *tap tap* of an opium pipe, its blue curls like clouds in a fake night; a rotting mango the flesh of a finger. Eyes down, watch your step . . . remember ah-Chor? Blinded for days.

Hei-Fong navigated the stairwells with ease, the building gradually revealing itself in intermittent pools of sulfurous light and the tentative cracks of doorways. They passed men in corners engaged in games of dice, their chatter rising and falling with their fortunes; a child receiving a haircut on a landing. The stench of the wet markets bled up from the basements, its copper tang of blood and the sea mixed with the starch of boiling rice. Up and up they climbed, her adrenaline soaring the higher they rose until she noticed the strangest thing. It wasn't fear she was feeling but life, the same thrill she'd had as a child hiding comics inside her Bible, rubbing garlic on the seats of the nuns, climbing the trees in Kowloon Park. What had happened to her over the years? Why had she allowed herself to forget?

AFTER THE GLOOM of the corridors his parents' apartment was open and pure. Scattered lanterns adorned the space, enabled by a street-facing window that kindled yellow through the muslin curtains.

Jin Lee came out of the minuscule kitchen and greeted Sook-Yin like a mother. "Wah! How well you look!" She twirled her around and examined her. "Very London London!" she said. "And how is your ah-Ma these days?"

"Very Kowloon," Sook-Yin said.

Hei-Fong called into one of the other rooms and at last a young woman appeared carrying a boy in her arms. The seams of her thin shoulders sagged, for he was even bigger than Mei-Hua.

"Ah-Jiao, this is Chor-Kit's sister. She's come all the way from London."

His wife attempted a smile but then the boy began to fuss again and she turned to Hei-Fong in irritation. "He's been like this all morning," she said. "See how he's dirtied my new dress?"

"Then put him down and let him walk! He's hardly a baby anymore."

Easy tears appeared in Jiao's eyes and Sook-Yin clicked her tongue in sympathy. *Men would never understand their burden.* She offered her arms to the child and then set him down in the shade of the carpet. "I imagine he dislikes the heat," she said. "My daughter is exactly the same."

Jiao gazed down at her son, who was now playing with the tassels of Sook-Yin's shoes with a look of mischief in his face. "You have children too?"

"Mei-Hua and Li-Li, yes."

"Two already?" she said, even though the news seemed to comfort her. "Don't you find it too much work?"

Jin pushed her way between them and clapped her hands. "Mothers, children, husbands! The secret to everything is food."

ENSCONCED IN THE warmth of the room, Sook-Yin was happier than she'd been in a long time. How different from Julian's parents' house with their place mats and *shoes off* orders. Here, they sat three abreast on the sofa, their chopsticks clacking in conversation as they met over dishes and bowls: rice and rainbow trout and choy sum fried in garlic, bitter melon with shrimp and char siu. She turned and smiled at Jin. "Your home is as lovely as I remember it. Do you think you will stay here forever?"

Jin nodded as she sucked on a bean shoot. "Ba-Ba talks about moving sometimes, but you can't buy belonging with money." Hei-Fong glanced in her direction, his raised eyebrow signaling his *told you so.* "Besides, ah-Fong would miss coming back."

"You mean he'd miss all his dodgy old friends!"

"Exactly! Even in a waistcoat, a cricket is a cricket. I wouldn't be surprised if he moved back himself one day."

"I hope that's not true," Jiao said, her chopsticks hovering in interruption. "I'm counting on a mansion someday . . ."

"And I am sure you will get it," said Sook-Yin. "I only meant that money won't change him." She smiled. "You should have seen what he was like at school. And ah-Fong a scholarship boy!"

Hei-Fong opened his mouth in mock outrage. "You can talk!" he said. "Who was it they always kept in detention for not knowing the National Anthem?"

"I knew it!" Sook-Yin protested. "It was simply that I didn't agree with it."

Jiao peered uneasily from beneath her lashes. It was no fun to be excluded from a private joke, and Sook-Yin dipped her head in apology. "We didn't know each other *so* well," she said. "It was more what my brother told me."

"*Now* she denies me," said Hei-Fong. "But when I am rich and famous—"

"Then your wife will get the best of you." Sook-Yin gave him a pointed stare and then raised her glass. "To your happy family," she said.

"Happy families," they said in unison and their glasses clinked and shattered the light.

THE SKY WAS cloaked in a purplish haze before Sook-Yin noticed the time and they were forced to take their leave. Back in the car she sat in silence as the last moon she would see in Kowloon rose slowly through the deepening shadows.

"Did the food not agree with you or something?"

She startled at the sound of his voice. "Not at all! Everything was delicious. And your mother as wonderful as I remember her."

"Then what is all this sad face?"

"I was thinking about the journey back to London. I almost wish I could go on the boat again."

"And float around for six weeks?"

Yes. Just floating and thinking.

She pulled her lip balm out of her pocket and took her time applying it. "Did you meet Jiao when you were out in the States?"

He shook his head. "My mother would have hated the women in Chicago. Our fathers got us together when they were managers at the textile factory."

"You mean like a business decision?"

"Why do you sound so surprised? Half the marriages in Hong Kong are the same."

"I don't know," she said. "You were never one for toeing the line."

Hei-Fong shrugged. "Rebellion is a luxury of the young. I had my fun in America. Now it's time to make sacrifices for the family."

Sook-Yin frowned at her lap. Ever since his reappearance in her life she couldn't help but revisit her memories: the promises of escape that they'd made, the last letter he'd ever sent to her—*Don't forget me, Sook-Yin. I'll come back for you.* She understood that time had changed things but is that how he saw her life in London? As though she'd been having too much fun to grow up? For a moment, she really hated him. "It can't be that much of a sacrifice. Jiao's a very beautiful woman."

"Do you really think I'm that shallow?" Hei-Fong narrowed his eyes. He was smiling but there was hurt in his voice.

"I know that beauty is useful. If you were a woman, you'd be a fool to deny it."

"But that's never been important to me. Man or woman it makes people lazy, whereas those that haven't been blessed have to work extra hard to survive. It keeps us on our toes, don't you think?"

"Thank you for the compliment," she said.

He laughed. "Ah, come on, I was joking. And I would apologize if I believed it bothered you but I think better of you than that."

"Even old friends like to be flattered . . ."

He sighed. "All right," he said. "Here is my compliment to you. Don't go back to London. Stay in Kowloon and get a job at the bank. Build a life here with your children."

Sook-Yin rolled her eyes. "You are talking in clouds now, ah-Fong! Did your mother put wine in the water?"

"I'm deadly serious," he said. "You have all the skills that they need. You've always been sharp and fearless and your English now is excellent. I would be happy to give you a reference."

"Are you forgetting that I have a husband?"

He scoffed. "But you'd take the boat and delay getting back to him . . . ? Let me ask you something," he said then. "Do you remember that blaze at your mother's house? The day you set fire to the cooking pot? I was there that morning with Chor-Kit. We were out on the balcony playing farmers and you kept asking to join in with the game."

Sook-Yin reddened. The memory she had thought of that night

in Gower Street as she tried to protect herself from Julian. Of all the things to bring up! "I've no idea what you're talking about . . ."

Hei-Fong gave her a sideways glance. "Anyway, the point of the story is this: I knew you would light that fire. I could see the longing in your eyes—it's the same look that you have in them now. You keep saying that you want to belong but you won't do it without someone's permission. So now I am telling you. Come back."

She crossed her arms. Ah-Fong may have been blessed with many gifts, but turning back time wasn't one of them. How easy it was to advise when the chance had already passed. "You misunderstood me," she said. "I only came here to have a great holiday. I have things to do in London."

"Like prove a point to your brother? Pretend you don't care that he sent you away?"

She felt her anger rising. He was ruining the time they had left together. Why couldn't he leave it alone? "Well, you know him better than anyone. Don't pretend he wouldn't love me to beg."

Hei-Fong sighed. "Does it mean nothing that *I* admire you?"

At least he hadn't tried to deny it. "Forget my brother," she said. "Maybe I have a point to prove to myself."

He tightened his grip on the wheel. "All right. It's your decision. Just promise me you won't be a martyr."

She nodded but her mind was made up; in truth, she'd known it since the day of the phone call. Ah-Chor, Julian, England. If the world wanted a fight she would give it one, but things would be different from now on.

THIRTY-FIVE

Lily

36th Day of Mourning

The anomalous chill that had descended on Hung Hom had reached the whole of Kowloon. The morning after my dinner with Daniel I was too hungover to do much of anything except take a pill and sleepwalk through coffee, but when noon arrived like an accusation, I forced myself into the shower.

I WENT THROUGH the objects from Mrs. Tam's box again. I'd started to regret my arrangement with Feng Mian. It wasn't simply about managing expectations but that, like Maya, she'd shown a gift for disguise, a skill that rarely came without guile, and I wished I'd been more circumspect. Far better to see Uncle Chor again, hear his side of the story. Like a name, there was always something more to it.

I picked up the invoice again and this time I saw there was a date on it: August 10, 1977—the same time we were living here. What if *Mumma* had spent the money? Part of me liked this idea; to think of a woman—the product of humble roots—having the audacity to spend all that cash: ten thousand on a single dress, or a ridiculously extravagant hat that she would never have occasion to wear. A tacky ornament. Was this something else that Uncle Chor had been mad about? And now Hei-Fong Lee had left us this fortune. The karma was enough to make anyone spit.

I RETURNED TO the Kowloon library. They hadn't been kidding about exam season. Red-cheeked from effort and the sun, young people with books and notepads spilled out like liquid from the tables or made piers with their shoulders against shelves, pens scratching. In the corner, a boy in headphones percussed to an invisible beat: *tssst da tssst da tttst da tssst da.* It was summer, and scrutiny was looming.

I was directed again to the back where the man who'd helped me before was parading among the machines in a practiced routine of activity: retrieving and scanning the microfiche and issuing warnings to acne-plagued teenagers to keep their fingers away from the glass and their drinks inside their bags. I wandered over and raised my hand.

"Oh, hi!" he said and then frowned. "I think desk must call you by mistake. I haven't had chance to look yet."

"Actually, I came to ask for your help with something else. I didn't realize you'd be so busy."

"That's okay. One minute." He asked one of his colleagues to take over and then pointed to a lone chair by the window, where I sat and pulled out the invoice.

"Is there anything you can tell me about this? I'm guessing it's some kind of receipt."

He took it over to the light and studied it. "Yes, is receipt. For debt. What you call IOU."

"A debt?"

"Where you get this, may I ask?"

I hesitated. "It was just in a box of stuff . . . among my research materials. I don't suppose it's anything—"

"For your project? Now it makes sense. This is in name of Hei-Fong Lee."

The hairs on my neck stood up. "Are you sure?"

He pointed. "These characters: Lee, Hei-Fong. Family name always first." He smoothed the creases on the paper. "And this is address at top. Somewhere in Kowloon Walled City." He looked at me over his glasses. "This look like gambling debt."

The remains of the old Walled City. The same place that Daniel had shown me on the way to the temple that morning. *My father grew up not far from there.*

"How would I get to this place?"

"No such place anymore. Now is Kowloon Walled City Park. Here, if you wait, I show you."

He left me and returned with a book. "When the British first lease Hong Kong, China refuse to give up this area. Initially, is military fort but gradually, after destruction, refugees come and build up. According to the principle of feng shui, the location is very lucky—facing south and overlooking the water. They build many hundred apartments, very tight together but no rules or laws to govern them. No one would come and visit—no doctors or dentists et cetera, so men start training themselves, try to make their own community."

He flicked through the pages and showed me a photograph. It looked like a council estate on crack; a conglomeration of ramshackle apartments without any single identity.

"Most families were poor but good there, but then bad people move in very quickly."

"What do you mean, bad people?"

"Drug dealer . . . prostitutes . . . gangs. You hear about triads?" I nodded. "Lots of triads in Kowloon Walled City. People say the clouds in the sky were made of opium. Even the rats were high."

"When did they pull it down?"

"The government been planning since 1987 but many residents stay put until '92. They didn't pull down till two years after." He tapped the date on the receipt. "This paper long time before that. Important piece of social history."

My mouth had turned sticky. Maybe we weren't the only family with secrets. What the hell lay in Hei-Fong Lee's past and why was the receipt in my grandmother's apartment? "And you're absolutely sure?" I said. "This refers to *Mr. Lee's* debt?"

"Mr. Lee and also this other man." He ran his finger around a group of characters. "Mr. Zhu Li an, Mi Le."

Part Three

ENDINGS

THIRTY-SIX

Sook-Yin

‗‗‗‗‗‗‗‗‗‗‗‗‗‗‗‗

March 1977

Sook-Yin peeled back the shrinkwrap from the plate and laid the last of her offerings on the table. At the recent half-term fundraiser, her *ma lai go* had been the talk of the school but this Easter she had outdone herself. As well as reprising her famous sponge cake she'd made several trays of coconut rolls, glossy buns with red bean paste, and a sticky tower of yellow sachima.

The vicar, engaged on his walk around the church hall, paused wide-eyed in front of her. "My goodness, Mrs. Miller," he said. "God must have blessed your hands when he created you." He caught a whiff of the tureen at the next stall with its hemic scent of oxtail. "And Mrs. Johnson, you've made stew. Again . . ."

They waited till he was at the tombola before both of them collapsed into giggles. "What an idiot," Sook-Yin said. It had become her favorite word and the one she used without caution whenever she thought now of Julian. *Idiot, idiot, idiot.*

ALTHOUGH IT HAD been four years since her return from Kowloon, the memory and its details had stayed with her; a hallmark she realized now, of both the trauma and the triumph she'd experienced.

Julian had been waiting at the airport for them, his face as pale and lined as a death mask as they emerged through the chaos of Arrivals. "Are you going to leave me?" he'd said and straightaway her nausea had vanished, replaced by a feeling she assumed was relief but which she subsequently learned was power.

"I need to think," she told him.

She'd kept him waiting, too. She never found out for sure what had happened in those awful weeks between his discovery and her return except for what the house in Brixton showed her. There was desperation in its freshly painted walls, in its humble but comfortable furnishings, in the lavish meal he'd prepared for their arrival. None of it was done very well but the effort it revealed spoke volumes to her and Sook-Yin had eventually relented. "Things are going to be different," she said, repeating the promise she'd made on that last day, and he had simply said yes.

But as was often the case with past hurt, the contentment that followed was fragile, shored up as much by Maya and Lily as the unspoken knowledge that the family were alone again. Harvey and Florence had emigrated to Sydney, but after a flurry of postcards and photographs—*we are outside the famous opera house; we are holding koalas at the zoo*—and a handful of long-distance phone calls, they might as well have moved to Antarctica.

The one exception was Hei-Fong, who communicated frequently by letter. He was advancing in importance through the bank; aspirations kept buoyant, he said, by her pledge of not being a martyr.

Unwilling to indulge in defeat, Sook-Yin filled the cracks of self-pity by turning her gaze to their home, filling it with extravagant Asian knickknacks that she found in the corners of antique shops or the touristy job lots in Chinatown: plastic fishermen on the hull of a sampan, a roll of red silk that she fashioned into curtains, water-damaged paintings of willows and dragons that in their contrast seemed to speak to her mood. Sometimes, in her darker moments, she wondered if she was simply creating the illusion of authenticity—like the Vesta spare ribs and "chicken chow-mein" that had crept into the freezers at Bejam with their pictures of slanty-eyed Chinamen. Yes, there were different faces, different colors in Brixton but no one understood *her* experience and Kowloon felt as distant as ever. Still today, as they had at half-term, her cakes were the first to go—ten pence for two this year!—allowing Sook-Yin the rare consolation of having something that people wanted.

MRS. JOHNSON POINTED at the clock as Sook-Yin swept the crumbs from her table. "Don't worry about that," she said. "Don't you have to get back for Julian?"

Sook-Yin had forgotten that he was on nights that week, another thing that she had insisted on and which she suspected had been his hardest compromise—a regular wage from a regular job. She'd lost count of the posts he'd walked out on and had issued an ultimatum: he could have his freedom or his family, but not both. Taking risks was a single man's game, and it was time for him to be responsible.

SHE WAS EATING dinner alone with the girls that night when all the lights in the house went out. At first, Sook-Yin was unbothered. Power cuts had been frequent of late and she had made it into a game, their bodies forming a chain in the darkness as they searched for candles and matches. "Another candlelight meal," she told them, kissing the air with her lips. "Very romantic. Like restaurant."

Maya craned her neck at the window that overlooked the row of back gardens. "Mrs. Johnson has power," she said. She took Lily and opened the back door, letting in the cool evening chill as they went to check the other houses in the street. "Nope . . . Yes . . . Yes!"

Sook-Yin stepped out and called to them. "Come in and I try it over."

She went to the hallway and pressed the light switch—on and then off and then on again. Nothing. "Maya, get torch and take Li-Li to bathroom. Wash your teeth and get into bed."

She took one of the candles from the table and then made her way to the cellar. She found the fuse box and shone the candle's light on it, flicked the red switch backward and forward, but the house remained in darkness. She sighed. They *could* spend the night at Mrs. Johnson's, but it would be better to let the girls go to bed and deal with it in the daylight.

She returned to the kitchen for the second torch in case Julian came home early but when she tried the drawer it was stuck. She wriggled her hand through the opening, felt a mound of paper jammed into the back, and freed it with her fingers. Envelopes. The red lettering was bright in the candle's flame. *Notice, Warning, Final Notice.* They hadn't even been opened.

She sat at the table with them, slitting open the top of each one and pulling out the letters inside. Most were from the London Electricity Board—a flurry of unpaid bills culminating in a threat to cut them off. The rest were from the council: *Rent Due, Rent Late, Final Warning,* but it was the last that made her heart jump. *NOTICE OF INTENTION TO EVICT.*

Sook-Yin fetched the rent book from the cupboard and frantically searched through its pages. Each Sunday she'd given Julian the money but there had been nothing recorded for weeks. Where had it gone?

She turned the candle's glow on the kitchen. The new tiles and cooker glared accusingly at her, as did the dresses for Li-Li and Maya still hanging unworn on the clotheshorse, the shiny black shoes in their Freeman, Hardy and Willis boxes. She'd told Julian they were an extravagance but he'd wanted to see their faces, the thrill of showing his parents should they visit for Sunday lunch.

Idiot, idiot, idiot.

She startled as the telephone rang but couldn't move her body from the table. What if it was more people asking for money? And what would happen if she didn't answer? Would they send bad men to the house with their shaved heads and their fists and their tight boots? She got up and checked the windows and doors, her lizard brain overriding her logic. Sniffed the air for smoke.

"Mumma, do you want me to get that?" Maya's voice floated down from the landing and before Sook-Yin had time to stop her she'd already picked up the extension. "Who do you want to speak to?" she said.

Sook-Yin hurried into the living room and snatched up the other handset. "Maya! Is okay. I have it."

"But who is it, Mumma?" she said, still speaking into the receiver.

"Mei-Hua Miller, put down the telephone!" The handset fell with a dull clang. "Hello?"

"How come you never write back to me?" Sook-Yin ran a hand through her hair. Not a bailiff's call, at least. "Has your husband been hiding my letters?"

The irony was almost too much for her. "I've just been busy," she said. "Are you only ringing to tease me, ah-Fong? It must be one in the morning over there."

He laughed. "I'm phoning so you can't get away from me. What's happened to Mei-Hua, by the way? She sounds so grown-up these days."

"Daniel too, I suppose."

"Going to be eleven pretty soon. Been in the States four years already."

"Yes. I read that in your letters. I suppose ah-Jiao is relieved." She listened through his heavy silence.

"So, what about you? How's Julian?"

"Working nights at the moment."

"Oh. Remind me what he's doing these days?"

"Warehouseman." She said the word in English, not knowing how to translate it. "Factory work."

"Didn't you say that he was a college man?"

She gnawed at the edge of her knuckle. "Yes, but the market is difficult. I'm sure it won't be forever. In fact, now that the girls are older, I might look for a job myself." The idea had only just occurred to her, but now she realized it made perfect sense.

"Who will watch the children?" he said.

"I will ask the neighbors for help. Not everyone can afford a nanny!" It came out harsher than she'd intended and she heard his intake of breath.

"What's going on?" he said.

"Nothing. What do you mean?"

"Come on, ah-Yin. It's me."

Sook-Yin pulled out a chair. She'd never been one to confide her troubles, but given Hei-Fong's knowledge of finance perhaps he could give her some tips. "You won't mention it to ah-Ma?" she said.

"All right, I won't say anything but tell me quickly because you're scaring me."

"I need some advice about money."

"All right . . ."

"I want to make the best of my savings."

"Are you and Julian in trouble?" He paused. "Forgive me, ah-Yin," he said, "but when people have money behind them, they don't usually sound so worried."

Sook-Yin closed her eyes. Alone in the darkness of the living room she might as well have been attending Confession. "We are a little behind on the rent."

"Tell me how much and I'll send it."

"That's not what I'm asking," she said.

"I can't teach a woman to fish if she doesn't have a rod to her name."

She heard the disappointment in his voice. Why couldn't she have kept her mouth shut? "We *do* have a rod, ah-Fong. Everything is going to be fine." She turned her head and shouted at the stair-well. "I have to go," she said. "The children are calling me now. Please send my love to our mothers."

She hung up and put her hands to her face. Maya and Li-Li would probably be asleep by now and her skin burned afresh with the lie, but she couldn't bear his kindness any longer. Or his pity. Whichever it was.

THIRTY-SEVEN

Lily

37th Day of Mourning

There comes a point when you've gone too far; when the road back is longer than what's ahead of you.

Had I been looking in the wrong place all this time? Trying to find the link between Hei-Fong and Mumma, I hadn't even considered a connection to Dad but even then it didn't make sense and this worried me, not only in the obvious way—with the danger and the risks of the Walled City—but in the way I would have to parse the recklessness the gambling suggested with the person I thought I had known. The idea was too ridiculous. Dad wouldn't even ask a policeman for the time or eat pineapple on his pizza. He was a hot-milk-and-in-bed-before-ten man. If he *had* got involved with the Lees it was because he'd been conned in some way, a victim of some elaborate Ponzi scheme or one of those pavement tricks. No. Like I'd first suspected after Maya's subterfuge, it was *us* that had left him with nothing.

TAKE OUR SATURDAYS at the Bon Marché in Brixton: Dad stooping beneath the weight of our desires as we heaped hanger after hanger in his arms. "The heart wants what it wants," he used to say for every pretty dress that we coveted, every pair of shoes that seduced us with no mind as to their use or their consequence. "Can't you see it makes him happy?" Maya said as we sweated and jostled in the changing rooms. We were doing this because we loved him, because it helped his grief to spoil us; a tangled and complex guilt that I'd never quite managed to shake. Like the relationship I now shared with Maya, I lost track of who was helping who, who was hurting who, and this was the way it went.

I RESISTED MY impulse to ask Daniel about it. Aside from insulting him outright, what exactly was I going to accuse him of? He'd been a child himself at the time and it was hardly a detail his dad would have shared with him, especially since he'd been in the States. There was also a chance I was wrong and that the whole thing had been a mistake, a one-off, and nothing to do with anything. I would go carefully. Not overthink things.

THE SKY WAS still dark when I got up. It was too early even for the ferry and in lieu of its usual clatter there was a glassy silence on the harbor.

I went downstairs for a walk, but as I was passing the lobby I caught sight of the piano at the back again. I'd noticed it the day I arrived but hadn't mustered the courage to try it. I glanced at the clock on the wall. Five a.m., and the place was deserted.

I arranged myself on the stool. Under my fingers the keys were warm, the sweet smell of the rosewood comforting. I eased myself in with some scales. Schumann's *Kinderszenen* came to me then: his bittersweet miniatures of childhood at once quirky and plagued with terrors. I segued into a Liszt sonata—a stupidly impressive party piece—and then Rachmaninoff's *Morceaux de Fantaisie*. On and on I went. I played for Maya and Dad and everyone else who had doubted me. I played in apology to Mumma and—

Scott.

His name landed on my tongue unexpectedly, green-lemon sharp with regret as I recalled our last encounter. The pointless cruelty of it. It was only now, with the luxury of distance, that I was forced to confront my behavior; my constant desire, just for once, to be the one who rejected.

I'd call him when I got back.

Life was too bloody short.

A SOUND MADE me turn my head. Sitting at one of the tables was an elderly Chinese woman stirring a pot of tea, the spoon clanking against the china. I pushed back the stool and stood, barely stopping to nod in her direction.

"Thank you, I enjoyed that," she called. I was ambushed by the crispness of her English, which seemed strangely at odds with her age.

"No one was supposed to be listening."

"Yes, I could tell," she said. "Still, I'm always here, so maybe you're the one that's intruding." There was a playfulness about her tone, a half smile playing at her lips. She picked up the pot and shook it at me. "First tea," she said. "You must."

I surprised myself by sitting and noticing the spare cup on the tray, obeyed her gesture to pour for us. "Are you a guest here, too?"

"I've seen you around," she said. "I've been coming to this place for years, so I know when something stands out."

I tilted my head toward the window. "You must have seen some changes, in that case. And more to come, no doubt."

She followed my gaze. "Whenever the winds of change blow, some build walls and some build windmills."

"And which one are you?" I said.

"My future is a thing of the past. It's the young ones you should be asking."

"There's definitely a mood . . . about the Handover."

I'd sensed it on the ferry and the streets, the way conversations would quieten, the nervous gazes toward the construction sites and the mantis-like blight of the yellow cranes that had popped up all over the city. More frequently on my walks, too, there'd been the odd flyer trodden into the pavement mixed in with the adverts for gold or slathered on girders and bins. Cartoon fists. Exclamation marks.

"Handover, return . . . betrayal. I've heard it called all these things."

I leaned towards her. "But that's what I don't understand. Hong Kong was taken by force. It's not as though people had much of a choice, then."

She gave a knowing laugh. "Death is the magic trick of history. Memories can be forgotten."

"So no one sees the stick for the carrot, now?"

She shook her head. "No one thinks Hong Kong is perfect. It's simply a matter of what they're used to. What they have become in the meantime. Look around you," she said. "Even a Kowloon beggar will defend his corner of the pavement. Besides, who can say what China is planning? Exploitation has no nationality."

"You don't seem too afraid."

"As I said, I'm not the person to ask. I have the protection of age and money, and at my last sleep I will dream in Cantonese. Not everyone will be as lucky."

There was something comforting about her presence. I'd always avoided situations like this: being enrolled into random conversations, happenstance meetings. I'd grown to wear it like a badge of pride, preferring to remain composed on the sidelines while others grew careless with their confidences. This had been especially true at university, all those conspiratorial female conversations that, according to my knowledge at least, had always proved unfounded in its shared experience. Now, as I'd done with Mrs. Tam, however, I hadn't thought twice about sitting down, as though being invited to drink tea with a stranger were the most natural thing in the world. Was I changing or was I belonging? Or was it simply that she was irresistible?

"Your English is amazing," I said. "I hope that doesn't sound patronizing."

"I learned it after my husband died. The younger members of my family all spoke it, and being alone can make you vulnerable. It helps to know when people are talking about you."

I laughed. "I know how that feels . . ."

"Are you here to play a concert?" she said.

"No. Nothing like that. I suppose I came to prove something to myself. Find some peace." I took a mouthful of tea. "It's not really worked out that way, though. Perhaps I should've gone to India like everyone else."

Partly to avoid her quizzical stare, I diverted my gaze to the chain around her neck. There was something magical about it: a gold cameo of a bird in flight encased in a bed of blue agate, quite different to the jade I'd seen. "I love your necklace," I said.

"Yes, I saw you looking at it. Much to my family's frustration, it's the only thing I wear these days. They have given up buying me jewelry."

"I'm not surprised. It's gorgeous."

"I'm glad you like it," she said. She stretched out her legs with a yawn. "Well, I'd better be going. They say a storm is coming."

"Bad luck for the fireworks, I guess."

"Bad luck for everyone," she said.

I stood and offered my arm and she took it and heaved herself up, even though she was as light as a cherry blossom. "It was lovely to meet you."

"I'm sure I'll see you again."

"I'll be on a plane back to London soon."

She nodded. "In that case, I'm glad I heard you." She patted me on the arm. "You play with pain," she said. "Make sure you look after your heart."

THIRTY-EIGHT

Sook-Yin

April 1977

O ver the next three weeks, Sook-Yin applied for twelve jobs without success. She trawled the shops and offices, sat at the kitchen table and replied to adverts as *Mrs. S. Miller* in the back of the *Evening Standard*, her hand faltering and cramping with effort. Getting an interview had not been a problem but as soon as they saw her face they told her the position had gone. She knew that this was a lie. She had seen the other women in the waiting room, blond and maxi-skirted with their neat manicures and Afghan coats. Their creamy skin.

The economy is in a slump.

It's that Jim Callaghan fiddling the books.

English jobs for English people.

"I fed up," she said to Julian after another wasted bus fare, another blister on the skin of her heel from wearing the cheap, smart shoes too tight for her. "Nobody want me here."

Julian, who was cuddling with Lily on the sofa, laughing at a children's TV program, looked over. "Something will come up. I know it. They simply haven't realized your brilliance yet."

"I should have stay in Kowloon."

He frowned. "But how on earth would I have met you, then? My life would have been thoroughly miserable."

"I mean that time I went back. I had the chance of a good job."

"Oh yes? Doing what, exactly?"

"A friend of my brother, Hei-Fong. He work in big Hong Kong bank now."

"A job in a bank?" Julian moved Lily onto the sofa. "Do you think he'd take you now?"

"What is the point of thinking that now? Now we stuck in London."

"But what if we all moved abroad? It worked for Florence and Harvey, and you keep saying I've never met your family. I could apply for a working visa ... I could ... I could ... I could ..."

His mouth was moving faster than his brain, the nervous twitch of excitement in his fingers and his rapidly blinking eyes, the same way as with the shop all those years ago. "And how we get there, Julian? What we do with house?"

"It's only money," he said.

Sook-Yin clenched her fists. The day after discovering the red bills she'd woken early and taken most of her savings in order to pay off the arrears, as well as a month in advance on the rent. She'd done these things in secret, desperate to stem the tide of her fears, but now her frustration spilled over. "Is that why we get letters?" she said. "Electric cut off light? Landlord try evict us?" She stomped to the cabinet and pulled out the paperwork. "Here! Red letter ... red letter ... final notice of turf out."

Julian's eyelids flickered. "Nobody pays their bills on time."

"*I* pay them to keep roof over head. In Hong Kong you go to prison!"

"Thank God we've been living in England, then." It took him a moment to absorb what she'd said. "What do you mean you paid them? Where did you get the money?"

Now she'd done it. Sook-Yin twisted the letters in her hand. "I been saving some of the housekeeping. Put away for rainy day." She folded her arms. "Isn't it just as well? If you use wages properly, I don't have to worry worry."

"My wages? Good luck with that." He waved his hand at the room. "You reckon this is a cheap place to live? I got it to make you happy, but we barely break even, Sook-Yin. Still, you sit back and enjoy the benefits and don't worry yourself about *that*."

Sook-Yin gazed at the carpet. He was right, she should have kept an eye on things, especially after the insurance with the shop. Even so, she hadn't asked for the luxuries. That was all on Julian. "So why you spend spend spend? Buy me new cooker for kitchen? Buy new shoes for Maya and Li-Li?"

"Because Maya needed new shoes. And you can't treat one and not the other."

"But that is nonsense," she said. "When I grow up, I wear my brother's shoes."

Julian turned back to the TV, the gesture putting an end to the matter. "Yes, so you keep saying, Sook-Yin, but we're not in the war now, dear. There's no need to keep punishing yourself."

AFTER SHE'D PUT the girls to bed that night, read them stories of princesses and happy endings, she sat down at the table and wept. Unlike Julian, with his head in the clouds, she'd had to contend with the truth of the world, find a path where none had existed. And that was the problem: she knew the precise moment she'd allowed things to go wrong. Standing on that ship in the harbor. How would her life have turned out if she had stood her ground with ah-Chor? It felt indulgent and cruel to think about, for she loved Maya and Li-Li like her own breath but she couldn't help thinking of what may have existed. Another life with someone else. Now Kowloon was back in her head and her perpetual longing curdled to a cruel taunt. There was nothing to be done.

Unless . . .

Afraid she would change her mind, she ran and picked up the telephone. "It's me," she said when he answered. "Yes, I'm fine, but forget that. I need to ask if I can trust you."

THIRTY-NINE

Lily

―――――――――
―――――――――

37th Day of Mourning

I'd been so focused on finding out about Mumma that I hadn't dwelt on the nuances of the Handover. I still wasn't sure what I thought of it. Being English—whatever that meant—I'd been schooled in the language of imperialism: red swathes on a classroom map, scratchy films about the dangers of "others"; entrenched but awful assumptions. If Hong Kong had been exposed to the same, encouraged to believe in its separateness, was it any surprise that it was nervous? Had the British made the city what it was or simply created a monster in their likeness, meddling with the genetics of the place until it no longer resembled one thing or the other?

MY CARD HAD finally arrived from the bank. I'd planned on visiting Uncle Chor again but it was still too early to call on him, so I decided to visit Victoria Peak. It would make a change to use my own money, to feel the independence I'd intended when I first arrived, plus I'd hardly explored the city. If the Shenzhen border was ever removed, I might never know the before for the after.

The tram was already sweaty with tourists migrating like a herd to the summit, and by the time we arrived at the top I'd had enough of the long lenses and baseball caps and turned back toward Findlay Road and the quieter Lion's Pavilion.

Even on a day like this—the sun pale and ungenerous in its haze—the view from the pagoda was incredible. Looking out from its ancient balconies, the V of the landing was like the hands of a giant holding the city within its embrace, the distant mountains majestic in their warning that for all the man-made razzmatazz we would never be more than tenants.

I leaned forward and peered over the balustrade where the sides of the cliff fell away to a dizzying perpendicular drop. Forget your gas towers, bridges, and shopping malls, this was the place to make your point: the last five hundred meters to glory, and all of it was beautiful.

"Lady, take photograph, please?"

A young man held his camera toward me and then arranged himself against the balcony. I lifted the viewer to my eye and zoomed in on the details of his chubby face, speckled with its dander of bum fluff.

Aside from the photo that Daniel had given me, I'd never seen pictures of us in Hong Kong. Not many in London, come to think of it. Christmases and birthdays perhaps, Maya always center of the frame, me losing a hand or a shoe. Half a face.

I pressed the shutter button and was about to hand back the camera when I changed my mind. "Hold on! Another one!" I said. "This time look out at the scenery." He smiled and gave me the thumbs-up and when he turned, I took the photo. I imagined him getting them back from the pharmacy and flicking through them with hurried fingers, searching for the ones to impress his friends with. *I was in Hong Kong.* And then he would come to mine—my frowning, windblown face—and his brows would knit in confusion. *What the hell?* he'd say. And then he would remember me.

I was coming back down on the tram when I got a call from the

Kowloon library to say that the information I'd requested was ready. Even after the shock of my last visit, it was important to know what they'd found. Uncle Chor would have to wait.

"OH, HI! YOU CAME," the man said, when I presented myself at the desk. "You almost like local now." I followed him again to the back and he pointed to the last vacant machine. "Sit down, please. I bring your stuff over."

It took him a while to return, his complexion freshly sheened and harried. "Excuse," he said. "Still so busy here. How is research going on?"

"Not great, to tell you the truth." I nodded to his box. "But I see you managed to find something."

"Only little little," he said. He laid one of the sheets on the glass. "I search for the date you give me but there was nothing in the main Hong Kong newspaper. Until, one day later is this . . ."

He focused on a page of what looked like a local rag and scrolled to a tiny paragraph. "Minor story," he said. He squinted as he translated. "*Woman killed in accident, October 13, 1977. Collision happen near Nathan Road, which was temporarily close to traffic. Victim, age thirty-three years, worked as teller at Dah Sing Bank.*" He sat back. "That about all I find."

"They didn't name the victim?"

"No, but this is not unusual. Many accidents happen in Kowloon. Journalists only report."

There was something soulless about it: a life reduced to three lines of print. Eerie, too, that it had happened near Nathan Road, so close to Chungking Mansions. If this story really *was* about Mumma, I'd probably walked right past the spot. My throat tightened. "This Dah Sing Bank," I said. "Does it still exist in Kowloon?"

He laughed. "It is one of the biggest. Many branches all over the city." He tapped his head. "Remember you ask about Hei-Fong Lee?"

"Yes?"

"Funny coincidence," he said. "Dah Sing is where he first made his money."

He removed the film from the plate and replaced it with a second one. "One more thing I find for your friend. An article with the date you give me. This from *Oriental Daily News*. October Obituary section: "*In loving memory of Chen Sook-Yin, February 24, 1944–October 13, 1977. Beloved mother and daughter. Survived by daughters Mei-Hua and Li-Li Chen. Forever in our heart.*" He turned to me. "Lady is thirty-three, also. Same age and date as accident, so I think it must be same one."

I pinched my fingers together. Mumma's name. *Our* names. This Dah Sing Bank had to be the connection.

"Still, there is something quite interesting." He leaned forward, his expression animated. "At first, it look like normal obituary . . ."

"Except there's no mention of a husband?"

"No. That's not what I mean." He zoomed further into the paragraph and pointed to a group of characters. "This phrase unusual," he said. "Not regular word for 'die.' Is more . . ." He struggled to find the translation. "What you call it? Emphatic?"

I frowned. "Specific, maybe?"

"Yes, *exactly*! Specific." He repeated it under his breath, enjoying the relief of its sound.

"How do you mean?" I said.

"This word . . ." He scratched his head. "This word is more like *sacrifice*."

FORTY

Sook-Yin

May 1977

S ook-Yin cradled the contents of the envelope: four one-way tickets to Kowloon, along with a receipt from Dah Sing Bank showing a generous transfer in her name. It wasn't the circus but it was
still an escape, and came from the one person who had never forgotten her. She had struggled to say the words on the telephone—*I'll pay
you back as soon as I can. I promise, ah-Fong, I promise*—but he had only
answered with one of his own:

Come.

He had repeated the offer of a job with him, and after they visited Maya's school even her headmaster had seemed amenable. "The
experience will be wonderful," he said. "She's already way ahead of
her classmates and she'll only miss a few months."

It was going to be six months, in fact, including the summer
holidays. Six months to prove to her family that she deserved to be
among them again.

She was still unsure how Julian would cope, with his funny pal-
ate and his "dicky tummy" and his *never been farther than Scotland*. She
pictured him walking like the po-pos with their parasols, seeking
refuge from the noonday sun among the lobsters and red bean ices,

and the image of it made her laugh, a moment of relief amid the worry. Still, there were limits to what a person was capable of and she couldn't speak for Julian. His impetus was so different from her own when she'd first arrived in London. For him, it was a vacation rather than an exile, a clean slate to make his mark on the world if he decided it was what he wanted, and if not, he was free to return. She knew it was only herself, now heavy with the burden of the loan as well as the weight of her family's expectations, who understood the fallacy of choice.

o o o o o o

When their plane touched down in Kowloon it was one in the afternoon and the May sun was already punishing. The air shimmered on the tarmac at Kai Tak, giving it the illusion of being studded with precious jewels rather than the oil and dirt that was there. As Sook-Yin descended the steps with the children she was reminded of an image from her school days: of holding some rock in geography or science, seduced by its beauty. *Fool's gold*, Sister Catherine had told her. It was amazing what the head remembered.

The journey had taught her something else, too: Julian was not a resilient person. At Heathrow he'd been buoyant with excitement, conspicuous in his brand-new suit as he strode through the gate at Departures flashing his British passport. The plane had been a different story. He'd spent the whole flight fearful and restless, whimpering and gripping her shoulder at the slightest bump of turbulence, refusing any food he didn't recognize, vomiting at the nearness of the rooftops on the approach to the island runway. It was like she'd adopted a third child, and by the time the engines had stopped she felt like she wanted to strangle him.

Ah-Chor had said he would meet them at arrivals, but when they finally negotiated customs and located their luggage at the fight for the carousel, it was Hei-Fong who waited at the barriers. He swept her up in a bear hug and ruffled the children's hair before he stretched out his hand to Julian. "The climate is different here," he told him as he wiped Julian's sweat from his grasp. "I hope you'll be able to get used to it."

Sook-Yin gazed around the terminal. "My brother couldn't make it?" she said.

Hei-Fong took hold of her case. "My sedan is better for baggage. Everyone's waiting at the house."

IN THE AIR-CONDITIONED luxury of the car, Julian swiftly recovered. Sook-Yin noted the unfurling of his back, the jut of his chin as he gazed out the windows at the sticky shirts of men on bicycles and the women fanning themselves at bus stops. She could hear the soundtrack playing in his head of all the songs he sang along to in London: Frank Sinatra, Elvis Presley, Perry Como. A king looking out at the insignificance of others.

The one thing she hadn't anticipated was his reaction when they arrived at the apartment. His lips drooped at the peeling paintwork, at the mold that embraced the windows and the slop from the market in the gutters. What else had he expected? His own parents' home was hardly a palace!

As soon as they went upstairs, however, he hurried to greet ah-Ma and her brother, his voice transformed to a cheerful crescendo in the knowledge of others' attention. Her mother stood at the margins, listening with a passive expression as Sook-Yin translated. *She is trying to gauge his measure. The reality of our marriage.* Once the introductions were finished, ah-Ma furnished the children with sweets and sent them to play on the balcony. "Big people must talking," she said.

It wasn't long before ah-Chor descended. "So what do you think of Hong Kong, Mr. Miller?" Sook-Yin clicked her tongue. Not even a chance to relax! "First impression?" he said.

Julian, half-draped on the sofa, crossed his legs. "My first impression is you should call me Julian. My second is that your city is exquisite."

"I have to tell you," said ah-Chor, "we were pretty surprised when we heard you were coming."

"But I've always wanted to visit Hong Kong."

"So you are here for a holiday, after all? Only, I heard that you'd applied for a work visa."

Sook-Yin glanced between ah-Ma and Hei-Fong. She had told them this in confidence on the understanding that nothing was decided. Which one of them had told her brother?

"Yes, I applied for a visa," said Julian. "No harm in expanding our horizons."

Ah-Chor pushed out his lips. "That's very brave when it's at your expense. To come to a different culture, I mean."

"'Think like a winner.' That's my motto. Plus, Sook-Yin was homesick, and a man is only as happy as his family."

"On that we agree, Mr. Miller." A light sweat had broken out on her brother's brow and he took out a pristine handkerchief and wiped his face and then his ears with slow, deliberate movements. "Hei-Fong tells me that you are a college man."

"English. Durham University."

"That is very impressive, I must say. I take it you have your certificates?"

Sook-Yin narrowed her eyes. In spite of the years she'd spent away from him, she knew her brother too well. He used words the way hunters used traps, hiding them beneath flowers and sweet grass, waiting for smaller animals to break their necks. *Ah-ma, you are such a clever woman. Why are you letting Sook-Yin take advantage of you? She's a no-good spinster in waiting.* "Is this an interview or something?" she said.

Ah-Chor raised his hand to silence her. "Please forgive all the questions, Mr. Miller. It's just that I know of some older students in need of a private tutor, and when I learned you were looking for work I thought it might be of interest. It would be a trial at first, until we checked your credentials."

Julian could hardly speak for the smile on his face. "I didn't imagine things would happen so fast, but I can send for my papers straightaway." He leaned over and squeezed Sook-Yin's knee. "What did I tell you?" he said.

"That is excellent news," said ah-Chor. "I will make inquiries at once."

Hei-Fong suddenly stood, his seat scraping against the linoleum. "I'm afraid you must all excuse me. I have a meeting of my own to get to." He leaned over and shook Julian's hand. "I'm sure I will see you again."

Sook-Yin watched him leave. It may have been a trick of the light, but as he let himself out of the apartment she could've sworn that he was frowning.

LATER, AS THEY lay in her old room, the children sleeping on the floor beside them, she revisited the conversation. Julian's jet lag had already defeated him and he'd been dozing on and off in the scorching heat since ah-Chor had left that evening. She sighed and his eyes slid open. "What are you thinking about?"

"I thought you asleep," she said.

"I'm trying but your head is too noisy."

Sook-Yin turned to him. "Be careful of my brother," she said. "Be careful of whatever he offer you."

"Why do you say that? He seemed perfectly friendly to me."

"Yes, but he not always nice person." She propped herself up on her elbow. "I tell you story," she said. "When I little, I get very sick and doctor tell me to take ah-Chor's urine. Every day he piss in a bottle and laugh as he watch me drink it. When I get better, he say to me, 'I save you. Your life is mine now.' So."

Julian frowned. "How old were you when this happened?"

"Six, or maybe seven."

"You must be remembering it wrong."

"No! Ah-Ma corroborate. This why I don't trust ah-Chor. He never want me around. It was his wish to send me to England."

Julian gave a cynical laugh. "Children say things like that all the time. Look at Maya. She loves to shock people. I bet if you asked him, he wouldn't even remember it."

Sook-Yin leaned back against the pillow. "Why you need ah-Chor's job when I can work for Hei-Fong? This is what we agreed."

"Ah, so *that's* what it's really about . . ."

"No! I only telling about ah-Chor."

On the surface, this had been her intention. But the more Sook-Yin considered it, the more she realized what a tangle she was in. For one thing, Julian had no idea about the loan. When he'd asked her about the money, she told him she'd sold some jewelry that ah-Ma had given her when she'd first come to London. How could she even begin to pay it back if she wasn't earning a wage of her own? But yes, he was right on the second count. After all the years raising the children she'd been looking forward to a job of a different kind. "Hei-Fong's bank will pay better money."

"Yes. I'm quite sure about that." Julian rearranged the pillow with his fist: *pap pap pap.* "You might have told me he was half in love with you."

Sook-Yin stared at him. "Why you talk such nonsense?"

"I saw it in his face at the airport. It was quite clear he wished that I hadn't come."

She felt her face redden in the darkness. "Hei-Fong old friend from school days. Plus, he marry with child."

"Since when did *that* stop anyone?"

Sook-Yin gave a dry, bitter laugh. "That is first true thing you say."

That stopped him. He reached for her hand and squeezed it. "Didn't I explain how sorry I was? How sorry I was for everything?"

She pulled away. "We not talk about this again. Now is new start, okay?"

He nodded. "Yes, all right. But it needs to be a new start for everyone. Your poor old brother included."

"All right, I promise I try."

"Good girl, and remember, I love you."

He turned over and within a few minutes his breathing deepened to its habitual snore. Sook-Yin stared up at the fan as it spun beneath the cracks in the ceiling. She hadn't lied about doing her best, but Julian was being naive. He'd only lived one life, after all, while she had already lived so many.

FORTY-ONE

Lily

37th Day of Mourning

Sacrifice

/ˈsakrɪfʌɪs/

noun

1. an act of slaughtering an animal or person, or
   surrendering a possession as an offering to a deity.

verb

2. to give up (something valued) for the sake of other
   considerations.

I returned the dictionary to the shelf in my room. Seeing the words in black and white—the seeming gulf between the definitions— hadn't made things any clearer. Maybe the man had been mistaken, or perhaps "sacrifice" was some kind of idiom. An interpretation. Poetic license.

I knew it wasn't something particular to the Chinese. History and politics had taught me that. Death brought a universal desire for a certain truth: *beloved father*, *dedicated daughter*, the sanitized epitaphs we hung out as their legacy rather than the disheveled laundry of their lives. Nor was it purely for their sakes either, but in hope of all the things we'd inherit. The progeny of heroes.

I'd been thinking about that a lot lately. That night at the restaurant with Daniel, I wasn't entirely honest about Dad. Most people knew it was a fallacy, anyway—the notion that parents love you unconditionally. It was more an unspoken principle, like eating healthily or trying not to smoke, turning our shameful impulses inward until they became an emotional weapon: the eye roll when they thought you weren't looking—*pow*, *thwack*; the too-loud sigh once you'd left the room—*bam*, *kerblam*. That was the other truth about Dad, and each gesture, intended or not, had found its target in me, as though my physical likeness to Mumma had been a constant reminder not just of his grief but his own self-loathing for failing to save her.

A few months after he'd gutted the Brixton house it was reborn in an absence of color; the drenching of its walls and furniture in a flaccid palette of beige and cream whose dunness only lent it more profundity. Please paint it, we wanted to say, paint it blue or orange or green. Just paint it and start being our dad again.

He always claimed it made things easier but as I got older I began to suspect that the ease of which he spoke was more a fear of disappointing us. The indulgent shopping trips were part of this evidence but there were other proofs too: the way he would defer on a Sunday morning to our choice of film at the ABC cinema as well as where we should go to eat afterward, as though relieved in some secret knowledge that we would have no one to blame but ourselves.

If *like father, like daughter* is true, then my own retreat had been forecast in a similar but opposite way through my small, petty acts of rebellion: the black-painted walls of my bedroom, which Dad tolerated by pretending to ignore them but which by my first return from Cambridge had been covered with more magnolia.

The job, like my act, was half-hearted—apologetic almost, so that lying at night in bed I could see the brush marks of the dark paint beneath, excavating its flakes with my fingernail in some piss-poor attempt to stir him. After my final fall from grace, when I finally returned home from the hospital, my vandalism transmuted to a sort of mocking. I had tried my worst and failed. I resorted to sleeping facing the window, until surrendering myself to the blackness I, too, lost the will to make any decision, even that of staying alive.

o o o o o o

Exhausted by the events of the day, I fell into a thin, unrefreshing sleep. As had often been the case of late it was haunted by dreams of Mumma, of ghost girls that floated in the ether and dragons that leaped from lotus ponds while a clock tolled, dirgelike, in the distance. When I jerked awake, the telephone was ringing.

"I'm sorry to disturb, Miss Miller." It was one of the receptionists from the front desk. "We have an urgent call to put through to you."

I sat up and without thinking said yes. It was only in the pause that followed that I panicked. Who would be calling at this hour? What if Maya had tracked me down? Found out about the trip from Nesbit?

"Hello? Li-Li? Are you there?"

I swung my legs off the bed. "Feng Mian—is that you?" I said.

"Yes. I need your help."

"What's happened?" I strained to hear what she was saying but only caught the end of a word—*vong* or *pong* or something—blurred by the sound of traffic. "Slow down, you're not making any sense.'

"Friends . . . we met up . . . separated. No purse . . . Everyone's split."

"All right, I get it," I said. "Do you want me to call Uncle Chor?"

"No!" The panic came back into her voice. "He's gone away for the night. I told him ... studying ... friend's house."

Jesus.

"Hang on," I said. I scrambled around for the lamp switch and then grabbed a pen. "Tell me the name of the place again."

"Mong Kok. It's about fifteen minutes from Tsim Sha Tsui. Take a red taxi toward the night market. I'll be outside the McDonald's on Argyle Street."

FORTY-TWO

Sook-Yin

June 1977

I n England, they call it a cram school."

Julian adjusted his collar in the mirror while Sook-Yin sat on the edge of their bed, flicking through his book of poetry. She ran her finger along the rows of bookmarks that stuck out from the edges of the pages, tried to read the verses that they marked out. *Thee*, and *thou* and *thine.* Why were there so many words for the same thing? And what sort of name was Bysshe? Like the sound of someone dropping something.

"Help me with this, would you?"

She put the book down and stood, making sure his top button was done up and the knot in his tie was straight. She had not seen this shirt before—white with purple spots on it. Ugly.

"How do I look?" he said.

"Why you always dress so hot? In summer, Hong Kong metro like furnace."

"Yes, but do I look *good*?" He frowned at her reflection. "You're not even looking, Sook-Yin."

She gave him a cursory glance. "Yes. Very handsome," she said.

Julian sighed. "I know you're still sulking," he said. "But we talked about this, didn't we? Someone has to stay home with the children."

Home. A month into his silly teaching job and he thought he was a local already. There was a new lightness to his voice, the loss of his stoop that made him look taller.

"Even ah-Ma agrees with me."

Was it any wonder, she thought? Each time he got his wages he'd make a big show about paying their rent—"This is for *you*, ah-Ma, in return for letting us stay here'—and Sook-Yin's fingers would tingle. She had yet to make a payment to Hei-Fong but she couldn't very well explain that.

She folded her arms. "You do not call her ah-Ma. In Cantonese you call her *ngoi mou*. The mother of your wife."

Julian laid a kiss like an egg on her forehead. *Plop.* "Have a great day," he said.

"HE'S DOING HIS BEST," said ah-Ma as they shelled peas with the children in the living room. "And your brother has done a great favor to him. Have you seen all the letters he's received?"

Sook-Yin chewed her lip. Yes, she had seen the letters—he had practically made a display of them, laying them out on the sideboard so she would find them when she returned from shopping: *Mr. Miller has turned Wei-Wei's life around! At last we can see a future! What a talented, kindhearted man!* Sook-Yin had nodded and smiled at them, patted his arm in encouragement while wondering if his head would still fit through the door. What would the parents say if they had seen his scattered laundry, smelled what he left in the bathroom? And the gifts! Good God, the gifts! The children had never seen so much chocolate.

She wrenched at the seam of a pea pod. "Ah-Chor has changed his song."

Her mother tssked. "You were always like this as a child. Always waiting to get him into trouble. You and that naughty Hei-Fong."

Sook-Yin put down the bowl and gaped at her. "It was the other way around if you remember. You used to criticize him yourself in your letters. '*Ah-Chor is so bossy and secretive.*'" And where *was* Hei-Fong, for that matter? She hadn't seen him since the day they'd arrived. In fact, he seemed to have forgotten her.

SHE WENT OUT onto the balcony, the concrete burning through the soles of her sandals and the heat lighting the fuse of her temper. She knew that being angry at her mother was easy, the path of least resistance compared with the complexity of feeling she deserved but which was too painful for Sook-Yin to contemplate. The truth was she resented ah-Ma's docility at times, her lack of fight; the way she continued to wear the mantle of her history—the ruin of Kowloon and her marriage—in her bent back, her deliberately ruined hands, not because she didn't want to forget but because she was afraid that she might. She would often see her mother's surprise, the way that she looked at Sook-Yin as if to say *Who brought you up? I didn't teach you to expect so much from life.* And maybe it was true: maybe it was only since being away that Sook-Yin had started to want something different, something better; to question the judgment of others.

So why couldn't she be happier for Julian? Back when they were in London, it was the thing she'd wanted most from him—to be steady and own up to his mistakes. There was little doubt he had found his vocation, and deep down she really *was* proud of him, so was it more frustration at her own quiescence or the fact that she no longer felt superior? The idea of this meanness stung her almost as much as her alienation. Even her husband was more at home here, as though in the time she'd been away—both too visible and invisible at the same time—she'd talked herself out of belonging anywhere.

FORTY-THREE

Lily

38th Day of Mourning

It was after midnight when I arrived in Mong Kok. Despite the lateness of the hour, it was even busier than Nathan Road, its bulging pavements replete with nightclubs and the spill of late-night eateries lit by the orbs of the market.

This time there was no mistaking Feng Mian. She was dressed in her weird kawaii shit, one foot propped against the glass of McDonald's in the confident assurance of her rescue.

The taxi pulled over and she climbed in, barking her address at the driver as she slouched into the seat beside me. "Nothing to say?" I asked, as we headed southward into the traffic. She reeked of beer and cigarettes.

"*Thank you?*" She pulled a wet wipe and mirror from her rucksack and made aggressive jabs at her makeup. It had begun to spoil in the heat and there were black circles around her eyes, her lips smeared in a Joker-esque frown.

"You know what I mean," I said. "Uncle Chor goes away for one night and you bunk off and go to some nightclub? What are you, even—thirteen?"

She glared at me over her mirror. "I'm almost sixteen, actually. And do you think I'm such a cliché?"

"*All* teenagers are clichés," I said.

She scrubbed at the corner of her mouth, playing for time. "It's the only place we can meet."

"You and your boyfriend, you mean?" She looked up, her expression a question mark. Too late to take it back. "I saw your note at Lockhart Road. I shouldn't have looked. I'm sorry."

She'd cleaned only half of her face and it gave her the ghoulish appearance of something temporary, midway through the throes of transition. She leaned over to the driver's partition and slid it closed. "Were you able to read it?"

"No. It was just . . . the *thing* at the end."

"I don't have a boyfriend," she said.

I shrugged. "It's none of my business." I couldn't afford to get involved in her antics. I was running out of time as it was. "And don't worry about looking for those other things. I'll talk to Uncle Chor myself. There's no need for you to get into trouble."

"Like that won't happen sooner or later . . ."

"I'm not going to rat you out . . . I never did to my sister."

"Yeah. I do believe that." She scrunched the wet wipe between her fingers. "I was at a meeting tonight. About the first of July."

"The first? As in the Handover?" I turned my body to look at her.

"We call it group action," she said. "I've been part of it for a year now. We always used to meet at the bookstore before some of the guys got busted."

"What do you mean? Busted for what?"

She made little air quotes with her fingers. "Inciting unauthorized assembly. Crimes of civil disobedience. Whatever the police can make up. That's why we moved to the clubs. So people would assume we were idiot kids."

I caught her pointed look. "What are you up to?" I said.

"We're planning to have a protest. Demonstrations have always been legal here but now Beijing is getting pretty nervous. We can only use the bookshop for messages and we always write them in code."

I made the mistake of rolling my eyes. "Well, that's all right, then."

She bristled. "Don't you care about democracy?" she said. "Once China has its claws into Hong Kong, it doesn't have to promise us anything, Basic Law or not. What does *One Country, Two Systems* even mean?"

My hands fluttered against my lap. "All right, I get it," I said. "But you won't be doing anything if you get arrested for underage drinking. And I'm sure Uncle Chor would love that."

"Can't you see that's the point?" she said. "It would be exactly what he'd expect. Not to mention what he'd prefer. A naughty girl he can take. A dangerous one scares the life from him."

Hell-raiser. I shook Mumma out of my head. "Look, I know Uncle Chor can be annoying, but I'm sure he understands how important debate is."

She laughed. "You really *don't* know him, do you? He wears the mask that suits him. Do you know what my sister told me? She heard that during the Cultural Revolution, when the Red Guards were hanging the intellectuals, he pretended that he was a fisherman. Why else do you think my parents trust him? If he found out about the rallies I'd be straight back on a plane to Beijing."

"Would that really be so bad?"

"Now I *know* you're related to Chor-Kit . . ." She didn't intend it as a compliment. "This is about our rights as Hong Kong people. Freedom of speech. Our own language. Not immediately saying 'how high?' when China tells us to jump." She frowned at me. "You of all people should understand that."

I rubbed at my temple. "So, what exactly happened tonight? How did you and the others get separated?"

"Someone must have sent their soldiers to spy on us. I don't mean police or anything—I mean some guys listening in at our table, pretending to spill drinks, that sort of thing."

"But didn't you say it yourself? People protest all the time."

"This isn't *London*," she said. "Remember Tiananmen Square?" *We must be visible, Lily. We have to fight the good fight.*

"Then what happened?"

"One of them started an argument. Said we were traitors to China, and when things got heated, we decided to split up. It was only later I found my purse missing."

I had a flashback to Chungking Mansions. "Maybe they were hustling for money."

"Either way, it doesn't matter. My ID was inside my purse."

"Shit." I leaned my head against the window. I hadn't signed up for *this*. "So why call *me*?" I said. "Why tell me all of this stuff when you could've called a friend?"

"You came and got me, didn't you?" I raised an eyebrow at her. "Because you seem okay? Because you haven't taken Hei-Fong Lee's money?"

I laughed. "I still might," I said. "I've got eleven days to sign the papers."

"If you were that sure, you'd have done it already." She gave me a triumphant look. "But you're still worried about what it might cost you."

FORTY-FOUR

Sook-Yin

July 1977

It was now ten weeks since they'd arrived in Kowloon, but aside from the views and the heat Sook-Yin might as well have been in London. Her intentions in coming back—to prove her worth to her family—had been smothered as much as they'd always been beneath the yoke of cooking and cleaning. Even ah-Ma's job at the factory mocked her.

She was making dinner when Julian returned that evening. "Don't bother about anything for me," he said. "I'm going out tonight." She had already started to dish up, the rice suspended on a spoon above the pot.

"What you mean?" she said.

The doorbell went before he could answer, but when she heard Hei-Fong's voice in the living room, she tipped the rice back and hurried out.

"How are you, ah-Yin?" he said.

She was too flustered to answer at first. "What are you doing here?" she said then.

Hei-Fong looked at the floor, his mouth set in a mutinous line.

"Boys' night," he said in English. "I heard your husband needs cheering up."

She sensed something distant about his tone. Hoped it was embarrassment. "It's the first I've heard of it," she said. "Is this going to be a regular thing?"

"I don't think so," Hei-Fong said. "But don't worry, I'll take good care of him."

SHE LAY AWAKE until two in the morning, her mind a boiling soup of confusion. She'd assumed Hei-Fong had been busy—couldn't count the excuses she had made for him—but had he been on the scene all this time? And had Julian been gossiping about her? She had heard it in his evening sighs—the signal of his suffering patience with her. He must've known this would hurt her the most.

When his space was still empty in the morning, however, she rose in a panic and went into the living room. Julian was asleep where he'd fallen on the sofa, the air thick with the sourness of alcohol and his trousers around his ankles. Her fists ground in little circles on her hips. She wanted to hit him with a saucepan! Instead, she roused and dressed the children, shushing their outraged laughter as they tiptoed out of the apartment.

Mrs. Chee was at the lobby window reading one of her gossip magazines. "Where are you off to so early?"

"Going for a walk to the market."

"In that case, I might tag along," she said. "The desk is never busy at this time."

SOOK-YIN LINGERED FOR as long as she could, squeezing the fruit and examining the vegetables at every stall they came to. "You must be making something special," said Mrs. Chee.

"Something like that." She stopped at the *lung so tong* stand, watching in amazement with Maya and Li-Li as the man crafted the strings

of hot sugar. She had done the same as a child, anticipating its fizz
on her tongue, its crackle and softness together. She erased Hei-Fong
from the memory. "Dragon's beard," she said, taking a long skein
from the man and hanging its strands from her chin. "All girls should
learn to be dragons." Mrs. Chee covered her face in embarrassment.
"Aiya, juk sai!" she said.

Sook-Yin turned and squinted at the storefronts. "Where is the
Army and Navy store? I wanted to pop in on Siu Je and ask her to
make me a dress."

"Siu Je? That poor woman died four years ago! This is where
she was. Remember?"

She pointed to a herbalist's practice and Sook-Yin stared at the
ledge above the doorway, trying to picture the old wooden sign.
She'd never gotten around to sending those photographs.

Mrs. Chee rubbed at her shins. "My legs are so tired, ah-Yin. We
must have gone ten times around the market."

Sook-Yin glanced at her watch. They'd been out for almost two
hours, long enough for Julian to wake up and panic about where
they'd gone. "Yes. We can go back now," she said.

They'd just crossed Hing Wah Road when an old woman
stopped them on the pavement, distracted by the sight of Maya. She
reached out and touched her golden hair. "Ho leng, ho leng," she
said.

Sook-Yin turned and smiled at the children. "This lady thinks
you are beautiful." Maya puffed out her chest.

"I think she was talking to me."

The woman nodded in confirmation. "Your employer's daughter?" she said.

"No. She is my daughter."

The woman frowned and pointed at Lily. "And this one?"

"Yes. The two. They are sisters." Sook-Yin realized the misunderstanding. "Their father is English," she said.

Mrs. Chee pulled at her arm. "Come on, ah-Yin," she said. "I
have seen her face before. That is not a friendly person."

Sook-Yin did not understand until the old woman stepped forward and spat at her. "Banana!" she shouted in her face. "Only yellow on the outside. You should be ashamed of yourself."

Sook-Yin looked down in shock at the sticky green phlegm on her sandals, her breathing erratic and rapid.

Banana.

Too yellow for the men in England and now too white for the people at home. Is that what it was? Her fists clenched, her feet driven to follow the woman who had disappeared into one of the market stalls. Mrs. Chee ran after her. "Leave it. Please," she said. "Not in front of the children."

Maya came toward them, her face a mixture of confusion and wonder. "What did she say to you, Mumma?"

"Nothing. She is silly old racist."

"Yes. But what did she *say*? Ow! You're hurting me! Stop!"

Sook-Yin looked down at her fingers, which had tightened like a vise around Maya's arm. She released them at once in dismay. "Sorry! It was only accident."

"You did it on purpose!" Maya shouted. "I'm telling Daddy you did that and I hope he gives you a spanking, you silly Chin-Chin Chinaman!"

Sook-Yin wasn't sure what happened next. All she saw was her hand on Maya's leg and the sound of a slap ringing out. "You tell him about this as well, ha?"

The market filled with Maya's wails. Sook-Yin left her standing in the street as she took Lily's hand and walked away. At the corner, she glanced over her shoulder and after a moment saw Maya running back to them, her thick sobs tangled like webs in her throat as she fought to catch her breath. By the time they reached the apartment, Sook-Yin could still feel the echo in her hand; the sting not of pain, but satisfaction.

FORTY-FIVE

Lily

39th Day of Mourning

I arrived at the promenade and stretched. I'd been planning to see Uncle Chor again but given what had happened with Feng Mian I'd decided to let the dust settle.

Try and get out for a run, stop examining yourself in mirrors, practice having conversations with people. I wondered if Maya would appreciate my progress. One and a half out of three wasn't bad.

I focused on my breath in the fresh air, the sound of my feet along the concrete, not having a heart attack, but I was barely beyond the pier when I got a stitch and had to stop. Fuck this. I crouched down to catch my breath as a fat cloud appeared on the horizon. Bloody story of my life.

The rain, warm and sporadic at first, was merely a prelude to the sky splitting open and by the time I'd limped back to the hotel I was soaked. I'd barely managed to make it to the front desk when I saw the receptionist nod in my direction and a young woman walked across to me. "Miss Lily Miller?" she said. "I wondered if we could talk for a minute."

The elevator dinged and I was forced to move aside as a boisterous group of Australians spilled out like a stain on the carpet, juggling their rucksacks toward the entrance. The elevator doors closed again. "It won't take long," she said.

○ ○ ○ ○ ○ ○

My embarrassment turned to irritation as my wet legs snagged against the lobby booth. Who ambushed someone like this—without the courtesy of a hot shower and a change of clothes? Someone on a mission, obviously.

I studied her profile as she spoke to the waiter. I'd been too surprised at the elevator to notice how peculiarly beautiful she was: pristine skin, the grace of a swallow, neat neck in a silky sweater . . .

"Two hundred dollars for a pot but they don't serve narcissus tea." The waiter had gone and she was staring at me. Even her frown was gorgeous.

"I'll get straight to the point, Miss Miller. My name is Felicia Yuen, a friend of Mr. Lee's family. They asked me to come to see you."

"About signing the papers?" I said.

"Not exactly." She fiddled with the strap of her Rolex. "Mr. Lee has not been himself of late. He has a number of big deals on the table and colleagues are worried he seems distracted."

My brain raced. I bet his mother had caught him hungover that day and sent her pit bull in chiffon to check me out. Her little personal assassin. What a gift I must have handed her with my sweaty joggers and see-through top. "His father *has* recently died."

"Yes. And that was a tragedy. But the death was not unexpected, so it seems unlikely that this is the reason."

"You'd be surprised," I said.

"Forgive me if I speak frankly, but it's only happened since your arrival."

I pouted. "I can't see how that can be right. We've hardly spoken since I got to Kowloon."

"You'd say it's untrue you have a need to be rescued?"

The waiter came back with the tea and she opened the pot and stirred it. Long enough for her comment to sink it. She raised her eyebrows in a mirage of sympathy. "That terrible incident at Chungking Mansions."

"Yes. That happened," I said. "I did offer to stay somewhere else but his assistant wouldn't hear of it."

She shook her head. "Hong Kong is difficult for the uninitiated. In matters of business especially, it pays to protect one's interests."

I smiled. "So Daniel *is* keeping his eye on me?"

Her mouth slackened at the mention of his name, too slow to regain its composure in the face of my apparent audacity. "Not at all," she said. "My fiancé is not that complicated."

Ants of heat crept over my neck as she indulged a smirk of satisfaction. He'd kept that quiet, hadn't he?

"Please be in no doubt, Miss Miller. The cost of the hotel is of no concern to us. However, the time for mourning is coming to an end and it is our dearest wish that you sign the papers." She made a show of examining my clothes. "I'm sure the money's the only reason you came, and we would like to conclude things quickly." She took a sip of her tea, its amber reflected in the gold of her skin.

"Not *exactly*," I mimicked.

"Excuse me?"

"My sister doesn't want the money. She didn't want me to come here either but my curiosity got the better of me."

"What *are* your intentions, may I ask?"

I leaned toward her. "Mr. Lee left us a very generous gift, with no explanation behind it. And while the money would be lovely, it's his reasons that I've been looking for, rather than your permission."

She put down her cup, her face a sudden picture of reason. "You want to know the connection with your mother?"

"Yes. Exactly." The harshness of her tone had gone and I was willing to concede that I'd misjudged her, especially as Daniel had been equally in the dark.

"Now I understand. Some of the other beneficiaries have been the same." She flicked an invisible thread from her skirt. "It is the most natural thing in the world to believe our ancestors were someone of importance. To carry on that legacy in their name." She frowned. "Sadly, I don't remember Hei-Fong ever mentioning her. Indeed, the other people have been similarly disappointed and now wish they had been content with their fantasies." She said something in Cantonese. "You do not understand," she said. "I was telling you an old Chinese proverb. 'When a man digs a hole for too long, he inevitably ends up with a grave.'" She stood and opened her handbag and laid a five-hundred-dollar bill on the saucer. "Enjoy the rest of your holiday, Miss Miller."

FORTY-SIX

Sook-Yin

July 1977

Three days after the incident in the market, Sook-Yin came back from a trip to Mong Kok and found Maya and Li-Li on the stairwell. Maya hung upside down from the railings, her hair dusting the surface of the stone floor while Li-Li fed her lychees.

"What are you doing? Spit out! You want to grow tree from your head?"

Lily giggled as Maya traipsed down the stairs. At the bottom she opened her mouth and deposited the four small stones, glistening with spit, into her mother's hand. "And where has your Po-Po gone?"

Maya pointed at the reception window. "In there."

The side door opened and Mrs. Chee put her head out. "I'm sorry, Sook-Yin," she said. "I didn't mean to keep them waiting but your mother was very upset."

"Why? Has something happened?"

Mrs. Chee pointed upward. "Perhaps you should talk to your husband."

Sook-Yin balked. It was only four in the afternoon and he should have been at work. "Please watch the children," she said.

SHE HEARD IT before she got to the landing: laughter, high and silly, punctuated by Julian's voice.

"... by that stage, poor Shelley was pretty disillusioned, and expressed it by changing Spenser's rhythms to show his own imperfection:

'... Alas! I have nor hope nor health,
Nor peace within nor calm around,
Nor that content surpassing wealth
The sage in meditation found
And walked with inward glory crowned—
Nor fame, nor power, nor love, nor leisure.'"

Sook-Yin pushed open the door of the apartment. Schoolgirls littered the space like blossoms, their perfumed bodies leaned forward on chairs or across the floor on cushions, heads turned as one toward Julian. "What are you doing?" she said.

He came over and put his hand on her shoulder. "Darling, I'm teaching," he whispered.

"Why you not teaching in school?" She glared at the girls. "My mother is very upset."

"I did try to explain to ah-Ma..."

"How you explain?" she said. "This is a house, not brothel! You make her feel very embarrassing."

One of the girls stood and addressed her in English. "Don't you know he was injured this morning?"

Julian put up his hand. "Thank you, Grace, but it's all right..."

In her annoyance Sook-Yin hadn't noticed but now she saw it. His left eye was bruised and swollen and he had a deep, drying cut on his bottom lip. "How you get this?" she said.

"I surprised an intruder at the school this morning. One of the first-aiders patched me up and told me to go straight home but I felt bad about letting the students down."

"You think is better to bring them here?"

"Mr. Miller hero," the girl said.

"Mr. Miller *is* a hero," he corrected. "Although I'm really not." He shook his head. "I should have tried harder to explain to your mother but she left in such a hurry."

Sook-Yin sucked in her breath. She was not only angry but afraid, too. Soon, other tenants would be returning from work and might question the noise from the apartment. Ah-Ma's shame was bad enough to contemplate, but worse still was her disappointment. She had opened her house to their family and would accuse them of taking advantage of her. But what did Julian care? It wasn't *his* mother's approval on the line. "You must get rid of girls," she said.

Julian's eyes widened. "Didn't you hear what I said? For goodness's sake, be reasonable, Sook-Yin . . ."

When he made no attempt to move, Sook-Yin gathered the girls' bags and coats and threw them onto the landing. "Goodbye, goodbye, goodbye. This is not school," she said. "You want pass exam? Try harder."

The girls trooped out to collect their belongings, barely pausing to acknowledge Julian, who stood dumbfounded at the entrance to the kitchen. Once they were alone, he exploded. "Did you intend to humiliate me?" he said.

"Sorry." She folded her arms. "Maybe I try harder to explain."

His face flushed to a shade of gammon. "There's no logic to you when you're angry."

"What make me angry is you! You come here and stamp on our culture, like you are master of Hong Kong. Seducing all the women."

"Do you realize how deranged you sound?" She frowned, unfamiliar with the word. "Mad, doolally, mental." He screwed his finger into the side of his temple and then snatched up his keys and jacket.

"Where you going?" she said.

"Hopefully to get drunk with Hei-Fong."

Her throat tightened. "Why you always meet Hei-Fong?"

"I don't know," he said. "Maybe because he helps me understand you. Because God knows *I* find it impossible."

SOOK-YIN CROUCHED ON a stool in the living room, rubbing lotion on ah-Ma's feet as they watched TV together. Her mother had been furious at first—*made to feel a stranger in my own home!*—but the penance of the massage had worked, as had the flowers and box of custard tarts that Sook-Yin had bought from the market. It was a price worth paying to be friends again, and now as they sat without Julian, she was surprised how calm she felt. How blissfully close to the past.

The telephone rang in the bedroom. "Maya, get that," she said.

Maya kept her eyes on her book. "But I can never understand what they're saying!"

"Just say 'wai?' and then listen. My hands too slippery to answer."

Maya trudged out of the room, muttering under her breath. "Hello?" she said in a grumpy voice. A moment later, she called through the door. "It's Uncle Hei-Hei. For you."

WHEN SOOK-YIN PICKED up the phone, he was laughing. "I'm Uncle Hei-Hei now?"

"You should be happy that she likes you." She kicked the door closed with her foot. Lowered her voice. "Why are you calling anyway? Is Julian drunk already?"

"Julian?"

"He said he was going to meet you."

Hei-Fong hesitated. "No . . . I couldn't make it in the end. I think he went with one of my colleagues. In fact, I've just finished work and I was hoping *we* could meet instead. I haven't seen you properly since the day you arrived."

"I thought you were trying to avoid me."

"Don't be like that, ah-Yin! I've been dying to see you for weeks. Things have been difficult, that's all."

"I see."

"Come on, let me take you for dinner. There's a really great restaurant I know."

"You're too late. I've already eaten . . ."

"Are you really going to make me beg?"

It was no more than he deserved, after all his gadding about with Julian. She lined up her lipsticks on the dresser. "I suppose you could take me for dessert."

"That's more like it," he said. "Hurry up and put the children to bed. I'll see you outside in half an hour."

SOOK-YIN WAITED ON the corner of the street, convinced the weather was playing tricks on her. She couldn't possibly need the toilet again. All she was doing was having coffee with an old friend—barely a comma in the sentence of her life now—so why the need to keep pressing on her bladder, to keep stepping from foot to foot like Lily after too many soybean milks? And why hadn't she been honest with ah-Ma? "I'm popping out for a walk," she said after putting the children to bed. She'd been conscious of editing the story, the same way she'd short-changed the girls on their bedtime book that evening.

"What happened to the middle?" Maya said, once she'd reached the Happy Ever After.

"Is better. Tonight, no sad bit."

Li-Li peered over the blanket. "Will you still sing us to sleep?"

"Little tonight. Okay?" Sook-Yin stroked her head and sang.

"A ripple I seem
On life's mystic stream
Tossed at the waters' will
So I dream I'll be
Like the poor ripple, free
When the troubled waters grow still."

IT WAS ONLY when she'd put on her coat that the conceit's dishonesty nagged at her. She was unpracticed at the art of entitlement. "I need to go back to the supermarket," she said. "Is there anything there that you need?"

"If the *char-siu bao* are still warm you could bring me one." Her mother turned with a raise of her eyebrows. "But only if you're passing, naturally."

EVEN ABOVE THE sound of the closing shutters, she would've known his loping walk anywhere. "You smell so pretty!" he said as he leaned into her shoulder for a hug. Sook-Yin kept her arms by her side.

"I think my mother must have bought a new soap."

This was also a lie. After the schoolgirls had left the apartment she'd found a bottle of perfume down the side of one of the sofa cushions. She hadn't meant to take it but then, curious, she'd opened the lid: honey, watermelon, youth.

"She should buy ten more. It suits you."

He drove them to a place she'd never been before, a little café in Lai Chi Kok where he ordered coffee and a plate of moon cakes that arrived still warm from the oven. She had never seen them outside of the festival. Sook-Yin closed her eyes and inhaled. The smell belonged in a box with their childhood. Heedless. Happier. Husbandless.

Hei-Fong ate with a reckless appetite, smiling at her with an open mouth. "Do you remember that time . . ." he said, and each story he recounted was golden: the day that the sprinklers burst during the hottest summer on record, the cow that broke the train on the railway line, on the ferry when ah-Chor had shit himself and ah-Ma had been forced to bring him home stinking and red-faced from crying. Sook-Yin remembered them all and eventually she begged him to stop because her body was aching from laughter.

"You will burst my stomach," she said. She waved her hand in front of her nose. "And then you'll have to carry me home like ah-Chor."

He brushed the tips of her fingers. "It's great to see you laugh. You always seem so sad these days."

"I like the way they've decorated this place."

She turned her body away, pretending to study the wicker baskets and dried starfish adorning the shelves; danced her fingers across the checked tablecloth. Hei-Fong followed her gaze. "Hah. It's quite homely, isn't it? You should bring Julian one day."

Sook-Yin wiped her mouth on her napkin, the spell of forgetting broken. "Is this where you bring your wife?"

His lips twisted. "Once or twice. In the early days."

The waiter returned and refilled their coffee cups and she tried to drink hers immediately but only burned her lips. "Now you are angry," Hei-Fong said. "You used to make that same face when you were little. Hey . . . do you remember that time . . . ?" He laughed but when she didn't respond he picked up a stray crumb from his plate and rolled it between his fingers. "How *is* Julian these days?"

"You see him more often than I do." She studied him, narrowing her eyes. "What is my brother up to?"

"I don't know what you mean."

"All this business with the job at the school. Bending his back to be nice to him."

"It seemed like a decent gesture."

Why was he still sticking up for him? Had he forgotten how cruel he'd been—what a misery he'd made Hei-Fong's life? Chor-Kit striding to school, leaving ah-Fong running in the dust. *Smelly dirty Hei-Fong, his mother stinks of fish guts and rotten meat. Only peasants live in the Wall.*

"Not from ah-Chor," she said now. "He's been against my marriage from the start."

"Perhaps he didn't think Julian would take it so seriously."

Sook-Yin looked up, surprised. "The teaching, or being with me?"

He took a sip of his coffee. "I can't speak for Chor-Kit," he mumbled.

Sook-Yin watched him a moment. "Did Julian tell you he got into a fight today?"

"What?"

"They had an intruder at the school."

"Did anyone call the police?"

"I don't know, but I wouldn't worry. He was well enough to go for a drink tonight." She pressed her finger into a smudge on the tablecloth. "Where do you take him?" she said. "What do you do when you're together?"

He shrugged. "Your husband likes his brandy, doesn't he? Expensive English habit."

Sook-Yin pinched the ends of her hair. "You will get your money," she said. "Didn't I give you my word in London?"

"Ah-Yin, you misunderstood—"

"In fact, if you'd given me that job you promised we'd be paying you off much quicker."

Hei-Fong jiggled his leg. "And that wouldn't look bad at all . . . The two of us, working together."

"Now you sound like Julian."

"It's easy for a man to get jealous."

"Jealous of what?" She was tired of him speaking in riddles. "Then why did you offer it to me?"

"Because I hoped you would come back alone!"

Sook-Yin sat back and blinked at him. Had Julian been right about that day at the airport? And was she supposed to be happy or sad at this?

He bent his head. "Why do you think I asked you to come tonight? Why I haven't been able to see you?"

Her heart thudded beneath her dress. It couldn't be true. It couldn't. "Go on . . ." she managed to say.

Hei-Fong reached for her hand. "I think Julian should stay home with you more . . . Be a good wife to him, Sook-Yin."

The sense of light-headedness left her. Instead of falling she had definitely landed. As surely as if the chair had been rocks. "Be a good wife?" she repeated.

"Show him the commitment is worth it."

She moved her hand away. Adjusted her voice till it was clean and empty. "Yes, you're right," she said. "He only came here to make me happy, after all." She looked at her watch. "It's getting late, ah-Fong. He'll probably be home by now."

"One last coffee?" he said.

"No, thank you, I've had enough. Will you be able to take me home?"

The journey back was silent and too long, the car not as comfy as she'd first thought. They were almost at Castle Peak Road when she remembered ah-Ma's request. "You can drop me here," she said. "I need to go to the supermarket."

ALL THE WARM char-siu baos had been sold. Only the dregs of the morning remained, their hardened surfaces pitted by the fingers of others. The man at the counter saw her looking. "Half price, going cheap," he said.

She caught her reflection in the darkened window. The harsh lights had leached the color from her skin, and she watched herself shake her head, her face as cold and blue as the rest of her.

FORTY-SEVEN

Lily

39th Day of Mourning

I found solace in the hotel minibar; flicked on the telly. It landed on some nature documentary and for a while I let it wash over me: a shadowy cloud of piranhas thinning out a basin in Venezuela; a dust bowl of buzzards descending on carrion; a saltwater crocodile eating a goanna. Could anything escape its nature?

Perhaps Miss Yuen had been fueled by rage—her curiosity about me and Daniel unfounded and purely circumstantial—or maybe there was more to it. What if the family had been following me around, aware I'd made the link between Hei-Fong and Dad and scared I'd broadcast his dodgy past? How powerful were the Lees in reality?

There was a simpler explanation; the one revealed in the way that she'd looked at me. Disgust. I'd done nothing to earn this money but here I was drawing things out, lingering at their expense. If I really cared about Mumma, why had it taken me this long to come out here, why hadn't I confronted Maya or Dad, pressed them on their silence? Because I was a loafer. A sponger. An ingrate. Morbid, maudlin Lily, determined to make everything about myself. I should have been brave when it mattered. Proved that I could be good.

My gaze fell to the bedside table and the shiny laminate beside the telephone.

First enter the International Code, for example
001+1 for the United States or 001+44 for the UK.
For further assistance, please dial 0 for reception.

I pressed the light on the clock. Coming up to six p.m., which meant nearly eleven in the morning in London. I got up and fetched my address book along with another miniature vodka and lifted the receiver. Dialed the number on the scrap of envelope.

Four things I can feel, three things I can hear, two things I can—

"Hey, is that Scott?" I said. I sat up and muted the telly. "It's Lily . . . Lily Miller, remember? We used to see Dr. Fenton in Clapham."

"Yeah, I remember," he said. I listened through his hesitation, imagining him picturing our night together or even worse, the morning after. Had he somehow sensed me down on my knees scrubbing the smell of him out of my laundry, bleaching the cups and shower tray? As if I hadn't insulted him enough. *Some of us prefer not to dwell on it.* The fact he hadn't hung up on me already proved him the better person.

"I'm just ringing to say I'm sorry and . . . yeah. That's it," I said.

"Right." It was difficult to interpret his tone, as though in the time since I'd been in London it had become lost in translation like so much else. "Well, no hard feelings, I guess."

I snorted and then he laughed too, even though he hadn't meant it as a joke. "Okay. Okay," he said. "How are you doing, Lily Miller?"

I let out a breath. "I'm fine. Which I suppose means alive, at least."

Hearing the words out loud, I realized I was cheapening the moment, defaulting to an attitude of habit. Less than a fortnight ago I'd been a virtual recluse in my flat, my diary a sea of white space punctuated only by trips to the clinic and my shifts at the charity shop. No! I was more than alive, I was *coping.* "Guess where I am," I said. I sat up and looked out the window. The sun had been lost to the clouds but the lights from the skyscrapers burned, bright as fireflies. "I'm only in Hong Kong." I heard the awe in my voice, as though I were part of the wonder.

"You mean Hong Kong like China?"

He'd be amazed how far a ghost girl could travel.

"Weirdest story," I said. "Some stranger left me a shedload of money."

"You're joking."

"God's honest truth."

"So, what—you're there on holiday? Shit, I'm pleased for you, Lily."

"Not *exactly*," I said. I pinched the sheet between my fingers. *Please ask. Let me tell you about it.*

"Actually, things aren't that bad for me, either."

The moment had passed. "Oh yeah?"

"They finally sorted me out with a new shrink. He's decent. I like him, as it happens."

"Right, that's good," I said. "Maybe I should come back. I kind of miss the twisted banter."

"Dunno what Groucho would say about that . . ."

I laughed. "Hey! You remembered, at least . . . Anyway, I thought I might shout you a drink when I get back. Take you out to a greasy spoon. The whole works. I'm a marvelous conversationalist these days."

"Yeah, sure. Maybe." His playing-hard-to get act was killing me. "Thing is, I'm kind of seeing someone at the moment."

"Uh huh." I let this sink in. *Seeing someone.* Ugh. Who even *used* that phrase anymore? "Wow. Good for you," I said.

"Maybe that's *my* weird story. She's been seeing the same doctor as me and we kept bumping into each other, you know, at the clinic and stuff? And then we got chatting one day, went for coffee a few times . . ."

I necked my vodka as he gabbled on. Finished it.

"...and she really loves talking, you know? About our problems and all that ..."

"Sounds amazing," I said. Christ. Just kill me now. Knowing my luck, he'd be singing "Kumbaya" next.

I rolled the empty bottle in my hand and then reached over and banged it on the table. "Hang on, Scott," I said. "Somebody's knocking at my door."

"Okay, okay, yeah, sure. Sorry. Going on, as usual."

I cringed at the defeat in his voice. Hated myself. "No, seriously, that all sounds great."

"Really?"

"Yes. Don't be daft."

"Thanks. That's nice of you, Lily ... You probably should see who that is."

"All right," I said. "And Scott?"

"Yeah?"

I pressed the scars on my legs.

... One thing I can taste.

"Everything's going to be wonderful."

I hung up and collapsed on the bed before I staggered back to the minibar and grabbed what was left of the vodka. Switched up the volume on the telly. The documentary on predators had ended, replaced by a new one on how to beat cancer. On the screen was a man about Dad's age. Bald from chemotherapy, he was extolling the virtues of a diet based on raw carrot and beetroot juice.

Mumma, Po-Po, Scott. Me, trying to be a better person; trying to be a person at all. I was always too late. Too late.

I toasted my bottle to the air. "Plus ça change ..." I said.

FORTY-EIGHT

Sook-Yin

August 1977

Astorm brewed over the city. For the last three days at least, the oppressive heat had teetered on the edge of surrender, the mackerel clouds gathering like a cluster of bruises. One more push and the sky would open.

Sook-Yin sweated as she stood in the kitchen, gutting fish and replacing their innards with coriander and garlic and ginger, her fingers staining. Being a good wife had kept her busy, even if the fruits of her labor had been questionable. Whatever she seemed to cook, whatever the degree of her effort, Julian ate in exactly the same way: hurried, preoccupied, absent. There had been another change too—his evening outings marked by reluctance and the weary slope of his shoulders as he soundlessly left the apartment. At first, she'd suspected an affair but there was no joy in it for something so new. She'd stopped asking if he was seeing Hei-Fong and feared her jealousy was no longer the reason. Julian had been taken over by something else.

Idiot idiot idiot.

"What smells so good in here?" Ah-Ma wandered into the kitchen, trailing Lily at the end of her hand.

"It's because Mummy smells of watermelons!"

"Silly Li-Li!" said ah-Ma. "That is smell of fish!"

Sook-Yin smiled. Her youngest child never failed to amaze her with the tiny things she noticed. "Po-Po's English is getting good," she said.

"Yes, but her nose is old."

Ah-Ma gave a playful swipe at Lily's bottom and then bent over and examined the counter. "You bought trout?" she said in Cantonese. "Expensive. Why not red snapper?"

"Trout is Julian's favorite."

"Will he actually stop to taste it? He always seems in such a hurry these days."

Even ah-Ma had noticed. Sook-Yin tried to keep her voice even. "You know what teaching is like. I'm sure ah-Chor has told you many times."

"Ah-Li, watch TV with sister." Ah-Ma pushed Lily in the direction of the living room and then shut the door. She didn't say anything at first, merely lingered and knitted her fingers.

"Is something the matter?" Sook-Yin said.

"I am a little embarrassed, ah-Yin. I didn't want to mention it at first, but your husband forgot the rent and, you know, with all of you here . . ."

Sook-Yin put down the spoon. "Why didn't you tell him straightaway?"

"Like you say, he's always so busy. I'm sure it just slipped his mind."

"Obviously, that's all it is." Sook-Yin peeled off her apron. "I will go and get it at once. This week's money, yes?" Ah-Ma shuffled her feet. Held up three fingers. "He hasn't paid you anything for three weeks?"

"Ah-Yin, if money is tight . . ."

"Ma-Ma, this is simply a mistake." She nodded at the cooker. "If things were bad, would I have bought trout?"

IN THE BEDROOM, she took her suitcase from the wardrobe, her heart thudding. *Please let it be there.* She let out a breath of relief when her hand touched the small pile of cash that over the weeks she'd concealed in the lining. Thank God she had insisted on housekeeping. She'd kept it to pay off some of the loan but there would be hardly anything left now. She peeled off enough for the rent and then put the rest back in the case, pushing it behind their coats.

"I'm sorry, Ma-Ma," she said, her fingers limp as she handed her the money. "He can be so forgetful sometimes."

"Of course, he is working hard." Her mother touched her hand. "You are a good daughter, ah-Yin."

SHE NEEDED TO get some air. The promised rain had changed its mind, her footsteps dragging as she walked through the thick heat. They would have words about the money later.

At the grocer's along the street she bought eggs and a single cigarette. The habit had never tempted her before—she'd always hated the smell on Julian, and even before that, on Peggy—but now she wondered about its attraction. She asked for a light at one of the stalls, delighting in the man's disgust, but managed only a few puffs on the corner, gagging at the taste and the smoke before throwing the rest in the gutter. Even her rebellion was petty these days, an instinct evolved only to hurt herself.

As she drew closer to the apartment, she saw a young girl standing near the entrance. The mouthy one who had been at ah-Ma's. She straightened at Sook-Yin's approach, pushing her foot against the wall like a swimmer. "I don't suppose you remember me?" she said. "Your husband teaches me over at the cram school. I wondered if I could speak to him."

Sook-Yin glanced at her watch. "Can't this wait until you see him in class?"

"He's definitely coming back, then?"

"What are you talking about? Why would he not come back?"

"But it's been nearly four weeks," she said. "Since the intruder attacked him, I mean, and we were wondering if he was all right."

The uneasy sensation in Sook-Yin's stomach threatened to block her throat. "Yes," she replied at last. "My husband has been a little unwell."

"I knew he was just being brave!" The concern in her face was pathetic. "We wanted to ask the other teachers but that day we all came to your apartment he told us not to bother the school."

"He said that?"

"In case it threatened their investigation."

Sook-Yin fumbled for the key in her pocket. "No, he was right," she said. "It is a serious matter. We will deal with it."

The girl pulled an envelope out of her bag, trailing a waft of perfume between them. "The whole class made him something . . . Could I give it to him, at least?"

"No. I will make sure he gets it." Sook-Yin snatched the envelope out of her grasp. "You'd better go home now," she said, as she pushed open the door with her hip. "Before the school finds out you were here."

SOOK-YIN HURRIED INTO the bedroom. If Julian had not been at work, then where? She paced the floor, upending the orphan socks and the T-shirts thrown down by the children until she found a pair of his trousers. She turned the pockets inside out, releasing a dusty cascade of tissues and tickets for the MTR. Checked the dates. They were stamped for consecutive days, matching up to his usual routine. But why would the girl have lied?

Grace.

The reverent sound on Julian's lips. The misty schoolgirl eyes.

I'm really not a hero.

Had she come to taunt Sook-Yin?

She tore open the envelope she'd taken, steeling herself for the words, the soppy ramblings of love hearts and kisses. Inside was a shop-bought card with a cheap picture of flowers on the front, and she wrenched it open. English messages were scrawled over its surface, each one in a different handwriting.

> To the very best teacher we ever had . . .
> Mr. Miller, we miss you, come back!
> Don't abandon us now!

She let the card fall to the floor and covered it with her foot as her mother surprised her at the door.

"What are you doing?" said ah-Ma.

Sook-Yin ran her hand through her hair. "I thought I'd make a start on the laundry. The children are so messy these days." She followed her gaze to the spilling wastebasket. "I'll do that, too," she said.

She waited for her mother to leave and then emptied the bin on the floor. Among the tissues and discarded newspapers there was another ticket for the MTR and a receipt from the grocery store for cigarettes and a bottle of water. Beneath these was a folded piece of paper, and she plucked it out and opened it.

She assumed it was another receipt until she saw the address at the top and the figure written below it: 10,000 Hong Kong dollars. Her stomach twisted at Julian's name, clumsily written in phonetic characters—*Mr. Zhu Li an, Mi Le*—but it was only when she saw the second name that her nausea finally overwhelmed her and she vomited into the empty bin, quiet and quick as a dog.

FORTY-NINE

Lily

―――――――――

40th Day of Mourning

The morning paper had arrived at my door. Since my trip to the library that first time, I'd asked for the *South China Morning Post* so I could follow the events in English. The coverage of the Handover had been pretty constant but that last week it had noticeably ramped up, the colony's liminal state an almost perfect parallel to mine.

According to the story on the front page, Hong Kongers were departing in droves—to Australia, Canada, the UK—fearful of the imminent changes. Migration was nothing new but the high numbers seemed conspicuous, comparisons being made to the early nineties and the fallout of Tiananmen Square.

Desire was only half the issue, however. No matter how many wanted to leave, only a fraction could actually afford it—the middle generations with steady incomes. The rest had no choice but to stay and see how *One Country, Two Systems* played out. The woman in the lobby had been right about that.

I drifted off while reading the op-eds, woken an hour later by a faint roaring over the harbor. The noise was choppy and distant at first, the way the air crackles and splits before a thunderstorm, but when I looked out the window the sky was blue and patched with soft clouds.

I stepped out onto the balcony as two Royal Navy Sea King helicopters flew over the top of the island. It was an escort for the royal yacht, *Britannia*, sailing into the port flanked by a flotilla of local boats, its Union Jack fluttering in the breeze. Caught in the ripple of the ship's wake, the pinpricks of the nearby sampans rocked in the water like overgrown buoys.

The convoy slowed and stilled and I went back inside and switched on the telly, scrolling until I found the news. I flicked among the various channels: Prince Charles acting as envoy for the Queen; the Hong Kong Executive Council meeting for their final session; two thousand troops from the People's Liberation Army to be deployed to stop civil unrest. Tung Chee-Hwa, Chris Patten's successor, had already put into motion a law restricting the freedom to demonstrate, effective as of midnight on the thirtieth. Even *if* Feng Mian could get away with it, would she really take the risk?

My mobile rang. I didn't recognize the number on the screen and it wasn't one that Daniel had stored. I pressed the button. "Hello?"

"Good morning, ah-Li," a voice said. I couldn't place it at first, and then —

"Is that you, Uncle Chor?" I said.

"I hope I didn't wake you."

"No. I've been up for a while." I shut the balcony door. "How are you? Is everything all right?"

"Oh, yes. Everything's fine." I waited. "Forgive me, ah-Li," he said, "but I think there may have been a misunderstanding. Would you like to come over this afternoon?"

"Yes, of course!" I smiled. "I've been planning to do that anyway, so you've called at the perfect time. I'll go to the pier and check the ferries. Be there as soon as I can."

"Thank you, that would be great. We'll talk about it more when you get here. Ring the bell when you arrive at the building."

FIFTY

Sook-Yin

August 1977

Julian looked older beneath the glare of the café lights. Sook-Yin had found him coming back to the apartment and confronted him with everything she knew—the loss of his job, the gambling—his body shrinking as he listened in silence. How reduced he seemed to her now, how unlike the man she'd first met at Harvey's restaurant. "Is funny," she said at last. "You always talk before. Now all of sudden you have nothing to say." She pressed her knuckles against the plastic of the table. "Why you lose job at school?"

Julian bent his head. "It was a silly misunderstanding."

She caught the remnants of scent on her collar undiminished by various washings. Resented it. It was an imposter's perfume now. "Misunderstanding with girls?"

"No! Is that all you—" Julian rubbed his face. "There was a mix-up with my references. The school said when they got them, they were terrible. It made me feel humiliated." He stared at her. "Why are you looking like that? I swear these people were reliable."

Sook-Yin shook her head. She didn't know what she believed

anymore. Who had betrayed her the most. "So instead you go gambling in that place? You know nothing about the Wall City. You are lucky you come out alive!"

"I was just trying to make things right again. I got in over my head."

"Because you always want to be boss man, Julian! Try to impress everybody. Now we bottom of barrel!" Heads turned in their direction, unfamiliar with her language but recognizing its volume. "That story you tell me about burglar . . ."

He pinched his fingers together. "It was a reminder. About the debt."

What else could it be? This wasn't some loan from the bank, negotiated over tea and civility. These people were nothing but crooks. Probably paying their own protection money.

"It was the last day of my notice at the school," he said. "I was lucky they gave me that, but someone must have followed me. I'd been trying to make up the money, hoped if I could get a head start on things it would tide us over until I sorted out my references. But you're right, I *was* ashamed. I couldn't face telling the students, and that's when I invited them back to your mother's." His shoulders sank. "We don't belong here," he said. "But I promise when we get back to London—"

Sook-Yin's head snapped up. "You think we are leaving Kowloon?"

"What else is there to do? Sook-Yin, we gave it a shot but now it's time to go home."

What is home? she thought. Had she ever been more than a refugee, living at the whim of others? She shook her head. No. Even if it took her ten years to pay the debt, she wouldn't let herself be exiled again.

SHE WAITED UNTIL the house was asleep that night and then crept out to the nearest pay phone. "I need to see you," she said when he answered. She could hear the sounds of their life in the background:

the canned laughter of some TV comedy, the distant clatter of dishes in a metal sink.

Hei-Fong lowered his voice. "Right now? It's almost eleven. Jiao and I were going to bed."

"Perhaps I should talk to *her*, then."

His tone became softer, more hesitant. "What's got into you all of a sudden?" Jiao's soft complaints drifted in from the kitchen. "A colleague from work," he told her before he rejoined the call with a fake laugh. "No! It's not good to get so stressed. Remember that saying we have in business—"

"The one that says you're a treacherous snake?" Sook-Yin let that sit for a moment. "I know about you and the gambling. If you don't come, I will call Jiao myself." She was satisfied by the length of his pause.

"Give me half an hour," he said. "I'll pick you up at the corner of Hing Wah."

SHE WAITED OUTSIDE the apartment, shivering more with each second that passed even though the night was humid. She'd come out with only minutes to spare, no thanks to Mrs. Chee, who'd kept her talking at the reception window. Sook-Yin had humored her idle gossip—the noisy tenants who'd moved in to flat 6, the rat infestation at number 16—one eye half-trained on the clock before she was finally able to interrupt. "I must catch the late shop," she said. "I need char sui for congee in the morning."

SHE IMMEDIATELY GOT into Hei-Fong's car, ignoring the narrowed eyes of the shopkeepers drawing conclusions along with their shutters. A parked sedan, in the middle of the night? In two days, maybe three, Mrs. Chee would be talking about that, too.

"What did you tell your wife in the end?"

"I said there was an emergency with one of the clients."

"She bought it?" She wasn't sure why she was surprised—knew how easy, how important it was for women to close their eyes to these things. Only hands that were empty of oars could afford to rock the boat. "Don't worry, I won't keep you for long."

"Ah-Yin ... Why don't you tell me what you think has happened?"

She pulled the receipt from her pocket and threw it at him. "Is this your idea of a friendly gesture? Getting my family into even more debt?"

His blush lit up his face. "Listen, it's not how it seems—"

"Do you think I'm so stupid that I can't read a number? This sort of money may come easily to you, but how in God's name are we supposed to cover it?"

He wound down the window and lit a cigarette. "The debt is paid," he said.

"What are you talking about?"

"Don't you see my name on the paper?"

"Yes, but I assumed—" Sook-Yin blinked. "The debt was only Julian's?" As soon as she'd said it out loud—when she remembered the bills in London, the unpaid rent and his extravagant tastes—she knew that it was true.

"That night at the restaurant," he said, "when you told me he'd got into a fight, I realized he must be in trouble. When I found out who it was, I paid it."

"You know these people?" she said.

"They have a reputation around the Walled City. Don't worry, I've spoken to them. They won't take his business anymore."

She put her head in her hands. "He didn't tell me you had paid the debt." No wonder Julian had seemed so unafraid. So willing to run away again. Yet despite her relief, something nagged at her. "How did you know?" she said. "That night when I told you he'd been beaten up, you said you realized he must be in trouble. Why would you have assumed that?"

He took a long drag on his cigarette. "Most men like to gamble," he said. "If it isn't women, it's money."

"But you only met him when he came to Kowloon. You didn't know anything about him."

"He's not as unique as he thinks. And what does it matter anyway? He's in the clear now, isn't he?"

Sook-Yin studied his face. "Does our friendship mean anything to you?"

He flicked his cigarette out the window and immediately lit another one. "How can you ask me that?"

"Then tell me the truth, Hei-Fong."

"What's the point? You don't want to believe me."

"I want to believe that people are good . . . but I am always waiting for the surprise."

He pressed his temples. "It was only meant to be a casual introduction. A one-off favor."

"Julian asked you to meet these people?"

"No. Not Julian," he said.

"Who, then?"

"It was your brother, ah-Yin. A little joke, he said. To put the Englishman in his place."

Sook-Yin's stomach fell into her shoes. "My husband's references . . ." she managed.

"Chor-Kit asked him to send them to him, since he was coming on his recommendation. He'd been hoping he'd mess up on his own, ruin himself in a couple of weeks, but when he didn't—"

"He forged the references and you took him gambling . . ."

She bent her head. Though she was still livid about Julian's stupidity, her anger was tempered with sorrow. The debt was bad enough but to rob him of a job he loved, of the chance to find his vocation, was something you couldn't put a price on.

Hei-Fong raised his hand in appeal. "That's not how it happened—I swear to you! After that one time, I told him I was out. I had no idea Chor-Kit was encouraging him."

"But you still did it! No questions asked!"

She wanted so much to be furious, but whether blinded by their history or something else, his actions didn't make sense. Hei-Fong may have been a crook in his time but he had never been a spiteful person, especially not to her. There had to be more than he was telling her.

"What does my brother have over you?" It was only a stab in the dark, but his flinch was unmistakable. Her chest tightened. "Tell me quickly, ah-Fong."

He rubbed his finger across the top of the steering wheel. "When I first returned from the States, I was finding it difficult to get a job. All that money my parents had spent on me trying to buy me a better life, but my past was always waiting. No one respectable would touch me, not with a criminal record, and I grew ashamed I couldn't do better. Chor-Kit put his neck on the line for me, that first time I applied for the bank. Falsified details of my work experience. I wouldn't have my job without him."

Everything fell into place. What a despicable person her brother was, waiting all this time to call in the favor. "But the dangerous people you knew. Why didn't you call his bluff?"

"Because where does it end, Sook-Yin? A favor simply breeds another favor. I wanted a life, a future. I wanted my parents to think that I mattered. You should know what that feels like."

"I never had that choice!"

All those years that had passed between them and her brother had never forgotten, never stopped wanting to play games with her. To control her, hate her, punish her, rule the roost as the man of the family. And what had she done to deserve it? She pictured those days in her sickbed: the hazy fits of her fever dreams, her spiking temperature, ah-Chor laughing as she drank his piss. *Your life is mine now, Sook-Yin.*

She wished ah-Ma had let her die.

Hei-Fong's voice crept toward her. "I tried to warn you, that night in the restaurant when I told you to keep Julian at home, but you shut me down immediately."

"I thought—"

"I know exactly what you thought. But you couldn't have been more wrong. In fact, in my darkest moments, I *did* wonder if I'd done it out of jealousy. Why should Julian have you when he is so weak?"

Sook-Yin turned and stared at him. To think she'd almost softened! "Who are you to talk of weakness, Hei-Fong? A man who kowtows to my brother? Can't you see he is nothing but a bully? It was the same when you were at school, the way he teased you about your family. The way he laughed about where you lived! You were always better than that." She reached for the latch on the door.

"I spoke out of turn, ah-Yin! Please stay and let me try to explain." He reached for her arm but she pulled him off. "Didn't I pay your husband's debt? Surely that counts for something?"

Sook-Yin could barely look at him. "No. You are wrong about that. This debt is *your* debt," she said. "Yours and my brother's, Hei-Fong."

FIFTY-ONE

Lily

40th Day of Mourning

The news of *Britannia*'s arrival had brought more people than usual to the harbor. Down at the crowded promenade faces filled the open windows of the pier, transforming the wooden squares into outsized, ever-changing photo frames. Some people clutched flaccid Union Jacks in a mournful half-salute like tourists at Buckingham Palace; others stood with their legs astride looking cynically over the water.

I found a space on the deck of the ferry to bathe myself in the sun's warmth, still baffled about Uncle Chor and what had caused the sudden change in him.

We were halfway across when it came to me. He must have discovered Feng Mian's little escapade and realized I'd brought her home. Hadn't there been a note of gratitude in his voice—an almost apology? It was obvious Feng Mian had exaggerated. Uncle Chor would have bawled her out, grounded her at worst, but for me there was an unexpected prize. In my small unselfish act I'd shown him that I was worth something. That I was trustworthy and good and invested. As much as I sympathized with Feng Mian's outrage, I had no desire to be part of her cabal. Uncle Chor was family, after all. What if now I could change the past—reunite the two halves of myself?

The yacht dominated the port at Central. Spectators had gathered here, too, taking photos of its temporary landmark against the gleaming towers of the island. Along the road at the Exhibition Centre, the tingling buzz of construction—heavy drills, the echo of hammers—drowned out the cries of plovers swooping across the bay, their wings clogged with yellow dust. The sense of change was within and without me and as I walked to Wan Chai my heart swelled.

I got there and rang the bell, feeling the thrill of hearing my own name when Uncle Chor answered the intercom. Li-Li Chen had arrived. When I stepped off the elevator he was waiting. "Good morning, ah-Li," he said. "Thank you for coming so quickly."

He ushered me into the kitchen, where a pot of coffee brewed on the countertop. "How was your journey?" he said.

"Great. The ferry was busy. I think Prince Charles arrived this morning and they're drilling away at the Exhibition Centre." *Digging their way to China.* Didn't they use to say that when Maya and I were kids? Who'd have imagined I'd see the day?

"For Chinese people it's quite a big deal. We must look our best for the party."

"Is that how you feel about the Handover? I saw some people on the pier looking pretty glum."

He began to pull out crockery: four cups, four saucers, four spoons. Was he expecting someone else? "You mustn't believe everything you read," he said. "No matter what the West likes to tell you, the adopted child has always had a mother."

I followed him along the hallway. It was the farthest I'd been in the apartment and I could see a large room at the far end flooded with light and annexed by other doors. I stopped as I got to its entrance, not quite sure of what was in front of me.

Feng Mian was slumped on the sofa, her face ashen, while beside her was a man in a dark suit, his hands clasped as though he were praying. It looked like a scene from the Resurrection and a nervous laugh escaped me. "What's going on?" I said.

Uncle Chor gestured to one of the two chairs. "Please, ah-Li. Sit down."

I peeled off my anorak and sat, stealing another glance at Feng Mian and getting a sickly feeling inside me. Maybe I'd called this wrong. "I'm a bit confused," I said. "I thought you'd called me to talk about Mum."

"You mother? Of course, of course!" Uncle Chor smiled as he handed me a cup. "I'd be happy to tell you some stories once we clear up a minor matter."

"All right. How can I help?"

He remained standing and looked out the window. "A few nights ago," he began, "I was away on university business when Feng Mian asked if she could study with a friend. She has important exams coming up and so I was happy when she suggested it. Sadly, as I now understand it, this wasn't the case at all."

"No?" The coffee tasted bitter on my tongue.

"I might have been none the wiser but the night watchman called me yesterday to say her purse had been handed in to his cabin. The person told him they had found it in Mong Kok." He turned and looked at me. "You may not know the area but it has an interesting reputation and not only for the things you can imagine. Of late, there have been worrying rumors that some students have been gathering there. Political reprobate students trying to cause trouble for Hong Kong. Even on the night in question two men were arrested by police."

I gripped the handle of my cup. "I'm not sure I follow the connection. Surely Feng Mian could have dropped her purse anywhere and someone else simply dumped it in that area."

"Yes, I considered this," he said. "Until I spoke with Feng Mian's principal." He nodded to the man on the sofa. "Dr. Kwan told me there have been similar problems with some of his older students."

I glanced at the man on the sofa, who looked as uncomfortable as I felt. "Feng Mian's been in trouble?" I said.

The man shook his head at the floor. "Miss Zhang has always been an excellent student. I find this quite hard to believe."

Uncle Chor, bewildered by this unexpected betrayal, hurried on. "Nonetheless, we were worried," he said, "so I asked the night watchman to review his tapes and he was kind enough to give me a copy."

My stomach flipped as he picked up a remote control and pointed it at the TV. I hadn't noticed till then, but it was paused on a black-and-white video that he then proceeded to play.

A grainy image of a building emerged, which I recognized as the front of the apartments, with the guard's cabin at the rear of the picture and a full view of the residents' car park. As the timer at the bottom ticked on, a Hong Kong taxi pulled into the space and the figure of a girl climbed out. Illuminated by the sodium lights, there was no mistaking Feng Mian.

I put my mug on the table. "Uncle, you mentioned a misunderstanding this morning . . ."

He paused the video and stared at me. "There was someone else in the cab that night, although it was too dark for the guard to see properly. A woman, he said. Not Chinese."

Ghost girl. Was I as invisible to him as I'd always been?

"I'm sure you understand this is a serious matter. If Feng Mian is involved in something illegal it has repercussions for all our reputations."

He pulled her tatty rucksack from behind the sofa and emptied it onto the floor. Out tumbled her bag of makeup, along with my leather jacket and the piece of paper I'd left from the hotel. "I know it was you in the cab," he said, "which can only mean one of two things. Either you were with Feng Mian that night or she forced you to bring her home."

I examined the toe of my shoe. I had no idea what story she'd given him, but if he'd been sure he'd have accused me by now. What he was offering me instead was a choice. Either Feng Mian had betrayed him, or I had.

I weighed up the odds. It was clear Dr. Kwan was a bust, so I *could* say she'd sacked off to a club. I doubted he'd even tell her parents. It would mean admitting he'd made a mistake, failed their trust, which would be anathema to a person like him. By contrast, I had everything to gain. I would have his gratitude and the key to my family, including all the answers I'd wanted about Mumma. Isn't that what he'd said? Why shouldn't I get to belong?

Uncle Chor took the seat beside me. "I want the truth, ah-Li."

My mouth opened and closed like a fish. I couldn't look Feng Mian in the eye. "I mean . . . Feng Mian . . ." I said. "I don't think this is really—"

His fist hit the wood of the table, sending the cups juddering against their saucers. "I demand you tell me!" he shouted. "Take some responsibility for your life!"

I flinched as if he'd slapped me. Even Dr. Kwan looked diminished in his horror.

It was then I realized something. Uncle Chor was no different than the rest of them. He was like Maya and Dad and Ed. A paper tiger. A control freak. Offering promises of solidarity in order to keep me quiet. What had my life been up until that point but an elaborate system of defenses complicit in the denial of any contradiction; from every song and rhyme and insult I'd endured throughout my school days to every boy I'd fucked in consolation.

It doesn't matter, Lily.

Please! Do whatever I tell you.

Do it so you can fit in.

What good had trying to fit in ever done for me?

"Yes. I was with her," I said then. "I came here for coffee without your permission, looking for information about my mum, and then last week I persuaded her to lie and come dancing with me in Mong Kok. She didn't want to do it. I forced her." I gave a dismissive laugh. "It's stupidly easy, isn't it? Manipulating people who are desperate for love?"

Uncle Chor looked like he might have a stroke. His color rose to a terrifying crimson before he eventually rose from his seat and muttered something in Cantonese.

"I'm sorry. I don't understand."

"I said you are the image of your mother. A stubborn idiot since the day she was born."

I raised my chin. "Mumma was not an idiot. But she wasn't what you wanted her to be. I know you didn't agree with her marriage. You probably bullied *her*, too."

He laughed. "You think I bullied my sister? How would you know?" he said. "When you cannot even remember her? I was trying to do what was best but she never wanted to follow rules, either. And look where it got her in the end."

I stood and walked toward him. "She died being loved," I said. "She died with two children who adored her and who will never forget her name. But you are bitter and cruel and lonely and I'm sorry it won't be the same for you."

He swallowed and pointed to the corridor. "Take your chaos out of my house. And do not contact Feng Mian again. If you do, I will call the police."

I'd bent down to pick up my coat when something else occurred to me. This was the last time I would ever see him. The last chance I would have to ask. "Please give me what you have of my mum's. Photos, letters, anything. There must have been things at Castle Peak Road after me and Maya went back to London."

He seemed surprised and then he smiled. "Nothing here belongs to your mother." He picked up my cup and made a show of wiping it. "Sook-Yin chose to give up her culture. And she became like you in the end. A banana. Nothing more than a tourist."

FIFTY-TWO

Sook-Yin

August 1977

Three days after the conversation in the car, Sook-Yin went to Hei-Fong's office. Slowly, it had started to dawn on her that she had choices in the matter, after all.

Dressed as he was in his immaculate suit, it was easy to imagine herself talking to a stranger. "I need the job you promised me," she said. "I will clean toilets, I will make tea for the staff. An honest job for honest money."

"You're going to stay in Hong Kong?" She tried to ignore the hope in his voice. "What about Julian?"

"My husband will stay here and look after the children." She let the word *husband* wash over him. There was a time when she was proud of it but now she used it merely as a weapon. "I know the language and the area," she said, "so it makes sense for me to work."

Hei-Fong held her gaze as he pulled a piece of paper from his drawer. She waited while he composed a letter, her body angled toward the window.

"Take this to Mr. Lau at the staffing office. He'll tell you what you need to know." His hand shook as he held it out to her. "I never intended to hurt you, ah-Yin."

She reached out and took the paper, unable to avoid his miserable expression, and then bent her head and exited in silence. There were many things she wanted to say, but she didn't trust herself to answer him.

In the basement, she took a seat on the bench and opened the letter.

Mr. Lau,

Please take this as my highest recommendation concerning its bearer, Miss Chen. I have known her for a number of years and find her ambitious and highly tenacious. Her English is also impeccable and I suggest a post in customer services, where she can benefit our international clients. In addition, with my authorization, two months' salary to be paid in advance with the purpose of securing her residence in Kowloon.

AFTERWARD, SHE FOLLOWED Mr. Lau's eyes as he read it, a bead of sweat appearing on his brow. He must have been about forty-five, his receding hairline coaxed down with Vaseline and his thin shirt dotted with the stains of an instant lunch; the same routine day in and day out without ever hearing such words about himself.

He set the letter upon his desk. "May I ask how you know Mr. Lee?"

"It is a family connection."

He nodded. "I have been here myself for a quarter of a century."

If it was a complaint then it was a veiled one and only to let her know that he had not shared her apparent advantages. She barely suppressed a laugh. "Twenty-five years?" she said instead. "Then the company must really value you."

His chest expanded a little. "I have always done my best."

Sook-Yin ran her fingers along the desk. "Mr. Lee mentioned customer services. Would that be possible?" She had already seen the sort of women they employed: attractive, trim-hipped dollies with powdered faces and bright red lips. She would never have dreamed of joining their ranks, or even of speaking to them in passing. Now, though, she held his eye, daring him to contradict her. Mr. Lau nodded.

"I am sure we can find a place for you. If you can present yourself tomorrow, I will put Miss Huang onto your training immediately."

THE SUN WAS a coin setting over the city as she walked back to the metro station. Sook-Yin lingered a little, enjoying the heat on her skin and the feel of the crowds around her. No one gave her a second look, no one stopped to call her names or pull their eyes in ridicule. She stood in line at a nearby noodle stand behind the salarymen and women; ordered a bowl of ramen and told the man to add extra broth, extra chilies. Felt for the first time that she had earned it.

WHEN SHE RETURNED to the apartment that evening, there was no sign of Julian or the children. Instead, Chor-Kit was on the sofa with their mother, picking his way through a bowl of sunflower seeds. "Where has everyone gone?" she said.

Ah-Ma pointed to the empty armchair. "I've sent them out for shopping. We need to talk, ah-Yin."

"All right."

Chor-Kit shook the salt from his hands. "I had an interesting phone call this morning, from one of the parents at the summer school. It seems your husband has lost his job."

"Is it true?" her mother said.

Sook-Yin sat. "I'm sorry to say it is. Julian was on trial while they waited for his references but when they arrived they were not what we expected." She glared at her brother. "Still, considering that ah-Chor saw them first it seems strange he didn't tell us. We could have sorted out the problem easily."

Ah-Chor scratched at a stain on his trousers. "That's a neat way of putting it," he said. "I recommended the position in good faith. It's hardly my fault he embarrassed himself, let alone the damage to my reputation. Still, what's done is done."

"If only that was the end of it . . ."

"What are you talking about?"

"I'm talking about the break-in at the school. Julian's not been right since it happened." Sook-Yin pointed to the top of her temple. "A terrible pain. Right here. Neither of us wanted it to come to this, but if there's a case for compensation we'll have to report it to the relevant authorities. Let them judge the conditions of his employment."

Ah-Chor coughed up a seed. "That's very unfortunate, naturally, but do you really want the school to suffer? These investigations take their time and you'll be back in London by then."

Sook-Yin raised her eyebrows. "Oh, we're not leaving," she said. He twisted his neck so violently it was a wonder he didn't break it. "That's where I've been this afternoon. I've found a job of my own, and it will pay more than enough till he recovers. It's at Dah Sing Bank, in the city."

Ah-Ma clapped her hands. "Wah, ah-Yin!" she said. "That is wonderful news."

"And do you know the biggest coincidence? Hei-Fong Lee is manager there."

"This means you will stay in Kowloon after all?"

"Yes. I'm going to look after you." Sook-Yin turned and smiled at her brother. "I won't make that mistake again."

SHE WAITED UNTIL the children were asleep before she broke the news to Julian. "My brother will leave you alone now. He think the school will find out about references." She giggled and mimicked him choking. "I make him very frighten about it."

Julian lay under the covers, his eyes flickering beneath half-closed lids.

"You not glad?" she said.

"You've made me look weak," he muttered. "I'm perfectly capable of fighting my own battles."

Sook-Yin tipped out a handful of lotion and rubbed it into her skin with sulky, vigorous movements. "Battle is over," she said. "I tell you not to trust my brother but always you fall into trap." How many times had she told him that no such fat goose lay in the road? She threw the bottle onto the table. Tomorrow she would start her training and she wouldn't allow him to spoil her excitement.

"And I'm to look after the children?" he said. "While you're out there doing your *job*?"

"First, is proper job. Second, we find school here soon."

"When neither of them speaks the language?"

"There is English-language school in Kowloon. Plus, after time they learn." Her hand paused on the way to the lamp. "Is this really about children?" she said. "Or me working for Hei-Fong Lee?"

"Well, now you mention it no, I'm not happy."

"Is that why you not tell me he pay your debt? Let me believe he is bad one?" Julian's throat bobbed. "Yes. I know," she said. She turned off the light and fell back in the darkness. "You want money. Here we have money. And now I go to sleep."

FIFTY-THREE

Lily

41st Day of Mourning

My room looked different when I woke up. The novelty of it had gone and all I saw was its artifice, the deliberateness of it. I wanted to unweave the silky sheets, grind down the crystal lampshades and reduce them to what they were: the bare plants and the minerals and sweat from the hands that wove and shaped them.

Riding back on the ferry yesterday, the diminishing shape of *Britannia* behind me, there had been a strange sort of poignancy; Britain and I both burning our bridges with a place that, just for a time, had felt like it belonged to us.

I had no regrets about Uncle Chor except for where it had left me, a conclusion strengthened by the rage of his parting shot. Would he have told me the whole of Mumma's story? I doubted it. As much as death was the magic trick of history, truth would always be an equal casualty, the same way that only the winners made maps. We forgot, we conflated, we dissembled. All I knew was that there were secrets there, unresolved hatreds. And that they'd started a long time ago.

THE FINAL INSULT came at breakfast that morning when I was waved over by the man at reception. "We're sorry you're leaving," he said. "I just wanted to let you know that the Lee family will take care of your bill."

My stomach clenched. I'd been so distracted those last weeks I'd forgotten to go back to the consulate. Thank God I had my bank card. At least I could pay for the emergency documents, another place to stay if I had to. Even so, the message was clear. I'd outstayed my welcome with the family.

I steadied my hands on the desk. "And *Mr.* Lee arranged this himself?"

"A representative of the family."

Felicia Yuen. It had to be. I concealed my annoyance beneath a fake smile. "It's come around so quickly. Could you please remind me of the day I check out?"

He ran his fingers across his computer. "Sunday, July sixth . . . There was also a delivery this morning." He retrieved an envelope from one of the pigeonholes and slid it toward me. "We hope you enjoy the rest of your stay with us."

I took the envelope to one of the sofas, surprised when I scanned the postmark and saw it bore the crest of the embassy. How had they known where I was? I tore it open.

Inside were travel documents outlining my return to London: one approved flight between Kai Tak and Heathrow, my passport listed as *Missing*. I read the accompanying letter. All the fees had been paid, meaning I only needed to report on the day.

Sunday, July 6.

APPETITE FORGOTTEN, I walked to the promenade. Fuck. Why hadn't I called the consulate? Arranged a return at my own convenience? It wasn't the point that I might've chosen the sixth, it was the fact I was being *sent* home with about as much ceremony as when we'd been kids. History repeating itself. And what did I have to show for it? A tacky souvenir for Babs, an extorted promise to swear her to secrecy. It was what my life had always amounted to: the feelings I never managed to communicate, the things I hid from others. I hadn't broken the circle at all. I imagined what Maya would say if my failed enterprise ever came out. *What on earth did you think you'd find there that I hadn't told you already? What do you have to say for yourself?* And I would answer as I always had.

Nothing.

I SAT THERE for over an hour, folding and unfolding the paper before I got up and went back to the hotel. As I came out of the elevator, I saw a package outside my room. It was small and carefully wrapped but there was no evidence of any postmark. *Miss Lily Miller,* it said. *Care of the Peninsula Hotel.* There was a familiar scent to the paper—balsam and Tiger Balm—like the air in Mrs. Tam's flat.

I opened it on the bed. There was a small box beneath the paper and inside it the cameo necklace that I'd seen on the woman that day in the lobby: the gold bird against the blue agate. I pulled it out and stared at it. It was even lovelier than I remembered, but why the hell had she given it to me? I searched through the paper again and found a card with a single line on it: *Prove to yourself.*

I laid it aside and called reception but they had no idea who'd left it. Had she wanted the gift to be a secret, and what would her family say when they found out? It must be worth a fortune.

Prove to yourself.

Maybe I still could.

I checked the date on the bedside clock and then read the embassy's letter again. Sunday, July 6. The fiftieth day of mourning.

Eight more days to find out the truth.

FIFTY-FOUR

Sook-Yin

September 1977

Had it not been for her experiences at the hospital, Sook-Yin might not have lasted that first week. Miss Huang was certainly formidable and as a result had earned various nicknames, which were whispered around the bank. She was not just a "dragon," but a "witch," a "demon"; "about as safe as a mongoose with a leopard." That Sook-Yin had yet to cry or take shelter in the company bathroom must have been a testament to something.

In direct contrast to her days as a nurse, however, the bank's rigorous instruction came easily to her: the names of the various loan managers; the hours when the bank was most quiet and therefore more amenable to certain demands; the thin line between friendliness and flirting. The growing asset of her employment seemed proven when by the end of that third week she found a steady stream of customers neglecting the prettier clerks in order to seek her out.

Her growing sense of achievement was nonetheless tempered by a certain mournfulness, the inevitable contrasts with her life at the nursing home bringing renewed regrets about Peggy. Cowardice had ruined their beautiful friendship; Sook-Yin's unwillingness to face up to the truth or be confronted on the choices she'd made were nothing but stubborn pride. Matron Connolly had been right about that. *Your problem, Miss Chen, as I see it, is merely your fear of being tested.*

She resolved to seek Peggy out, rekindle the bond between them if Peggy would have her back. She would ask for her advice. Be braver.

ON FRIDAY, she was tidying her station when Miss Huang pulled her aside. "Was it you who moved those leaflets to the front desk?"

Sook-Yin reddened at the shrillness of her tone. "Yes. Did I do something wrong?"

"May I ask who gave you permission?"

"No one told me," she said. "I was thinking of peaches and custard."

The other tellers looked up from their stations, their expressions a mixture of nosiness and pity. "Sometimes," Sook-Yin continued, "people don't know what they want until it is right in front of them. They might come here to put money in the bank, but when they see a leaflet for a loan they realize a bigger possibility, especially here in the shopping district. Although it may not be right to say it, some people think they can buy their dreams."

Miss Huang folded her arms, her face devoid of expression. "You may go back to your desk now, Miss Chen."

SOOK-YIN DWELLED ON the conversation, growing paranoid as the day went on and the rest of the clerks avoided her. It was almost the close of business and she was looking forward to retreating for the day when Miss Huang approached her again. "Mr. Lee has requested to see you. Please go to the fifth floor immediately."

"Mr. Lee?" she repeated in a small voice.

"Don't keep him waiting, Miss Chen."

She avoided the elevator for the stairs, praying that by the time she arrived the flush in her cheeks had subsided. Hei-Fong was behind his desk. "Ah, Miss Chen, a word, please," he said. His face looked terribly serious, and as she went to close the door, she could barely keep her legs from shaking.

"I hear you've been causing trouble. Miss Huang couldn't wait to tell me."

She kept her eyes to the floor. "I thought as much," she said.

"Three new loans this morning and now she has all this work to do."

Sook-Yin looked up with a start and saw that he was grinning at her. "Three?"

"Pretty big ones, too."

She rested her hand on the chair, supporting herself. "You didn't call me here to get rid of me?"

"Get rid of you? I want to kiss you." She didn't know which one of them turned redder. Hei-Fong straightened the pens on his desk. "Anyway, now you're this big success can I assume that I'm forgiven?" He tilted his head at her silence. "I can see you're still thinking about it. Well, how about you think over coffee? I really miss our conversations."

Sook-Yin squeezed her fingers together. In truth, she had missed him too—his laughter, the sound of his voice. And now, as when they'd been children, they had something in common to talk about, especially as Julian had shown no interest in her work. "I suppose that would be all right . . . I'm almost finished for the evening."

He hesitated. "I was actually thinking about the weekend. It might look a little strange if we left together."

Sook-Yin colored. "Yes, that was silly. I didn't think."

"It's only because—"

"Business is business," she said. She rocked on the balls of her feet. "Was there anything else you needed to tell me?"

"Only that Miss Huang is very impressed with you. And that is saying something." He lowered his voice. "I will definitely call you this weekend."

"As you wish," she said, and then she turned and left the office.

BUT HEI-FONG DID NOT call that weekend, or any of the weekends after that. On the rare occasions when she saw him in the bank she was torn between looking and avoiding, not wanting him to see her disappointment, and though initially she'd been willing to concede that they were back on equal ground, she came to realize that they were not. Instead, as always in her life, she'd allowed a man to become her boss.

Matters were not helped by the situation with Julian. Her new position as the family provider continued to increase the rift between them, and he grew proud of sleeping till noon and having her see his unshaven face, to breathe in the rankness of his odor. The trouble with ah-Chor had killed all the fight in him. She recalled the letters he'd received from the students' parents, how she'd discovered them one day in the kitchen bin, torn up among the wet rubbish; her heartbreak as she tried to rescue them. But as much as she remained sympathetic, so too did her patience wear thin. He had to be better than this. He had to learn to be a fighter.

Meanwhile, the children grew feral in their boredom and ah-Ma would return from the factory to find them alone on the street, pilfering bruised fruit from the gutters or pressing their faces at the bakery window. "They are getting a reputation," she said when Sook-Yin returned that evening. "I hate to come between a husband and his wife but I have my own feelings to think about."

"Is Julian rude? Have you argued?"

"If he spoke to me at all we might have. And to be honest, I would prefer it. Instead, he wanders around like a ghost all day. It gives me the creeps, ah-Yin. Plus I am an older woman. It looks bad to be alone with your husband. It would be better if he found a job."

"Then who will look after the children?"

"Since they've cut my hours at the factory I am happy to do it myself. But when will you enroll them in school?"

Sook-Yin picked at her nails. With all her focus directed at work, it had completely gone out of her head and now the new term was about to begin.

"Have you changed your mind about staying?"

She shook her head. "No. I am staying," she said. "I will talk to Julian about it."

AS USUAL, he was intransigent. "What you don't seem to grasp," he said, "is how disruptive this has been for the girls. You can't take them out of one culture and plop them into another with nothing but a feeling of goodwill. It isn't fair, Sook-Yin. All they know is how to be English."

"What about me?" she said.

"*What about me?*" he mocked. "This whole enterprise has been nothing *but* about you."

"I do not mean that," she said. "I go to England by my own. I have to learn to adapt."

"But Maya doesn't want to adapt."

"Always you think of Maya."

"She's homesick. She wants to go home."

"Then what do you want me to do?"

"You have to decide, Sook-Yin." He threw himself onto the bed and flicked unseeingly through his book. "Which family do you want to belong to?"

FIFTY-FIVE

Lily

___

42nd Day of Mourning

It's amazing what guilt does to people.

Given everything that had happened that last week, I was no longer sure who Maya's words related to. My whole time in Hong Kong had been like this—reassessing what I'd taken as fact, rewriting the story of my past—but like Reggie's jigsaw, there were still missing pieces.

No more secrets.

I picked up the telephone and dialed the number.

"Maya Cochrane's office?"

I paused. It was unlike her to answer her own phone. Maybe they'd fired that Sloane in reception.

"Hey. It's Lily," I said.

"Blimey, a whole twelve days?" The sound of her laugh was like sunshine and in that moment I wanted to stop time, lie in its warmth. "You lasted longer with the nuns than I thought."

Shit. I'd forgotten about that.

"Did you dig a tunnel or go over the fence? . . . By the way, your cheese plant died. Sorry, I think I overwatered it. And don't tell my ego, but I've really missed you . . ."

I blocked out the sounds of her joy, imagined jumping into a swimming pool, the shock of the water closing over my head. *You have to tell her. Now.* "Mays . . . don't be mad but I lied. I'm actually in Hong Kong. I came out here and I need to talk to you."

I heard the wordless change in her breath. The awful tremolo.

It all came out in a torrent then, from the robbery at Chungking Mansions to the secret aggressions of Hei-Fong Lee's family. If her lack of interruption was disconcerting, the void that followed was even worse. "Maya?" I said. "Are you there?"

"You promised me we had an agreement. I *told* you I'd give you that money."

"It wasn't about the money," I said. "I just needed to know why it was left to us. I wanted to know about Mumma. But Uncle Chor's been properly weird, like there's this big conspiracy or something. At first I assumed it was the whole cross-culture thing, Mum marrying Dad and all that, but it's definitely not the whole story."

"Uncle Chor?" Her voice was flat. "Why the hell would you ask him for anything?"

"I know, but I need you to listen." I glanced across at the desk where all the papers and photos still lay with their edges curling in disapproval at me. "The more I look into the past, the more everything leads back to Dad."

"What the hell are you on about, Lily?"

"He lied about the letters, Maya. Our grandmother *did* write but he returned them all. She died never knowing what had happened to us."

"I don't know why you're saying this."

"I've got one of the letters right here! It has our Brixton address on it."

"Then there must have been a reason," she said, before she added more confidently, "he was hurt because they sent us away."

Her scrabbling was unexpected but unsurprising. We'd spent our lives on this psychic raft—constantly trying to readjust, return to a state of equilibrium while splinters peeled off around us. "Yeah,

I get that, but still . . . What if Dad *was* the connection to the Lees? I think something may have happened between them, something dodgy in Hei-Fong Lee's past, and that's why he left us the money. Think about it, Maya. Is there *anything* you can remember?"

"Seriously, Lily, you sound ridiculous. And don't you think I'd have told you if I'd known?"

"Like you told me about Dad's estate?" She made a little noise at the back of her throat. "I know he was skint at the end, Mays. Ed told me the money was yours."

"What the fuck—"

"Honestly, leave it, it's fine. In a way I'm glad he told me, because I wouldn't have come out here otherwise. But I'm still missing the bit from before. Why the hurry to get us back to London?"

"We've been through this. You know why! . . . Because Dad had gone home for an emergency and they didn't want two kids on their hands. *They* were the ones who were wrong and what you're suggesting is really hurtful. After all the things that Dad did . . ."

"For me, you mean?"

"For both of us."

"It wasn't Mum's fault that she died!"

"No. I know. But she did. And no matter how shocked they were, her family behaved appallingly."

I sighed. "So why not tell me that Dad had nothing left? Why keep offering to give me money?"

"Because all we have is each other!"

"Not you . . ."

"Fucking Ed?" she said.

"No. Not Ed. Just . . . life. Other people's approval. And coming back here, it's changed me, Maya. That's something else that you were wrong about. There really *are* things I remember, things that have always been a part of me."

"A whole twelve days and you've *discovered* yourself?" She almost laughed. "So the twenty years before that mean nothing?"

"What? They do! I love you! What are you so afraid of?"

"Nothing! It just seems weird. You've never shown any interest before."

I'd lost count of the things I could have said to that: We have to look forward, not back. Are you asking to get beaten up? Chinese, Japanese, yellow knees. But not now. It wasn't the time.

"Lils, you were barely five. Whatever you think you remember, it's been changed. Think of all that time you spent in the hospital—"

"Why do you always bring it back to that? Like every little thing I believe is because I'm mad or dangerous or something?"

"Fuck off, Lily, I don't."

"Yes, you do!" I said. "But I'm better now, Maya. I *am*." I was mortified at the wobble in my voice. Resented the fact that Maya was listening. The way she'd always been listening.

"Don't do that, please," she said. "I'm so bloody hormonal right now you're going to set me off, too."

"It's fine," I said. "*I'm* fine."

"I want you to listen to me, Lily. You're always going to be the person you are. You'll always be funny and quirky and awkward and that's nothing for you to be ashamed of. And Dad understood that too, right? He knew what it was like to go through Hell. All we ever wanted was that you were okay."

"I know that."

"Then you've got to stop punishing yourself. We've got so much to look forward to. Promise me now you'll stop."

"Okay."

"I mean it."

"I said okay!"

There was the sound of her turning pages, the scratching relief of her pen doing the thing she was best at. "Did you say you got your card back?"

"Yeah. It came to the hotel."

"And where is it they've put you up?"

"It's called the Peninsula. In Kowloon."

"For God's sake, Lily," she said. "That's about a million quid a night!"

"The Lee family said they'd take care of it."

She blew out an exasperated breath. "Fine. I'll pay the bill when I get there. And tell them you're not taking that money. You haven't signed anything, have you?"

"No . . . but wait. What do you mean, when you get here?"

"Well, obviously I'm coming to get you."

"No, Mays, you don't have to do that . . . especially not in your condition."

"My legs aren't pregnant, you idiot. Besides, it'll be an excuse for a break together. I mean, you'd like that, wouldn't you?"

My chest thudded. I had to think quickly. "To be honest, I want to come home. Plus, I don't have my passport, remember? I have to take the embassy's flight." She continued to flick through her diary. "Maya? I'm *definitely* going to come back. I'll be on the bloody plane on the sixth."

She tutted. "And you promise you'll come straight to mine? I'll pick you up at the airport."

"Fine."

I heard the door to her office open followed by a terse exchange with Ed. Fuck. He was definitely in the shit. "You'd better go," I said. "Honestly, it's all okay. I'll call you before I get on the plane."

"I'll be waiting, Lils. I mean it."

I WAS EXHAUSTED after I'd hung up. That's the thing about families. About sisters. The thing you have to accept. That along with all of the good stuff—the laughs, the contentment in silence, the sharing of private experience—you also know when something is wrong.

FIFTY-SIX

Sook-Yin

September 1977

As Sook-Yin stood on the edge of defeat, a strange transformation came over the household. It began at the start of that next week when on her return from work she found Julian and her mother in the living room, laughing and dancing to Elvis Presley. Julian was singing along, his voice tuneless and unselfconscious, and standing alone at the edge she felt again that childhood panic of missing something warm and loving and secret. The girls were wearing new dresses and what had happened to Maya's hair? Normally poker straight—the only thing she'd inherited from Sook-Yin—it was now a fuzz of wayward curls that made her look alarmingly older.

She walked over and switched off the cassette. "Have you all gone mad?" she said. "I could hear you from Hing Wah Road!"

Ah-Ma let go of Julian's hands, her half-mortified, half-resentful look like that of a child caught sleeping on duty in the paddy fields. "It was only a little fun," she said. "To celebrate your husband's good news. The school has paid him his compensation."

"The school?" Sook-Yin said in English.

Julian smiled. "The money arrived this morning."

Ah-Chor had surrendered after all. In spite of her surprise she couldn't resist a little smile herself, not that she intended to gloat or lower herself to his standards. It was enough that both of them knew it. "First things first," she said. "We need to get children in school and then look for teaching job for you. Get proper reference from London."

His smile wavered. "All right. But at least let me dream for tonight."

THE NEXT DAYS came and went and although there was no news on him finding work, Sook-Yin noticed a definite change in Julian. Instead of sleeping till noon, he got out of bed when she did. He shaved and cut his hair and when Sook-Yin returned in the evenings the smell of washing would drift down from the balcony, the children's clothes like bright pennants on the line. Dinner was nearly always ready for her. Even ah-Ma's demeanor had changed and she would arrive home to the sound of their chatter, broken but somehow musical, like two different species of bird who had nonetheless learned to communicate. Sook-Yin felt a new level of pride in him. At last he was learning to fight.

THE NEXT WEEKEND, he took the girls to Lai Chi Kok—the amusement park in the bay—and she looked forward to a day of relaxation. She decided she would get her hair done. Maybe even her nails as well.

She was getting ready to leave when the phone rang. "Is that you, ah-Yin? It's Jin. Hei-Fong tells me you work at the bank now. He reckons you're quite the natural."

Sook-Yin squeezed the base of the receiver. Had he also told her they hadn't spoken in weeks? "That's kind of him," she said.

"Even so, you need a break now and then. How about you come shopping in Central? I find it so boring on my own."

"Why don't you go with Jiao?"

"She doesn't want to ride the ferry. She keeps saying she'll catch a chill. Can you imagine—at the end of summer? The only thing she'll catch is laziness! Besides, don't you think I'd prefer it with you?" There was the quiet determination in her voice that always made her questions seem more like an order. Sook-Yin chewed her lip. Her hair would have to wait for another day.

THE HARBOR'S STENCH was overwhelming as she waited for Jin to arrive. She rubbed the day's warmth into her arms, tracing the small brown freckles of youth that danced on the surface of her skin. One day, she would be old and they would blur into countries, continents, the way that ah-Ma's had started to turn. But not today.

She couldn't believe it when the taxi pulled up and Mrs. Lee got out with Hei-Fong. She crossed her arms as they approached the jetty in case they saw the sudden thrum of her pulse. Why had they tricked her like this?

"How pretty you look!" Jin said.

"I thought you were coming alone."

"And who's supposed to carry the bags?" Jin gave a mischievous smile as she looked from one to the other.

"It's good to see you," he said.

MUCH TO HER relief, Hei-Fong had no patience for shopping and took himself off to a café to drink tea and read his newspaper. "Call me when you're ready to pay," he said.

Sook-Yin grew increasingly distracted as Jin dragged her from shop to shop, the dresses and jewelry and books soon melting into a homogenous blur. "Lovely," she answered each time she was asked for her opinion on a pattern or the particular turn of a sleeve, until Mrs. Lee stopped and stared at her.

"We cannot have it all, ah-Yin. We need to make a decision."

IT WAS AFTER three when they reboarded the ferry, and complaining she was weary from the heat, Jin elected to sit inside, leaving the two of them alone on the deck. Sook-Yin reached for something to say. "Your mother is good company," she managed.

He bent and peered into the cabin where Mrs. Lee was looking through her carrier bags. "She had a good time, I can tell. And yet your arms are empty."

"I don't mind," she said.

"Just as well I bought you this, then." He handed her a small velvet box and gestured for her to open it. Inside was a pendant on a chain: a gold bird on a deep blue background.

"What is the meaning of this?"

"Let me put it on you," he said. He ignored her protests and put it around her neck. Stood back to admire it from a distance. "Yes," he said. "Very beautiful."

"But why? I don't understand."

"You have worked so hard these past weeks. I wanted to get you a treat."

"Then I hope Miss Huang has one too."

He shuffled his feet against the deck. "Would you be angry if I told you I'd lied?"

"About what?"

"You must know the reason I bought it."

She shook his words away with her hand. "I told you, I want to forget all that. As you said, the debt is paid. You don't need to be sorry anymore."

"And yet I am," he said. "I'm sorry that time has been cruel to us. Sorry that I see you all day and can't hug you or talk to you or kiss you. Why do you think I've been staying away?"

Sook-Yin pressed herself to the railing as a falling wave pitched beneath them, swelling and then steadying the ferry. All these years, she thought, the countless ebbs and flows of their lives in which she had imagined these words: sitting in the trees in Kowloon Park; watching him parade around the Walled City; somehow conjuring his eventual return to her. But time had no patience for imagining, and now they had two spouses and three children between them. It was already too late. Too late. "You cannot say this now."

"Then when *can* I say it?" he said. "Unless you don't feel the same way? I made a promise to come back for you, ah-Yin. If I'm wrong, I'll never mention it again."

Sook-Yin closed her eyes. "Not wrong," she said, "but impossible."

"Nothing in life is impossible. We only need the guts to do it." He reached over and clasped her hand. "Please tell me you'll think about it." He startled at the approach of his mother. Whispered. "Ah-Yin, please tell me you will."

She looked across at the approaching pier, felt her home within touching distance. What was it that Peggy had said? *It's not too late, you know . . .* Was it ever too late to be happy?

"All right, I will," she said. She squeezed and then released his hand as Jin walked over to join them.

"It's getting a little chilly in the shade." She looked between the two of them. "It seems chilly out here as well. What on earth has happened between you?"

"We were only discussing business," said Sook-Yin.

"Business and love," she scoffed. "It's what I tell Ba-Ba all the time: *Don't moan about business or love unless you are prepared to do something about it.*" She reached into her bag for her camera. "Let me take a picture," she said.

Sook-Yin took a step to the left. "No. It will not look good."

"Nonsense! Stand closer together. Let me get the skyline behind you."

She shuffled over reluctantly. "I will keep this photo in my pocket," he whispered.

"What?"

"That way, I will always have you beside me."

Sook-Yin turned toward him and the shutter fired in time with her heart.

FIFTY-SEVEN

Lily

43rd Day of Mourning

The day after talking to Maya, I was surprised by a phone call from Feng Mian. She rang from a pay phone in Wan Chai and asked to meet me at Victoria Park. I was to go to the main entrance in Causeway Road, a short walk from Tin Hau station, and wait beneath the statue of the old queen.

It was a typical Hong Kong morning—a threat of sultriness beneath the haze—and the place teemed with the sounds of normal: a family of four meandering on a nature trail; the discordant chatter of workers on their lunch break; the pulsing metronome of a nearby tennis game. Hard to imagine how anything could change but maybe that was the point. Erosion was a stealthy business.

She came dressed like the first time I'd met her, in a demure little pinafore and ankle socks, only this time instead of her roller skates she walked a pristine little dog on a leash. I examined it beneath the visor of my hand. "New family member?" I said.

"Don't talk for the moment. Just follow."

I couldn't imagine why anyone would notice us, plus it was hard to keep walking behind her with the dog pissing every two minutes, but eventually she turned onto a path that gave out to a canopy of heavy trees and sat on the grass. Relieved of the shortness of its chain, the dog wandered over and sniffed me. I'd assumed it was a terrier at first, but up close it looked more exotic.

"He belongs to a neighbor," she said.

"Looks like he belongs on a throne. Doesn't he mind you pulling him about?"

"Apart from going to school, he's the only reason I can leave the apartment."

I mouthed a silent *Oh* as I picked at a fallen leaf. "I'm sorry I couldn't have helped more."

"Are you joking?" she said. "I could've been back in Beijing by now. It was pretty cool what you did, Li-Li Chen."

"It's not as though I'd have got what I wanted."

"Is that the only reason you did it?"

"It wasn't the reason at all. As I'm sure you know very well."

She smiled as she lay down in the shade. "Do you know this park?" she said.

"No. It's the first time I've been here. I really like it, though."

"This is where they hold the vigil for Tiananmen Square. Every year on the fourth of June. No one is allowed to remember it in China."

I looked at her and nodded. "Not commemorating isn't the same as forgetting, though. That counts for Hong Kong, too."

I lay back as Feng Mian fell silent, although I could feel the heat of her gaze beating through the veins of my closed lids. "Is it okay to be frightened?" she said at last. I opened my eyes. Shuffled sideways and touched her sneaker with my shoe.

"It's more than all right. It's natural. I know it's hard to see it that way—with the Handover and Uncle Chor—but pretty soon you're going to be a grown-up and you'll be able to make your own choices."

"I hope I'm like you," she said.

"Definitely not. I forbid it."

A loud beeping rang out from her watch and she stood and

brushed the grass from her dress. "My alarm. I have to go. Chor-Kit knows how long my walks take."

"Can I go with you to the exit at least?"

"I don't like goodbyes," she said. She pulled an envelope out of her pocket. "This is for you, by the way."

I laughed. "Did you actually make me a card?" I flipped it around and looked at it. On the front were some Chinese characters. "What does it say?"

"Don't you know?" She bent down and kissed my cheek and then whispered into my ear. "It says 'Property of Li-Li Chen.'"

I WATCHED HER recede from view and then opened the envelope. Inside was a piece of notepaper—Hello Kitty, obviously.

> Dear Li-Li,
>
> Thank you for what you did. I'm sorry for all the trouble I caused and that we can't be friends anymore. It's safer that way. For both of us.
>
> Now, for my half of the bargain. These were the only things I could find but they should be enough to tell you that your uncle Chor is a liar.
>
> Stay golden, Je Je (big sister),
> Lots of love,
> Feng Mian xxx

I tipped the envelope onto the grass and two photographs fluttered out. I moved to the light to see them better. The first was a picture of Uncle Chor. He was probably no more than ten in it but I recognized the set of his jaw, the arrogance of his expression. Alongside him there was another boy, taller and a little chubbier. He had one hand around Uncle Chor's shoulder, the other holding a trophy of some sort. On the back was an inscription in Chinese and the date: 1951.

The second photo was a faded color one. Uncle Chor was in it again but this time he was in his late thirties. The man with him had his back to the camera but they appeared to be shaking hands over cocktails in some restaurant or other. The inscription looked similar to the first one, only with a date of 1977. It might even have been taken while *we* were there. Why these photos specifically?

AT THE HOTEL, I studied them again. In the first one Uncle Chor and the boy were younger than I'd first assumed. They were wearing identical sports jerseys, the trophy a gesture of some triumph or other. They must have been at school together. I threw the pictures onto the bed. Uncle Chor was almost smirking, his eyes following me around the room like one of those statues of Jesus.

They should be enough to tell you that your uncle Chor is a liar.

Was it possible?

I went across to the desk and picked up the receipt from Mrs. Tam's box and took it over to the window. This time, it wasn't Dad's name I was looking for. It was the characters written beneath. The same ones on the back of the photos. *Lee Hei-Fong*, they said.

FIFTY-EIGHT
Sook-Yin

October 1977

Autumn brought more business to the bank. People had returned from their summer vacations, and with the start of the
new school year and the pressure of books and uniforms came a
renewed demand for money. As much as Sook-Yin sympathized, she
also welcomed the distraction. Life with Julian had continued to be
good and she'd been afraid to think of Hei-Fong and the conversation that they'd had on the boat.

She'd been presented with an impossible puzzle. On the one
hand there was Julian—the man she had made a life with, the father
of her children. It may have emerged from the seeds of something
difficult but there was no doubt that over the years his presence had
been dependable. Even his betrayals had been mitigated by good
intent; from a desire to do better, *be* better.

Yet her assumption that this was love was not quite true. It was
more like survival, coping, and like blowing on the embers of a fire
it was something that had always needed work. Hei-Fong was more
like an inferno, its heat urgent but temperamental and which ever
since her return to Kowloon had kept her in a state of waiting; not

playing Chinese chess with ah-Ma, not watching *God of River Lok* but staring out the window, desperate for the sound of him. And so, it had come to this: What exactly was the meaning of a marriage? The slow burn or the bright inferno? And which one would sustain her the longest?

o   o   o   o   o   o

Her queues at the bank remained a challenge and Miss Huang had taken to patrolling them, forcibly moving this customer or that to the other, shorter lines. Normally, the process went smoothly but that morning there seemed to be a problem.

Eventually, Miss Huang approached her. "Do you know that person?" she whispered.

Sook-Yin, along with her colleagues, looked to the back of the queue where an old woman was stooped over a wooden cane. "No. I've never seen her before."

"Well, she believes she knows you," she said. "And she refuses to see anyone else."

Sook-Yin was known to be good with the clients. She spoke softly to them and longer, and had gained something of a reputation as the person you'd want to see if you had a particularly awkward problem such as debt or a difficult record. She saw the life that existed behind a face and now, as she looked at this woman, she imagined a complex history that deserved a little kindness. "It's all right, Miss Huang," she said. "I don't mind dealing with her myself."

Miss Huang nodded and walked away, seemingly satisfied that despite her own defeat the old woman would have to wait a while. Indeed, it was another twenty-five minutes before she was finally at the front of the queue.

"I'm so sorry to have kept you waiting. I heard that you asked to speak to me."

The woman squinted at her name tag. "You are Miss Chen Sook-Yin?"

"Yes. How may I help you today?"

"Siu-Je, it is a personal matter. Is there somewhere more private we can talk?"

Sook-Yin looked askance at the other clerks. "I'm afraid that requires an individual appointment and all our rooms are booked for today."

"That is a shame," she said. "What I had to say would be to your advantage."

Sook-Yin laughed softly. "My advantage?"

"No matter, my dear," she said. "But remember later, I tried."

She watched her walk away. Beside her, Miss Po raised an eyebrow. "That's a new one," she whispered. "Perhaps she had a tip for Happy Valley."

Even as Sook-Yin laughed, something about the woman had bothered her. It was then she noticed she'd left her walking stick. "Hold my queue," she said. "I'd better run and see if I can catch her."

Outside, she peered along the street but the woman had disappeared. Sook-Yin lingered for a moment on the corner, unsure why she was suddenly afraid.

"You decided to come, then?" a voice said. When she turned, the woman was waiting.

Sook-Yin handed her the cane. "Now we are alone and you can tell me. Whatever your problem is, I'm sure that it can be dealt with."

"Such personal service, Miss Chen. Now I understand." She pointed to a nearby bench and they took a seat together.

"I can't stay long," said Sook-Yin. "My colleagues will wonder where I've gone."

"All right, I'll get to the point. Your husband is playing with fire."

"My husband? What are you talking about?"

"He took out a loan with a friend of mine and now he needs to pay it back."

Relieved, Sook-Yin exhaled. "You have made a mistake," she said. "I know about this already and you'll find the debt has been paid. I have the receipt at home."

"My apologies if I spoke in error . . ." There was something disingenuous about her tone as she fumbled inside her waist bag and pulled out a piece of paper. "I presume you mean this one?" she said.

Sook-Yin took the paper, holding the woman's gaze in defiance before she looked down and read its contents. Her heart stopped at the numbers she didn't recognize; the unfamiliar address at the top and then, at the bottom, her own. *Guarantor: Miss Chen Sook-Yin, Flat 10, 430 Castle Peak Road.* She struggled to find her voice. "When?" she managed.

"The date is there at the top. Three weeks ago, I believe. Take your time," she said. "I can see you've had a surprise." She let out a breath. "Marriage, childbirth, affairs . . . It is always the woman who suffers. Sadly, by not keeping up his repayments your husband has forfeited the privilege of favors. And obviously, you understand the concept of interest." She spread her gnarled fingers across the top of her walking stick. "Your older daughter is remarkably beautiful. I can hardly believe she came out of your belly."

Sook-Yin's head jerked up. "What do you know of my daughter?"

"Your husband brought both of your children when he first came to collect his money. My friend couldn't stop looking at Mei-Hua. Did you like what I did to her hair?" The yellow cloud of curls. The same day Julian had got his *compensation.* "I am doing you a favor, Miss Chen."

"By coming here and threatening me?"

"It is only a friendly warning. My friend calls me his good messenger."

"Then send your message to my husband!"

"Oh, we will," she said. She laid her hand on top of Sook-Yin's—as dry and cold as a lizard's. "And I can guarantee he won't borrow again."

Sook-Yin swallowed. "When do you need the money?"

"We will give you until next Friday." She pointed at one of the storefronts. "I will come to that café to remind you on Thursday and give you further instructions. Meet me as soon as the bank has closed."

FIFTY-NINE

Lily

43rd Day of Mourning

Everything was starting to add up: the Lees pretending not to know my family; arranging my flight home with the embassy; sending Felicia Yuen. Everyone had secrets, it turned out. Wander a few miles here or there, look under rocks instead of through windows, and eventually you'd uncover their roots. Maybe it was never that I didn't belong but simply that everyone had something to hide from me.

Mostly, I was furious with Daniel Lee. I cringed thinking about that night in the restaurant and all his bullshit about doing penance. *All the things I'd shared.*

I tried to call his cell phone but it immediately went to voice mail. I waited and tried again. Nothing. It was an hour before it rang back.

"Hello, Miss Miller?" a voice said. "This is Miss Leung, Mr. Lee's secretary. I can see you've been trying to reach us. How can I help you, please?"

Us. Like the bloody *Godfather.* "It's actually a *personal* call?"

"I see. Well, I'm afraid Mr. Lee is very busy. Perhaps I can take a message?"

I drummed my fingers against the table. "Please tell him to phone me," I said. "Or I'll come to the office and confront him in person."

Another two hours went by and eventually my patience broke and I took a taxi to his building in Wan Chai. Even amid the towers of Gloucester Road it was singularly impressive, rising head and shoulders above its neighbors with a soaring profile of mirrored glass giving way to a palatial lobby.

I walked over to the central reception where a woman, all lipstick and rouged cheeks, stood like an on-board hostess preparing to offer me hot towels. "I'm here to see Mr. Lee."

Her smile maintained its cheerless rictus. "Which Mr. Lee do you mean, miss?"

"Mr. *Daniel* Lee?" I anticipated the stare; the forensic exam of my jeans and T-shirt; her slightly too high laugh.

"You have an appointment, I take it?"

I pulled the business card out of my bag on which he'd written his private number and slid it across the desk. "If you could call him," I said. "Tell him Lily Miller is here and that it's a matter of urgency." I surprised myself with my boldness, the lack of apology at the sound of my own name. The woman read it and dialed a number, speaking hurriedly to someone in Cantonese. Could her eyebrows get any higher?

"Someone will come down to you now."

After five minutes or so, one of the elevators in the lobby sprang open and a prim-looking woman came toward me. "I'm Miss Leung," she said. "I believe I spoke to you earlier." I was just about to protest when she spun around on her heel and gestured for me to follow. "Mr. Lee's office will see you now."

My stomach tightened as we ascended the building, my irritation turning to uncertainty. What exactly was I going to say to him? We emerged near the top of the tower into a greenhouse of several offices, each with a vertiginous view of the harbor as terrifying as it was beautiful. I followed behind the woman, reaching out to the walls for ballast and leaving sweat marks from my fingers on the thick glass.

At the end was a sectioned-off space comprising its own reception and bedecked with miniature palm trees. The woman pressed a button on her desk and then gestured to one of the inner rooms. "You may go in now," she said.

As soon as I opened the door, all doubts about the wisdom of my visit were lost to surprise. Daniel was not in his office. Draped in his place across a sofa was a handsome older woman, flicking through a copy of Chinese *Vogue*. She glanced up but didn't rise. "You must be Miss Miller," she said. She left the slightest of pauses, long enough for a brief appraisal of me. "My name is Jiao Lee. Daniel's mother."

I could have guessed as much. She was the vixen among the foxes, the queen amid the worker bees in her tailored blush-pink trouser suit. I came forward and shook her hand. "It's a pleasure to meet you," I said.

"I'm afraid my son is at one of his meetings. But when Miss Leung received the call from reception, I couldn't resist the opportunity to meet you." She lit a slim blue cigarette and blew the smoke in my direction. "Someone so tall should sit," she said. "Your shadow is blocking the sun."

Fair enough, I supposed. All that glass without anyone seeing you. I perched on one of the armchairs.

"Would you care for some English tea?"

"Thank you, but no," I said.

"I agree, it's quite disappointing here." Her accent was clipped and perfect. Years of elocution, no doubt. "I hear you'll be leaving us soon?" She offered a fatal smile. "Please don't be offended, Miss Miller, but I have always maintained the habit of knowing exactly where I stand. I'm sure that you would agree?"

"I've not always had that choice."

She tapped her cigarette on the edge of the ashtray. "You must be referring to the visit from Miss Yuen. I did advise her not to go, but she is young, and young people, I find, tend to have an un-guarded curiosity that is not always in their best interests."

"What exactly was she curious about?"

Mrs. Lee gave a tinkly laugh. "You don't have to be coy for my benefit. Insecurity isn't merely an English affliction." She raised an eyebrow. "She believes my son is quite taken with you. But as I said, Miss Yuen is young and has yet to understand the insignificance of a passing infatuation."

I folded my arms. "You don't need to reassure her on my account."

"I wasn't referring to you." She yawned as she examined her nails. "Daniel knows the marriage will happen. As soon as the mourning for my husband is over."

My body folded. "Mrs. Lee, I never intended to disrupt your loss, but your husband was the one who asked me here and I'm simply looking for the reason—"

"Why he set this farce in motion?" She crushed her cigarette and waved the smoke away. "Hei-Fong was quite the joker in his time. Elaborate ruses. Impromptu pranks. Most of all, he loved puz-zles. Each year, on our anniversary, he'd organize a treasure hunt around Hong Kong. Off I would go in the car, imagining some ring or some necklace at the end of it, a new horse at Happy Valley, but each time it would be the same thing."

"Which was?"

"The prize was always himself."

I saw her disappointment even now. "And what is the point of *my* treasure hunt?"

"I assume it's the money, naturally."

I shook my head. "Sorry, but I don't think it is. You implied yourself that money was too easy. He could have simply sent that to us in London but he wanted me back in Kowloon, like there was something he needed me to know."

She ran her fingers around the edge of her pearls. "You have more confidence than Miss Yuen gave you credit for. And a great imagination, Miss Miller."

"Do I? Because I've been following the clues myself, you see. Not left by your husband, perhaps, but clues all the same. I couldn't work out the connection at first, which was why I was so baffled by the money, but then I found photos of your husband with my family. Receipts." I leaned toward her. "I know that he knew my father and that they gambled in Kowloon Walled City. That my mum's death might not have been an accident. Was your husband feeling guilty, Mrs. Lee?"

She rose with an irritated flourish. "I think this meeting is over."

"Did you know my father?" I said.

She patted her hair. "I did not."

"But you'd be unlikely to say if you did, right? Not someone with your reputation. The scandal of something to lose."

Her voice rose to an indignant soprano. "You dare to accuse us?" she said. "Did *you* even know your father?"

"Of course I knew him!"

"Then perhaps you should visit your memories again. If you had, you wouldn't have come."

"What the *hell* is going on here?"

Both of us turned at the voice. Daniel was standing in the open doorway, his face a mixture of confusion and anger. "They can hear you all the way down the corridor."

"Miss Miller was just leaving," his mother said. "Have you finished your meeting at last? I have a headache. I need to have dinner."

"What were you talking about?" I sensed his gaze on my face, which I knew was pink and hot. "Are you all right?" he said. I nodded and he turned back to his mother.

"It was a silly misunderstanding," she said. I'd expected her to be angry and was shocked when she bowed her head. She said something to him in Cantonese.

"No. It sounds like I *don't* know."

"Daniel. It's a private matter."

"All right, then let's discuss it in private." He looked at me again. "Do you trust me?" he said.

"What?" My voice was barely a whisper.

"Do you trust me, Lily?"

I hesitated, surprising myself when I answered yes.

SIXTY

Sook-Yin

October 1977

As soon as her shift was over, Sook-Yin ran down to the wages office. "Ah, good, Mr. Lau, you're here. Would it be possible to speak with you a minute?"

"What can I do for you, Miss Chen?"

She took a seat. "It is a rather delicate matter, but I need an advance on my salary."

He finished the haw flake he'd been sucking on. "It's not really our practice, as you know, but I'm sure a day here or there would be fine."

"I was actually hoping for a couple of months." In truth she'd wanted more, but in light of Mr. Lau's caution had been forced to dial back on her request.

"A couple of months, Miss Chen? Are you in some kind of trouble?"

His eyes glinted and Sook-Yin hesitated. Although Mr. Lau was decent enough, she knew how easily a grudge could fester and be weaponized into gossip. She prayed to the gods for forgiveness. "My mother needs an urgent operation."

"Say no more," he said. He raised his hand toward her, the news at odds with the nearness of dinner. "But two months would need a higher authority. Have you spoken to Mr. Lee? I'm sure your connection would stand you in good stead."

"No. I don't want to do that."

"I'm sorry, but this is where we are. Between a rock and a wall."

Sook-Yin stood. "That is okay," she said. "Thank you for listening anyway."

AT DINNER SHE barely spoke, each mouthful tasting like a bullet. Julian, by contrast, was as cheerful as ever, laughing and joking with the children. *Smoking and eating and drinking as though pleasure were going out of fashion.* Her charitable thoughts about the marriage fell away. What had Harvey's kindnesses amounted to except a lifeline to hang herself with?

Even worse than Julian's denial was his assumption that she would pick up the pieces. Hadn't he given her own name as a guarantor? Now that Hei-Fong had paid his first debt, perhaps he believed this was simply the way of things.

LATER, AT HER request, he put the girls to bed in her mother's room so they could talk on their own. When he opened his book instead, Sook-Yin fought back the urge to scream. Stared at the side of his head.

He turned the page with a casual finger. "I thought you said you wanted this job."

"This is nothing to do with job."

"That's not what it sounds like from here. In fact, it's making you a total misery." His eyelids fluttered. "What is it, then?" he said. "Are you having an affair or something? Is that what you've come to confess?" He laughed softly with a wounded certainty. "I suppose your family planned this from the start. Who is it? Your old pal Mr. Lee? With your cozy little job at the bank, hmmm? Seeing him every day. I must have been an—"

"Yes! You are idiot, Julian. I am not having affair. I trying to stop bad people from killing us!"

His eyes froze at the top of the page. "What do you mean?" he said.

"You think I wouldn't find out?" Sook-Yin lowered her voice but it only made the words more menacing. "Shark send little old woman to bank today. Threaten me, threaten children, threaten you. Is very easy you lie to me, huh? Tell me ah-Chor pay your compensation. But you think is easy to lie to these people? This time, I tell you, they kill us."

The book slid out of his hands. "Sook-Yin, they're just trying to frighten you."

"Where is the money, Julian?"

"I've already worked out a plan. I'll go to the bank. I'll beg."

"You would rather be dead than beg! This is why we have problem in first place. You don't know these people. You think your colonial master help you? Your English accent? No accent when body is chop up!"

"Stop it, Sook-Yin! Please!"

"The truth is frightening now, eh? Now you see reality. This is not Hei-Fong people. This is very bad people."

"Then why don't we leave Hong Kong? Pack up tonight and go?"

"Because you give them ah-Ma address! If we go, they come after my family." She was appalled when he started to cry.

"What are we going to do?"

"*I* do," she said. "Like always."

She got up and turned on the main light and then reached into the wardrobe for the suitcase. Inside, she found her jewelry box and tipped it onto the blankets. She took out a watch and examined it and then lifted the satin tray. Beneath was the string of beads that she'd bought on the boat at Suez. She cradled the stones in her hand before putting both things in a sock. "Give me your wedding ring," she said, taking off her own along with her diamond engagement band. Julian did as she asked. "Tomorrow, I sell this," she said. "Try to get money for shark. When is paid, we go back to London."

Even amid his uncertainty Julian couldn't disguise his hope. "Do you mean that—really, Sook-Yin?"

"Yes. I really mean it. We go back to London soon. And then I divorce you," she said.

○ ○ ○ ○ ○ ○

The next day, during her lunch break, Sook-Yin took the sock to the market. She was already familiar with one of its stalls—a buyer and seller of jewelry that she'd often visited while browsing the area. "See anything you like, miss?" the man asked. "I will give you the best price in Kowloon. Jade, silver, gold."

"Are you still buying?" she said.

His smile dimmed. "That depends. Let me see it."

Sook-Yin handed over the jewelry, and he took the loupe from around his neck and squinted at one of the wedding rings. "This is only nine carats. Foreign."

"It is English gold," she said.

The man ran his teeth around the edge. "Yes, and hard as a rock." He turned his attention to the watch—a Seiko that ah-Ma had gifted her when she first went over to London—and shook it against his ear before setting it aside on the table. Picked up the string of beads.

"This is the best one," she said. "The workmanship is Egyptian. It is practically an antique."

He turned it in his hand. "This is children's jewelry," he said. He held it up to the light. "Not even semiprecious. Plastic."

"No, you must be mistaken. It was very expensive at the time."

The man smiled. "I think your husband has played you. Still, it's pretty enough. I could probably sell it as costume jewelry."

Her face flamed. It was he who was taking her for a fool. It wasn't possible she could have been that naive. "What can you give me?" she said. He ran his hands along the items on the table and then added them up on his abacus. Wrote a figure on a piece of paper. Sook-Yin gaped. "Is that all?"

"Lady, this is not Chinese gold. And this diamond is no more than a chip. Believe me, I'm doing you a favor." He shrugged. "Take it or leave it."

"Fine."

He nodded and counted the notes. As he held them out, he noticed her necklace. "I like this one," he said, gesturing with his head. "This is proper gold."

Sook-Yin touched her throat. She had put the bird necklace on that morning, more in defiance than anything else. Now that Julian knew where he stood there was no need to deny its existence.

"You sell this, I give you three times."

It was then she knew the true value of it. Hei-Fong wouldn't have bought her rubbish knowing the declaration he intended to make. "That one isn't for sale."

"Five times. My final offer."

Five times would help her a lot. Not the whole amount by any means, but a good way toward it at least. She paused but then shook her head. "It's not for sale," she said.

WITH WHAT WAS left of her lunch break she hurried to a different branch of Dah Sing and withdrew what was left of her wages. By the time she'd waited in line, she was late getting back to work and her face was gray from worry.

Miss Po tapped her foot on the carpet. "Where have you been?" she said. "You've made me miss my break. I had to tell Miss Huang."

"It doesn't matter. I'm sorry."

"You look terrible. Are you ill or something?"

Before Sook-Yin could answer, Miss Huang appeared at her elbow. Why couldn't anyone cut her some slack? Hadn't she always been a good worker? "I'm sorry for my lateness," she said. "I was at the pharmacy and there was a long queue."

"Never mind that," Miss Huang said. "Mr. Lee has been asking to see you."

HEI-FONG STOOD AND closed the door. "What's going on, ah-Yin? Mr. Lau told me you've been asking for money." He must have noticed her frown. "Please don't be angry at him. He didn't want me to hear it from someone else."

"It wouldn't have come to that if the other staff minded their business."

"He said your mother was ill? Is there anything I can do?"

Sook-Yin stared at her feet. "It was only an excuse," she said.

His eyes grew wide. "Surely it's not your husband again?"

She had no loyalty to Julian anymore, not beyond saving her family from trouble. She knew that. So why did she hesitate? Because she'd recognized Hei-Fong's expression and did not want his pity. She wanted him to love her for her virtues rather than feel sorry for all her mistakes.

"After a fashion," she said. "I need the money to divorce him."

Hei-Fong sat heavily on the sofa. "When did you decide?"

"It's been building up for a while now. He wants to return to London and I wish to stay in Kowloon. Aren't you pleased?"

He took her hand and pulled her down to him. "Yes, I'm pleased!" he said. "My God, ah-Yin, I'm delighted."

She smiled. "I am wearing your necklace," she said. "I'll wear it every day when we're together."

"It looks even more beautiful than I remember." He wetted his lips. "Does Julian know that I bought it?"

"No, but he will guess. He already thinks we are having an affair."

He pressed his palms to his knees. "What did you tell him?" he said.

"I told him—" she stopped. "Does it matter?"

"No, you know I don't care but it doesn't hurt to be careful. It should be me that tells my wife."

"I doubt Julian would tell her," she said. "They've barely said two words to each other. Besides, he has other things to think about."

"Even so."

"Then when do you think we should tell her?"

Hei-Fong stood and fetched a letter from his desk. "This is strictly between you and me," he said, "but the board of directors are looking to promote me. It will mean more money and shares in the company. More training in how to do investments."

Sook-Yin barely glanced at it. "That's very nice," she said. "But it doesn't answer my question."

"Can't you see it does? With this promotion I can rent you an apartment. Visit you and the children at weekends."

Something caught in her throat. "What do you mean by this?"

Hei-Fong batted the air. "My wife will see sense eventually. Besides, divorce is a costly business."

"You are suggesting I am kept as your mistress?"

He took her hand again. "You must not use that word, ah-Yin. You are my one and only love."

"Below your reputation . . ."

"Why are you saying that? There's Daniel to think about, too."

"But Li-Li and Mei-Hua are unimportant?"

Would she be the one in bed when Daniel came knocking on the door looking for his mother's housekeeping? Would she be the one he resented? What exactly was the point of the future if you couldn't make good on the mistakes of the past? "We have all made sacrifices," she said, pulling her hand away. "I am too old now to be a dirty secret."

Hei-Fong put his head in his hands. "You need to see this from my point of view. Do you know how difficult this is? How many lives I'm trying to juggle?"

Sook-Yin pursed her lips and stood. "Yes. I know," she said.

NO LONGER CARING about the time, she went to the staff room and made herself tea. She took an old box from the bin, filling it out with tissue before she laid the necklace inside and took it down to the mail room. "Mr. Lee needs this sent right away," she said as she filled out the label in her best hand. "Can you make sure that it goes today?"

SHE WAS BACK on the main floor of the bank when Miss Po approached her station. "Was everything all right upstairs? I hope I didn't cause any trouble."

"No. It was not what I expected."

As soon as she said it, she realized; knew that Hei-Fong had given her the courage to finally do what she needed to. All this time she'd been breaking her back, racking her brain to come up with a solution when the answer had always been there. The one person who lay at the root of things—her banishment, her trouble, her misery.

And now she was going to confront them.

SIXTY-ONE

Lily

―――――――――――
―――――――――――

43rd Day of Mourning

Partly through spite I'd ordered room service: a whole lobster with all the trimmings, as much caviar as I could stomach, along with two bottles of chardonnay. If Mrs. Lee was determined to see me off, the least she could do was drown my sorrows.

Half an hour later there was a knock at the door, but when I opened it, Daniel was outside. "Can we talk?" he said. I stepped back and he came into the room, shutting the door behind him. He glanced at the menu on the bed.

"Your mother's buying me dinner."

He fetched a bottle of water from the minibar and then sank into one of the armchairs. Loosened his tie. "I'm sorry for what happened at the office."

"She's quite the force of nature. Did she say anything after I left?"

"She doesn't want to discuss it."

"Well, then." I caught my reflection in the console mirror. I'd been crying and my face was a mess and I was surprised how little it mattered. I took a seat in the opposite chair. "So why did you bother to come? I'll be out of your hair in a few days and you can all get on with your lives."

"I wanted you to believe me."

"Right. Big ask at the moment. I don't know what I believe anymore."

He held out his hands in appeal. "I was seven when they sent me to America! The first time I even heard of your mother was in my father's will."

"Yeah, I know, I get that. But I don't understand why you didn't question it, especially after that photo of me and my sister."

He pulled at his earlobe. "My mother claimed that the picture was a random thing, that perhaps your mother was a servant he once had. When you told me she'd died in an accident I didn't want to insult her memory."

I laughed. "You must have more money than sense! Who leaves a servant's children a million pounds?" I got up and paced the room. "Do you know what makes it worse? That with all your talk about honoring the dead, this was never about what your dad wanted. It was only about clearing your conscience. You had no interest in working it out."

"I can't argue with that," he said.

"You're not even trying to justify it!"

He rolled the bottle in his hands. "Tell me you've never made excuses for your family. That you were always brave enough to confront them when something didn't seem right. That you weren't afraid of them rejecting you. Why the hurry to send me to the States? Was it for the opportunities or because I wasn't good enough? Not the son they hoped to have had? You asked why I didn't question it, but you didn't question *your* family either."

"I did! And they fobbed me off. They said I couldn't remember living here, that our Chinese family hated us. That there was no point living in the past. They shut me down every time I questioned it until in the end I stopped."

"But that's exactly my point. The minute we stop asking questions we become complicit in the silence. We surrender to make *our* lives easier."

"Oh, I've had a wonderfully easy life!"

"I'm not suggesting it was easy," he said. "Only that we played the part so we could belong."

A knock at the door made us both jump, and when Daniel went to open it there was a waiter standing outside with the stupid dinner I'd ordered. The lobster was bigger than my head, its claws bright red and ridiculous. Daniel tried to keep a straight face as he tipped the waiter and saw him out. "You'd better eat that," he said.

"Oh, fuck off," I said, but I smiled. "I only got it to punish your mother."

He took the silver spoon and prodded the caviar. "Maybe we should share it," he said.

OVER DINNER, I showed him the photographs. He wiped his fingers and picked up the earliest one. "This is a picture of my father."

"Yeah, I know. And that's my uncle Chor beside him. Unfortunately, he's a bit of a wanker. Does his name sound familiar at all?"

He turned it over and read the writing. "Chen Chor-Kit," he said. He shook his head and picked up the second photo. "It seems like they were old friends but my father never mentioned him. Perhaps they simply lost touch."

"Or else they fell out about something."

"Why didn't you show me these pictures before?"

"I only came into them recently. That's why I turned up at your office. I suspected you'd always known the connection and had been trying to hide it from me."

"Even after that night in the restaurant? You didn't trust me at all?"

"It's one of my things," I said. "Try not to take it too personally." I folded and unfolded my napkin. "Why did your parents do that, anyway? Send you off to America, I mean."

He shrugged. "Like I said, sometimes I thought it was me, sometimes that my mother was not a natural parent. She knew children were important to the marriage but she preferred the good things in life."

"Children *are* the good things," I said.

"Yes, but there is love and then there is duty. I think she confuses the two of them sometimes."

"Is that why you're marrying Miss Yuen?" He almost choked on his mouthful of wine. "Didn't you know she paid me a visit?"

"What did she want?" he said.

"I'm not really sure." I was actually enjoying his discomfort. I smiled and raised my glass to him. "Good luck with that one, anyway."

He tapped his fingers on the stem of his glass. "It was an arrangement between our families. To keep the money flowing between us."

"How very Chinese," I said. "In that case I've no idea why she was threatened by *me*."

He laughed. "Is that what she said?"

"It's what your mother told me."

"You shouldn't sell yourself short." Two perfectly round disks of scarlet appeared on each of his cheeks and he pretended to study the photos again. "Have you thought about what you're going to do?"

"No. Not really," I said. "Your mum has made sure that I'm leaving, meaning I'll probably never know the whole story."

"You should still be proud of yourself. I can't imagine coming back here was easy."

Maya's voice popped into my head. *You've got so much to look forward to. Promise me you'll leave it alone now.* "Honestly? You don't know the half of it. I've told some lies myself, although I *did* make a friend."

"A friend?" The way he said it made me smile.

"I should be so lucky! But she gave me a gorgeous present." I pulled the pendant from my shirt and showed it to him. "Look."

He reached out a finger, stared at it. "Where did you get this?" he said.

"Why?"

"I'm serious. Where did you get it?"

I frowned. "I met a woman in the lobby one morning. She was wearing it and I told her it was beautiful. The next thing, it was outside my room, all wrapped up and addressed to me." His face paled. "That's the truth. What's wrong?"

"Lily," he said, and his voice broke. "That necklace belongs to my grandmother."

SIXTY-TWO

Sook-Yin

October 1977

Ah-Chor had never made it to Central. Despite his years of posturing, he lived in the same small bungalow in the modest enclave of North Point. Without the softening touch of a wife its yard was pitted and sparse, a brown plot of unturned soil that only attracted weeds. What better proof, she thought, of a life getting what it deserved.

Sook-Yin watched him awhile through the window, humming tunelessly to himself as he prepared a bowl of instant ramen and then adorned it with strips of cold pork belly. When he didn't answer her knock at the door, she went back and rapped on the glass.

"Aiya! Are you trying to kill me?"

"I've been knocking for days," she said. "Come over and let me in."

He gave a sad little glance at his bowl and then walked through and opened the front door. "Why are you here?" he said. "I just got home from work and I'm trying to have my dinner."

"You can eat it after I talk to you." She followed him into the living room.

"I hope this is important," he said.

"You are going to give me twenty thousand dollars."

"Eh?"

"I am deadly serious, ah-Chor. And I need it by the end of tomorrow. I will pay you back as soon as I can."

Ah-Chor laughed. "We always said you were going to go mad. Wait until ah-Ma hears about this one!"

"Go ahead," she said. "And I will tell her what you did, too." His lips twitched. "I know what you did to Julian. How you managed to forge his references, take him gambling in the Walled City. You decided from the start to ruin us."

He folded his arms. "Where is your proof?" he said.

"Hei-Fong confessed it all to me."

"You believed that sewer rat over your family?"

"I am willing to take my chances. Hei-Fong is an influential man now and corruption is a serious crime. What do you think your bosses would say?"

Ah-Chor stuttered toward the sofa. "There's no need to hurry into anything. Let's sit down, at least."

"I do not want to sit down. All I need is what you owe me."

"You are stressed ah-Yin, I can see that."

Sook-Yin stamped her foot. "It is all your fault I am here!"

He seemed taken aback by her fierceness but then raised his chin and sneered at her. "Did I put a gun to your husband's head? He is an ant that thinks he's a god. It was his own weakness that ruined him. Besides, if you are so desperate for money why don't you ask your criminal lover?"

"Hei-Fong is not my lover." The sound of his name hurt her heart.

Ah-Chor laughed again. "He's dumped you, hasn't he?" he said. "How is it we all see sense except for you, Sook-Yin? You would rather keep your feet in the fire than admit that it's too hot. That is how stupid you are."

"I need the money to divorce my husband."

Ah-Chor clutched his chest and pretended he was having a heart attack. "*Finally* you admit your mistake!"

"It is my own decision," she said. "I'm not doing it because you will it! My children are not a mistake."

"Your half-breed children," he said. "Do you know that's what ah-Ma calls them?"

"Liar! She loves my children."

"No. She pities them," he said. "The same way she pitied our father's bastard when they laid him in that grave."

She blinked back mortified tears. "Why are you so horrible? I know it was your idea to send me to London. You poisoned ah-Ma's mind against me."

"As if she were strong enough to do it herself! After our father went off with that whore it fell to me to be man of the house, to protect our family's reputation. Do you think I would have let you sabotage that, a brainless washerwoman? You were nothing but an embarrassment."

"Are you that obsessed with appearances? Think that everyone spends their time looking at you? I deserve some closure, at least. Tell me the truth, ah-Chor! Tell me why you hate me so much. Is it really because I'm stupid?"

"We're not talking about this," he said.

Ah-Chor turned away and for the first time she found herself doubting it. There was a new uncertainty in the stoop of his back, in the flick of his gaze across the carpet. He pinched the skin between his fingers. "Why?" His voice was flat. "Because you were always their favorite! I saw what ah-Ma did—saving you pieces of chicken in a bowl, taking your side in arguments while I was breaking my back at school so I could earn a name for the family. You couldn't even finish your education, but did they ever love me as much? Tell me they were proud of me? No. Everything was ah-Yin, ah-Yin! And then you returned like the prodigal daughter and I saw it happening again."

For a long moment she was stunned into silence. How was it even possible that all these years she'd focused on her own shame, her belief that her brother was embarrassed by her, that she was wrong? Despite this, her cynicism crept in. What if he was lying even now, adding another brick to the wall of her guilt? She wouldn't have put it past him.

She was surprised when he crossed the floor and opened a large box beside the sofa, found herself holding her breath as she recognized the things within it: the tin cup that he'd won with ah-Fong at the under-10s badminton tournament, a selection of medals for swimming and chess. He reached for something beneath them—a small textbook of mathematical functions—and showed her its inscription: *To Chor-Kit, from Ma-Ma and Ba-Ba. Good luck for all your success.* He laughed. "They couldn't even write *with love*."

Sook-Yin bowed her head. It was like looking through the wrong end of a telescope, yet having lived through rejection herself she saw his pain was true, even if its source was mistaken. "You are wrong," she said to him then. "Ba-Ba may not have cared enough to stay, but ah-Ma loves you. She does! She's always saying how she wants you to be happy."

"I don't need your pity, Sook-Yin."

"But you have spent your life being sad for something that is only a lie . . ."

He waved a hand toward her. "It's fine," he said. "I will live. When has love ever helped me before?" He rubbed the words from his face, as though aware he'd said too much. "So, you need this money pretty badly?" His tone had become softer, kind even.

"Yes."

He walked over to the credenza and counted out a handful of notes. "I only keep this much at home. I can get you the rest in the morning."

"Thank you, brother," she said. She reached out to take it but he pulled his hand back.

"Your life is truly mine, now. So first, I would like you to beg." Her face fell. "Come on, get down on your knees. Admit that your life belongs to me."

"Ah-Chor, why are you doing this?"

"As you said, I am sad. Seeing you beg will give me pleasure."

Sook-Yin stared at him in disbelief, imagined cutting the smirk from his face line by evil line. What a fool she had been for caring. Finally, she got down on her knees and her voice, when it came, was clear and loud. "All right, I will say it," she said. "My life does not belong to you or this family. It is mine and mine alone."

SIXTY-THREE

Lily

―――――――――
―――――――――

44th Day of Mourning

Aafter the calm of the night came the storm. When I woke, alarmless at seven, diagonal rain was lashing at the window, the sky a wounded smudge interspersed with electric light. Later in the taxi it was worse, and aside from the blurry glimpses of the highway I could have been going anywhere.

Only when the rain had started to exhaust itself and I finally caught sight of the peninsula did I realize how far we'd traveled; farther south than Uncle Chor's at Wan Chai, toward the site of Stanley Prison. The weather slowed to a drizzle and I wound down the window. The green smell of the trees enveloped me along with the heady scent of freshly bloomed bougainvillea. "Where are we?" I said to the driver.

"This is Tai Tam," he said. "Red Hill Peninsula close now."

In the distance I saw a group of apartments overlooking the mouth of the bay. The vista looked vaguely Mediterranean with the sun hitting the pale pastel houses stacked neatly on the curve of the headland. It was less ostentatious than I had imagined, as though, like Jin Lee herself, they only needed to announce themselves with a whisper.

Following the revelation about the necklace, Daniel had called his grandmother and she'd agreed to meet me that morning. But even with the promise of answers, I was unsure.

Ten minutes later we arrived at the complex. The apartment, though modern in build, was rendered in a colonial style with large arched windows of tinted glass and a sherbet-lemon exterior. I got out of the taxi at the side entrance and followed a flight of stone steps to an unruly garden on the roof of the building.

"We meet again, my dear."

Daniel's grandmother, as I knew her now, was sitting on a pale pink lounger directly overlooking the bay, half-covered by a woolen blanket. I went over and gave her a hug. "You deceived me," I said.

"Where do you think Hei-Fong got his love of mischief?" She gave me an inscrutable smile. "And I think he would have loved you. You played his game very well."

Not ready for whatever this was, I walked to the edge of the roof so I could distract myself with the view: the faint chill of the wind on my face, the serrations of the grass along the bay, the smell of waiting rain. These were the things I would hold in my memory. The distinct line between before and after.

"You have an incredible home," I said.

"It is a good reward for a bad life." She pointed to the bay. "Those were all fishing villages at one point, but they took a beating once the Japanese invaded. The reservoirs and dams, you see? It was a very strategic territory. He who controls the water . . ." She patted her blanket. "But you have not come for a history lesson. At least not about Tai Tam Bay."

"I find history fascinating," I said.

"Another story for a different day. It's not good to have too many sad endings."

I looked at her. "Is that what I've come to hear?"

"Everything is open to interpretation."

The terrace door slid open behind her and Daniel appeared, carrying a large tray laden with tea things. He set it down on the table in front of us. "I'm glad you made it," he said. I glanced at the fluttering curtains.

"Is your mother here too?" I whispered.

He smiled and put a finger to his lips. "My mother would really hate this."

"Your mother is an idiot," said Mrs. Lee. She flicked a finger at him. "Leave us now please, *syun zai*."

I stepped forward. "If he wants to, I'd like him to stay." Daniel nodded his thanks and we took a seat on the small wicker sofa.

"Very well," Mrs. Lee began. "You must ask me what you want to know."

"I suppose I want to know everything."

She snorted. "That is not only impossible, but foolish. You are not learning the piano now."

"All right." My throat was scratchy and dry. "Did Hei-Fong . . . my mum . . ." I said.

"Whatever you think of my son, he was not responsible for Sook-Yin's death."

Even if some part of me had suspected this, it seemed a relief to Daniel, whose leg visibly relaxed against mine. He opened his mouth to say something but his grandmother held up her hand. "He *was* a fool to his name, though—something he regretted till the day he died."

"I need to hear it from the beginning," I said. "I assume they met through my uncle Chor. He and your son were at school together?"

"Hei-Fong was a scholarship boy. In those days your family was poor too, but not in the same way as us. We lived in Kowloon Walled City, the lowest of the low in those days, but even then, he aspired to greatness. He worked hard enough at school, but he also got in with bad people. It was inevitable in a place like that. Our meat, our rice, our shoes. All of it probably stolen. Debts that had to be paid in kind. When your uncle became an academic, he agreed to give ah-Fong assistance—made certain aspects of his past disappear, which allowed him to enter the bank."

"So, did the two of them fall out? Did my uncle think that Hei-Fong betrayed him?"

She wrinkled her brow. "In what way?"

"By going against his family." I reached down into my bag and showed her the receipt I'd found. "This was among my Po-Po's effects. I think your son got my father into gambling."

She read it and shook her head. "Hei-Fong *paid* your father's debt."

"I'm sorry?"

"I know these receipts," she said. She pointed to the remnants of the copper stain. "That seal means he took the debt over. Sadly, your father was not a wise man."

I was getting the feeling she was right. That there was worse to hear. Despite this, I felt sorry for Dad: his ambition, his stupidity, his weakness. And where did Hei-Fong fit in to it? Was it love, or guilt, that had paid Dad's debt? I touched Daniel's arm. "I'm sorry for asking," I said. "But did something happen between my mum and your son?"

Her lips tightened. "There was no affair," she said, "although they loved each other from childhood." She picked at a spore on the blanket and then let it be taken by the wind. "By the time they were willing to admit it, both of them were committed to other people. They each agreed they would leave their marriages, but Hei-Fong grew frightened of what he would lose. His job, his reputation, his public face. All the things he had worked for. And your mother quite rightly refused to be his mistress." She gestured to the pendant around my neck. "That necklace was his last gift to her." She pulled a photograph from under her blanket. "This was taken on the day he bought it. The last time that I saw ah-Yin."

Daniel took the picture and held it between us. It had been taken on the Harbor Ferry—the skyline sparser than the way it looked now but unmistakable in its shape. Hei-Fong and Mumma were standing together, their faces caught in profile as they turned toward each other. There was an unmistakable glow to her face, a freedom or happiness that made me swallow, while Hei-Fong's expression was studied, as if he were committing her features to memory in a candid instant unintended for posterity. By any other name it was love, and our looking became an invasion.

Judging by the redness of the trees, the picture had been taken in autumn, and like everything viewed from the past there was a terrible inevitability about it, the sense that the moment had gone and could never be recovered or undone. My heart clenched at the date on the back: September 25, 1977. Mumma couldn't have known what lay around the corner—that beyond her thin cotton dress, the smiles and promises and secrets, in little over a fortnight she would be dead.

"The necklace came to me one morning in a box. There was no letter or explanation and so finally I confronted my son. If it's any consolation at all, he knew that he was an idiot." She directed her gaze at Daniel. "What is the use of love if you are not prepared to do something about it?"

Daniel's voice, when it came, sounded thin. "I suppose my mother knew?"

"She certainly suspected," Jin said. "But then, she won in the end and that was all she needed."

"There's still something I don't understand," I said. "If Hei-Fong *paid* my father's debt, why did it make my uncle angry? I mean, I know he disapproved of her marriage but it was his sister that his friend was helping, and surely that protected my uncle's reputation."

"You really *don't* understand," she said then. "It was your uncle who started it all. He was the one who led your father into gambling."

"What?"

"Sometimes we fall victim to our baser instincts." She smiled but there was no joy in it. "The bond between siblings runs deep, Miss Chen, and not always in favor of the current. I don't know any of these things for sure, but I know what Hei-Fong told me and I have no reason to doubt it. He blamed himself enough for what happened. Sook-Yin was convinced that her brother was ashamed of her, but I've long wondered if it was almost the opposite—fear that he could never be loved in the same way. Whatever your mother had done—become a millionaire, married an emperor—Chor-Kit would still have punished her because she had the one thing that he wanted. Sook-Yin was happy in Kowloon. Why did she end up in London?"

For a moment I couldn't say anything. It all made a terrible sense now—Uncle Chor's bitterness, his anger, his ambition. Jesus. I'd been closer to the mark than I'd thought with him. I thought about me and Maya. No matter the arguments we'd had—even our rivalry for Dad's affections—she would never have considered abandoning me. How could Uncle Chor have lived with his conscience?

"What happened to my mum, Mrs. Lee?"

She pressed her lips together. "That is where my story ends. I do not know for certain."

"Do *you* think it was a random accident?"

"That was how they chose to record it. But Hei-Fong had his suspicions." She looked at me. "I take it you've never questioned it before?"

"No. Why would I?" I said. "I've been told a different story my whole life. That she'd simply looked the wrong way on the street. When I first heard about your son's bequest, I had no idea about the family connection."

"You thought Hei-Fong was driving the car?"

I reddened. "If I'm being honest, it crossed my mind, yes. And then Maya, my sister—" I hesitated. "She said it was amazing what guilt did to people."

Her gaze became curious. "Mei-Hua decided not to come to Kowloon?"

I shook my head. "I didn't tell her I'd come until this week. And then she was furious . . . worried."

Mrs. Lee looked a little disquieted. "That is very interesting," she said. "Miss Chen, I want you to remember something. Though an act may appear to be done from hate, it can come from a need to be loved in the end."

"All right . . ." My heart was pounding again.

"My daughter-in-law was right about one thing. All the answers you needed were at home. But you were too afraid to ask the right questions."

"I don't understand," I said.

"The day your mother was killed. Your sister, Mei-Hua, was with her."

SIXTY-FOUR

Sook-Yin

October 1977

Sook-Yin's legs were heavy as she climbed the steps. Two days before the deadline and she was no closer to finding the money.

The apartment was eerily quiet and she called out into the darkness until ah-Ma shuffled out from the bedroom. "I assumed you were working late," she said. She reached over and switched on the lamp, which lit the space with a sickly gloom. "I went to lie down for a nap."

"Where is everyone else?"

"Mrs. Chee took the girls for tofu. And Julian has gone out for a walk."

"A walk? Do you know where he went?" Despite everything the two of them had been through, she did still care about him. You couldn't disregard eleven years in a heartbeat. What if the old woman had lied to her? Had lured Julian into a trap?

"I'm not his wife!" Ah-Ma laughed. "All I know is he looked quite sick today." She straightened the cover on the sofa. "I hope he will be well tomorrow. I promised ah-Li I would take her shopping. Mei-Hua gets too much attention and it will do them good to do something separate." She straightened at Sook-Yin's silence. "Have I said something to upset you, ah-Yin?"

"No! Thank you. That will be nice for her." She went over and hugged her mother, working herself up to say the words. "Ma-Ma, do you love my children?" Ah-Ma flinched, as if the words had burned her.

"What a terrible thing to ask me! I can't remember a life without them." A cloud passed over her features. "And why are you saying this anyway? Are you going to leave, after all?"

"No, Ma-Ma, I'm not leaving."

"Then why are there tears in your eyes?"

"They are only happy tears."

Ah-Ma searched her face for the lie. Squeezed her elbow. "Then I am going to make har-gao and chili beef! Let us get old and fat together!"

She disappeared into the kitchen but then returned with a thick padded envelope. "I almost forgot," she said. "This was left for you downstairs at the front desk."

Sook-Yin's stomach turned. "Who left it?" she said in a whisper. "Why didn't they bring it upstairs?"

"Why so upset? It's here now."

"And you're sure Mrs. Chee has the children?"

"Yes! I said so, didn't I?" Ah-Ma tilted her head, her lips pushed out in confusion. "What on earth's got into you, ah-Yin? Aren't you going to open the envelope?"

"I will," she said. "In a little while."

IT TOOK HER an hour to work up the courage. *It's nothing*, she told herself. *Your imagination is working overtime.* Nonetheless, she was careful with the envelope, sliding her nail along the flap so as not to disturb what was in there. She would just peek into the top at first.

The seal had compressed the contents and the package immediately sprang open. Not a finger, not blood, but banknotes! Sook-Yin let out a gasp of surprise and then pulled out a sheet of paper. There were only two characters written on it:

恭喜

(Congratulations)

She tipped out the cash and counted it. Twenty thousand and one dollars exactly. Her first instinct was that Hei-Fong had sent it, although the message didn't make sense and how could he have known the exact amount? She ran her finger over the notes—crisp and fresh from the bank.

Ah-Chor?

She hugged the stack to her chest, her shock overtaken by relief. Was it her show of defiance that had made him realize the meanness of his ways, the falseness of his grudge against her? Had he finally seen her as an equal? It didn't matter. When this was all over, she would go to see him. Try to mend their bridges. Be a family together.

She went to the wardrobe to put the money in the suitcase and then changed her mind. Julian had seen her take her jewelry from it, and what was to say he wouldn't check on the off chance? She looked around the room. On top of the wardrobe was a tin of Chinese checkers. She remembered it from her childhood, its exterior dusty and covered with abandoned webs. She took it down and prized off the lid. The space inside was perfect.

"What are you doing, Mumma?"

Lily and Maya appeared in the doorway as Sook-Yin pushed the money inside it. "'Chinese checkers,'" Maya read. "Can me and Lily play?"

"Sorry, Maya, this game very delicate. It come all the way from my childhood. Po-Po will be angry if you break it. How about I find you cards?"

Maya shrugged. "Okay."

Sook-Yin put her hand on her head. "Good girl. Good girl," she said. "You have nice time with Mrs. Chee?"

"Uh-huh. She bought us yummy hot tofu in syrup. I wish Daddy had been able to come but Po-Po sent him out for a walk."

"Po-Po sent him?" Sook-Yin blew out her cheeks. She had been imagining things, after all.

Maya nodded as she opened a drawer and retrieved the pack of playing cards. "She said he was looking yellow." She took Lily's hand and skipped out of the bedroom. "Maybe he's turning Chinese after all!"

SIXTY-FIVE

Lily

44th Day of Mourning

I don't remember the journey back to the hotel, although I remember the rain returning. All afternoon, without my notice, the preparations for the Handover had been happening and the promenade was awash with umbrellas as people staked out their places for the fireworks. I switched on the TV in my room. There was blanket coverage on at least four of the networks and I watched the scenes on repeat: Chris Patten cradling the Union Jack as he left Government House for the last time, the farewell ceremony at the Prince of Wales Barracks. Strange to think that less than ten miles away something truly historical was taking place, such a momentous sense of an ending, and I had no idea what I should be feeling or whose side I was really on.

I poured a vodka and drank it on the balcony. Despite the rumbles of thunder from the hills it was a near-perfect evening on the harbor, the breast of the water so calm that the lit floats barely shuddered on its surface. A panda and then a dragon drifted by, a field of lotus in garlanded splendor. Was it really as easy as it seemed, this changing of one state to another, the inevitability of confronting your destiny?

"Today is a day of celebration, not sorrow . . ."

I had lived through other moments like this—that feeling of standing on the precipice of something already set in motion that I couldn't see past or take back—but now as I looked toward Central there was only one that came to mind. That last day in my room at Cambridge.

AS SOON AS I'd woken that morning it had felt wrong in all the right kinds of ways, the sun only augmenting my clarity. My latest essay—a good one on Mozart—lay waiting to be delivered to my tutor, its edges straightened and perfect, my pen arranged alongside it. There was a pleasing closure to its tableau, a message that needed answering, and this, too, I'd laid on my desk. The sealed envelope addressed to them both.

Dear Dad and Maya, I'm sorry.

I'd been remembering something as I wrote it, something about the way they'd always joked I was the unwitting genius of our family and how one day I would make them famous. But over the years I'd realized how untrue that was, that all that time I'd just been part of the audience, watching someone else's rhythm and trying to turn the pages in time. If I *had* been in sync for a moment it was only an accident of physics, like monkeys pressing on typewriters or the way a stopped clock on the wall still manages to be right twice a day.

People were always telling me that the fear of getting over depression was worse than the illness itself, that fear of how to be someone else. That wasn't my problem. I already had so many versions to choose from: the healthy me who wanted rid of her meds, the perfectionist sister-daughter, the conjurer me whose other half had vanished. And, conducting them all, this depressive sick version of me who wanted to see how much she could rock the boat, and *that's* not who I wanted to be. Not when our lives had capsized already.

It was Elise who saved me that day. *I just had a weird feeling*, she said. *Something was telling me to check on you.* I'd seen too much of human behavior to ever believe in Fate, but I believed in the subconscious. In timing. Isn't that what had brought me to Hong Kong—to face a different kind of music?

MY FIRST REACTION at Tai Tam had been fury. It was like someone had torn up my history book, juggled the fragments of my life in a bag and asked me to reassemble myself from its pieces. Only now, as I stood on the balcony—facing down my twenty-year assumption that it was me who had been the victim—did I understand the feeling as guilt.

Maya had seen Mumma die.

The unerring success of my sister's life suddenly made a terrible sense to me: the consolation of prizes and money, the false flags she'd presented as living. She was both afraid and grateful for her life in a way I had never appreciated, haunted in a way I would never understand. Why hadn't she ever told me?

I drank through the rest of the evening, numbing the edges of my shame with alcohol and the spectacle of fireworks, the sky florid and black by turns and the clock ticking down to the hour.

At ten to twelve I glanced back at the TV to watch the final minutes of the ceremony. It was both as solemn and pompous as I'd imagined, until an instant before the stroke of midnight something weird happened. They'd lowered the Union flag and were waiting to raise the Chinese standard when there was a delay of several seconds. Prince Charles looked as awkward as ever but it wasn't this that caught my attention. Rather, it was the essence of the thing—the moment when Hong Kong belonged to nobody. It was independent. Free at last. I thought of Feng Mian and Victoria Park. Hoped that somewhere she was stealing her own march.

ALONG THE PROMENADE I was jostled by the departing crowds as they returned to the routine of their lives. The air was thick with the smell of sulfur; the huge tower they'd erected on the harbor eerily fragile and spent, yet apart from these few small totems it seemed that nothing epochal had happened. Until tomorrow, and tomorrow, and tomorrow.

Within the hour it had started to rain again, the hesitant dimples of earlier giving way to a heavy downpour that lashed the pavements and filled the gutters. I sat on a bench and let it soak me.

At half past one I walked back to the hotel and caught my reflection inadvertently in the mirrored glass. I looked ghastly: a cold and pale risen Lazarus haunted by a past that should have been dead.

And then, near reception, I saw another ghost. I was convinced I'd imagined it at first until it pulled a face and floated toward me. "Hello, Lil," it said. "You might look happier to see me."

SIXTY-SIX

Sook-Yin

October 13, 1977

For the first time in a number of weeks Sook-Yin spent the day at work without worry. "Look at you, all happy," Miss Po said as they tidied their desks that morning. "Anyone would think you had won Mark Six."

Sook-Yin smiled. Although she was due to meet the old woman, the prospect no longer terrified her and that was as good as winning the lottery. Vanity, or pride perhaps, had almost made her bring the money that morning but she'd decided against it. Now was not the time to break rules.

As the close of business approached, however, tangled weeds took root in her stomach and she jumped when Miss Huang approached her. "Are you staying for Mr. Yu's drinks?" she said. "His little retirement party?"

Sook-Yin had completely forgotten about it. "What time is it going on until?"

"Only a couple of hours or so. We're putting a few tables out on the floor but the cleaners will get mad if we stay too long."

"In that case I would love to," she said. A celebration seemed strangely appropriate. She might even have a glass of champagne.

Guiltily, she fetched her coat as everyone else began preparing the space—blowing up balloons and pinning up banners. "I have to run and meet someone at the café," she said as she passed Miss Po. "Don't eat all the cake without me!"

THE OLD WOMAN was nowhere to be seen. Sook-Yin peered through the steamy window and then ordered a glass of iced tea and took it to a table outside. Waited.

She'd been there almost half an hour before the woman appeared. She looked sprightlier than Sook-Yin remembered and no longer carried a cane. "You are later than we agreed," she said. She glanced in the direction of the bank, worried that her absence had already been noticed.

"My sincere apologies, Miss Chen. I had a troublesome client to deal with."

Her words cast a shadow on the table. Even now it seemed impossible that such an innocuous-looking old woman should trade in this sinister business. But maybe that was the point. She was invisible only to those who didn't matter.

"Did you manage to get the money?"

"Yes."

The woman smacked her lips in approval. "You must be a very resourceful young woman. Why don't you buy me a tea to celebrate?"

What was the point of arguing? One more day and it would be over. Sook-Yin got up and went into the café. There was a longer queue at the counter now—the usual line of commuters buying drinks for the journey home—and she tapped her foot, growing restless. At last, she bought a pot of green tea and brought it out to the table. "Here is your drink," she said. "Now please tell me the arrangements for tomorrow."

The woman appeared not to hear her at first. Her head was turned in the opposite direction, distracted by something that was happening down the street. Sook-Yin followed her gaze and saw two people running toward them: a shock of long blond hair conspicuous next to the black. To her horror, she recognized Miss Po. She was pointing in the direction of the café, and holding her hand was Maya.

Sook-Yin mouthed her daughter's name as Maya broke free and barreled toward her. Miss Po raised her chin in salute and then turned and headed back to the bank. "Maya! What are you doing here?"

"I had to come . . . in a taxi . . . oh, Mumma, Mumma, Mumma!" Filled with relief at seeing her, Maya let free the sobs she'd been holding in.

"What is it? Is it Po-Po?" said Sook-Yin. Grotesque images flashed through her mind, too quickly to get a solid grasp of them—a burning building, a sunken ferry. "Has something happened to her and Lily?"

"Daddy! . . . It's Daddy! It's Daddy!"

Sook-Yin gripped her shoulders, even as she tried to stay calm. "Maya! Tell me what has happened."

Maya's expression crumbled. "He . . . he . . . Mumma . . . he's gone . . ."

SIXTY-SEVEN

Lily

45th Day of Mourning

The queue for taxis at the airport was ridiculous."
Maya stood by the balcony door, her growing bump an
alien silhouette against the now dormant panorama of the harbor.
"I'm so bummed that I missed all the fireworks."

She prattled on as she always did, amplified by her jet lag: how
snowed under she'd been at work, the state of the weather in London,
the lack of dietary choice on the plane. Safe, unimportant chitchat
that gave the impression of filling a space. I sat on the bed saying
nothing. I'd not even changed or dried my hair and everything stuck
to me like flypaper. I shivered.

Maya turned and stared at me. "Why are you being *so* quiet?"
She came over and pulled at my T-shirt. "And get this off," she said.
"You're going to catch a chill. You never knew the meaning of a
coat." She fetched one of the robes from the bathroom and then
stood there, holding it against herself. "It's because I surprised you,
isn't it? And now you don't think I trust you. Tell the truth."

"But you don't."

"I was worried about you, that's all. And I'm here now, so let's just

366

enjoy it." She arranged the robe across my shoulders. "I'm going to make myself a coffee. I want to try your fancy machine. Want one?"

"Why don't you trust me, Maya?"

"For God's sake, Lil," she said. "Do we have to do this now?" She walked across to the console and ran her fingers through the pods of coffee, the selection of exotic tea bags. "You know I bloody trust you. You're my sister. My old skin and blister." She sounded high on something. Exhaustion, perhaps. Or nervousness.

This is it, I thought—the moment our lives had been leading up to. It didn't have to go any further. We could have coffee, enjoy our holiday. Become strange, old sisters together. And I was tempted. I was so so tempted. If I asked, would we lose what we had or would we gain the things we'd never had? I took a breath.

"So why have you never told me?"

"Told you what?"

"That you were there when Mumma got killed."

Her finger froze on the lever before it resumed its tireless passage, slower and less certain this time. "Who said that?"

"It doesn't matter, just tell me if it's true."

Her cup jangled as she tried to position it. "Bloody thing's alive," she said. "Or maybe I'm just tired. Should I have hot chocolate instead?"

"Leave the bloody machine!" Her body flinched and she put down the cup. "I want to know if it's true."

She blew the air from her cheeks. "All right, it's true. So what?"

"What do you mean, *so what*?" I stood in disbelief. "Maya, all these *years*. How can I believe you about anything? What else have you been hiding?"

"Nothing! My God, just stop!"

I pushed past her and went to the desk.

"I want you to look at something." I rifled through all of the items until I found the receipt from the box. "This was left at Castle Peak Road from when all of us were living there. I know Uncle Chor got Dad into gambling and that Hei-Fong Lee paid this first debt, but I need to know were there more? Did it have anything to do with what happened?" Maya lowered herself on the chair as though it were made of needles. "Think hard about it, Maya. You were always his golden child. He used to tell you everything."

She scoffed, avoiding my gaze. "Like you weren't Mumma's, you mean?"

"For Christ's sake, Maya," I said. "You're the only way I can settle the past."

"What's the point? It's over."

"It's never over when you still remember things. And I do remember, Maya, even though you told me I was imagining it. When you let me think I was ill."

For the first time she actually made eye contact, raised her brows in astonishment. "You *were* ill, Lily," she said. "You've been depressed for most of your life. You tried to hang yourself at Cambridge. If Elise hadn't found you that day . . ." She shook her head. "You were a suicidal fucking lunatic."

The words landed like blows on my skin. Every plaster she'd stuck over her honesty, every gag she'd bitten back through the years was being ripped off in a single moment. Well, then.

"Are you saying you didn't feel like that, too? I don't believe you. No one goes through something like that and comes out the other side as normal."

"Well, I did. I dealt with it," she said.

"How? By running yourself into the ground? Marrying a man five years off his pension? We could have dealt with this together, rather than you hiding it all away from me."

"I didn't lie to you, Lily."

"You're the fucking lawyer! You lied by *omission*, Maya. When you gave me that money from Dad, when you befriended Elise, when you tried to stop me from coming out here." I was struggling to control my breath. "No more lies," I said. "Aren't you the one that's always looked after me?" I took her hand but she wrenched it away.

"Don't be nice to me, Lil."

"What?"

"Don't be *nice*. I don't deserve it."

"It's fine. We *can* get past this."

Her dead smile stopped me in my tracks. "I always thought you were brighter than that."

"Why are you being so horrible?"

"Because we're not going to get past this. Don't you see? I'm not some bloody martyr. The whole reason I didn't tell you was because I knew you would hate me. Why couldn't you have left it alone?"

I fell back onto my knees. "Why would I hate you? Maya?"

Her eyes had that thousand-yard stare again, lost to a place I couldn't reach. "Because it was me," she said. "*I* killed Mumma, Lily."

SIXTY-EIGHT

Sook-Yin

October 13, 1977

Sook-Yin froze. "What you mean?" she said.

"He took his passport . . . the money . . . I think he went back to London."

"Which money? Which money?" she demanded. Her legs had turned to liquid.

"He found some money in the bedroom."

Sook-Yin collapsed on the chair. The old woman appeared beside her and tapped the table with her fingers. "So now we have a problem," she said.

"I can get your money," Sook-Yin told her. "You will just have to give me more time."

"Of course, my dear," she said. "I can see your luck is bad. But I will need a little insurance."

"But I have nothing to give you. All the money I had was there."

"Not money . . . your daughter," she said. Sook-Yin stared at her. "I promise we will take good care of her. Like a beautiful doll on a shelf."

"No! The deadline is not until tomorrow."

"Exactly. Plenty of time for the rest of you to leave. A little incentive will focus your mind." She held out her hand toward Maya. "You remember me, my dear?" she said in English. "We have very fun when you visit."

Sook-Yin pushed Maya away. "Maya, go back to bank. Tell them to lock the door."

"Mumma, no, you're scaring me."

"I will come for you in minute. Everything will be okay."

As her daughter turned and ran, the old woman whistled through her fingers and a man appeared from nowhere. Maya was almost at the entrance to the bank but he was young and his stride was long and his arms caught her like a moth in a net. He picked her up and was lost in the crowd.

"Mumma! Mumma! Mumma!"

Sook-Yin turned to plead with the woman but she was gone. "Help me! Someone!" she screamed. Eyes reacted but failed to notice, or if they did, they chose to ignore her.

The pavements were too crowded to see the woman but Sook-Yin ran in the most obvious direction until she arrived at the junction. She scoured each of the side streets in turn until halfway down on the left she caught sight of Maya again, being pushed into a waiting car. Its exhaust was already smoking. Now it was pulling away.

Sook-Yin ran harder to keep pace with it, her feet slipping from the curb to the road and the blood growing hot in her lungs. Her only hope had been the clog of the traffic but the side street was moving freely.

She didn't know how much breath she had left when in the near distance the lights turned to amber. The car was at the front of its lane and was forced to slow a little with the promise of opposing traffic. Sook-Yin was almost level with it. Her fingers grazed the passenger door and she tried in vain to open it, blood welling from the rags of her nails as she clawed at the plastic seal. Beyond the black windows she could hear Maya's wails.

There was only one thing for it.

She ran ahead of the car, blocking its path to the intersection despite the screams of horns around her. How could they not have noticed her? Why wasn't anyone doing anything to help?

At the same time that the signal turned red she caught the blur of the car surging forward. It was jumping the light, straight for her. Sook-Yin raised her arms and shouted, unaware of the brute force of metal, just the feeling of her body in space surrendering to gravity. Falling. She heard the wail of a baby's cry, the winter crack of branches as her bones snapped deep within her. Then nothing but a deafening silence.

Against the oily warmth of the tarmac she tried to catch her breath, but instead of air there was only liquid. A hot day ... the sun on the beach ... a high tide tickling her chest. Then she was drowning, suffocating in thickness, the shore so remote in the distance.

Her eyes flickered open to the sky. It was too early for it to be dark but the stars were bright around her, the constellations of ah-Ma and her children: Mei-Hua, big and strong, and Li-Li, born in a fire. How she wished the same for herself. To be reborn in summer out of flames, her power mighty as a dragon and her entitlement righteous as a goddess.

SIXTY-NINE

Lily

45th Day of Mourning

I don't remember the car hitting her," Maya said. "Over the years I blocked it out."

She folded and unfolded her arms, tucking her legs beneath in an attempt to make herself smaller. To make herself disappear. "Afterward, they panicked and let me go. Uncle Chor said I couldn't tell anyone. He told me to say it was an accident and if I didn't, they'd come back and find us. I was terrified they'd kill you or Po-Po. That's the reason Uncle Chor sent us back. As much for us as them in the end."

Her words fizzed, unintelligible as static. This was supposed to be our redemption: the end of Busoni's Piano Concerto, the negative test for cancer, the bit on those daytime chat shows where the host says *you're not the father* and everyone goes home happy. That was how these things ended, wasn't it? A good reward for a bad life.

"Dad took the money?" I whispered.

"I just wanted something to be normal. You understand that, don't you, Lil?"

Yes . . . No. How could anything be normal again? This was the man I'd worshipped my whole life. I'd depended on his quiet

373

resilience, his uncomplaining lack of entitlement, our disagreements no more than tantrums. Our kind, unassuming dad for whom nothing had been too much. It was only then that I saw his generosity had been stained with a different truth. Only then that it stank of guilt.

"It wasn't you," I said. "It was Dad who killed her, Maya."

"He didn't know, Lily. He didn't know!"

"He took her fucking money!"

"Don't you understand?" she said. "He didn't take it . . . I gave it to him."

My head snapped up as a fat tear crept out of her eye.

"That day you went shopping with Po-Po, when the two of us were alone in the flat. He seemed different. Kept pacing the floor of the living room saying that Mumma didn't love him anymore now she had a rich boyfriend to take care of her. That money always won in the end. That's all he kept repeating—*I've lost.* I wanted to cheer him up, wanted him to be proud of me. I said we could pretend to search for treasure, and that's when I took down the tin where I'd seen Mumma hiding the money. You should have seen his face. He looked so fucking happy I assumed everything was going to be okay. And then I watched him leave." She bent her head and sobbed. "It was me that killed Mumma, Lily. And all my life I've been trying to pay for it. I just wanted you to love me. I'm so sorry, I'm so sorry, I'm so sorry."

I couldn't move my legs; my instinct for anger and hate was like a tsunami rising to the surface. How could she have been so stupid? Betrayed us all like that for a smile, for someone's approval? Only gradually did the feeling recede with the realization of how similar we were. How much the same we had always been. Like father, like daughter. Like sisters.

"You were only a kid," I said. "You didn't know what was going to happen."

"But I'm sure that Dad didn't know either. He just assumed Hei-Fong Lee would take care of things."

I shook my head. Even now she was trying to protect him. "He really did a number on you, didn't he?"

She stared at me. "He was all we had! If either of us had said anything we might both have gone into care. I might never have seen you again."

"You made me love him!" I said.

"Because I wanted you to have that chance. For at least one of us to have that chance. If I could spare you that pain, why wouldn't I? Why wouldn't I pretend you couldn't remember? Give you a better story? And you saw how he tried to make up for it, how he knew he never could. That's why he made everything about Mumma disappear, because every time he saw it, it reminded him of what he'd done. He was actually glad when he got the cancer. Said it was all he deserved." She bit her lip. "I need you to believe me, Lily. We never did any of it to hurt you. We didn't mean for it to turn out like this."

"Me a suicidal fucking lunatic, you mean?"

"Yeah. I guess. Pretty much."

"That makes two of us, then." I put my head in my hands. "I know you thought you were doing the right thing, but it wasn't your choice. It wasn't your right to steal my memories. I always thought that you were ashamed of me."

"What?"

"I thought the reason you wiped out the past was because you were embarrassed to be my sister. That you hated the fact of where we'd come from."

"No. No!" She looked at me. "How could you think that, Lil? You're the only reason I'm still here."

"But I never knew where I fit."

She grasped my hand. "*Nobody* knows where they fit. We spend our whole lives changing ourselves for some idea of being accepted—*make me richer, prettier, more successful, make the enemy of my enemy my friend*—when all we can do is belong to ourselves. The way Mumma did in the end." Her body sagged in the chair. "I'm so fucking tired," she said.

"I know. We need to sleep on it."

She turned and glanced out the window. "I had to get a room down the street. Everywhere else was sold out. I can't even be arsed to walk to the lift."

"There's plenty of room here for both of us."

LYING UNDER THE covers I kept thinking about those origami truth-tellers, how often we'd made them as kids, the time we'd spent in their execution. I love you, I hate you, I love you. *Pick a color, pick a color, pick a color.*

Maya held my hand saying nothing. But that was okay, she didn't need to. I knew she'd be there in the morning.

SEVENTY

Lily

49th Day of Mourning

On that last day I took her to the peak, Maya huffing all the way up the slope. "You know I'll probably go into labor?" she said.

"Stop whining. The view will be worth it."

We finally got to the top and I saw the gleam appear in her eye as she looked out on the whole of Kowloon, the harbor like a lake beneath us, the farthest skyscrapers as tiny as matchboxes. Yes, we were tenants, but also gods.

Maya navigated the perimeter of the walkway, tasting the air with her tongue.

"All right, Fatty, was it worth it?"

"Hell, yeah." She leaned her arms on the railings, rested her chin against them. "FYI, Ed's been having an affair."

I turned. "What the fuck?" I said.

"God, it's been happening for years but I never had the guts to confront him. I was too afraid of losing everything, and I don't mean the money . . . the fairy tale." She sighed. "Dad used to love those stories—do you remember?"

"He never read them to me." I wrinkled my nose. "I remember him crying at *The Sound of Music*, though. When Julie Andrews

377

leaves Chris Plummer." I pressed my hand to my forehead. "*'That, my girls, is dignity.'*"

"God, what an idiot."

We laughed.

"Has it made you hate him?" she said.

"Why? Would that make you sad?"

"It would make me sad for you. Not to understand how much he loved you."

"I do understand. I *do* love him. It's just I don't like him very much at the moment."

"Fair enough," she said.

"What about you?"

"I'm swearing off men for a bit."

"Don't bloody blame you," I said. We did our half smiles. "What changed your mind? About Ed?"

"Thinking about Mumma . . . but mainly you." She pulled her hair from her eyes. "You're my bloody hero."

"Thank you for your sarcasm."

"No, I mean it," she said. "You came out here on your own, for a start. I'd never have imagined you would. And then standing up to Uncle Chor?" She fanned her face. "You give no fucks about anything."

"That's not true," I said. "I wouldn't be here if I didn't care."

"With me, or in Hong Kong?"

"Yes."

She fell silent and then pointed at the harbor. "That photo that Hei-Fong Lee kept. It was taken in Hong Kong Park. You practically fell into the waterfall, gave Mumma a heart attack. Your trousers were soaking wet on that lion."

I kissed her shoulder. "Thank you," I said. "That's nice."

Maya sighed and rubbed her stomach. "I suppose I've got all that to come."

"All that worry, you mean?"

"No. All that love," she said.

I squeezed her hand. "*Are* you doing all right?"

"Yes. I'll obviously fight for the house."

"I didn't really mean about Ed."

"I know . . . and I'm sure we will be. But you'll have to move in if you want the piano."

"I'll think about it," I said. "But I might be pretty rich soon, so you'll have to turn my pages."

Maya winced and looked at me. "Listen, about that . . ." she said.

I'D ARRANGED TO meet Daniel for dinner in one of the restaurants around the harbor. "How are you, Lily?" he said.

"Better, I think. I'm good."

He leaned over and shook Maya's hand. "You look more like your sister than I imagined."

Seeing the way that he stared at her, I acknowledged my small stab of jealousy and then put it out of my mind. I couldn't expect things to change overnight.

Over the meal we talked again about the music school. "You'll have to send me pictures," he said. "I'd like to know my father's money did *some* good."

I exchanged a look with Maya. "Actually, we've come to a decision. I'm going to take a loan from my sister." I held up my hand at his protest. "Hear me out," I said. "Irrespective of your dad's feelings for our mum, money wrecked our family in the end and it seems a bit weird to take it. The only person I want to owe is Maya."

Daniel wiped his mouth on his napkin. "I both understand and admire that," he said. "But there is more than one way of breaking a circle."

"And today's the forty-ninth day of mourning."

"What if the clock stops here? Take as long as you need. Say you'll think about it at least?"

I looked at Maya and she nodded. "Okay."

"And let me visit you in London? It would be great to meet the kids that you help."

"Sure," I said. "You must." I sensed Maya's stare like a laser.

"Do you . . . have children?" she said. Blunt as a yak's razor, as always.

"No children. Not even a wife." He smiled at me. "In fact, I recently called off my engagement."

"Oh! I'm so sorry," Maya said.

I prodded the air with my fork. "Actually, no, that's *great* news."

"Lil?" Maya's foot questioned mine beneath the table and I answered with a kick of my own. *Bloody go, me.*

THE MOON WAS appropriately muted as we said goodbye at the harbor. For all the promises we'd made, none of us knew what lay around the corner, what particular synergy of experience or accident might presage the perfect storm toward tragedy. All we could do was hold the rope in the moment, one foot in front of the other. Mumma taught me that.

SEVENTY-ONE

Lily

‗‗‗‗‗‗‗‗‗‗‗‗‗‗‗‗
‗‗‗‗‗‗‗‗‗‗‗‗‗‗‗‗

1st Day of Living

All this junk," I said.

We were kneeling in Maya's basement, sorting out Dad's boxes from Brixton in preparation for making the playroom.

"Is there *anything* here you want?"

I peered at the boxes of stained Tupperware, the ancient Moulinex blenders and Fanny Craddock cookbooks.

"Ugh, sorry," I said. "Not really. It's all a bit retro, isn't it, and not even in a Babs sort of way."

"Photo album!" Maya said, holding it up in the air. I grabbed it out of her hands and began to flick through it. There was Dad in Piccadilly Circus standing beneath the Coca-Cola sign, Dad in a Chinese restaurant, Dad holding baby Maya. I laughed.

"Jesus, Mays. You were huge!"

I went back faster through the pages, hoping to catch a glimpse of Mumma, and then, right at the front, I saw it. A photo taken back in her nursing days. She was wearing some prehistoric uniform and alongside her was another woman, her blond hair stark against Mumma's black, even beneath their caps. I pulled it out and turned it over. *Sook-Yin and Peggy, 1966.* I thought of the picture in Mrs. Tam's box.

"Mays! Look at this," I said. "Do you remember a person called Peggy?"

Maya's brow wrinkled as she studied the photo. "No . . ."

"I found a picture Mum kept from her in Hong Kong. I get the sense that she was important."

"We'll have to look for the wedding album. I'm presuming there *is* one somewhere." She stood and ferreted through a couple of boxes before something on the ledge caught her eye. "I almost forgot," she said. "There's this to deal with as well . . ." She showed me a small plastic box.

"That better not be some of Mumma's ashes."

"No, you buffoon." Inside was a large key on a plastic fob. "Dad kept a storage unit for years. I didn't have any idea until they wrote to him after he died. Wanted to know if he needed to renew it."

"A storage unit? What's in there? You said we'd cleared the house."

"I know I did," she said. "I've been too scared to look until now."

THE UNIT WAS in a group of garages in Herne Hill. The land was ripe for redevelopment and I was amazed it hadn't been sold to make way for the Eds of the world.

I pulled open the shutter door and reached over to turn on the light switch. Fluorescent tubes hummed like midges into life and for a moment we were stunned into silence.

There were boxes against all the walls, some too full to contain their contents: conical-headed lampshades; framed paintings of dragons and willows; silk embroideries punished by the sun. Like a smash-and-grab in Chinatown.

"Bloody hell," I said.

Maya and I looked at each other and then waded over to the closest of the crates, tossing out armfuls of straw and newspaper. I pulled out two plaster foo dogs. One of the faces had rubbed off and been redrawn badly in black pen. "I've seen these before," I said. It felt like someone had grabbed me by the collar and pulled me backward through time. "They used to be in our hallway in Brixton. Dad tried to wash them one day in Fairy Liquid and redrew the face with a permanent marker."

Maya smiled. "Well remembered, genius. Mum thought she was going mad when Dad told her it had always been cross-eyed."

I laughed as I pulled out a wooden puzzle box, its faded landscape familiar in the light, its superglued cracks. "And this used to be in their bedroom. All this stuff belongs to Mumma."

We rifled through more of the contents, pulling out long-forgotten treasures until we were standing in enough for a small shop. Dad had been keeping these memories for both of us, to rediscover without his notice. Without the weight of his guilt.

I sat and let out a breath. "Do you think he loved her, after all?"

Maya ran her fingers along a painting. "Yeah, I think he did. Mumma was everything he wanted to be. Independent. Resourceful. Brave. What's not to love?" she said.

I picked up a tasseled lampshade and balanced it on my head. "Do you remember when I wore this to school? For the Chinese New Year celebration?"

"Didn't they put your coat in the bogs?"

"No. That was a different time. That was when they wrote *Coolie* on my back."

"You were fucking savage," she said. She rested her hands on her belly; more like the Grampians now than the Fens. "What do we do with it all?"

"We're going to put it back together and love it. I can use loads of it to decorate the music school. You could put a few bits in the playroom."

"Okay." She came over and we hugged each other. "We'll have to work out a way to get it out of here."

I stood and took it all in, excited by the idea of its legacy, of sharing our story with others. None of that hiding anymore. "We'll hire a van," I said then. "As though we're normal people. We'll just take it one day, and go."

Acknowledgments

This story began in the spring of 2020 when, in the course of moving house, I discovered a collection of old-fashioned floppy discs languishing at the bottom of a box. These transpired, on closer examination, to be my late mother's diaries, documenting her life and experiences as a Chinese immigrant to the UK from the early 1960s to just before her unexpected death in 2009. As well as being frequently hilarious, they also told a poignant tale of displacement and grief, of losing her identity and of finding a different one amidst the challenges of a strange new world. Honest in a way that only diaries *can* be, reading these words was like seeing my mother for the first time, finally allowed beneath the veil of uncomplaining stoicism that she'd always worn as a way to fit in.

No less revelatory was the realization that I had unconsciously adopted the same strategy and had arrived at a point in my life where I was no closer to understanding where I belonged in the world. Growing up Eurasian in the 70s and 80s, I'd been constantly told that I was "half" this or "half" that, an unfortunate but accepted shorthand that only enforced the belief that I was incomplete and didn't fit anywhere. It was only then that I started to understand how much our mutual silence had effectively robbed us, not only of a deeper personal connection but also the opportunity to celebrate a major part of my cultural heritage.

It may seem strange that I decided to title the book after the racial slurs directed at its protagonists, but that was always a very deliberate decision on my part. For if the women of the novel teach us anything, I hope it's how empowering it is to reclaim those words aimed in harm and to rise above them in action and strength of spirit. We are all more than the names we are given or the labels that others assign to us.

Despite their very personal connection, Lily and Sook-Yin's stories are a tribute rather than a memoir, a universal mystery for anyone who has ever questioned where they belong or struggled to have a voice, irrespective of language. I hope so much they spoke to you.

This story was never meant to be a novel. The fact that it became one is down to the influence of so many wonderful people, some of whom I'll invariably forget to thank here. If I do, I hope you know who you are. To my indomitable, awe-inspiring agent, Claire Wilson, for her endless support and kindness and for understanding that being "other" is not a bandwagon but a lived experience, and to Peter Straus who not only arranged our perfect marriage but who taught me to "hold my nerve"; to all at the RCW Literary Agency for your tireless passion to get this story into other people's hands, especially Tristan Kendrick, Sam Coates, Safae El-Ouahabi, and Aanya Dave, whose first sight of me was falling down the stairs in a leopard print coat and who hugged me anyway. To my amazing team at Hodder UK, especially my brilliantly sensitive and astute editor Sara Adams for her lucky cat and gimlet eye, who not only read my words but shaped them from the deepest place; to Bea Fitzgerald, Joanne Myler, Alice Morley, Sofia Hericson, Juliette Winter, Ellie Wheeldon and Maria Garbutt-Lucero—the best girl gang ever on a book about kick-ass women. To everyone at HarperVia in the US who took me under their wing with such belief, passion and enthusiasm, especially the incredibly wise Judith Curr and my editor supreme Tara Parsons who constantly wows me with her intellect and insights, plus all the rest of the team: Juan Mila, Rosie Black,

Alexa Frank, Ashley Yepsen, John McGhee, Amy Sather, Kim Nir, Grace Han, Yvonne Chan, Brieana Garcia, and Stephen Brayda. To Dominique Pleimling at Eichborn Verlag and to Grazia Rusticali at Edizione Piemme; to Emily Hayward-Whitlock from The Artist's Partnership who, with such humour and fierceness, has made my dreams from a former life come true. I feel privileged to be working with such powerhouses of talent so early on in my career.

This story was never meant to be a novel, but for those people who saw that it might be I give so much thanks and love: to David Evans and the team at DHA (with my enduring sadness that we only have access to one universe); to Debi Alper and everyone at Jericho Writers for seeing the sparkle in the rough and allowing me to polish it on your time; to all at the Scottish Book Trust, especially the poet Don Paterson, whose comments on that seedling of a draft gave me the strength to persevere; to Aki Schilz and The Literary Consultancy for championing BESEA writers and sharing our experiences when no one else would. You are the gentle giants who allowed me to stand on your shoulders in order that my voice could be amplified, and I promise to pay it forward. My endless gratitude for the generosity of time and incisive feedback from my early readers and friends Fíona Scarlett, Jenny Ireland, Neema Shah, and Laura Danks, and especially Julia Kelly whose late-night texts, deep solidarity, and permission to be vulnerable first grew this dream into a reality.

This story was never meant to be a novel and if it weren't for the following, who distracted me daily with laughter and support, it might have not been one sooner: my wonderful virtual writing tribe the #VWG on Twitter, especially Simon Cowdroy and Emma Williams, who have been the most brilliant cheerleaders imaginable. If happiness is a warm puppy, you get the closest. It seems unfathomable that in the twenty-first century I still have real-life champions, but that being the case I need to thank the most enduring of them—Elaine Marney, Harriet Waterhouse, Mel Stidolph, Alison Willoughby, Caroline Ip, and Ben Court. You have seen me at both the best and the worst of times and through both your care was unwavering.

This story was never meant to be a novel but the proof that anything worth doing should have both truth and heart at its core is down to my wonderful family who have always had an abundance of both: Jim, Dexter and Lucy Wellman, Liam and Dominic Heneghan, Liv Dajivek, Anthony Deans, William and Josie Logan, Rhonda Tonner, and Chuen Kong. I owe a special debt of gratitude to my beloved sister Angie Wellman, who is not only the best sibling in the world but whose help in collating our mother's diaries was such a big part of this project, all of it a labor of love. Once upon a time, there were three of us of course, and a particular sadness and no small fraction of my heart belongs to my other beautiful sister, Janet Heneghan, whose irreverent chutzpah I cling fast to each and every day. You were right, my darling, the days are precious and you lived them magnificently.

This story was never meant to be a novel, but the ultimate reason it became one is because of my mum, Alice Wing-Chan Au-Yeung, whose words began this journey in more ways than I can express. It is an immense privilege to hold her legacy in my memories and in my genes and to honor it in these pages. Thank you Mumma for your gift and for teaching me the power of questions. I'll tell you properly one day when we meet again.

This story was never meant to be a novel, but to all my future readers who decide to take a chance on it, thank you thank you thank you. Authors are nothing without their audience: the readers, booksellers, bloggers, fellow writers, and influencers who so generously give up their time to spread the word. I see you and I salute you. If you enjoyed this book, or know someone who might, please do pass it on so others can remember these incredible hidden women. Most of all, thank you to the libraries everywhere who are the arteries of our culture; who continue to feed my curiosity and help me and so many others see worlds beyond worlds.

This story was never meant to be a novel, and neither were these acknowledgements, so finally thank you to Bert and Ren and of course to Stimpy for being in my life in the most special of ways. You say "cringe," I say love.

A Note on the Cover

In *Ghost Girl, Banana*, Lily delves into her family's past and seeks to find a place in the world. I used frames to echo the reframing of Lily's identity as she discovers more about her past and introduced the dragon to depict the spirit she shares with her mother, a woman she barely remembers. I hoped to combine the old and new by pairing old imagery with a colorful and bright, contemporary design approach.

—Grace Han

Here ends Wiz Wharton's
Ghost Girl, Banana.

The first edition of this book was printed and
bound at Lakeside Book Company
in Harrisonburg, Virginia, March 2023.

A NOTE ON THE TYPE

The text of this novel was set in JY Aetna (Newstyle 2), created by JY&A Foundry in 1994. JY Aetna is a revival of Bembo, a font originally designed by Francesco Griffo in 1495. Bembo would first appear in print the following year, debuting in de Aetna, a travelogue by the popular writer Pietro Bembo. JY Aetna derives its name from Pietro Bembo's original work. Stylistically, the font restores Bembo's quaint letters and original x-heights, lending it a stability and quiet grace that has made it a reliable choice for printed matter.

HARPERVIA

An imprint dedicated to publishing international voices,
offering readers a chance to encounter other lives and other
points of view via the language of the imagination.